Abandoned

Memories

ESCAPE TO PARADISE

✳✳✳ BOOK III ✳✳✳

MARYLU TYNDALL

SHILOH RUN ▲ PRESS

An Imprint of Barbour Publishing, Inc.

ESCAPE TO PARADISE BOOK 1
FORSAKEN DREAMS

ESCAPE TO PARADISE BOOK 2
ELUSIVE HOPE

© 2014 by MaryLu Tyndall

Print ISBN 978-1-61626-598-4

eBook Editions:
Adobe Digital Edition (.epub) 978-1-63058-528-0
Kindle and MobiPocket Edition (.prc) 978-1-63058-529-7

All scripture quotations are taken from the King James Version of the Bible.

This book is a work of fiction. Names, characters, places, and incidents are either products of the author's imagination or used fictitiously. Any similarity to actual people, organizations, and/or events is purely coincidental.

Cover design: Faceout Studio, www.faceoutstudio.com

Published by Shiloh Run Press, an imprint of Barbour Publishing, Inc., P.O. Box 719, Uhrichsville, Ohio 44683, www.shilohrunpress.com

Our mission is to publish and distribute inspirational products offering exceptional value and biblical encouragement to the masses.

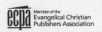
Member of the
Evangelical Christian
Publishers Association

Printed in the United States of America.

*Behold, I give unto you power to tread on serpents
and scorpions, and over all the power of the enemy:
and nothing shall by any means hurt you.*

LUKE 10:19

Dedicated to everyone who feels weak,
for when you are weak, He is strong.

CAST OF CHARACTERS

James Callaway—Confederate Army surgeon turned Baptist preacher, James signed on as the colony's only doctor but suffers from a fear of blood. Feeling as much a failure at preaching as he does at doctoring, James endeavors to rid the colony of all immorality, but instead ends up in a fierce battle between good and evil.

Angeline Moore—Signed on as the colony's seamstress, Angeline is a broken woman with a sordid past, which she prefers to remain hidden. Tough and courageous on the outside, inside she longs to be loved. She mistrusts all men and claims she can take care of herself, but the colony's doctor keeps hindering her plans. To make matters worse, she is constantly haunted by visions from her past.

Magnolia Scott—A spoiled plantation owner's daughter, who at first hated Brazil and hoped to return to Georgia, Magnolia, instead, fell in love with Hayden Gale. Now she is learning to value character over beauty as she receives God's love and distances herself from the constant belittling she received as a child. If only the reflection of her soul would become more radiant.

Hayden Gale—Con man who joined the colony in search of his father, whom he believed was responsible for the death of his mother. At first bent on revenge, Hayden, by the grace of God, has now forgiven the man and wants to make a good life for himself and his new wife. Instead, he finds himself thrust into the middle of a spiritual battle.

Colonel Blake Wallace—Leader and organizer of the expedition to Brazil, Blake is a decorated war hero who suffers from post-traumatic stress disorder. By God's power, he has learned to forgive his enemies and now hopes to start anew with his wife, Eliza. But when strange disasters strike the fledgling colony, Blake feels the weight of responsibility grow even heavier.

Eliza Crawford Wallace—Blake's wife and Confederate Army nurse who runs the colony's clinic. Once married to a Yankee general, she was disowned by her Southern family and nearly ostracized by the colonists when the truth came out. Eliza is impulsive, stubborn, courageous, and kind—qualities she will need in the upcoming battle.

Patrick Gale—Swindler, con man, and all-around crook, Patrick came to Brazil in search of gold. He is Hayden's father and ex-fiancé to Magnolia—and the man who swindled her family out of everything they had.

Mr. and Mrs. Scott—Once wealthy plantation owners who claim to have lost everything in the war, they had hoped to regain their position and wealth in Brazil by marrying off their comely daughter to a Brazilian with money and title. Unfortunately, their plans came to naught.

Wiley Dodd—Ex-lawman from Richmond, Dodd is fond of the ladies and in possession of a treasure map that points to Brazil as the location of a vast amount of gold.

Sarah Jorden—War widow who gave birth to her daughter, Lydia, on the ship that took them to Brazil, Sarah signed on to teach the colony's children.

Thiago—Personal interpreter and Brazilian liaison assigned to New Hope to assist the colonists settle in their new land.

Moses and Delia—A freed slave and his sister, along with her two children, who want to start over in a new land away from the memory of slavery.

Mable—Slave to the Scotts.

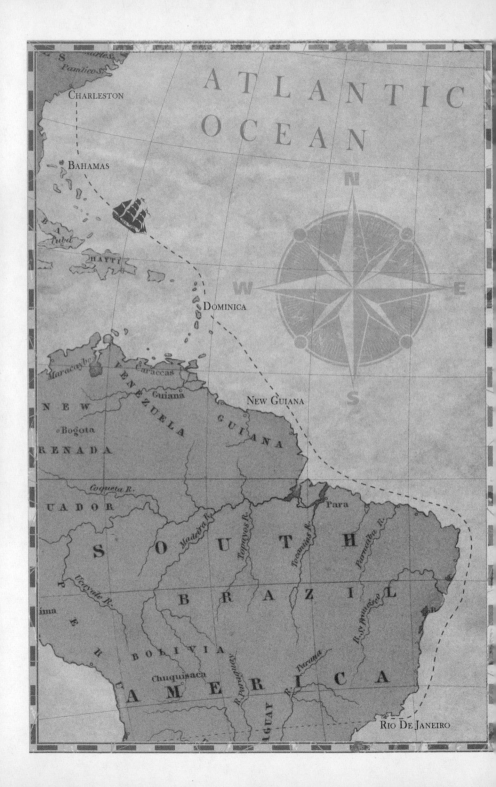

CHAPTER 1

October 18, 1866
The jungles of Brazil

The ground shook like a ship in a sea squall. Dirt and rocks pelted Angeline. . .striking. . .stinging. Her heart seized. Covering her head, she spun and staggered back the way she'd come—up toward the tunnel entrance and into the temple, where at least she wouldn't be buried alive. Unless the roof of the ancient shrine caved in. A violent jolt struck, launching her against the rock wall as if she were made of paper. Pain radiated up her arm. Her legs quivered like the ground beneath them, and she fell onto the shifting dirt.

The hand that engulfed hers was rough like old rope, powerful, yet warm. An equally powerful arm swung around her waist as tremors wracked the tunnels. "Hang on. You're safe," James spoke in her ear, covering her head with his own. Pebbles rained down on them. Coughing, Angeline flung a hand to her mouth when the quaking finally stopped.

She drew a deep breath, her lungs filling with dust scented with spice and man and James. And standing there, ensconced in his embrace, fears that had risen so quickly when the ground had begun to shake suddenly vanished. She hated herself for it. She pushed from him. The stench of sulfur and mold instantly swept away his masculine aroma and resurrected her terror.

James stared at her oddly while he said to the men, "I told you we should not have brought the women."

Brushing dirt from her skirts, Eliza, who stood in front of them with her husband, Blake, turned to face him. "You had no say in it,

Doctor. We insisted. Did we not?" She smiled at Angeline. "There's nothing to fear from a little shaking."

Angeline wasn't so sure. But then again, she didn't possess Eliza's courage and strength. Few women did. Those qualities, along with a multitude of others, were the reason Angeline admired her friend so much—the reason she'd cast aside her fears and agreed to venture into the eerie temple they'd found in the middle of the Brazilian jungle.

And then down into the tunnels beneath.

Yet at the moment, Eliza looked as if someone had dumped a bucket of chalk powder on her head. If Angeline weren't so frightened, she'd giggle at the sight. But her alarm at being so far below ground during an earthquake stifled any laughter. She never should have come along. The men had insisted on investigating a loud explosion they'd heard last night that had shaken the ground all the way to their settlement of New Hope. When they feared it came from the temple, Eliza's concern for Mr. Graves mounted, but now that Angeline had seen the ancient ruin and experienced the stink and heat of the narrow tunnels that spanned beneath it, she wondered why anyone would want to return. Or live here, as Mr. Graves had done since they'd arrived in Brazil.

Mr. Graves was one of the reasons Angeline had joined them today—to witness for herself the madman "digging his way to hell," according to some of the colonists' reports. Exaggerated reports, she was sure, but after Eliza had regaled her with further tales of gruesome obelisks, prison alcoves hewn in rock, strange Latin and Hebrew inscriptions, and Graves's obsession with releasing powerful, invisible creatures, Angeline's curiosity had gotten the best of her—regardless of James's insistence that she remain in town. Or maybe because of it. Angeline grew tired of men dictating to her. Telling her how to live and what to do and how to behave.

And using her like a dried-up commodity.

So, she'd come. And now, despite the heat and the terror and the pain, the look of approval in Eliza's eyes made it all worth it. Almost.

"We ladies don't fear a little earthquake, gentlemen. Do carry on." Eliza's courage caused Angeline's shoulders to lift just a little. The woman was nearly two months along with child, yet here she was burrowing into the depths of the earth right beside her husband.

Oh, how Angeline longed to be brave and independent like Eliza. Not weak and submissive as she'd been her entire life. Angeline had not only come to Brazil to start a new life but to become a new person. To put both her past life and her past self behind her. If only she could. . .

The ground trembled again and she pressed a hand against the wall. Sharp crags pricked her fingers as they slid over rock that seemed to sweat in the infernal heat. "If there was an explosion here last night, I'm surprised these tunnels didn't collapse."

"Indeed," James said, shifting his torch to his other hand, "though these walls appear to be solid enough." He ran a sleeve over his forehead, leaving a streak of mud. "Still, being below ground makes me nervous."

"I couldn't agree more." Blake, an ex-colonel in the Confederate Army and the leader of their colony, raised his torch and wiped dust from his wife's nose. He planted a kiss on it and shook his head. "I told you it wasn't safe."

"Which is precisely why I didn't want you coming here alone." Eliza brushed dirt from his shirt. "Besides, we have to discover if Mr. Graves is injured."

The colonel huffed his frustration and glanced at James with a shrug. But James was still examining the tunnel walls. "Odd. I wonder how primitive cannibals managed to score these tunnels out of rock."

"This place is filled with nothing but questions." Hayden's voice preceded his appearance from the shadows behind them. "The main one gnawing at me now is why we are bothering to check on Graves when he's made it plain he wants nothing to do with us." He ran a hand through dark hair moist with sweat.

"Where are Patrick and Dodd?" the colonel asked.

"They spotted the gold moon and stars above the altar." Hayden's lips slanted. "Need I say more?"

James snorted and leaned toward Angeline to whisper, "Are you sure you want to continue?"

"Yes, I've come this far. I might as well go on." Though her bodice was glued to her skin and sweat trickled down her neck and the fetor that rose from deep within the tunnels was enough to wilt a sturdy oak tree, she would prove herself brave. At least this once. Anything to keep James gazing at her with such admiration.

"Let's get on with it, then," Hayden said, urging them forward. "I've got a new wife to return to."

Eliza smiled and looped her arm through her husband's. "She was so sweet to take over the clinic in my absence."

"I'm glad she did," Hayden replied. "I wouldn't want her coming to this vile place."

Vile indeed. Angeline had forced her eyes shut at the sight of the images of torture carved into stone obelisks that littered the temple yard above. As well as the huge fire pit where no doubt the cannibals had roasted their victims so many years ago. Thankfully, James had ushered her past it all and into the temple before she'd had time to visualize the scenes in her mind. Something she was prone to do, especially with bad memories.

Trying to not lean on James for support, she followed Eliza and Blake as they descended an uneven set of stairs into a dark hole that grew hotter and hotter with each step. The walls narrowed. Air abandoned the space as if too frightened to go farther. She couldn't blame it. Coughing, she gasped for a breath, but only the foul odor of death and decay invaded her lungs. James patted her arm. Torchlight cast ghostly shadows over walls and ceiling. Angeline shivered and nearly tripped.

"Almost there." Blake's voice reverberated through the narrow passage.

They descended another set of stairs cluttered with dirt and rocks then crawled one by one through an opening that led into a large cave. Stalactites and stalagmites thrust from floor and ceiling like giant fangs of some otherworld creature—its mouth gaping wide to receive them. Blake lit torches hooked on walls about the chamber. Their flames cast talon-like shadows leaping over rock and dirt. Angeline's gaze flew to two empty alcoves carved upright into one of the walls. Her breath caught in her throat. Eliza's description did them no credit, for they were much larger, much taller, and so perfectly hewn from stone that Angeline could only stare in wonder.

"Mr. Graves!" James shouted, his voice echoing like a gong. "Mr. Graves!"

Nothing but the *drip*, *drop* of water and howl of wind replied.

Angeline took a tentative step toward one of the alcoves, her eyes fixed upon the iron shackles lying loose at the bottom of a long vertical pole. Her mind tripped on the impossibility of such a place existing beneath an ancient temple, of smooth alcoves carved in a perfect semicircle out of solid rock, of a metal pole and chains that formed some ungodly prison.

A blast of heat swamped her, coming from nowhere, yet all around. Air as hot as a furnace seared her lungs. Sweat moistened her face. The tunnel began to spin. James clutched her arm and handed her a canteen. She took several gulps, allowing the hot but refreshing water to slide down her throat.

"How could Graves stand to be down here so long?" Hayden said from behind them.

"Graves!" Blake shouted. Lifting his torch, he slid through another opening to their left, Eliza on his heels. With a heavy sigh, James followed, escorting Angeline through the narrow crevice into yet another cave. Most of this chamber was filled with large rocks stacked to the ceiling as if the roof had collapsed. The smell of sulfur and feces stung Angeline's nose, and she covered her mouth as her gaze latched upon a single empty alcove carved out of the wall—the same as the two in the cave above.

Leaping atop a boulder centering the room, James raised a torch and tried to peer above the mound of rocks. "There's another alcove back here. I can see the top." He jumped to the ground and approached the empty one then kneeled to examine the broken chains at the bottom. The clank and jangle of iron thundered an eerie cadence through the cavern. Angeline tensed. Dropping the chains, James stood and lifted the torch to reveal writing etched above the alcove. In a foreign language. No, two different languages from what Angeline could tell. James's Adam's apple plummeted, and he snapped his eyes to Blake's.

"Same as the other?" Blake asked.

James nodded.

Hayden approached, glancing up at the writing. "Destruction?"

But James didn't answer. Instead, his wide eyes focused on something on the ground hidden from the rest of them by the boulder.

"What is it?" Blake circled the large rock, glanced down, then turned to stop Eliza from following him.

But it was too late. She shrieked and buried her face in her husband's shirt.

"What's wrong?" Angeline started forward, but James darted to her and held her back.

"It's Graves."

Blake groaned. "Without his head."

CHAPTER 2

Angeline hated funerals. They reeked of finality and no more second chances. They spoke of an eternity hounded by memories one could never escape, mistakes one could never rectify. The last funeral she'd attended had been her father's. She could still see Reverend Grayson in his long black robes, Holy Book in hand, his words dribbling on the fresh mound of dirt, empty and meaningless as the drizzle of rain that had battered her face. She could still see the crush of people—black specters hovering beneath billowing umbrellas—come to pay their respects to a beloved member of their community, a pillar of Norfolk society, businessman, scholar, man of God. Pushed through a window to an early death by a misguided man inflamed in anger. She could still see Uncle John and Aunt Louise standing on either side of her. Her aunt wearing an impatient scowl, her uncle a look of interest. Though that interest was not on the funeral or the reverend or the crowd. But on her—a devastated seventeen-year-old girl. She hadn't known at that time just how far his interest would take him.

Or how far it would take her.

"Mr. Graves made few friends among us." James's voice drew her gaze to where he stood before a fresh heap of dirt, much like Reverend Grayson had done that dreary day three years ago. Only this time, the sun was shining and they weren't in a graveyard in Virginia but in the middle of a lush jungle in Brazil.

Tall, thin trees surrounded the clearing, their vine-laden branches bowed as if paying respect to the dead. Colorful orchids and ferns twirled up their mighty trunks. Luxuriant lichens swayed in the breeze. Birds of every color flitted through the canopy, providing music for the ceremony—albeit a bit too cheerful for a funeral. But not many of the colonists mourned the loss of Mr. Graves. Stowy shifted in her arms, and Angeline caressed the cat who'd been her dear companion since the ship voyage to their new land.

"He spent his time in Brazil deep beneath the earth on a quest for power that made little sense to most of us," James continued. The preacher-doctor looked nothing like Reverend Grayson either. Where the reverend had dark short-cropped hair, James's light hair hung in waves to his collar. Where the reverend was a thin, gaunt man, James was tall and built like a ship—like one of her father's ships. Where the reverend had an angular face, James had a round, sturdy face with a jaw like flint and eyes of bronze that reached to her now across the fresh grave.

She lowered her gaze. That was another way the two men were different. With just one glance, one brush of his skin against hers, James could evoke a warmth that sizzled from her head to her toes. She'd never felt such a thing from a man's touch. And a preacher, at that. Sweet saints, the shame!

"Perhaps we failed Mr. Graves somehow by not trying harder to befriend him. If so, may God forgive us."

Angeline knew the remorse in James's tone was genuine. He truly cared for each and every colonist. Yet she still could not reconcile this man before her with the one she'd met a year ago in Knoxville, Tennessee.

"May God forgive Mr. Graves for sins that would keep him from entering heaven's gates."

Forgiveness. Bah! Angeline well knew there was a limit to God's forgiveness. And from what she knew of Graves, he, like her, had far exceeded that boundary. A breeze, ripe with the scent of orange blossoms and vanilla, wafted through the clearing, fluttering ferns and spinning dry leaves across the ground. A butterfly, its wings resplendent with purple and pink, landed atop Eliza's bonnet as if she were the only worthy subject in the crowd. Beside her, her husband, Colonel Blake, hat in hand, stared at the ground with his usual austere, determined expression.

The butterfly took flight and settled on Sarah's shoulder. Ah yes, another worthy soul, Sarah Jorden, Angeline's hut mate, and one of the sweetest, most godly women she knew. Her baby Lydia, now five months old, was strapped to her chest and thankfully asleep at the moment. Being the resident teacher, children flocked to Sarah as they were doing now, tugging on her skirts, vying for her attention. Delia grabbed her two wayward lambs and ushered them away, casting apologetic looks at Sarah. Angeline wondered if the freed slave woman was happy here in New Hope, where she endured much of the same racial aversion she would have experienced back in the States. Delia took her spot beside her brother, Moses, at the back of the crowd.

"Oh death, where is thy sting? Oh grave, where is thy victory?" James spoke with enthusiasm as if he actually believed the poetic hogwash.

The shifting canopy scattered golden snowflake patterns over the crowd. A sunbeam set the butterfly's wings aglitter as it danced through the air, skipping over Mr. and Mrs. Scott. The wealthy plantation owners were under the impression they still lived on their Georgia plantation and the colonists were their slaves. Yet no one paid them much mind. Angeline smiled. Especially their daughter, Magnolia, the object of Mr. Scott's glower at the moment.

But Magnolia didn't seem to notice as she stood hand in hand with her new husband, Hayden, at the foot of the grave. The butterfly landed on their intertwined hands, bringing another smile to Angeline's lips. Despite the somber occasion, the couple couldn't hide their happiness, nor the loving glances they shared—glances that held such promise. A promise of intimacy and love Angeline would never know.

"For God so loved the world, that he gave his only begotten Son, that whosoever believeth in him should not perish, but have everlasting life. . . ."

Wiley Dodd's eyes locked upon hers as the butterfly passed him by. She tore her gaze from the hungry look on his face. The ex-lawman remembered her. She was sure of it. She could see the mischievous twinkle in his eyes, the knowing glances when he passed her in town. Why didn't he simply tell everyone her secret? What was he waiting for? Despite the heat of the day, her fingers and toes turned to ice.

The butterfly landed on her arm, instantly warming her. She hadn't time to ponder the implications when the crackle of flames sounded in her ears. Glancing up, she expected to see a lit torch, but none was in sight. Neither did anyone else seem to hear the sizzle that grew louder and louder. Wind wisped through the clearing, fluttering black feathers atop a hat that drifted at the outskirts of the crowd. No, not just any hat.

Heart slamming against her ribs, Angeline peered across the grave and through the assembled colonists, trying to make out the woman's face, but the lady wove through the back of the mob, her hat bobbing in and out of view. A hat of ruby velvet, trimmed in a black ribbon with a tuft of black feathers blowing in the wind. Angeline knew that hat.

"I am the resurrection, and the life: he that believeth in me, though he were dead, yet shall he live," James droned on.

The lady stopped. The crowd parted slightly, and the woman tilted her head toward Angeline.

Aunt Louise!

The butterfly took flight. And so did Aunt Louise. But not before Angeline saw a devious smile curl her lips. Setting down Stowy, Angeline clutched her skirts, barreled through the colonists, and plunged into the jungle after her.

"Aunt Louise!" Greenery swallowed a flash of ruby red in the distance. Thrusting leaves aside, Angeline headed in that direction, ignoring the scratch and pull of vines and branches on her gown. "Come back!" Why was the woman even here in Brazil?

Batting aside a tangle of yellow ferns, Angeline burst into a clearing and stopped, gasping for air. She scanned the mélange of leaves in every shade of green for a glimpse of ruby or flutter of black feathers. The *caw, caw* of a toucan echoed from the canopy, drawing her gaze to a golden-haired monkey scolding her for interrupting his mango lunch.

"Aunt Louise!"

There. A flash of red. Lifting her skirts, Angeline plowed through the greenery, her eyes locked on one target: the insolent smirk on her aunt's face. The red grew larger in her vision. The smirk wider. Until finally Angeline stopped before the lady. She caught her breath while studying every inch of her father's sister, wondering how two siblings could be so different, wondering why the woman had despised Angeline more than any relative should. Despised her from the feathers atop her promenade hat to the tiny lines strung tight at the corners of her mouth, to the pearls on her high-necked bodice, the black velvet bows on her pannier skirts, and down to the tassels on her patent leather boots. Boots that tapped impatiently on the dirt as they used to do on the wooden floor back in her Norfolk home.

"What are you doing here?" Angeline asked when her breath returned.

Louise cocked her head. "I could ask you the same. Aren't you supposed to be polishing the silverware like I ordered?"

Angeline stared at her. That was the last chore her aunt had assigned her to do before. . .well, before her life disintegrated. "What are you talking about? I no longer live in your house."

Finely trimmed brows rose. "And why is that, *Clarissa*?"

Angeline cringed at a name she hadn't heard in years.

"Ah, yes. Now I remember." Her aunt strolled about the clearing, the swish of her skirts an odd accompaniment to the drone of insects. She spun to face Angeline, spite pouring from eyes as dark as the feathers atop her hat. "Because you're a vulgar strumpet who stole my husband's affections!"

Blood surged to Angeline's heart, filling it with shock and fury. "I did nothing of the kind." She couldn't tell the lady what had truly happened. It would be far too cruel. Even for a woman who had done nothing but mistreat her.

"I curse the day you entered our home," her aunt hissed. "I knew you were wanton refuse just like your mother."

The woman might as well have forced a bag of rocks down Angeline's throat for the way it made her stomach plummet. Her mother had died giving birth to her, leaving a hole within Angeline, deep and vacant. Yet as the years passed, she couldn't help but hear the whispers floating through town behind raised fans and smug looks. When she questioned her father, he told her that her mother was the most kind, loving, compassionate person who ever lived and to ignore any rumors to the contrary. So she had. Until she moved in with Uncle John and Aunt Louise and their constant degradation of her mother's character eroded the memory implanted by her father.

"I was only seventeen," Angeline said. "I wanted you to care for me.

I *needed* you to care for me—like a mother cares for her own daughter." She hung her head. "But instead you worked me to death."

"I wanted no children. Nothing to steal John's attention from me." She fingered the emerald weighing down her finger then stretched out her hand to examine it in the sunlight. With a snort, she snapped her hand to her waist. "But there you came, young and beautiful, a bouquet of lace and curls no man could resist."

"I had no choice. I had nowhere to go."

"Humph." Aunt Louise gazed out over the jungle as if she stood on Granby Street in Norfolk.

Angeline took a step toward her, the longing for a mother's love shoving aside her misgivings, her memories, giving her a spark of hope that it might still be possible. "Did you ever love me, even just a little?"

Aunt Louise swept eyes as cold and dark as an empty cave toward Angeline. "No one will ever love you." Then, spinning on her fancy heels, she shoved through the foliage and disappeared.

Batting away tears, Angeline darted after her. She had to tell the woman what had really happened. No matter the pain. No matter the cost. She had to make her understand. She had to beg her forgiveness.

After Angeline had sped off in a frenzy, James could barely concentrate on the rest of the funeral. What would cause the woman to dash away in the middle of a ceremony? Certainly not her grief over Graves's death. As it was, her departure caused quite a stir in the otherwise solemn occasion, so he hurried through the remainder of his eulogy before closing his Bible, handing it to Blake, and dismissing the gathering. Now, as he shoved through the leafy jungle, he could think of only one thing that would cause her to run. And that one thing sent an icicle down his spine. That and the fact that whoever *or whatever* had beheaded Graves might still be on the loose.

Destruction. The name etched above the empty alcove. The name of the third being described in the ancient Hebrew book Graves had found in the caves and given James to translate. A being that, it appeared, Graves had somehow freed from its prison. Having seen firsthand what the first two beings, *Deception* and *Delusion*, could do, James feared more than anything the power of this third beast. That was, if he hadn't gone completely mad and all this nonsense about a fierce battle, the judgment of the four, a molten lake, and invisible angelic beings was just that. Pure nonsense.

But for now, he was more concerned with Angeline's safety. Shoving aside a tangle of hanging vines, he caught a glimpse of her standing in the middle of a clearing talking to the air. His chest tightened. Suspicions confirmed, he sprinted toward her, but she took off again. He lengthened his stride, ignoring the scrape and jab of branches on his arms as he kept his eyes on her blue skirts flickering in and out of view through the maze of leaves. She stopped again. James rushed toward her, calling her name, but she didn't seem to hear him. Instead, she stood near the brink of a tall precipice. What he saw next made his blood freeze. Gathering her skirts, Angeline started for the edge.

CHAPTER 3

Aunt Louise halted between an acacia tree and a massive fern. She turned and gave Angeline a grin of victory. Gathering her breath, Angeline hoisted her skirts and darted toward her. Still her aunt remained... smiling...gloating. Making no attempt to run. Perhaps she'd decided to speak to her after all. Good, Angeline had more than a few things to say to the woman who had caused her so much pain. She wasn't a young girl anymore. She wasn't timid, in mourning, or desperate for love. Nor was she at her aunt's mercy for survival. This time, the conversation would be different. Just a few more steps... "So, are you ready to—"

Strong arms grabbed her from behind, cinched her waist. "Let me go!" Angeline tried to pry off fingers that tightened like vises. She lunged to break free, staring at her aunt's smirk that now faded to disappointment.

"Angeline, stop!" The male voice blared in her ears. Her behind hit the ground. Her back flattened on leaves. And James's face absorbed her vision. "Holy thunder, woman, what are you doing?" Lines of terror spiked from the corners of his eyes.

Angeline pummeled his chest with her fists, but she might as well have been pounding on steel. He pinned her arms to the dirt.

Panic tied her stomach in a knot. Too many men had forced her to her back, held her down against her will. Memories pierced the fear. Bestial grunts and groans, hands groping where none should touch. The struggle against muscles too strong to move. Like now. She kneed the man above her, grinding her fists in the mud. "Get off of me! Get off of me!"

Releasing her, he leapt back, hands in the air. "I wasn't. . .I wasn't. . . doing anything untoward, Miss Angeline. Forgive me."

Breath clogged her throat. She rose and inched backward on wobbly arms, staring at the man she least expected to make advances on her. The preacher-doctor, James.

But they weren't advances. Not from the look of concern in his eyes. Nor the remorse that followed. Not a speck of desire could be found in either. She knew desire. Could spot it in a man a mile away.

"You were about to run off a cliff." He gestured with his head toward the right as he collected his breath.

Making no sense of his words, she glanced toward the spot where she'd last seen Aunt Louise. But there was nothing there but the jagged edge of a precipice and the empty space beyond carpeted with spindly treetops.

Air fled her lungs. The jungle reeled in her vision, and her arms gave out. Before she hit the ground, James caught her and cradled her against his chest. She couldn't be sure whether it was the feel of that rock-hard chest or the sight of the cliff where none had been before that made her head spin. But spin it did.

"There was no cliff. . .just jungle. . ." she muttered. "And my aunt was there. . .no cliff."

James brushed hair from her face. "Your aunt? Did you see her?"

"Yes. . .Aunt Louise!" Alarm forced its way through the fog in her mind. She pushed from James. "Did she fall? We have to help her!" Struggling to rise, she refused his help and started toward the overhang.

"No." He pulled her to a stop, caressed her hand with his thumb. "It was a vision. It must have been a vision." Concern poured from his eyes.

Angeline tugged from his grasp and swallowed. Like Mr. Gordan, whom she'd seen last month. "But she looked so real. She spoke to me."

"They all do." He led her to sit on a boulder then knelt and eased a strand of hair behind her ear. The intimate gesture sent heat firing to her toes. She wiggled them, wondering if it was simply nerves. But it was far too delightful to be anything other than what she feared—the thrill of a man's touch. Not just any man. Looking away, she shook it off. She wanted nothing to do with men ever again. Especially this

21

one: preacher, doctor, drunk? She had no idea which. Nor could she forget their brief encounter over a year ago.

Thankfully he seemed to.

Yet, if he was nothing but a womanizer and carouser, why did he affect her so? Both in the past, when she'd met him on the streets of Knoxville, and now, when he seemed so different. People change. Isn't that what they said? She wanted so badly to believe that. She *had* to believe that or the rest of her life would surely be doomed.

Nerves strung tight, James rose to his feet. If only to put some distance between him and Angeline. The woman drove him mad. In a good way. In a dangerous way. Truss it, he'd almost lost her! He breathed a silent prayer of thanks to God for helping him reach her in time. One second later and she would have been gone. He couldn't imagine New Hope without her. He couldn't imagine life without her. Although they had no formal understanding—and if the lady had a lick of reason, she'd never agree to one—they *had* formed a friendship these past months. Possibly a bit more, if he sensed things right.

Sunlight filtered through the canopy, weaving gold threads through her hair, the color of burgundy wine. A sudden thirst overcame him, and he licked his lips and shifted his thoughts to the funeral then to the spider skittering up the tree at the edge of the clearing, anything but on her. But then she raised moist eyes to his, the same shade as the lilacs circling the vine behind her. And just as striking. She bit her bottom lip, full and soft as a rose petal, and looked at him with such need, such innocence.

He took another step back. He must focus. He was the town preacher, not the town rogue. For once in his life, he must resist this tempting morsel. For once in his life, he could not fail. He ran a sleeve over his forehead and studied the cliff.

"You didn't see the drop-off?"

"No."

"That means they are turning deadly." He frowned.

"The visions?"

"And whatever or *whoever* is causing them."

"I still can't believe Aunt Louise wasn't real." Her voice trailed off as she wrung her hands in her lap. "She tried to kill me. But why?"

James shook his head, wishing he had answers.

"You think they have something to do with the temple?" she asked. "The empty alcoves and broken irons and Graves's death?"

He nodded and smiled at the way she wiggled her nose, shifting her sprinkling of freckles. Adorable as always. A flock of green parakeets with black heads landed on the branches of a nearby tree and began chattering, while uneasiness crossed her violet eyes. She fingered a button of her bodice. Another thing he admired about her—her modest attire. High-necked blouses, long sleeves, and her hair always put up in a bun, though now some strands broke free and dangled in the breeze. Angeline was a lady in the truest sense. In fact, all the women in New Hope seemed to possess the highest of morals. Something James was extremely thankful for. He'd had his fill of unscrupulous women back in Tennessee and would not allow them to taint the new Southern utopia they were building here in Brazil.

"And this Hebrew book you're translating. . ." She broke into his musings. "The one Graves gave you before he died. Will it tell us more?"

"That is my hope."

"Who do you think killed the poor man?" She rubbed her throat, no doubt thinking of the manner of his death.

"Whoever it is, you have nothing to worry about, Miss Angeline. Blake and I will protect the colony." He had hoped to set her at ease, to erase the fear lining her face. Instead, she slanted her lips and huffed.

"Don't placate me, Doctor." Her sharp tone surprised him. "I may be a woman, but I don't wilt like a flower. In fact, I shed my petals years ago."

But not all her thorns. James smiled, remembering the gun she'd pulled on him last month when he'd surprised her at the river. He scratched the stubble on his chin. "Truth is, I don't know who killed Graves. But I do believe there is something peculiar going on. Something supernatural, even." He shrugged. "Demons, angels, curses, who knows? Something only God can help us with."

Her snicker brought his gaze back to her. "You don't believe in evil, Miss Angeline?"

Her eyes sharpened. "Evil? Absolutely." She stood and brushed dirt from her skirts as if she could brush away memories of that evil.

"It's God I have trouble believing in." She raised her chin.

That would certainly explain why the lady never attended church. "I'm sorry to hear that." What had happened to this beautiful woman? Whatever it was, James longed to know more about her, to ease her suffering if he could. Memories of their ship voyage from Charleston to Brazil rose to prick his suspicions. Perhaps she had not seen a vision at all just now, but had intended to fling herself off the precipice. It wouldn't be the first time she'd attempted to leap to her death. Yet she had seemed much better since they landed in Brazil—happier, more settled.

A breeze rose from the ravine and swirled through the loose strands of her hair. Her gaze shifted to the cliff. "How did you know? Where I was?" Her brows—the same lush russet as her hair—scrunched together. "How did you know I was in danger?"

"You ran so quickly from the funeral, I assumed something had either frightened or upset you. So I followed."

"Your duty as town preacher, no doubt? Comfort the afflicted? Save the tortured soul from hell?" The cynicism in her voice stung him. But he refused to let it show.

"Something like that." He chuckled. "Though, I must say, you do make my job sound rather nefarious."

A tiny grin flitted across her lips. "My apologies, Doctor."

"Please call me James."

She glanced down as if he'd asked her to reveal her deepest secret. He would ask her to do just that if he thought she'd tell him. The warble of birds and buzz of insects filled the awkward silence. James shifted his boots over the ground, littered with dried leaves. "When I saw you heading for that cliff. . ."—he'd felt his heart tumbling over with her—"and you weren't slowing down. . .I. . .I'm just glad I made it in time."

His heart cramped even now. . .even though she was safe. And he realized for the first time how much he truly cared for her. In all his twenty-eight years, he'd never truly cared for a woman. He'd never had time. From an early age, he'd spent his days studying Greek, Hebrew, and theology under his father's tutelage, and his nights resisting the delights other young men his age embraced: courting young girls, attending parties and plays, playing All Fours or Faro at the local tavern. All innocent enough activities, but out of reach for a preacher's son studying to follow in his father's footsteps.

Angeline moved toward the cliff, stared into the canyon, and hugged herself.

Trouble was, James hadn't wanted to be a preacher. He'd wanted to be a doctor. So, after proving himself an abject failure at pastoring, he ran away to apprentice under a physician in Charleston while attending the Medical College of South Carolina. The news broke his father's heart. And his mother's. Especially when the war began and he volunteered to serve.

Blood. There had always been so much blood. Day after endless day. Night after endless night. It was as if the world and everything in it had been painted red. And no matter how he tried, he could never scrub the stain from his hands. He stared at those hands now. They shook at the memory, and he fisted them at his sides.

A dark cloud rolled overhead, stealing the sunlight and settling a smoky dust on the scene. And now here he was in the fledgling colony of New Hope—a haven for Southerners after the war—preaching again. Not doctoring. He chuckled at the irony, drawing Angeline's gaze over her shoulder. "Something amusing?"

"Just pondering life's twists and turns." The most recent twist had him bearing the spiritual well-being of an entire town when he couldn't even bear his own.

Thunder bellowed, and a gust of wind brought the spicy scent of rain upon a gentle mist. He found himself remembering what she had looked like drenched from seawater. . .how her blouse had clung to her underthings, mapping out her bountiful curves.

She whirled about, caught him staring at her, then narrowed her eyes as if she perceived his thoughts. "We should go."

No, he wasn't fit to be a preacher at all.

"Yes, of course." Though he hated to leave. Though he knew these rare tête-à-tête's were beyond appropriate. Yet he so enjoyed them.

They set off side by side, crunching the leaves beneath their shoes and brushing aside foliage as they went.

"If you should see another vision, Miss Angeline, please oblige me and do not follow it."

"I will try," she responded with a slight smile, "but I so desperately needed to talk to this particular one."

James understood that all too well. He had tried to refrain from talking to the vision of his dead mother a few weeks ago, and he'd been no more successful than Angeline. "I suppose that's why they appear. They know we can't resist them."

"Perhaps they are just cruel tricks of our imaginations. Memories rising to taunt us."

"I doubt it. If so, all the colonists' imaginations are ravaged with the same plague."

She swatted a leaf, not even flinching at the large beetle that grazed upon it. "We all have our demons, do we not, Doctor?"

James touched her arm, stopping her, always amazed at how petite she was—at least a foot shorter than his six feet. "Whatever your particular demon is, Miss Angeline, whatever is bothering you, I hope you know you can talk to me." He cleared his throat. "As your pastor of course."

She tugged from his grip and forged ahead. "If I talk to you of my demons at all, Doctor, it will not be as my pastor."

The rest of the hike back to camp was made in silence as James pondered the unusual woman beside him. Part angel, part dragon. Both terribly wounded. By the time they burst onto Main Street, black clouds broiled low over town like a witch's cauldron. Though most of the colonists had no doubt taken refuge in their huts, Blake, Hayden, and Magnolia stood beneath the cover of the meeting shelter, peering up at the frightening sky.

James started toward them when a bright flash turned everything white as if someone had struck a giant match over the scene.

Thunder roared. The ground shook. He blinked, waiting for his vision to clear when Blake's shout pounded in his ears. "Fire! Fire! The sugar mill!"

Chapter 4

Setting down the bucket, Angeline leaned back against a tree and tried to settle her rapid breath. She plucked a handkerchief from her pocket and wiped the perspiration cooling her face and neck as she examined what was left of their sugar mill. What once had been the building's frame lay in piles of smoking, charred remains. Several of the town's men, including James, stood staring at the ruins, water pails locked in their grip as if there were still some chance to save it. The colonists, who had only moments before formed a human chain of water from the river to the mill, began to drop like wounded birds to the ground, their chests heaving, their haggard faces aghast at the futile result of their hard efforts.

Magnolia appeared beside Angeline, her normally flawless skin streaked in soot and sweat. Wincing, she stretched her fingers on both hands, no doubt from the same ache that afflicted Angeline's after an hour of hoisting buckets full of water.

"I can't believe this happened. Of all the places for lightning to strike." Magnolia fingered her hair, attempting to stuff strands back into their pins.

"I agree. Any other building would have been better."

"My parents' house, for one." Despite the dire situation, Magnolia gave a sly smile as her gaze traveled to her mother and father standing in the distance, eyeing the disaster with shock and dismay—as they had done through the entire ordeal.

A month ago, Magnolia would have been by their side, thinking herself too superior for such menial work. Especially too superior to bring herself to such a state of perspiration and filth to save a mere mill. What had changed her? Marriage? Angeline glanced at Hayden, the roguish stowaway who'd stolen Magnolia's heart. Word was he'd been a confidence man before coming to Brazil. The swindler and the Southern belle. An odd match, indeed.

Cursing under his breath, Hayden tossed down his bucket, splattering water over the dirt.

Magnolia cocked a brow. "I better go calm him down." After giving Angeline's hand a squeeze, she joined the men standing just feet from the smoking remains.

Angeline did the same. For the first time since she'd been a young girl, she had friends—friends who cared, friends on whom she could rely. Though if they knew her secrets, she doubted they'd have much to do with her at all. Smoke burned her nose and throat. James's bronze eyes swept her way, at first hard and pointed but then softening around the edges. He tapped her on the nose then held up a finger covered in soot and smiled. Heat surged up her neck.

"You brat!" She laughed and wiped her nose.

Blake cursed and took up a pace before what was left of the mill, instantly stifling their playfulness. "It took us a month to cut down trees, shape the logs, and erect this frame."

Angeline felt sorry for the leader of their new colony. It was a hard enough task to organize such a diverse group of people while struggling to create a new town and eke out a living in the jungle. He certainly didn't need any further setbacks.

"Perhaps we can salvage the rollers." Eliza, his wife, gestured to the round iron objects used to press sugarcane that now lay in a glowing heap inside the building. "And the gears. It appears the fire didn't destroy them."

Blake nodded and rubbed the back of his neck. "Yes. Thank God for that."

"And we still have the donkeys." Magnolia pointed to the two animals tethered off to the side. One of them brayed in response.

"Indeed." Blake heaved a sigh and turned to face the colonists, raising his voice for all to hear. "Thank you all for working so hard! You pulled together when we needed you the most."

"A lot of good it did us," one man shouted.

Moses, the burly ex-slave, lowered himself to a stump and wiped sweat from his forehead. With no thought to his own safety, he'd been up front with Blake, James, and Hayden, enduring the full heat of the flames. His sister, Delia, and her two children approached him, and he swept both little ones on his knees in a tight embrace.

"Where'd the lightning come from?" Mr. Lewis, the old carpenter, pulled a flask from his coat and leaned against a tree.

Thiago, the Brazilian guide the emperor had assigned to their colony, glanced upward and scratched his head. "Look at sky now."

All eyes snapped above, where sunlight speared the canopy.

"It was black as night a minute ago," Hayden said.

"It is curse," Thiago added with a shiver.

As if he were searching for something, James's gaze spanned the sky then lowered to the wide river from where they'd drawn the water, before taking in the rows of huts that made up their town.

Eliza slipped her hand into her husband's. "The good news is we have plenty of time to rebuild the mill before the sugar is ready for harvest."

"And at least no one was hurt," Angeline offered, trying to lighten the dour mood.

Eliza nodded and placed a hand tenderly over her belly as if she could caress her child before it was born.

Magnolia leaned against Hayden, and he swept an arm around her, drawing her close.

Angeline's closest friends had found love on this journey. Love and marriage and happiness. She should be happy for them. She *was* happy for them. She hadn't come to Brazil to find a husband. A husband was the last thing she needed. Or wanted. Then why did the sight of her friends arm in arm make her feel so alone?

James shifted his stance and glanced her way. Was he as lonely as she? No matter. Lonely or not, she must avoid the doctor—for a number of reasons. The one foremost in her mind was the way she'd felt all hot and tingling when his body had been atop hers, when his warm breath had wafted over her cheek, when his arms had kept her from tumbling to her death.

To her death? Sweet saints, she'd almost darted off a cliff! Her legs wobbled at the memory.

James finally lowered his bucket to the ground and stretched his back. No matter how hard she tried, she couldn't keep her gaze from traveling his way. Damp, sooty hair stuck out in all directions and hung to his collar where it curled at the tips. A muscle twitched in his tight jaw, and dirt blackened the tiny scar on the right side of his mouth. She remembered the night he'd received that scar. She had tended to the wound in a room above a tavern in Knoxville, Tennessee. But she wouldn't ask him about it, lest he ask her where she'd gotten the scar she kept hidden on her arm.

Nevertheless, he'd been so kind to her today in the jungle. So caring. He'd made her feel safe. But she didn't want to feel safe with him. She never wanted to feel safe with any man again. Out of the two men she'd ever trusted—the two men she should have felt the safest with—one had died and the other had betrayed her. She took a step away from James.

No. She would not be fooled again.

The colonists struggled to rise and began ambling toward the river to clean and refresh themselves. Angeline was about to join them when James grabbed Blake's arm. "Have you considered this may not have been a natural act?"

The colonel's dark brows dipped together.

Hayden snickered. "I suppose you think some invisible beast did this, eh, Doc?"

Magnolia glanced at her husband. "Come now, Hayden, how can you deny what we've all seen?"

"I didn't want to say this in front of the others"—James scanned the five of them who remained—"but we all saw it firsthand. The empty alcove. The next beast gone. Have you ever seen a sky turn that black and oppressive in so short a time? And the lightning. Did it strike anywhere else? And now the sun returns within minutes?" He shook his head.

"It *is* rather strange." Eliza hugged herself.

"Perhaps what we should be more concerned with," Blake said, his face drawn tight, "is who killed Graves and why. And whether the murderer is still close by."

"What if it isn't a *who* at all?" James lifted a brow toward Blake.

Blake seemed to be pondering the possibility while Hayden

offered a cynical chuckle.

"Regardless," James continued, "we should post extra guards at night."

"Indeed," Blake agreed.

Angeline felt her admiration rising for the doctor as it did every time he spoke with such authority. Though Blake was the leader of the colony, James had assumed a position of power right beside him. As had Hayden. Wise and strong, the three of them had engendered the confidence of the people. And Angeline's confidence as well. Even though she didn't always agree with James's position on spiritual matters, she trusted his judgment.

"What does your Hebrew book say?" she asked.

His eyes met hers. "Not enough at the moment. I need to translate more of it."

Blake rubbed his leg where an old war wound still pained him. "Well, until you do, let's assume this was nothing more than a natural disaster. I don't want to scare the entire town with fables and myths."

"Speaking of myths and fables," Eliza said. "Where are Dodd and Patrick? We could have used a few more men to help."

Hayden huffed. "Where else would my father be but out searching for gold?"

⊷⊰⊱⊶

Taking a small brush from his pocket, Patrick Gale swept dirt from a boulder and took a seat. A drop of sweat trickled down his back, making him squirm while loosening a curse from his lips. "Blast this infernal heat!" He gazed up at the maze of vines and branches webbing the canopy, where birds of every color and size skipped and chirped and whined and essentially made nuisances of themselves. So many! Studying the shoulders of his Marseilles cotton shirt, he was relieved to not find spatters of bird droppings. "Over there. I said to dig there." He pointed his jeweled finger to a portion of the creek a few feet from where the imbecile, Dodd, had planted his shovel.

Dodd leaned on the handle and gave him his usual exasperated glare. "Apologies, your *lordship*, but perhaps if you got off your bottom and helped now and then, I wouldn't make so many mistakes."

"We only have one shovel." Patrick spread the three maps on his lap.

Squatting, Dodd cupped water onto his head, allowing the liquid to saturate his golden hair and trickle from the ends onto a chest bare except for tufts of hair scattered across it like brambles on a plain. "I'm the one doing all the digging, Patrick, while you sit in the shade and study those maps."

That the man had ever been a sheriff astounded Patrick. Though one might consider him brawny enough, the deficit of a single intelligent thought must have made the job difficult at best. Dodd shook the water from his hair, spraying droplets over the dirt. Ah, yes, that's what he reminded Patrick of—his grandfather's dog, a Greyhound to be exact. Thin, powerful, with the same sharp, crooked nose, and just as clumsy and witless.

Patrick waved away a swarm of gnats. "How many times must I inform you, Mr. Dodd, that if we are ever to find this gold, I must spend my time examining every detail of these maps? Since you have been in possession of two of them for months and have made no progress, might I suggest that it may take a superior mind to decipher them? In which case, the best use of my time is in their study, and the best use of yours is digging where I tell you to dig."

Dodd spit off to the side, no doubt an indication of his thoughts on the matter. "If you're so smart, then why have you led me to dig in three different spots in the last two weeks and we've come up empty each time?"

A *caw*, *caw* rang above them as if even the birds laughed at the idiocy of such a question.

"This is not science, my friend. This is a puzzle, a code which one can interpret different ways depending on the position of each map in relation to the others." Patrick stared at the maps. "Whoever designed these was a genius. Quite impressive."

"So you have said." Dodd gripped the handle and thrust the shovel into the gravel lining the creek bed then tossed the silt atop a growing pile on land. "All I have to say is we better find the treasure soon or I'll be taking over the map deciphering." He forced the shovel in again.

Patrick shook his head. It was like dealing with a child—an unruly child. And if he'd wanted to do that, he would have raised Hayden instead of left him and his mother when the lad was but two. But Dodd must be tolerated, for he provided the brawn for their venture.

At the mature age of forty-three and with his experience and skill, Patrick had certainly risen above such menial work. He'd certainly risen above living in a hut and eating bananas like a monkey as well. Ah, the struggles he endured to line his pockets with gold!

To make matters worse, not only must he suffer in this bestial jungle, but he was forced to watch his ex-fiancée, the lovely Magnolia, stroll about town on his son's arm, the two smiling and cooing at each other in a nauseating display of marital bliss. Why she chose him over Patrick, he'd never understand. Though Hayden had inherited Patrick's good looks, he'd definitely received his plebian mannerisms and limited wit from his sweet mother. And to think Hayden had become a swindler like Patrick. A very bad one at that, to look at him now. Impoverished, living in a thatched hut in the most pathetic attempt at a colony Patrick had ever seen. No, Hayden was going nowhere.

Not like Patrick. He had plans. Big plans. Wind stirred the crinkled edges of the map, and he pressed them down, gliding a finger to the drawing of the well in the center. He folded the map across the figure then folded the other two maps at the precise points he'd determined and slid all three together. Yes. Yes. It was definitely this creek. He was sure of it. The treasure had to be here.

"Hurry up, Dodd. Hurry up, our gold awaits!" he shouted with exuberance.

Sweat streaming down his face, Dodd's blue eyes speared him with disdain, but Patrick waved him away with a snort.

"*More gold than ye can carry,*" the old pirate had told him over a sputtering candle in the back room of a tavern in St. Augustine. "*More gold than ten men can carry. Why, ye'll be the richest man in America.*" The man had looked to be near one hundred years old. He had a glass eye in one socket, no teeth in his mouth, and three missing fingers on his right hand. But Patrick believed him. The old pirate knew things no one else could.

That's when Patrick had decided to come to Brazil. As luck would have it, the end of the war drove many Southerners in the same direction. All he had to do was organize a colony, collect everyone's money, and he had a free ride to the land of promise.

Only the land of promise had turned out to be filled with insects the size of a fist, snakes that could strangle a man while he slept, and endless heat and hunger. And the map led him to one empty dig after another. Until he figured out it was only a piece of a much larger map.

The sweet crunch of a shovel into gravel drifted over his ears like a symphony. The gold had to be here. And when he found it, he intended to rid himself of the bird-witted Mr. Dodd. He'd also rid himself of his promise to pay back the Scotts and to invest in this primordial hovel they called a town. New Hope, indeed. There was nothing new or hopeful about the place. And Patrick couldn't wait to shake its dust from his boots.

CHAPTER 5

Magnolia sidestepped a massive root and continued down the path to the river's edge. "Mable, I'm so happy my mother released you for the day."

"I's glad too, Miss Magnolia. I thank you for your kindness." The slave girl's voice teetered on the edge of nervousness as she hurried along beside Magnolia. "If she knew what you were doin' she'd be stormin' mad."

"Don't you worry about her, Mable. She will never know." Magnolia winked. A habit she'd acquired from Hayden. "Wells, I thank you just the same, Miss." The Negro beauty graced Magnolia with a rare smile that flashed a row of alabaster teeth. No wonder Moses found the woman comely and charming and sweet. She was all those things and more. Why hadn't Magnolia noticed how special Mable was when she'd been her personal slave?

"I'm so sorry, Mable, for all the times I mistreated you." Magnolia swatted an oversized fern aside.

"You diden mistreat me, Miss."

Halting, Magnolia gave the slave a look of reprimand. "Yes I did, and you know it. I was rude and condescending and behaved like a spoiled chit. While you were always kind to me."

Mable looked down at worn shoes peeking out from beneath her equally worn skirts. "You've changed, Miss."

"Yes I have." They continued walking as the drone of insects heightened with each hop of the sun across the sky. It was not even noon, and perspiration already spread a sheen over Magnolia's arms.

She looped one of those arms through Mable's. The slave tugged away. "People will see us, Miss."

"I don't care a whit. God has changed me, Mable. He exists and He loves me and He loves you too! And He doesn't like slavery. All are equal in His eyes." It was a revelation the Almighty had shown Magnolia recently, and she wished more than anything she could force her parents to free Mable, but they were having none of it. Their excuse was they couldn't afford to pay her, and the girl had nowhere else to go. For the time being, Mable seemed content with her station in life, but Magnolia had other plans.

Plans that included the large black man standing at the edge of the river, staring across the wide expanse of sparkling blue and green. The man who caused Mable to stop and gasp in delight as she and Magnolia burst from the leaves onto the tiny beach. The young slave girl stepped on a twig, and the snap brought him around and split his face in a wide smile.

"Go." Magnolia released her. The girl hesitated. "You have only a short time."

"Thank you, Miss." Her eyes glassy, Mable sped toward the stocky freedman and disappeared in his bearlike embrace. Magnolia knew she should turn away and continue on with her business, but she couldn't help but stand and soak in the glow that beamed from both their faces as Moses led Mable to sit on a boulder and took her hands in his. A glow Magnolia knew all too well with Hayden.

When one is fortunate enough to find real love, it should not be denied. Especially not because of the color of one's skin. My, but she *had* changed. She patted the mirror weighing down her right pocket and wondered if that change would at all be seen in her reflection.

A bee buzzed around her head, interrupting her musings. Batting it aside, she made her way to the river's edge, set down her bucket, and lowered herself to a rock. A much easier feat without the crinoline she'd finally discarded for good. The gush and roar of the river bathed her in peace while sunlight rippled silvery jewels over water as blue as the sky. She pulled the mirror from her pocket and laid it facedown on her lap. Colorful flowers painted on porcelain stared up at her. A chip cut into the gilding that circled the painting, no doubt broken during her long trek to Rio de Janeiro through the jungle with Hayden. Ah, such fond memories! Yet, despite the flaw, the mirror her father had given her all those years ago was still beautiful.

But would she see beauty on the other side? Or was the prophecy spoken over her by the old woman—or perhaps angel—in the church still in effect? She hadn't looked at her reflection in weeks—too fearful to see no change at all. Mable's laughter drew her gaze to the couple holding hands and beaming at each other like lovesick children. She faced the river again. Taking a deep breath, she flipped the mirror over and held it to her face. She'd become so accustomed to her aged reflection, she no longer gasped in horror. Brittle gray hair sprang out above creviced, loose skin; thin cracked lips; and eyes that hid behind drooping lids. But wait. She touched her cheek. Wait. Not as many lines wrinkled her skin. She brushed fingers over her lips that now held a tinge of pink. And her hair. . .a few strands of blond sprang from among the gray. She *had* improved! Her heart was growing less dark, more filled with light. Thanks be to God!

Hearing footsteps, she quickly stuffed the mirror back into her pocket and turned to see Sarah approaching with baby Lydia strapped to her chest and two buckets in her hands.

"Ah, marriage agrees with you, Magnolia. I've never seen you smile so much!" Sarah set down her pails and gazed over the river. Across the rushing water that spanned at least twenty yards, an armadillo emerged from the thick jungle, stared at them for a moment, then dipped his snout in the swirling current.

"I never thought I *could* be this happy," Magnolia said, hearing the lively bounce in her own voice. "Hayden is everything I could ever want in a husband and more. He's absolutely—" She halted when she saw the dazed look of sorrow in Sarah's eyes. "Oh, do forgive me. I'm going on and on when you. . .when. . .I wasn't thinking."

Sarah smiled. "That's quite all right."

"I can't imagine enduring the pain of losing a husband." Magnolia would simply shrivel up and die should something bad happen to Hayden.

Gurgling, Lydia reached up to touch her mother's face, and Sarah kissed the child's chubby fingers, gazing at her daughter with love. At least she still had something left of her husband. "The war stole many men from their wives," Sarah said. "But Franklin is in a better place now."

Magnolia nodded as she watched the armadillo disappear into the jungle again. "A month ago, I would have laughed at such a declaration. But now I understand."

Sarah brushed a strand of brown hair from her eyes. "It is wonderful, isn't it, knowing how much God loves you? Knowing Him?" She spoke with the excitement of a young woman in love, putting Magnolia's own zeal for God to shame.

"I'm only just beginning to know Him, but yes, it's better than I could have ever hoped."

"I've seen a great change in you in such a short time."

"If only I could change faster." Magnolia ran fingers over the mirror hidden in her skirts.

"Be patient." Sarah knelt and dipped a bucket in the water. "Allow God to work in His own time."

Magnolia took the other bucket and lowered it to the swirling water. "I miss sharing a hut with you."

"But I imagine you enjoy your new companion far better?" A devilish twinkle appeared in the teacher's eyes.

The insinuation behind those eyes set Magnolia's face aflame. A flicker brought her gaze down to the ever-present gold cross hanging around Sarah's neck, a symbol of her genuine heart and saintly ways. Sarah Jorden, the epitome of piety and grace. Then why had God taken her husband from her at so young an age? "Do you ever get lonely?"

Sarah set her bucket down. Water sloshed over the brim, and she dipped a hand in and brought it to her neck. "Sometimes I miss the feel of a man's arms around me."

"I am sure Thiago would be happy to oblige you in that regard." Angeline's spirited voice startled them, and they looked up to see the russet-haired beauty approaching, pail in hand, and ever-present black cat following on her heels.

A tiny smile peeked from the edge of Sarah's lips. "You shouldn't say such things, Angeline. I hardly know him. Besides, he has some strange beliefs about God."

"Sweet saints." Angeline set her bucket down and scooped up Stowy. "Why is that so important?"

The smile on Sarah's lips faded. "Because our paths would eventually go in very different directions. No, I have no interest in the

Brazilian guide, nor does he have any in me, I assure you."

Angeline bit her lip and stared at the river, caressing Stowy. Magnolia wondered if she thought of James. The poor lady always seemed so conflicted, so sad. Magnolia should pray for her. What a grand idea! She'd never done that before—prayed for someone else.

"James is a godly man." Angeline confirmed Magnolia's suspicions as the woman kissed Stowy and set him down. But her next statement shocked Magnolia. "Perhaps you should pursue him, Sarah."

"Me?" Sarah chuckled. "I've never been much for competition. Whenever you're around, the man is drawn toward you like a bee to nectar."

⚜

Both women grinned at Angeline, mischief twinkling in their eyes. Grabbing her pail, she brushed past them to the river's edge, not wanting them to see her expression, whatever that may be. For she didn't know which of the emotions spinning inside her—joy, terror, excitement, or sorrow—revealed itself on her face.

"Don't be silly. He's simply being kind like any preacher would."

"He *does* know his scripture well," Magnolia commented. "He's been teaching me and Hayden in his spare time."

Angeline didn't want to hear about God and scripture. She heard enough of such pious talk from Eliza and Sarah and James, and now Magnolia. The Southern belle had been one of the few women Angeline could count on to not mention God in every conversation. What had happened to her? A leaf floated by on the current, and Stowy batted it then pounced down the bank in pursuit. Squatting, Angeline dipped her pail in the water. "Seems we are all in need of water at the same time."

"I need some for my garden before the children arrive for their lessons," Sarah said.

Magnolia gestured to her left and smiled. "I came for them."

Shielding her eyes, Angeline glanced at Moses and Mable down shore, hands locked and heads dipped together. "It is a good thing you are doing, Magnolia."

"It's the least I can do. They deserve a chance at happiness too."

Angeline frowned. Why did happiness always have to involve a

39

man? Couldn't a woman be happy alone? She hefted her full bucket. "I'm bringing this water to the men in the fields. They should be taking their noon break soon."

"Men? Or perhaps one man in particular?" Magnolia gave her a sly look.

"You are incorrigible!" Angeline shook her head as the three ladies started back. Though Mable reluctantly parted from Moses, neither the girl's smile nor the skip in her step faltered all the way to town. When they emerged onto Main Street, she thanked Magnolia, said her good-byes to Sarah and Angeline, and started back to the Scotts. Thiago, the handsome Brazilian, appeared out of nowhere to help Sarah carry her buckets.

"No interest in him at all, hmm?" Magnolia leaned toward Angeline after they'd left, and they both giggled. "I'll accompany you to the fields. I wouldn't mind seeing Hayden." She smiled at Stowy trotting along beside Angeline. "That cat follows you everywhere."

"Not everywhere."

"I remember the day you found him on board the *New Hope*."

Chasing rats in the hold of the ship, if Angeline recalled. Even so, the cat had been riddled with fleas and near starving. "He's been a good friend." Loyal, trustworthy, caring. More than she could say about most people.

They crossed the street that ran through the center of their tiny settlement, separating two rows of bamboo huts, about twenty in all, housing forty-two colonists. Actually more than that, now that Patrick Gale had shown up a couple weeks ago with his own group of settlers. Blake had assigned a few men to build more huts, but it was slow going since he needed all able hands to work the fields. Would they ever turn this crude outpost into a civilized town? Angeline hoped so as she and Magnolia took a well-worn path to the edge of the fields.

Surrounded by jungle on three sides, sun baked the plowed land, luring green stalks of sugarcane from the ground where they'd planted the splices they'd brought with them on the journey. Barely a foot tall, they spiked across the fields on one side while tiny coffee sprouts dotted the other. The coffee beans would take at least three years to ripen, but the sugar would be ready within a year. Plenty of time to rebuild the mill and process the cane for market. Spotting the ladies, the men tossed picks and shovels down and headed toward the shade.

Angeline had come to Brazil to start a new life. To erase the memories of her past and start over. To be a lady. Or at least *try* to be one. So far she'd been accepted and had gained the respect and care of others. Now, as she watched men come in from the fields, men she'd grown to care for as brothers, an odd feeling welled inside her. A sense of being normal. Of being part of a family. Maybe her risky move to Brazil had been a good decision after all.

If only the ex-lawman, Dodd, would keep his mind busy with gold and not with trying to remember her from the time they'd met back home.

If only the half-clad man heading her way would stop sending her head into a spin.

And her heart.

Against her will, Angeline's gaze locked on James. She'd seen him at a distance without his shirt. But never this close. Thick-chested with his shirt on, the lack of it revealed mounds of corded muscle rolling under taut skin—gleaming like a golden statue of some Greek god. And this man was a preacher? Not like any preacher she'd met. Sweet saints, she'd seen men without their shirts before—far too many of them. Why did the sight of this one send a buzz over her skin? Stowy meowed and leapt onto a stump, gazing at him too. "Indeed, Stowy. Indeed," she said out loud without thinking.

Magnolia raised taunting brows in her direction.

Angeline smiled. "Just admiring from afar."

Except now he was close. Thankfully, he grabbed a shirt hanging on a branch and tossed it over his head. She must avoid him. She tried her best, but he followed her. Offered to carry the bucket while she ladled water for the men. He didn't speak, just smiled at her with that knowing smile of his that made her feel safe and cared for. Skin flushed with sun and health, he smelled of sweat and loamy earth. Since arriving in Brazil, the sun had painted gold threads in his wheat-colored hair that now blew in all directions in the swift breeze. Drat! She was looking at him again.

Blake accepted the ladle and gulped down water, thanking her. "This time next year, God willing," he spoke to the men lounging around him, "we should produce enough sugar to pay off our debt for this land."

"And buy better farming tools." Hayden sat on a log beside Magnolia.

"And new fabric for a gown," Magnolia said, making everyone laugh.

"Anything for you, Princess." Hayden slid hair behind her ear and kissed her cheek.

Mr. Lewis, the old carpenter, stood off to the side chopping logs for fires. Angeline headed toward him, offering him water. New fabric would be nice, indeed. They hadn't had any new cloth in ages, leaving Angeline, as the town's seamstress, with not much to do but mend tears and holes.

Lewis slogged down the water with a "thanks" before returning to work. Did the man ever take a break? Shaking her head, Angeline finished serving everyone, ending with James, who took a hearty drink himself before plucking Stowy from the ground and curling the black cat against his chest.

Angeline gaped at the sight. "He won't allow anyone to touch him but me."

"And me, it would seem." James grinned.

Of course. She sighed. God was no doubt playing some cruel trick on her. Wasn't it bad enough the man affected her to distraction? Did Stowy have to like him too?

"Lewis, take a break, man," Hayden shouted.

"Naw, I want to get this wood chopped before it gets dark." The old carpenter wiped sweat from his forehead and continued hefting his ax in the air. Though he tipped the sauce a bit too much and not many people took him seriously, Mr. Lewis never shied away from hard work.

Angeline felt rather than heard something zip past her. She *did* hear the *thwack* of blade in flesh. Followed by a blood-chilling holler. Jerking around, she saw one of the farmers, Mr. Jenkins, drop to the ground, his shoulder a burgeoning mass of red and a bloody ax lying on the ground beside him.

CHAPTER 6

I can't." James backed away from the examining table where Mr. Jenkins lay moaning in pain. His wife stood on one side of him, gripping his arm and dabbing sweat from his brow, her face mottled in terror. Eliza stood on the other, pressing a fresh cloth to the man's shoulder. Like an army of red marching across a white plain, blood saturated the rag within minutes. James's stomach vaulted. His hands shook. He snapped his gaze away. Unfortunately it landed on the faces of his friends staring at him in confusion—and judgment—Blake, Hayden, and finally Angeline, whose look of disappointment lured his eyes to the dirt floor of the clinic.

"Hold this." Eliza ordered before the swish of her skirts sounded and she dipped into his vision, demanding he look at her by her strong presence alone. "I've never stitched a wound so deep before. Please, James. I need you."

He swallowed hard and glanced at Magnolia holding the dripping cloth in place then over to Mrs. Jenkins, who cast a pleading look over her shoulder.

"Maybe you can talk Eliza through it," Hayden offered.

Approaching, Blake gripped his shoulders. "You can do this. I know you can."

James wasn't so sure. In fact, the tremble now moving from his hands down to his legs said otherwise. Nodding, he gathered what was left of his strength and took a shaky step toward Mr. Jenkins, focusing on the tortured expression on the man's face instead of the blood bubbling from his shoulder. But the red menace crept into his vision like a rising flood—one that would surely drown him.

Eliza began preparing the needle and sutures. Magnolia's frightened glance measured James as he slowly made his way to her. She slipped a clean cloth over the wound and tossed the bloody one into a bucket. *Splat!* Blood dripped from the table—*drip. . .drop. . .drip. . .drop*—like a doomsday clock ticking away the last minutes of Mr. Jenkins's life. Ticking away the last minute of James's consciousness, for he was sure he would faint any second. He inched beside the table, legs like pudding, heart slicing through his chest like the blade had sliced through Mr. Jenkins.

Afternoon sun angled through the window, lighting the macabre scene in eerie gold. Mrs. Jenkins sobbed and leaned to kiss her husband. One of her tears dropped onto his face, and James watched as sunlight transformed it into a diamond rolling down his cheek.

Such beauty in the midst of pain. James drew in a deep breath, trying to settle his nerves, but the metallic scent of blood filled his nose and sent the contents of his stomach into his throat. He rubbed his eyes. The room grew hazy. . .

The examining table became an operating slab in the middle of a medical tent. Mr. Jenkins transformed into a soldier, his chest ripped open, his kidney cradled in James's hands. The *thu-ump, thu-ump, thu-ump* of the man's heart grew dim. . .distant. . . .

"What are your orders, Doctor?" A nurse, apron sprayed with blood, stared at him with eyes filled with panic. The same panic that had kept him frozen in place.

"Doctor? He's dying. . .he's dying. . .do something!"

"James." Eliza touched his arm. She handed him the needle. . . slowly as if she had no energy. "Are. . .you. . .ready?" Her words were garbled and distant. Like she was there, but not there. He faced Mr. Jenkins. The soldier remained. An officer. The single gold star on his collar stood in stark contrast to the blood oozing from his midsection. The nurse continued shouting, "We're losing him. . .he's dying! Doctor. . .Doctor. . ."

James dropped the kidney. It disappeared. Along with the nurse and the wounded officer. He drew a breath. Just a vision. Not real.

But once, years ago, it had been *very* real.

"Pour rum into the wound," he ordered, taking a step back. His head grew light. "Stitch the blood vessel." Another step back. The room spun. "When the bleeding stops, suture the wound." He turned, pressed a hand over his heaving stomach. "I can't. I'm sorry. I can't." Ignoring their protests, he barreled out the bamboo door to a burst of fresh air and stumbled forward, praying for strength to return to his legs before he made a complete fool of himself and toppled to the ground.

People stared at him, whispering. No doubt mocking him as he charged down the street and dashed into the jungle, foisting the brunt of his anger out on leaves and vines that stood in his way. And all the while wondering why the cruel visions continued to assail him. Especially since it had been over two years since he'd left the battlefield. Did they come from these invisible beasts the Hebrew book described, or were they just figments of his tormented guilt? He remembered that injured major well. It was the first time he'd held a man's kidney in his hand—a kidney shredded from a cannon blast. He'd tried to remove it to save the man's life. He had failed. The poor soldier died in a pool of his own blood.

Halting, James pressed hands to his knees and heaved onto the ground. When there was nothing left in his belly, he wiped his mouth and gazed up in the canopy, where life went on in a myriad of chirps and chatters as if he weren't completely losing his mind below. Only a madman saw visions of men who died long ago. Men who died under his knife. Under his hands. Hands that still trembled. He held those hands up before him now. Not a doctor's hands anymore. He'd failed at that profession. He'd also failed at preaching, but God had given him a second chance at that. This time he was determined to be a good preacher, to avoid temptation, and to be a spiritual guide to the colony.

If only he could stay away from blood.

Angeline woke with a start. Her heart raced. Heat stormed through her. Tossing the coverlet aside, she swung her legs over the edge of the cot. Another nightmare. Just like all the others. A kaleidoscope of haunting images from her past: rain splattering on her father's muddy grave; the vacant, lifeless look in Uncle John's eyes as he stared at the ceiling; Aunt Louise's maniacal laugh of victory; dim taverns, male hands reaching for her, groping. Lowering her chin, she rubbed her eyes. The odor of stale beer and sweat clung to her nose. Would she never be rid of it?

A gray hue lit the window. Almost dawn. One glance told her that Sarah and Lydia were still fast asleep on the other side of the hut. At least she hadn't woken them as she'd done so often these past months. A ghostly tune rode upon the wind stirring the calico curtains. Angeline cocked her ear. Was she hearing things now as well? An off-key piano banged "God Save the South," a tune she'd heard many a time at the Night Owl tavern in downtown Richmond.

Rising, she tore off her night rail and quickly donned her blouse and skirt. Did visions play piano? Tired of being bullied by whatever or whoever was causing these nightmares, she intended to find out. As she passed the foot of her cot, she brushed fingers over Stowy curled up in a ball. The cat opened one eye then nestled farther into the coverlet, obviously too lazy to join her. After slipping on her shoes and stuffing her pistol in her belt, she burst onto Main Street to a blast of dewy air and the smell of musk and orange blossoms.

Still the music continued. More angry than frightened, she charged toward the meeting shelter when a shadow leapt in front of her. Shrieking, she barreled backward, heart bursting. The music stopped. A nebulous form drifted in her path. "Who is it?" Struggling to breathe, she plucked out the pistol and leveled it at the shape.

"Just an old friend." The voice rang familiar. Eerily familiar.

Moonlight speared the clearing, and the figure of Dirk materialized—Dirk Clemens, if she remembered correctly. "You're not real." The gun shook in her hands, defying her statement.

"That's not what you said back in Richmond, dear heart." His voice was sickly sweet.

"Get out of my way." She attempted to shove him aside with the barrel, but the pistol swooshed through air, sending her off balance. She tripped, quickly regained her footing, then spun to face him. He grinned and cocked his head. Her heart crawled into her throat. *He's not here. He's not here.* "Leave me alone!" Turning from him, she dashed down the street.

"You can't fool these people for long. They'll soon know *what* you are."

His sordid chuckle faded as she rushed onward, vision blurring, drawn by a lantern in the meeting shelter. Surely the women weren't up already preparing breakfast? No, it was James. Sitting at the table, leaning over a book.

Like a beacon of hope and light, he drew her to him, longing for the safety and comfort of his presence. Head bent, eyes narrowed, brows bunched together, he didn't seem to hear her approach. Wiping tears from her cheeks, she hesitated, hating to disturb him. A breeze sent the lantern light rippling over him like waves upon the sea. She was within a few yards of him now, so close she could hear his deep breaths, see the dark stubble on his chin, the way the wind swayed the tips of his hair over his collar. Dawn's prelude cast a heavenly glow around him that left her speechless. Somewhere a whippoorwill sang. She dared not move, dared not breathe. She could stare at this man forever. Just watching him seemed to unravel her tight nerves, slow her heart, and steady her breathing.

He looked up then. Right at her as if he'd sensed her presence, known she was there. Surprise melded into delight before the burn of shame torched his bronze eyes. No doubt at his performance in the clinic yesterday.

Laying down his pen, he stretched his back. "Forgive me, Angeline, I didn't hear you."

"It is I who am sorry, Doctor. For disturbing you."

He released a heavy sigh. "Don't call me that. As you saw today, or yesterday, rather, I am anything but."

"I imagine you are a great doctor."

"Imagining it is all you'll be able to do, I'm afraid." He snorted.

Angeline wanted to tell him that perhaps he could overcome his fear someday, but she'd heard too many useless platitudes in her life to foist one on this wise man.

"I'm sorry you had to witness my atrocious behavior." A muscle twitched in his jaw as he stared at his book.

"We all have our fears."

"And what are *your* fears, Miss Angeline? Nothing seems to rattle you, save visions flying off cliffs." He gestured toward the pistol stuffed in her belt and grinned. "God help those visions should they ever turn into flesh and blood."

Angeline smiled and took a step closer. "I wish they would." For she would have blown each one back to hell where they belonged. She ran her fingers over the gun's brass-plated handle, finding comfort in the hard metal, in the power resident within. She'd sworn to never allow a man to touch her against her will again. But how could she fight things that weren't even there?

James stood, concern bending his brow. "Did you see something?"

She stared at him, hesitating to add fuel to his supernatural fancies. "Outside my hut. . ." She glanced that way. "Someone I knew from long ago."

He took her hand and led her to a stool. "Sit down. You're trembling."

"I'm all right." She took the seat anyway. Mainly because his touch sent a spire of heat through her that she didn't want him to notice.

"The visions are getting more intense." He took a seat opposite her, leaning elbows on knees, and studied her with such unabashed concern, she squirmed.

"Is that the Hebrew book?" She gestured toward the volume on the table. Bound in cracked, aged leather, the yellowed pages crinkled at the edges and contained strange letters that looked more like drawings than words.

He nodded with a deep sigh, gazing at the book as if it held the secret to life. A breeze ruffled the ancient paper as the croak of frogs and buzz of night insects serenaded them.

"Any clues as to what's happening?"

"Many, yes. None I think you would believe." He gave a cynical snort.

"Those pesky invisible beasts again?" She grinned, desperate to wipe the frown from his face.

Eyes aflame with conviction met hers. "Yes. Chained in a catacomb below the temple for many years—maybe thousands."

She wanted to believe him, she truly did. But all this God and angels and devil stuff? It was beyond ludicrous. If there was a God, why had He ignored her all these years? "I don't understand. If these beings are so evil that they had to be chained up, why would anyone release them?"

"I don't think the cannibals knew what they were doing or what lay beneath the temple they were building."

"And Graves?"

James rubbed the scar angling down the right side of his mouth. "Graves sought power above all else. Somehow they convinced him that would be his reward. Poor fellow." His forehead tightened as he stared at the strange letters.

"You *do* realize how silly all this sounds?"

"Yes." He smiled. "And I tell you at great risk to your good opinion of me." His tone bore humor, but his eyes begged acceptance.

"You are right about my good opinion, Doctor. And I assure you, it is intact." Oh my, she shouldn't have said that. Lowering her gaze, she stared at the hands in her lap then across the dark jungle surrounding the meeting area. "So what happens next?"

"I don't know. I fear my command of Hebrew has faded over the years." He rubbed his eyes and seemed to slump in his seat. "It's been quite awhile since I studied under my father."

"You've been up all night, haven't you?"

"Couldn't sleep."

Something she could well understand. "So what will this newly released beast do? *Destruction*, was it?"

"Yes, and I have no idea. But if his name is any indication. . ." He chuckled.

Rising, Angeline pressed down her skirts, only now noticing she'd forgotten to pin her hair up. Drat. She so wanted to appear a proper lady to this man. She expelled a ragged sigh. "Why can't everything just be normal? I simply want our colony to succeed and everyone to be happy."

James stood. "We all do."

"Why, if it ain't the two lovebirds up to watch the sunrise?" Dodd's taunting voice scraped over Angeline. Turning, she faced the man as he strolled into the clearing, a malicious grin twisting his lips.

"We were only talking," Angeline said.

"*Sure* you were."

James slipped in front of her as if he could barricade her from the fiend. If only he could. "What do you want, Dodd?"

"Nothing." He scratched his mop of blond hair that had become even more unkempt with each passing month. "Heading out early with Patrick to search for gold and wanted to find a banana or mango or something to fill my belly." He made his way to the end of the table and plucked an orange from the basket of fruit.

"Apologies for the interruption." He tossed the orange in the air, caught it, and grinned at Angeline before he sauntered away, immensely pleased with himself, though Angeline could not imagine why.

"Odd man," James commented.

Unnerving was more like it. Dodd had the power to bring Angeline's entire life to ruin—if he truly remembered her.

The hum of crickets soon gave way to morning birdsong as Eliza and a few other women approached with yawns and sleepy eyes. Sarah, holding baby Lydia, swept a knowing glance between James and Angeline, muttering something about how she should have known where Angeline had run off to so early. Which, of course, caused James to squirm and Angeline to drag the woman away before she said anything else to embarrass her. Besides, Angeline should help prepare breakfast.

Before they'd even managed to boil water for coffee, Blake strode into the meeting area making a beeline for his wife. Despite his limp from a war wound, he moved as though he were still a colonel in the Confederate Army marching before troops. That authoritative demeanor abandoned him, however, when he halted behind Eliza, wrapped his arms around her and leaned to whisper in her ear. Whatever he said brought a blush to her cheeks and a smile to her lips as he locked hands with hers and laid them upon her belly.

Angeline turned away from the touching scene, joy and sorrow vying for dominance within her as she continued to slice bananas to be fried for breakfast.

A clap brought her gaze to Thiago, who rubbed his hands together and sought out Sarah, shouting, "Good morning, all. Where is coffee?"

Grabbing his book, James smiled at Angeline and started to walk away when a high-pitched whining filled the air. Soft at first, like the trill of a flock of birds, it grew louder with each passing second. Others heard it too. James spun around.

"What is that?" Angeline asked.

"Stay here," he ordered as he and Blake shoved through the leaves on the north side of the clearing.

Ignoring his command, she followed the men through thick brush that led to the edge of the sugar fields. In the east, trees scattered light from the rising sun into threads of gold over the terrain. Something moved in the distance. No, not something. The field moved. Darkness shifted and rippled over the ground as if someone had tipped over a giant bottle of ink.

Thiago burst through the leaves and leapt into a tree, climbing to the top with an agility only a native Brazilian could muster.

"What is it, Thiago? What do you see?" Blake shouted.

"Ants. Army ants! Thousands of them!"

CHAPTER 7

"I can't find Stowy." Angeline's frenzied gaze shifted first east then west down Main Street, while the increasing high-pitched drone of army ants sent a cold rod through James's spine.

Grabbing her hand, he pulled her in the other direction. "The cat will be all right."

"I will not leave him." She tugged from his grip and tore down the street. Growling, James sped after her. He had no idea how much time they had left before ants overwhelmed the town. Nor did he wish to find out until he and Angeline were safe in the river with everyone else. He glanced between two passing huts toward the sugar fields. Alarm charged his legs into a sprint at what he saw—a black horde swallowing up everything in its path like some biblical plague. And it was nearly upon them. Daring another glimpse, he rushed headlong into—*thump*!

Blake grabbed James's arms, his face sweaty and red. "What are you doing? Get to the river!"

"It's Angeline." James tensed as his gaze caught her green skirts up ahead. "She's looking for her cat."

"There's no time for this tomfoolery!" Blake shouted over the eerie whine. "Get her to the river if you have to carry her there."

James nodded and sped away. Gladly. He wouldn't mind at all hoisting the stubborn redhead over his shoulder. If only to teach her a lesson. She should listen to those in charge who knew what was best for her, not run around half-cocked looking for a mangy cat!

There. He caught a flash of her russet hair disappearing in the trees on the other side of the meeting shelter. Heart pounding against his ribs, he darted after her. Since they didn't know how wide the trail of ants stretched, Thiago told them the river would be their best chance to avoid being overwhelmed. Or eaten! Though army ants weren't known to attack humans, they did eat insects, snakes, toads, and the occasional small mammal. *A mammal like a cat.* Even so, their powerful bite made you wish for death, particularly when there were hundreds swarming your body. Hundreds that, if they got inside your nose and mouth, could smother you. Just thinking about it made the hairs on James's arms stand on end. What a horrible way to die.

Punching through leaves and branches, he skirted the edge of the fields, horrified at the sight. As if the sea had breached its boundary, a tidal wave of black and brown swept over the terrain, moving rapidly toward him, drowning everything in its path.

Everything.

That meant the crops too—the sugar and coffee. A hollow cave formed in his stomach. He'd been so frightened for the safety of the colonists, it hadn't occurred to him that they were losing everything they'd worked so hard to accomplish in the past two months. Squawking drew his gaze upward where a crowd of birds screeched and trilled, flapping and diving for insects driven out from hiding by the advancing army—an army that was advancing far too fast! And with scouts, apparently, as a few moved ahead of the pack, crawling over leaves and twigs in a haphazard path. One scrambled atop his boot. He shook it off, terror pricking his heart.

A flash of green snapped his gaze to the left. At the edge of the field, Stowy pounced on the intruding ants as if they were but a few common insects to be toyed with while Angeline dashed toward him, skirts and hair flailing and voice crying, "Stowy! Stowy!"

James took off in a sprint, calculating the distance between them and the ants, realizing as he did so, that by the time he arrived, they'd be smothered alive.

Hayden tugged Magnolia toward the river.

"Must we go in the water?" Clutching her skirts, she wrinkled her nose.

"Yes."

Resisting her husband's pull, she halted at the bank and gazed over the colonists. Eliza and Sarah beckoned her onward, their skirts billowing atop the rushing river. Thiago handed Lydia back to Sarah then treaded knee deep before the frightened group of people. "Move back. More. Move back." He gestured with palms up. Soon everyone waded farther into the current until the water reached their waists. Even Magnolia's parents! Her mother clung to her father, her face as white as the eddies that swirled and lapped at their clothes.

"Magnolia, you must come in!" It was the first words her father had spoken to her since she married Hayden. She returned a tentative smile.

She hated rivers. "There's dirt and bugs and snakes."

Hayden gestured behind her. "Or ants. Whichever you prefer, Princess." She gave him a sassy grin and glanced over her shoulder. A pulsating black sheet flowed toward her. The closer it came, the more she could make out the individual ants with their spindly legs and spiked antennae.

She leapt into Hayden's arms.

Chuckling, he carried her into the water and set her down. Despite the heat of the day, a chill etched up her back as the current knotted her skirts between her legs. Yet no sooner had her slippers sunk into the silt than the ravenous horde struck the water's edge. For a moment she thought the ants would form ships with their hideous bodies and sail out to get them, but, although a few did get caught in the tide, the rest split down the middle like the parting of the red—or in this case, black—sea and scurried down the bank of the river and off into the jungle.

Still they came. Endless waves of ants as big as a man's thumb, scurrying, scrambling, eating everything that stood in their way. Magnolia's legs grew numb. No doubt sensing her exhaustion, Hayden moved behind her and pulled her against him, wrapping his arms around her waist.

A somber mood descended on the colonists as they fought to keep their balance in the strong current while watching the endless swarm strike the shore. Other than the whine of the ants and the rush of water, the jungle was quiet—terror silencing its creatures. Sweat formed on Magnolia's brow.

A few of the women began to sob. One man cursed.

Magnolia glanced over at Blake and Eliza. The colonel stared straight ahead, his eyes as cold and hard as a river pebble. She imagined he'd worn much the same look after losing a battle in the war. For they all knew the truth. They'd lost this particular battle. The ants had devoured their crops and left them with nothing.

Looking for the rest of her friends, Magnolia scanned the group of colonists. Panic soon overcame sorrow. "Where are Angeline and James?"

⚓

Angeline leaned over to scoop up Stowy, ready to scold him for his disobedience when from the corner of her eye, she saw the ground advancing toward her. No, not the ground—a wall of ants. And they were only a foot away! No time to ponder how they got there so quickly, no time to chastise herself for her foolishness, she clutched Stowy to her chest, intending to run, but her legs felt like tree stumps—heavy and rooted in place. Her heart crumbled into dust as ants swarmed her, first swallowing up her slippers then swelling up her stockings. Pain like a hundred matches torched her skin.

Arms of steel clamped her waist and hoisted her up, smashing her against a thick chest. Stowy let out an angry wail, but Angeline managed to keep a tight grip on the cat as they bounced up and down in the arms of her rescuer. Her legs stung, her arms stung. Ants crawled over her and onto James's arms and neck. His hot breath gusted her cheek. His jaw bunched. His eyes focused. His pace slowed. He let out a growl that seemed to boost his strength to run faster.

Angeline closed her eyes. How could she have been so stupid? She'd put them both in danger, for a cat. But not just any cat—Stowy.

James let out another bestial groan.

"Put me down. I can run," she shouted then shrieked as an ant crawled on her face. She slapped it away. The land sloped upward. James ascended, huffing and panting like a steam engine. His face grew red. Sweat dripped from his jaw. He ground his teeth and continued. Finally at the crest of the hill, he set her down and leaned forward on his knees, gulping in air as if he'd surfaced from a deep lake.

Setting Stowy down, Angeline slapped ants off her skirts and blouse, trying ever so hard not to shriek like a typical goose-livered female. But when she felt something crawling on her thigh. . . Screaming, she turned her back to James, lifted her skirts and punched the vermin away. Two vermin, in fact. The hugest ants she'd ever seen! When she faced James, he smiled at her, his hands still on his knees, his breath still bursting from his lungs.

And an ant on his face. She dashed toward him and struck his cheek.

He shot back, eyes blinking. "Not exactly the response I expected after saving your life."

"There was an ant. . ."

"Thanks." He rubbed his jaw. "I think." Then, as if concerned more of the pesky critters were on him, he raked furious hands through his hair, shaking it over the ground. Nothing fell loose, but when he righted himself, he looked like a soft-quilled porcupine.

She would laugh if she weren't so frightened. "Are we safe here?" She peered down the hill.

"For now. They seem more interested in our fields and town."

"So many of them." Angeline gathered Stowy to her chest and slid beside James. Through the tangle of trees and vines, a dark wave flooded the land below. "Where are they all coming from?"

"Where are they going?" James added. "And more importantly, why, of all places, did they choose to devour *our* fields?" Hopelessness drained the life from his normally cheerful voice as the continual drone of destruction rang through the jungle. A gust of wind stirred leaves overhead, dappling him in sunlight and setting the perspiration on his forehead aglow.

Sweet saints, he'd risked his life for her!

"Thank you for saving me." Angeline swallowed as visions of her and Stowy smothered in ants filled her mind and resurrected pain from a dozen bites still burning her skin. Heart racing, she glanced down, expecting to see her skirts covered with the evil vermin. "I still feel them on me." She thrust Stowy at James and frantically brushed her arms and skirts, slapping and striking and punching. Panic sent her heart spinning along with her body as she ran hands through each strand of hair.

James gripped her arm, stopping her. "There's nothing on you,

Angeline." He leaned over until their eyes locked—his calm and as strong as their bronze color, hers flitting between his until their peace flowed onto her. She nodded and took a deep breath.

"Did they bite you?" James asked.

"My legs. They still sting."

"I should examine them."

"No need." She looked away. If this man's touch on her arm made odd things swirl in her belly, what would his fingers do on her bare legs? Best not to find out.

Stowy meowed and reached for Angeline. James held him up. "And you, you pesky varmint. We were nearly eaten alive because of you."

Angeline smiled at his playful tone. Most men would be furious at Stowy and even more furious at Angeline for going after him. But James was no ordinary man.

No ordinary man would have risked his own life to save hers either. Twice now. No, three times. Once aboard the ship and twice in Brazil. Which made her indebted to him. And she hated being indebted to anyone. Neither did she like being rescued. Being rescued was for weak women looking for a hero. And Angeline knew there was no such thing as heroes. Or happy endings. Never before had anyone swooped in to rescue her when she'd been in danger. Men had swooped in, that much was true, but much like these ants, they had stung and stung and then left her covered with bites and scars.

No, she didn't need a man to help her. She didn't need or want *anyone*.

"Why are you always rescuing me?" Her curt tone snapped James around to face her. Shock transformed into confusion and finally into anger.

"Because you are always doing foolish things."

Angeline wanted to tell him to leave her alone the next time he thought her foolish, but the whine of the ants suddenly grew louder and a line of the vile pests appeared over the ridge of the hill. Grabbing her hand, James plunged deeper into the jungle. With one arm tucked to shield Stowy, he shoved aside leaves and branches with his shoulder, forming a safe cocoon for Angeline following in his wake.

She tried to focus on her legs moving and her lungs breathing and not the feel of James's hand forming a fortress around hers, guiding her to safety. She wanted to let go of him and find her own way. She wanted to never trust anyone again. But, for the life of her, she couldn't seem to release her grip.

Finally, he halted, shoved her behind him, and turned to stare down the path.

Ants continued to advance, their scouts weaving down the trail ahead of the pack. Not just down the trail, but now coming at them from every side. Where had they come from? There was nowhere else to run. Angeline squeezed her eyes shut.

They were going to be eaten alive.

A grunt, followed by the sound of tree bark scraping and James's voice, drifted from above. "Grab ahold!" She pried her eyes open to see his hand reaching down from a low-hanging branch. A sheet of ants marched toward her, inches from her feet. Slapping her hand into his, she heard him groan, felt her feet leave the ground, her legs failing. Ants swarmed the dirt beneath her and stormed up the trunk. Sweat slicked her hand. It started to slip from James's grasp.

CHAPTER 8

Dangling in midair over a horde of army ants, Angeline gazed up at James. His tight grip on her wrist slid. Just a fraction. But it slid. Sweat dripped off his chin. His determined gaze pierced hers like a rod of iron forming an impenetrable bond between them. "I won't let go. Do you hear me? I won't let you go."

With a torturous groan, he hoisted her up, grabbed her waist, and set her on the branch beside him. The ants continued their insatiable crunch and snap over the jungle floor below, but she dared not look. "Won't they climb up the tree?" she breathed out, trying to settle her heart. Stowy leapt into her lap and meowed in complaint.

"I don't think so. Thiago said this species stays on the ground or beneath it."

Yet even as he said it, the little pests continued to skitter up the trunk.

"Come." He stood, pulled himself up to a thicker branch above, and reached down for her and Stowy. He did the same again and again until they were high above the ground.

"Where did you learn to climb so well? You're nearly as good as Thiago." Angeline took his hand one last time as he hoisted her onto the final branch.

"Summers in Tennessee."

He found a spot where several branches grew together, forming a flat area as big as a cot. Plopping down, he helped Angeline to sit beside him, his breath bursting in his chest. Hers was too, especially thinking the ants had followed. But when she dared a glance down,

59

none were in sight, at least not on the tree. The ground, however, rolled and swayed like storm clouds at night. Leaning her head back on the trunk, she lowered her shoulders and ran fingers through Stowy's fur. The cat seemed to understand their tenuous predicament and curled up in her lap.

"You're trembling." James swung an arm around her and drew her close.

"Who wouldn't be?" She wiggled from beneath his touch. "With a horde of army ants beneath our feet." She hated that she'd put a frown on his face, but she rarely allowed anyone to touch her—especially a man.

Taking the hint, he moved away. "If I act inappropriately, you still have your pistol." He gestured toward the weapon stuffed in her belt as a rakish grin appeared on his lips.

She laughed and plucked out the pistol, laying it beside her. "I'd forgotten all about it." Though as uncomfortable as it was pressed against her belly, she didn't know how. She raised a coy brow. "Don't think I won't use it, Doctor."

"Oh, I have no doubt, Miss." He lifted his hands in surrender. "You can count on me to be a gentleman."

Yes, she did believe she could. But that only made things harder. She looked away. "I suppose I should thank you, yet again."

"Not if you don't mean it."

A breeze swirled through the leaves of the tree, dousing her with the scent that was uniquely James—all musk and man. "Of course I mean it. . . . I *do* thank you. It's just that. . ." She sighed. "Never mind." Bundling Stowy close to her chest, she suddenly wished she weren't alone with James. He had a way about him that made her want to share things she wouldn't share with anyone. She supposed it was the preacher in him. His duty to care for people and listen to their problems.

He stretched his legs out, dangling one over the side of their wooden platform. "But you'd rather not accept anyone's help, is that it?"

She searched his eyes for any mockery but found only concern. "Do you find that so odd?"

"For a lady, yes."

"So you assume all women are weak and in need of help?"

His brows shot up, and a grin touched his lips. "Whoa, I didn't say that. I meant no disrespect, Angeline."

She looked away. "Forgive me. I suppose it's just the stress of being chased by killer ants." She forced a smile, trying to lighten the conversation. It wasn't James's fault she trusted no one.

Placing a finger beneath her chin, he turned her to face him. "There's no shame in needing help." His eyes seemed to look right through her, and she found the sensation unsettling to say the least.

She jerked from his touch. "It depends on the price."

❦

Price? The woman baffled James. They'd barely escaped a rather unpleasant death—one he'd pulled her from twice—and all she could talk about was not wanting his help. Or anyone's. "There is no price."

"Maybe not this time," she mumbled, petting her infernal cat.

James rubbed the back of his neck. What had happened to this poor woman? He so desperately wanted to know more about her. Why did she oftentimes carry a pistol in her belt? What made her turn from lady to dragon in a matter of seconds? Why did she seem so frightened of Dodd? Why, when she thought no one was looking, did a deep sorrow linger in her eyes?

The drone of ants lessened below, though the ground still moved. She followed his gaze, and her breath seemed to heighten.

"We are safe here," he reassured her. "If they were coming up, they would have done so by now."

"I fear for our friends. I hope they are all right."

"I'm sure they made it to the river." He drew his knees up and placed his elbows atop them. "Where we should have gone."

Angeline frowned, the freckles on her nose clumping together. "You should have gone without me."

"Despite your aversion to rescuing, I couldn't do that."

"And *I* couldn't leave Stowy either." She lifted the cat and planted a kiss on its head.

James suddenly wished he were in Stowy's shoes—or paws. He shook the thought away. It was such wayward thinking that had caused his many falls from grace. Angeline was a lady of the highest morals who didn't deserve to be ogled or thought of with impurity. Despite the fact that she looked so incredibly beautiful and vulnerable at the moment. A sheen of perspiration made her skin glow and transformed curls framing her face into dangling rubies. The rest of her russet hair tumbled in waves over her shoulders, down her back and into her lap, where Stowy played with a strand clutched between his paws. James swallowed.

Thankfully, the screech of a macaw sounded, followed by the chorus of birds returning to their song, jarring his thoughts. What was wrong with him? They'd almost been smothered by ants, their crops were ruined, and all he could think about was how being close to Angeline made him feel so alive.

She peered through the canopy, her gaze scanning the ground below, where the swarm of ants had thinned considerably. "How long before it's safe to return to New Hope?"

Eyes the color of the violets his mother used to grow in their garden in Knoxville searched his. Only, the violet in Angeline's eyes was more like a bottomless pool of swirling emotions. Emotions he longed to explore, along with those lips of hers she so often bit when she was nervous. He looked away. "We should wait until there's not an ant in sight. I don't want to risk getting trapped."

Nodding, she leaned back against the trunk and folded up the sleeves of her blouse against the sultry heat. A flicker of sunlight brushed over a pink scar on her forearm. He'd seen scars like that before. Many of them. All caused by knives embedded in flesh. But why would such a lovely lady like Angeline have been the victim of such violence? His gaze shifted to the ring she wore on a chain around her neck. Normally she kept it tucked within her bodice, but perhaps it had loosened during their mad dash through the jungle. Since it appeared to be a man's ring, he'd always wondered about it but had been afraid to pry.

Now seemed like the perfect time.

"That ring you always wear around your neck, it must be important to you."

Her lips flattened. "I realize, Doctor, that we find ourselves inappropriately alone, but that does not grant you entrance into my personal life." Her strident tone surprised him. Though he didn't know why. The woman could switch moods faster than a chameleon could colors. Flinching at the sting in his heart, he held up his palms. "Douse those flames, your dragonship; I was just asking."

"Dragonship?" A sparkle lit her eyes, softening the hard sheen of only a moment before. "Sweet saints, where did that come from?" She laughed.

"Sorry. Old habit." James shrugged, thrilled to see her anger flee. "I used to read stories about dragons when I was a little boy. They fascinated me." He shrugged. "Were dragons good? Evil? How did they make the fire that came out of their snouts?" He winked.

"So am I to be compared to a dragon now?" She laughed as the tension dissipated between them. "You are a strange man, indeed. A doctor, or rather preacher, who is fascinated by creatures that don't exist."

Her gaze snapped to his, and he knew she also referred to the invisible beasts he claimed were tormenting the colonists.

A bird landed on a branch and eyed them curiously before beginning a serenade in a variety of tones and notes and pitches that would shame a symphony orchestra.

Despite the joyful tune, she grew quiet. After several minutes, she lifted the ring and fingered it like it was the answer to all her prayers. "It was my father's. He gave it to me on his deathbed."

Sunlight cut a swath through the canopy and swayed over the ruby in the center, setting it aflame.

"It's beautiful," James said.

"Yes." She stared at it as if lost in another time.

"When did he die?"

"I was only seventeen."

"And your mother?"

"At my birth." She swiped away a tear, and James felt like a cad for bringing up such morbid memories.

She held the ring up to him. "My father told me I was the ruby in the center and he and my mother were the topazes on either side, watching out for me." She smiled but her voice caught.

"They must have loved you very much," James said. And with their death, this poor lady was left an orphan at only seventeen. Had family taken her in?

She withdrew the ring, kissed it, and slipped it beneath her bodice. "So now you know." She sounded disappointed.

"I can keep a secret."

"It's not a secret. It's just mine to know and no one else's."

"Then I am indeed honored you shared it with me."

She gave him a sly smile. "You coerced it out of me, sir. Took advantage of my weakness."

"Weakness? You? Never."

An expression akin to disbelief shadowed her face before she glanced away. He longed to bring those violet eyes back to his.

"Friends share things about their lives." He shifted on the hard bark. "It helps them know each other." Did she consider him a friend? He hoped so, though he wanted so much more.

She scooted away and peered down through the branches. "The more a person knows about someone, the more power they have over them."

Shock kept James silent. For several minutes, he watched her pet Stowy and gaze at the ground, no doubt searching for ants. Strands of hair blew in the breeze across her waist. "I want no power over you, Angeline."

"No?" Turning, she raised a disbelieving brow before glancing down again. "Everyone wants something."

James scratched his jaw. What had happened to make this lady so cynical?

"The ants are gone," she announced.

He inched beside her and peered through the lattice of leaves toward the distant fields. Small patches of dark still moved across ground that looked gray and empty in the blaring sun. "We should wait awhile longer. Just to make sure."

Regardless of whether the lady or the dragon appeared, James was rather enjoying his time with Angeline. When they climbed down from this tree, only God knew what they'd have to face: the loss of their crops, all their food, perhaps even their town. And he could only hope and pray there'd been no injuries. Or deaths. But for now, he would relish being close to a woman he'd spent five months with and yet felt he hardly knew. Every moment in her company only endeared her more to him. And made him want to dig deeper and deeper to understand everything about her. He'd never felt that way about a woman. Never thought he'd find a woman interesting enough and pure and good enough to marry. Yet, here was a woman he could care for. Here was a woman he could love. Perhaps his philandering wasn't his own fault at all. How could any man resist a woman who flaunted herself before him like a French praline?

"I lost my father as well," he said hoping to resurrect the conversation. "Just a few years ago."

She stopped petting Stowy. "Then you understand."

"Yes. Though I was much older than you, it was hard nonetheless."

She nodded but said nothing. He wanted to continue talking. . . wanted to find that connection they seemed to have earlier. But he couldn't tell her that he'd been responsible for his father's death—that he might as well have shot the man himself. Instead he said, "I was not the same person back then."

This piqued her interest as she swept an attentive gaze his way.

Prompting him to continue. "I've done some horrible things that I'm not proud of. Shameful things."

She didn't seem surprised, nor did she inquire what things. Instead, she simply stared at him with an odd approval as if he'd just informed her that he bore the bloodline of the prince of Wales.

⟳⟲

Angeline could hardly believe James would divulge such information. Yet once he said it, she could hardly stop herself from pressing him to reveal more. Most of her mistrust of the doctor—aside from him being a man, of course—stemmed from their brief encounter over a year ago in a Tennessee tavern. Though she doubted he remembered her, was he now confessing the sins of that night?

"We've all made mistakes, Doctor," she said, releasing Stowy to wander around the branches. "The important thing is that we move past them and become better for them."

He scrubbed the dark stubble peppering his jaw. "Indeed. And also that we repent and allow God to change our hearts."

She scoffed inwardly. It was she and she alone who had changed her life. Not God. But she wouldn't tell James that and start another theological debate.

"So what *were* these sins, exactly?" She raised a brow, half teasing, half desperate to know.

"Ah, who is being overbold now?"

She smiled.

"Drinking." He hesitated, searching her eyes, then lowered his gaze. "Women." Was that red crawling up his neck? "Too many of both."

Memories of him lying on a ratty, stained bed above a tavern that blared and thumped with music and laughter drifted through her mind. He'd been so drunk, he could hardly stand. And covered in blood. Too much to have come from the gash at the side of his mouth. But he'd been kind. And sad. Terribly sad about something. Which is why she remembered him from all the others.

Now, she laid a hand on his and said the words that screamed true within her—words she wanted so desperately to be true. "You are right. You're not that man anymore."

This brought his eyes up to search hers, the hope within them conflicting with the pain and despair that had filled them that night long ago. He pressed a thumb on the scar on the right side of his mouth. "Thank you for saying that."

If only she believed it of herself. Shoving aside her morbid thoughts, she offered him a smile. "And now we both know a secret about the other."

"Mine is much more incriminating."

"But safe with me."

He nodded, and his trust in her caused her heart to swell.

Stowy pounced on James's leg and began gnawing at his trousers. "Hey, you little rascal!" Clutching the cat, he flipped him on his back and knuckled his tummy. Stowy pawed James's hand in a mock battle for dominance he was sure to lose.

Watching how gentle and playful James was with Stowy, Angeline's heart felt lighter than a feather. Perhaps she *could* trust this man. He *had* changed, hadn't he? He'd made mistakes, but he freely admitted them. And when he could have lied about his past, he'd been honest with her. Besides, hadn't Angeline changed? Hadn't this new life in Brazil offered her a second chance? How could she deny the same to James?

Setting Stowy between them, James raised his gaze to hers. A breeze ripe with oranges and mossy earth swirled around them, toying with the hair at his collar as they stared into each other's eyes, searching, wondering, hoping. . .daring to trust.

Raising his hand, he cupped her jaw and swept a thumb over her cheek. Angeline's heart quickened. A tingle ran across her skin. He glanced at her lips and licked his own. And she knew he wanted to kiss her. More than that, she desperately wanted to kiss him back.

CHAPTER 9

J ames! Angeline!" Blake's baritone shout jarred them apart, drew them embarrassed to the edge of their tree terrace to see their friends combing the jungle below. With an odd reluctance, James had assisted Angeline and Stowy to the ground, ending their precious time together—moments that had given him hope for a promising future.

A hope, however, that was dashed as he now stood beside Hayden and Blake and some of the other colonists before their desolate fields. Where once stalks of sugarcane had poked through fertile ground, where once coffee seedlings budded fresh leaves, now there was naught but barren dirt dotted with bare twigs. Stunned silence shrouded the group, save for the occasional sob from the women and curse from the men.

A few leftover ants skittered about, separated from their army, their fate in the hands of angry colonists who stomped the life from them. One man even pulled a pistol and shot one, causing everyone to jump. Finally, however, when it became obvious no amount of staring would bring back their crops, the group assembled, one by one, in the meeting area, somber and dejected, and—all but James and Angeline—soaked to the bone. Blake stood in front of the crowd, Eliza by his side, while James took a spot beside him, should the leader of the colony need reinforcement.

Yet from the expression on the colonel's face, he needed much more than reinforcement. He needed encouragement. And hope. Something they all lacked at the moment.

"What are we gonna do, Colonel?" one of the farmers asked before

Blake could even begin.

"We are going to plant again," he responded without hesitation.

The colonists' groans were silenced by a lift of his hand. "We still have most of the sugar splints. Though the ants stripped them, they didn't eat them entirely. With some care, they should sprout again. The coffee might too, though we still have some seed if need be."

"Preposterous!" Mr. Scott, Magnolia's father, bellowed. "Start over again?"

"But we have no food," a woman whined.

Eliza stepped forward. "We still have rice and beans. They didn't eat through the burlap sacks."

"And we have fish from the river," Angeline offered.

"And fruit and wild boar from jungle," Thiago said. "I can teach men to hunt better."

Mr. Lewis took a swig from his flask and wiped his mouth on his sleeve. "All that work wasted."

"It will be wasted if we give up." Hayden ran a hand through his moist hair.

"I say we quit and go home," one of the ex-soldiers shouted, glancing over the mob. "Enough is enough."

"Besides, how can we pay the emperor what we owe him for the land now?"

"We will pay him when we can pay him," James said. "Come now, surely you aren't ready to give up after one setback? Not after all we've endured to make it this far."

Shadows crept out from hiding as the sun lowered in the sky, bringing a breeze that caused many of the colonists to shiver in their wet clothes.

"We've had more than our share of trouble," one man yelled.

Another farmer slapped his hat on his knee. "At least back in Georgia, I wasn't in debt."

"But we are still alive!" Angeline said, sharing a smile with James that caused his heart to leap. "No one was hurt. And our huts, tools, and dried food are intact."

Standing beside his sister, Moses, the freedman, scooped one of her children in his arms. "I says we stay." His gaze met Mable's, who stood beside her owner, Mr. Scott.

The elderly man let out a bloated grunt. "And, pray tell, who cares what a slave thinks? I, for one, plan to leave."

"Freedman, Papa. He's not a slave anymore." Magnolia nodded at Moses before turning to her mother, who wrung her hands together in her usual worried fit.

Breaking through the crowd, Patrick Gale sauntered into the clearing like a king surveying his subjects. "True, we expected hardships in this new land, but we certainly didn't expect complete destruction. I say none of us should feel guilty for leaving now."

Grunts of assent rang through the air.

James frowned. Of course the man wanted people to leave. Fewer people to stake a claim on his gold. If he ever found any, *and* if he intended to share it with the colony like he promised. Dodd, his partner in the mad treasure quest, sat off to the side, nodding his agreement.

"Go back to what?" Blake shifted weight off his sore leg. "Back to destruction, devastation, and tyranny? Why, I'd rather deal with nature's blows than man's, wouldn't you?"

A few nodded. Wind whipped leaves by feet that were bare and muddy due to wading in the river.

"What if the ants come again?"

Crossing his arms over his chest, James shrugged. "What if they do? What if our crops fail or our cane press breaks or the river dries up? Life is full of struggles. But also blessings. Remember, God is on our side."

Several colonists shook their heads in dismay, but Eliza smiled his way. "Indeed, Doctor. And He will see us through."

As if disagreeing, the last rays of sunlight withdrew through the trees and left them in darkness.

Lanterns were lit, but most of the colonists retired to their huts, too tired and wet to argue anymore. James was surprised when Angeline didn't join them. Especially after the harrowing day she'd endured. Instead, Stowy still in her arms, she stoked the coals in the brick stove and put on some water for tea then joined him and the remaining colonists around the fire Blake lit in the center of the clearing.

Flames reflected over her loose hair, casting it in a fiery red that reminded him of the dragon he'd called her earlier. Holy thunder, he'd nearly kissed her! Her gaze briefly met his, but she bit her lip and quickly looked away, as if embarrassed.

Blake's somber tone brought James from his musings. "So, are you thinking what I'm thinking, Doc?" The colonel led his wife to sit on a log and lowered himself beside her.

"If you're thinking this could be the work of *Destruction*, then yes." He scanned his friends' reactions, not wanting to seem foolish but not wanting to hide his suspicions either. Especially should they be true. "First Graves's death, the earthquake at the tunnels, the lightning strike, and now this. Either we have encountered a string of terrible luck or something else is going on here."

"What on earth are you talking about?" Dodd scratched his thick sideburns and spat in the dirt.

"We are talking about the ancient Hebrew book I'm translating, the one Graves found in the tunnels. We're talking about the cannibal temple, the empty prison alcoves beneath it, and these odd visions and disasters that keep happening. They are linked somehow."

"Nonsense!" Patrick's tone was spiked with haughty disbelief as he adjusted his necktie. "I, for one, have encountered no visions. And these disasters are nothing but misfortunes common to any new settlers. Tell them, Diego!" He motioned toward Thiago.

"I am called Thiago." The Brazilian guide didn't hide his disdain for the man. "But *sim*, they are all natural events." He moved beside Sarah, who sat on a chair, baby Lydia in her lap.

Magnolia slid her hand into Hayden's. "But so many disasters so close together?"

Patrick's slick gaze took her in like a crocodile would a rabbit, before he shifted eyes toward his son, Hayden. Though there was a physical resemblance, the similarities between them stopped there.

Hayden drew his wife closer. "Though I hate to agree with Patrick, I'm not ready to believe that some evil supernatural beast has caused our visions and all these misfortunes."

"I hope you are right." Blake rubbed his eyes and tossed another log in the fire. It crackled and spit, sending sparks into the night.

"I do as well." James lowered to sit on a stump. But he doubted it. He must interpret more of the book. It was up to him, and him alone, to figure out what was happening. Not only because he was the only one who knew Hebrew but also because he was the only one who was fully convinced that something spiritual was afoot. A sudden weight pressed on his shoulders. Of all the people to bear such responsibility... *God, what are You doing? I've done nothing but fail my entire life.*

Even the rising croak of frogs and crickets seemed to mock him.

"What will happen if some of the colonists leave as they've threatened?" Hayden shifted his stance. "We will lose good men. Good workers."

"Regardless," Eliza said. "None of *us* are leaving. We all believe God brought us here. We must fight and not give up."

"God. Bah!" Patrick snorted before shaking his head and turning to leave. "I shall leave you with your foolish notions."

Good riddance, as far as James was concerned. Magnolia seemed to agree as she released a sigh and leaned against Hayden.

James faced Angeline. "What about you, Angeline? Do you wish to leave?"

She caressed Stowy's fur a moment before lifting her eyes to his, causing his heart to nearly break at the pain he saw within them. "I have nowhere else to go."

Neither did James. There was too much pain back in the States. For him. For all of them. They had no choice. They must make a life here in Brazil, or they would have no life at all.

A month passed. New sugar stalks sprouted and coffee was replanted, and soon the fertile Brazilian soil pushed up infant sprouts in a promise of coming abundance. Though ten colonists had packed their things and started on foot for Rio de Janeiro, the spirits of those who remained lifted with each passing day—each passing day in which no further disasters struck. The river provided an abundance of fish and the jungle a bounty of fruit. And Angeline's nightmarish visions had decreased. Even Dodd seemed more preoccupied with finding his gold than gawking at her. Perhaps the worst was over. Perhaps God was indeed on their side.

Angeline couldn't help but hum a cheerful tune as she flitted about her hut in preparation for the day. She had several shirts and trousers that needed mending as well as a torn quilt. And in the afternoon, she would assist Sarah in teaching the children. Yet, if she was honest, it was the thought of James that had her in such good humor. His attentions toward her had become more frequent and intense, made all the sweeter by her growing knowledge of his character and honor. Yes, he *had* changed. He wasn't the same man she'd met in Tennessee over a year ago. Why, he'd even encouraged her to attend Sunday services, and she had found him to be a good preacher, fervent and heartfelt. This was a man she might well be able to trust. A man who could make her forget her past—sweep away the horrid memories like so much dust—and give her hope. Hope that she could live a normal life and find happiness like a normal woman.

A voice sounded from outside the canvas flap that served as a door to the hut she shared with Sarah. Her heart jolted in her chest. She knew that voice, a deep throaty voice that held a zest for life and a hint of hope. Checking herself in the small mirror on the wall, she pinched her cheeks and swept the flap aside. A bouquet of violet hibiscus and pink orchids filled her vision, flooding her with beauty and fragrance. Behind them, James's smile sent a streak of warmth down to her toes.

"Good day," he said. "I came across these in the jungle this morning and they reminded me of you."

If she didn't know how sincere he was, she'd laugh at his mawkish attempt at wooing her. Yet, despite his age of eight and twenty, he bore a charming boyishness that made her blush.

And she hadn't blushed in years.

"Why, thank you, Doctor. . .I mean James," she corrected herself and plucked the flowers from his hand. "They are lovely."

"Indeed." His bronze eyes poured life and love into hers, momentarily mesmerizing her. She could stare at them all day—at the depth of promise they held. But people were beginning to stir from their huts, curious gazes drifting their way.

The soothing rush of the river and flutter of leaves in the breeze whisked over her ears, accompanied by the happy warble of birds. A sleepy-eyed Hayden walked past, smiling at her and giving a knowing wink to James. James shifted his boots on the dirt and ran a finger down the scar angling the right side of his mouth as his gaze flitted about the town.

"Did you want something, James?"

"Yes. I. . .I hoped you would accompany me on a stroll after supper.

Down to the beach. It's so lovely there in the evening."

"A stroll?" She teased with a grin. "Alone with you?"

The right side of his lips curved upward as he leaned toward her. "I hope you know by now that you can trust me, Angeline."

His breath warmed her cheek. "I do."

"I have something to ask you."

Her legs turned to noodles, and she leaned on the door frame. *He was going to ask if he could court her!* He'd hinted about it often enough the past few weeks, though she had refused to believe it was possible. Her being courted by so fine a gentleman! Her being treated like a true lady.

Wiley Dodd emerged from his hut across the way, smothering her hopes with his frown. "How quaint." He chuckled. "Another early morning rendezvous. And flowers too?"

Releasing a sigh of frustration, James slowly turned to face him. "Shouldn't you be looking for gold, Dodd?"

"There's more than one type of treasure, Doc." He flashed his brows and winked at Angeline.

"But only *one* that can satisfy your insatiable greed, so be on your way, Dodd. And learn to mind your own business in the future." James's brass tone held an undeniable warning that sent emotion burning in Angeline's throat. Never had a gentleman stood up for her before.

"Threats, threats." Dodd clicked his tongue. "And from our preacher too. What is the world coming to?" He peered around James, his eyes locking on Angeline. "Have a pleasant day, Miss Angeline."

Acid welled in her belly. She tore her gaze from his. Why wouldn't the man leave her be? His petulant whistle as he strolled away grated on her worst fears.

James turned and took her hand in his. "Don't let him bother you. He's harmless."

Angeline wasn't so sure.

"Till supper then?" He placed a kiss on her hand and started down the street, glancing one last time at her over his shoulder. Diving her nose in the bouquet, she watched him walk away in that confident, boyish gait of his, light hair rippling in the breeze, white shirt, tan trousers tucked within his black work boots that stomped toward the fields for his day's work. A feeling welled up inside of her she'd never known before, an ache so palpable she pressed a hand over her heart.

She loved James. At least she thought it was love. He stirred her body, soul, and spirit like no man ever had. Like she never knew a man could. But more than that, she cared for him, wanted the best for him. But therein lay the problem—one that was becoming more real the more her feelings grew. For if she truly loved him, she'd run as far away from him as she could.

⚜

Dodd slapped aside an oversized leaf with his shovel and trudged after Patrick. The man claimed to have discovered some new secret twist on the treasure maps during the night and was once again leading the way to the "gold that would make Dodd a king." After three such grand declarations and nothing to show for it but sore muscles, blisters, and empty holes, Dodd's frustration level was rising—along with his doubts.

"If this new information of yours don't produce gold, we are switching roles. I'll be the brains and you can be the brawn."

"Don't be absurd, man." Patrick's ever-annoying imperious tone continued to eat away at what was left of Dodd's patience. "We must remain in the stations nature has given us. It will work out for the best in the end. You'll see."

"Nature ain't given me the station of digging, I can swear to that." Or trekking through a jungle so sultry it felt like wading through a hot bath. What Dodd wouldn't give for a real hot bath. And a shave and a drink. And a woman. Which brought his thoughts back to Angeline and the memory of her and the doc acting all intimate that morning.

Patrick halted and Dodd barreled into him, releasing a string of curses. "For crying's sake, tell me when you're going to stop."

"What has got you in such a foul mood today, Dodd?" Patrick fingered his goatee and scanned the jungle.

Dodd did the same but saw nothing but a web of green and brown strung between thin trees that reached for the sky. "How can you tell where we are going? Everything looks the same."

"That's why I'm the brains, my friend." Patrick continued marching forward as a band of yellow monkeys raced through the canopy, chattering like gossiping women at tea.

"I'm guessing it's a woman," Patrick said.

"What's a woman?"

"The reason for your foul temper."

Dodd cursed the man's blasted intuition.

"It's the seamstress, isn't it?" Withdrawing a handkerchief, Patrick dabbed his neck. "That voluptuous redhead."

"None of your business," Dodd growled, crushing a lizard beneath his boot.

"Ah, but it is my business, especially if I am to endure your company day after day. Why not make a play for her?"

"She doesn't want me. We have a past."

"Ah, interesting. Tell me more."

"I'll tell you nothing."

Patrick chuckled. "She and the good doctor seem to be forming an attachment."

Which was exactly what grated on Dodd. "What's that to me?"

"Only that if you want her, you must be a man and take her."

"Like you did Magnolia?" Dodd snickered.

Patrick turned on him, eyes like slits and jaw distended. "I allowed my son to have the wench." He poked Dodd's chest with his jeweled finger. "And you'll not forget it. I will have any woman I want after I find this gold."

Dodd smiled as the man resumed his march. The only pleasure he'd had on these torturous excursions were the few times he'd gotten under the pompous horker's skin. Yet, he could not deny the wisdom in the man's words. Dodd was in need of female companionship. And there was a perfectly lovely female for the taking, one that he could force to do whatever he wanted. Then what was he waiting for?

Dipping a cloth in the brook, Angeline wrung it out and brought it to her neck and face. She wanted to look her best for her stroll with James, but her day had been so busy, she hadn't had time to bathe properly. Besides, after Dodd discovered the women's bathing pool a few months back, they really hadn't found a new spot where the ladies felt safe from prying eyes.

A flock of parakeets darted from branch to branch in a nearby tree chirping and playfully pecking each other's beaks, drawing a smile from Angeline. Water trickled over a mound of boulders as it made its way down the creek bed while Stowy sprawled on a flat rock, soaking in what was left of the sun before it dipped behind the trees. Angeline moistened her cloth again. Sitting on a fallen log, she allowed the cool water to soothe her skin, all the while wondering at the peculiar feeling of happiness that invaded her soul. A happiness that brought back fleeting memories of her childhood before her father had died. Had it only been four years ago? It felt like a lifetime, so foreign were these sensations of contentment and joy.

Visions of the past few years attempted to barge into her thoughts, but she shoved them back. Today she would accept James's suit. Today she would put her memories behind her and become a real lady. She had already changed her name, why not change her past along with it? James need never know anything different. How could keeping her secret be wrong when she knew she could make him happy? Yes, she would make him very happy. She loved him, and love could never be wrong.

Unbuttoning the top buttons of her collar, she dipped the rag in the creek again and dabbed her chest. *Thu-ump, thu-ump, thu-ump*, she could feel the pounding of her heart against her fingers, proving her excitement for the coming evening. The crunch of leaves snapped her to attention. Plucking her pistol from her belt, she slowly stood and swerved to aim at a shadow emerging from the jungle. Retreating sunlight slicked over blond hair, slid down a pointy nose, to finally ride on the smug shoulders of Wiley Dodd.

Chapter 10

"What do you want, Dodd?" Though the barrel of the gun quivered in Angeline's hand, she kept it leveled at the vile ex-lawman.

He strutted toward her, his grin reminding her of Stowy after he caught a mouse—pleased with himself and very, very hungry. A hungry gaze that now lowered to her unbuttoned shirt. Taking a step back, she determined to shoot the man if he came any closer.

"You have a bad habit of spying on women at their bath, sir," she spat.

He clipped thumbs in his belt and eyed her. "I meant no offense, I merely came to talk."

"I have nothing to say to you." She gestured toward the jungle with her gun. "Now, leave."

"Ah, but you had plenty to say to me that night at the Night Owl."

Angeline's heart plummeted. She wanted to say she knew of no place by that name. She wanted to call him mad. But they both knew she'd be lying.

He grinned. "I see you understand me quite well, my dear."

"I am not your dear, and I don't understand at all. Who cares if you remember me from some tavern?" She lifted one shoulder. "What is that to me?"

"Nothing to you, I'm sure. But everything to your doctor beau. You *have* noticed how he abhors immoral women? Why, he talks about it all the time—how he wants to keep our new town free of such vices as harlotry and the like."

Nausea bubbled in her stomach. Of course she'd noticed. It was all she'd thought about the last month as she and James had grown closer. "Well, it's a good thing there aren't any harlots here."

He raised a taunting brow. "Aren't there?"

She lowered the gun, all hope lowering with it. "I knew you recognized me. You knew the minute we boarded the ship that brought us here, am I right?"

He circled her, assessing her as a panther would a rabbit. "Who could forget such a face?" He halted in front of her. "Or such a figure."

A lizard skittered up a tree behind him, the perfect example of the man before her. Slimy, slick, and sneaky. "Then why wait until now to say something?"

He cocked his head. "Because, my dear, I knew you would never come to me of your own will, so we could. . .how shall I say?"—he tapped his chin—"Become reacquainted?"

A hiss followed by a growl drew her gaze to Stowy, who glared at Dodd from his perch on a rock. Even her cat could spot a bad seed. "I wish no reacquaintance with you."

"Was our one night so terrible?" He ran a finger down her cheek. "Your moans of pleasure still ring in my ears."

"Moans of disgust, you mean." She jerked from his touch and snapped angry eyes his way. "Yet men like you always think them from delight."

A slight tic appeared at the corner of his lips. His eyes narrowed, and for a moment, she thought he might strike her. But then he thrust a finger in the air as if testing the wind. "But since you brought up the topic of pleasure, that is the reason I'm here."

The sun dipped below the trees, hiding its warmth and light from the hideous scene.

Stowy circled the hem of her skirts.

"I am a lonely man."

"That does not surprise me." Scooping up her cat, she stormed past him, but he clamped her arm. Tight. She winced.

He spun her around. "Then we will be lonely together, for once the good preacher hears about your prior profession, I do believe he'll have nothing more to do with you."

Though Angeline had known the threat was coming, hearing it out loud sent such a wave of agony through her, she nearly crumbled to the ground. Would have crumbled to the ground if the beast weren't still gripping her arm. She tore away from him, her breath coming hard and fast.

"Why? Why are you doing this now?" When she'd fallen in love. When she finally had a chance at happiness.

Blue eyes sparked with mischief. "Because now you have a reason to do as I say, my dear. Before James showered you with attention, you may have been willing to have your reputation besmirched. But not now. Not when you have everything to lose."

Everything to lose. Yet, hadn't she lost it all the second Dodd had set foot on the ship? Or was it the second her uncle forced himself on her all those years ago? Perhaps she never really had any chance of happiness at all. Tears flooded her eyes, and she lowered her chin.

"Come now." Dodd approached and leaned to peer up at her. "It won't be so bad. You will come to me in the night. Once or twice a week will suffice. I'm not greedy. And during the day you may carry on your callow dalliance with the doctor or preacher or whatever he is. You see, unlike your pretentious preacher, I am willing to share. What you see in the man is beyond me."

Anger dried her tears, and she lifted her head. "He's everything you are not."

"Yet I will have *you* in my bed while he carries on like a sheep-headed minion." He smiled. "What do you say to that?"

She stared at him, knowing she had no cards to play. No choice but to obey. Just like she'd had no choice in what she'd become. Dodd absorbed her with his gaze again, and the thought of him touching her sent a foul taste creeping into her mouth.

"Cat got your tongue?" He chuckled, reaching to pet Stowy, but the cat hissed at him again. Frowning, he withdrew his hand. "Well, you best get your voice back, my dear, because I'll expect your answer in two weeks. Yes, yes, I'm not completely without compassion. I will grant you some time to consider your options. Enough time to realize you have none."

And with that, he kissed her on the cheek before she could stop him then turned and strutted away, whistling a discordant tune.

Clutching her skirts, Angeline made her way to the water's edge and dropped to the ground. Groping for the rag through blurry vision, she found it and scrubbed and scrubbed and scrubbed her cheek until her skin was raw and stinging and her tears fell in a puddle on the sand. She'd been wrong. So completely wrong. It was impossible to escape her past, to put her memories behind her. She would always be what she had become. Her dream was shattered—her new life abandoned.

Angeline was not at supper. After James had frantically searched for her, Sarah informed him that she wasn't feeling well and had retired early. Though desperate to see her and concerned for her health, he forced himself to stay away from her hut and instead barely touched his meal of papayas, beans, and fish, while the rest of the colonists chatted idly around him. And why, in the name of all that was holy, was Dodd staring at him with that impish grin on his face? Continually staring and smiling like the blunderhead he was.

Rising, James handed his plate to Mr. Lewis, whose appetite for food matched his lust for liquor. He took it with an appreciative nod as James grabbed the torch he'd prepared to take on his journey to the shore—he and Angeline's journey—and dipped it in the fire. He'd even left the fields early to assemble logs on the beach so they would have a fire to sit around while he asked if he could court her. Perhaps he was just a foolish romantic, but he wanted everything to be perfect. Perfect for the perfect lady.

Shoving aside leaves, he plunged into the jungle, seeking some time alone to nurse his disappointment. Which was silly. The woman couldn't help feeling ill. He only hoped—no, prayed—it wasn't anything serious. *Lord, please take care of her. I intend to make her my wife with Your permission.* No sooner had he lifted the silent prayer than he realized he hadn't been very diligent in praying recently. Nor had he asked God's blessing to court Angeline. There'd been so much to do after the ants destroyed everything. Parts of the fields had to be re-plowed and replanted, the sugar splints tended to, huts repaired, the mill rebuilt from the fire, as well as their normal tasks of digging irrigation ditches and foraging for food. Plus James had been spending so much time with Angeline. An unavoidable smile lifted his lips as he thought of those precious moments. Still, that was no excuse to ignore God. He was the preacher, for heaven's sake! Was he destined to fail at it all over again? Just like he'd done with his father. Like he'd done with that woman who had destroyed him. He marched ahead, plowing through a curtain of vines, hoping he hadn't been showered with spiders or beetles or other insects. Insects that now buzzed in their nighttime chorus.

A growl echoed through the trees. Distant but ominous, it caused the hair on James's arms to prickle. Yet it was the sound that followed that made his stomach twist in a knot. Crackling like a fire but not coming from his torch. He knew that sound all too well. He swerved the flame through the darkness, the blaze flaring like the tail of a comet. The crackling increased. A figure—all smoke and mist—emerged from the leaves. James stood his ground, heart beating through his chest.

"Who are you?" he demanded.

The figure took form and shape and stepped into the light. Skirts of violet poplin floated over the ground, festooned with pink velvet bows. Satin embroidery drew his gaze to the creamy skin bursting from her low neckline, where her hair, the color of pearls, dangled in lustrous spirals. Eyes as green as the jungle around them looked at him with longing. *Tabitha.* Blood rushed through his veins and began to curdle in his mind. She smiled. He took a step back and blinked, trying to erase her from view. Still she remained, cocked her head.

"Don't you remember me?" she said in that honey-sweet drawl that had once sounded like music to his ears.

Of course he remembered her. She was the woman who had ruined his life. "You're not here."

An adorable pout appeared on her lips. "Why, what a horrid thing to say, dear James. After all we've meant to one another."

James knew she was a vision—from one of the fallen angelic beasts. She had to be. But she looked so real. Her skin was as sparkling and luminescent as he remembered. Her lips plump and moist. Her curves in all the right places. It was the sight of those curves and the peek she'd given him when she leaned forward in the front pew of his church that had become his demise. Week after week. Sunday after Sunday. The way she stared at him as he preached from the pulpit, the way she eased her tongue over her lips, the desire in her eyes, every movement a dance of seduction that had driven him mad.

"We meant naught to each other," he said, though he wondered why he spoke to a vision. "You seduced me."

"Did I now? Or was it *you* who drew me into your lair?" She stepped toward him, the rustle of her skirts joining the buzz of insects. "And what a lion you were." Her tone dripped with desire as she looked him up and down.

Shame seared his belly and rose up his neck at the memories: the clandestine rendezvous, the long nights of passion. The way he felt nauseous with guilt the next day. The lies. The deception. Her irresistible pull on him again and again. Even now, even as an illusion, she stirred his body to life.

He rubbed the scar beside his mouth—the one her husband had put there. "You're a wicked woman. Nothing but a pig with a gold ring in her snout who lures men to destruction!" he quoted from the Bible. Proverbs, in fact, had much to say about loose women.

Feigning a look of pain, she sighed and twirled a lock of her hair. "You came of your own free will, if I recall."

Tearing his gaze from her, James stormed through a tangle of leaves and headed back toward town.

"You have another woman now, don't you?" Her voice trailed him. "You think she is better than me? You are a bigger fool than ever, James Callaway!" The sound of her laughter bounced off trunks and leaves and rang in his ears all the way back to camp. All the way to his hut, to his cot, where he plopped to sit and dropped his head in his hands. Reaching beneath his bed, he pulled out a small chest, opened it, and brought a Bible to his lap. His father's Bible. He breathed in the smell of it—leather and fire smoke and aged vellum—and pictured his dad sitting in his favorite high-back chair by the fireplace in their home, reading the words on each page over and over as if they were precious.

"This is yours now, son." The hands, strong yet veined with age, handed the book to James. "Read it every day. Memorize its words and they will bring you life. Abundant life!"

James could have died happy right there for the look of pride in his father's eyes, instead of the usual disappointment ever since James had forsaken the church and run off to become a doctor. To make matters worse, during his long absence at war, his mother had died of heartbreak. And fear. Fear that she'd never see her son again. But James *had* returned, like the prodigal coming to his senses, and now he would take over the pastorate of his father's church—the Second Baptist Church in Knoxville, Tennessee.

Rain tapped on the thatched roof, jarring him back to the present. Clutching the Bible to his chest, he blinked back the tears burning his eyes. Tabitha had tricked him and led him astray. And now his father was dead. "I'm so sorry, Father. I failed you. I failed you in the worst possible way."

Chapter 11

"Why won't you look at me?" James asked Angeline as she hovered over the brick oven beneath the thatched roof of the meeting shelter.

Swerving around, her skirts flinging about her legs, she gave him a tight smile. "I *am* looking at you. I'm just busy at the moment, Doctor." Her voice sounded stilted. She turned and continued to slice the wild onions, mushrooms, and herbs Thiago had found to add flavor to the rice. Rain tapped a baritone cadence on the thatched roof and formed puddles in the dirt across the town square. The deluge had not lessened since it began last night.

"I've been searching for you all day." James shook his arms, sending droplets through the air. "Are you feeling well?"

"Well enough, thank you." She continued her work. Wisps of hair, stirred by a breeze, danced over her neck while the musky scent of moist jungle filled his nose.

"I was sorry to hear you were ill last night. I so longed for our stroll on the beach." He took a step toward her and swiped a hand through his wet hair. The rain had kept the colonists in their huts most of the day, save a few hardy souls who scavenged the jungle for food. And James, who had scavenged the town for Angeline. He had searched every hut, looked in the frame that would become the barn, hunted through the burnt mill, ventured over to the beginnings of the Scotts' house, but Angeline was nowhere to be found. Until a few moments ago when a flash of blue skirts and red hair sent his heart racing and his legs darting to the meeting shelter.

Still, she said nothing. Thunder grumbled, shaking the roof and loosening a few raindrops onto the table.

He dared another step closer. The fire swamped him in smoke. Coughing, he blinked the sting from his eyes and touched her arm, staying the knife in her hand. "What is wrong, Angeline?"

A tremble passed through her. She drew in a shaky breath and stiffened her jaw, still avoiding his gaze. "I'm helping prepare supper."

"I didn't ask what you were doing." Voices sounded in the distance. He leaned toward her. "Why are you treating me like I have the plague? Did I do something to offend you?" Though he couldn't imagine what. Tabitha came to mind, and sudden terror flooded him. Had she appeared to Angeline? Had she told her what he'd done?

Violet eyes, brewing with turmoil, lifted to his. But there, he saw it—a speck of affection hid beneath the angst. Or was he only hoping? She opened her mouth to say something. . .

"There you both are." Eliza darted beneath the frond roof, removed the cloak from her head and shook out the water. "Thank you for starting the rice, Angeline. That's just what I was coming to do."

Other feminine voices rode on the wind accompanied by the splash of boots in mud.

Releasing Angeline, James stepped away. *Confound it all!*

Lifting her skirts, Magnolia ducked beneath the roof. "Now look at my gown." She slapped at the mud clinging to her hem while Mrs. Jenkins, Sarah, and a few other women joined them. "When is this rain going to stop? I feel like a waterlogged goose."

Eliza chuckled. "Surely it can't last much longer." Shoving a wet strand of hair behind her ear, she leaned to inspect Angeline's work. "Would you believe Blake is still sleeping? One day of rain and he's as lazy as a sloth." She smiled and glanced up, but instantly frowned, no doubt at the tension strung tight between James and Angeline. Tension that threatened to eat away at his gut if it wasn't resolved soon.

Slapping her hands together, Eliza skirted the table, mumbling something about helping skin the fish.

Taking Angeline's elbow, James turned her to face him. "A word, please?"

"I have work to do." She glanced over her shoulder at the ladies chattering and donning aprons. "Besides, people will hear."

"Then whisper." He leaned toward her ear. "Why are you angry?"

She smelled of rain and coconut and sweet onions, and he longed to see her smile at him again. Lightning flashed and the droplets pounded even harder, splattering mud onto the raised bamboo floor.

"I'm not. We'll talk later." She tugged from him and started to go but not before he saw tears mist her eyes.

He pulled her back. "I'm not letting you go until you tell me what has you so upset. If someone has hurt you. . ." If so, he'd forget he was a preacher and pummel them into dust.

She jerked from his grasp. "You can't always rescue me, James." Anger burned in her eyes. . .anger and something else. Despair? "Sometimes you just have to let go."

"What does that mean?" A sudden chill bit through his wet shirt.

She swallowed and stared off into the jungle, where rain streamed off the tip of a giant banana leaf like a spigot. A drop squeezed through the roof and landed on her forehead. James reached to wipe it, but she swatted him away. Thunder bellowed. "It means let me go, James. Let *us* go."

⌘

The words felt like barbed spikes as they passed over her tongue. Sharp spikes that stung her lips, her ears. And her heart. James stepped backward into the rain. Water cascaded down his face, blurring his expression of shock and agony and beading in his lashes that hung limp over pain-filled eyes. She wanted to take it all back, retract every word, and lose herself in his arms forever.

But she couldn't.

Rain slicked his hair and dripped from the curled tips to his collar. His wet shirt clung to every line and muscle in his chest. Still he stared at her. "I don't understand. I thought. . .I thought we cared for each other."

Blood pooled in her head. Behind her, the women's voices grew muted and distant. "We do care." She forced a smile. She would give him that much. A friendship to cherish.

Lightning flashed a deathly gray over him, enhancing the benumbed look on his face. Flattening his lips, he nodded then turned and walked away.

Taking her heart with him.

Impulsively, she sped after him, tears joining the rain on her cheeks.

He must have heard her for he stopped and faced her, confusion bending his brow.

She must be strong. If she stayed away from him, if she pretended not to care, Dodd would have no leverage over her. Then perhaps she wouldn't have to give herself to the lecherous swine. She wouldn't have to go back to her old way of life. And James would be spared the pain of discovering the truth. Even if Dodd eventually told him, it was better to break James's heart now than crush it later after they entered a doomed courtship. Either way, things must end between them.

But she could tell him none of this.

Instead they stood, rain sheeting between them, water dripping off their chins and lashes.

"I'm sorry," she finally said. Then fisting her hands, she forced herself to turn and walk away. Tears came as hard as the rain.

Dreams were not meant for her—not for little girls who had become harlots.

⚓

Distant groans wove their way through the slumberous maze in Hayden's mind. *Tap, tap, tap,* just like the thrum of incessant rain on the roof of his hut—the thrum he'd become so accustomed to these past three days, it actually helped him fall asleep. That and the feel of his wife cradled in his arms. The last thought brought a smile to his lips while another whimper finally burst through his mind, jerking him awake.

Magnolia thrashed beside him. "No. Don't leave me! Don't leave me!"

Leaning on his elbow, he drew her trembling body close. "Princess, wake up. You're dreaming." He shook her gently then kissed her forehead. With a moan, her eyes popped open, her chest heaving against his. Releasing a breath, she flung her arms around him.

"Hayden, it was such a terrible nightmare." Her voice quivering, she clung to him as if he were a lifeline in a storm.

"I was all alone in a tiny boat at sea."

Nudging her onto the pillow, he brushed hair from her face and planted a kiss on her nose. "Shhh, it's all right now. Only a dream."

"It was so real, Hayden. I was old. All wrinkled and gray-haired and feeble. And I had no oars." Tears dampened his fingers as he caressed her cheeks. "You and all our friends were leaving me. . .sailing away on a big ship, and I had no way to get to you."

He cupped her face in his hands. "It's the enemy feeding on your fears of being old and useless, you know that."

She nodded as another tear spilled from her eye. Hayden kissed it away before it slid into her hair then drew her close again. If only he could kiss away all her fears, all her pain as easily. "Do you know how beautiful you are? Both inside and out?" Did she really know? Had Hayden been able to convey to her just how much she meant to him? How precious she was?

He felt her relax as she squirmed closer.

"Magnolia, you are useful to everyone in this town. You are kind and cheerful, and you make us all laugh. Besides that, Eliza finds your help in the clinic invaluable."

"You are right." Joy returned to her voice. "God *has* given me purpose. And He has shown me what true beauty is." Turning on her side, she curled her back against him, erasing all slumber from his body and stirring it to life.

He ran fingers through her hair. "I love you, Magnolia. More than life itself," he whispered in her ear, his passion rising.

"And I you," she mumbled, her voice trailing off.

Hayden caressed her arm, brushing fingers over her soft skin, and thanked God yet again for giving him such a wonderful wife. Yet when he lowered his lips to hers, only the deep breaths of sleep responded to his kiss.

Smiling, he laid back on the pillow with a sigh, willing his body to relax. Another time. She needed her rest. She'd had so many nightmares lately. Hayden's own visions had increased as well. In fact, each day a parade of people he'd swindled in the past accompanied him wherever he went, showering him with either looks of hatred or tears of agony. He ignored them most of the time. Citing scripture often sent them scurrying—something he'd learned from the doc. Another thing he'd learned from the doc, as well as from the hours Hayden had spent with God, was that Hayden was forgiven. God had adopted him into His family. He had a new Father and a new life. No silly vision of the past would ever change that.

An hour passed, and unable to relax, he rose, tucked the quilt beneath Magnolia's chin then donned his trousers and shirt. Maybe a walk in the cool night rain would settle him.

All the rain did was soak through his clothes into his skin and finally send a chill through his bones. He slogged down Main Street, once terra firma but now nothing but a puddle—a rising puddle that squished beneath his boots, cloaking them in mud. When would this rain end? He was about to turn around and head back to the warmth of his wife and his bed when a flickering light coming from James's hut tugged his curiosity. At least he wasn't the only one not sleeping. Besides, he'd been meaning to speak to the doc about something.

Hayden found James leaning over a makeshift desk, a Bible on one end and a candle and large open book on the other.

Hayden cleared his throat.

James spun on his seat. "Hayden, I didn't hear you." He rubbed his eyes and set down his pen.

"It's the rain. It drowns out everything." Hayden shook the water from his hair then noticed his trousers dripping on the floor. "Sorry."

"No matter. After three days of rain, everything is wet anyway."

"Where are your bunkmates?" Hayden gestured toward the empty cots.

James sighed. "Off making rum is my guess. You know Lewis." He tilted a pocket watch on his desk to see the time. "But at one in the morning, they should be back. What brings you here so late? Have a seat." He gestured toward the only other chair in the room.

Hayden remained standing. No sense in soaking the furniture as well. "Magnolia had a nightmare again."

James nodded as if the information didn't surprise him. "Many are suffering from nightmares." He leaned forward on his knees, his shoulders slumping. "I wish I knew what to do. I can't seem to stop these demonic visions and dreams."

"I doubt any preacher could." Hayden gestured toward the old book on James's desk. "Perhaps you'll find the answers in there."

James nodded as lightning burst outside the window. "Let's hope so. But you didn't come to talk about that."

"No."

James leaned back in his chair, the candle casting shadows over his face. "Well?"

"It's Angeline."

He frowned, but then alarm shot across his face. "Is she all right?"

"Yes, yes, she's fine." Hayden held up a hand. "Surely you would know better than I."

"No." James lowered his chin. "I haven't spoken to her in a few days."

Hayden finally took the seat. "I thought you two... Word was that you were going to ask to court her?"

James frowned. "It didn't work out that way."

"I'm sorry." Hayden couldn't imagine the pain he would have felt if Magnolia had turned him down.

Yet it was probably for the best. Hayden had noticed the doctor's interest in Angeline when they'd first set sail for Brazil. Then when he'd observed the playful dalliance between them here in town, he'd ignored it as innocent flirting. However when they began to spend more and more time together and he saw the loving glances between them, he'd become worried. Angeline had an obligation to tell James the truth. She should have told him the truth already, before they'd grown so close. And despite Hayden's hatred of meddling in other people's affairs, he could not risk the safety of his good friend. How could he ever forgive himself if something horrible happened? No, if Angeline accepted James's suit, Hayden was obligated to tell him he was courting a murderer.

CHAPTER 12

W hat about Angeline? Did she say something about me?" James could tell from the look on Hayden's face that whatever he had to say wasn't good news.

"It's nothing." Hayden shrugged and moved to the window where James had attempted to cover the opening with palm fronds—two of which had already blown off and the rest now bent in the wind. "It doesn't matter anymore."

Rising, James stretched the ache that spanned his shoulders and had now begun to migrate to his heart. He had tried to avoid thinking of Angeline the past few days, had buried himself in his translation. But fleeting glimpses of her around town without so much as a word or a smile had left him feeling as dry as a desert, despite the deluge outside. Now, Hayden had gone and brought her to the forefront of his thoughts again, resurging his loss. "If she's in danger, please tell me."

The flap opened and a blast of rain-saturated wind shoved Blake inside. He shook water from his coat and ran a hand through his wet hair. "I thought I heard voices." His glance took in his friends before he slapped Hayden on the back, sending a spray into the air.

James smiled. These two men had become like brothers to him. Brothers he'd never had, being an only child. "If I'd known I was going to have company, I'd have asked Lewis for some of his rum."

"Blaa!" Blake stuck out his tongue and shivered. "That stuff tastes like seaweed."

"Ah, it's not so bad when you really need a drink." Hayden chuckled. Thunder rode through the town, shaking the tiny hut. A few droplets squeezed through the extra fronds James had fastened on the roof. Soon there'd be no dry place in the whole colony. "The storm worsens."

"Which is why I came." Blake gestured for Hayden to take the only empty chair, but when the man shook his head, the colonel slid onto the seat, stretching his leg out before him with a wince. "Can't sleep lately."

"A common problem it would seem," Hayden said as he attempted to steady the canvas door that flapped and flailed like an injured goose.

Blake pinched the bridge of his nose. "Eliza's been suffering from terrifying visions of the war, and my nightmares have gotten worse. And this storm"—he glanced up as the pounding of rain intensified, reminding James of the war drums that haunted his dreams as well—"there's something strange about it. I feel it."

So had James. Which is why he'd been up studying more of the ancient book from the temple. He glanced at that book now with its Hebrew letters scrawled from right to left. Next to it, his own scribbles in English darkened a separate parchment in an attempt to translate a language he'd barely learned as a child.

Lightning flashed white through tiny slits and holes in the fronds that made up the wall. Wind snaked around corners in an eerie tune, sputtering James's candle.

The flap opened again, and Eliza pushed past Hayden, fear sparking in her eyes until they landed upon her husband. "I woke and you were gone." She moved and fell against Blake.

He embraced her. "I'm sorry, love. I didn't want to wake you."

"You know I hate it when you're not beside me."

James had never seen the woman quite so needy before, but he supposed the incessant storm had everyone on edge.

"I was just telling the men about your visions and my nightmares," Blake said.

"My visions have increased recently as well," Hayden added.

"Yes." Picking up his pen, James tapped it on the edge of the book. "Things are definitely getting worse."

"Have you discovered anything new in your translation?" Blake rubbed his leg as a barrage of rain struck the east wall, quivering the fronds.

"I'm finding out bits and pieces about the power of these beings and why they were put in chains. The first one, *Deception*"—he glanced at his friends—"has the power to deceive people by feeding them lies buried within half-truths. The lie could be anything from something about another person, or your own self-worth, the existence of God, to a lie that *Deception*, himself, isn't even real."

Hayden's lips slanted in skepticism.

Ignoring him, James continued. "The next one, *Delusion*, has the power to create visions, mirages, various illusions."

Blake rubbed the back of his neck while Eliza took his other hand in hers. "We've all experienced that, haven't we?"

A clap of thunder slammed the skies. James jerked, blood pumping, wondering if someone or *something* didn't wish him to continue.

Hayden held the flap down against another burst of wind. "And the one Graves released?"

"*Destruction*," James said. "He has the power to alter nature. He cannot kill anyone directly, but he can change their surroundings in order to destroy them."

"The lightning strike, the ants." Blake ground out, rubbing his jaw. "Possibly."

"But where did these beings come from?" Hayden asked.

"From the pit of hell is my guess," James said. "Apparently, these particular fallen angels had become extremely powerful or perhaps they broke the boundaries God had set for them—some cardinal rule they were not permitted to break. In any case, God decided to lock them up until the end of the age. He sent Gabriel and other angels to do battle. The four evil beings lost and were chained beneath the earth near"—James shook his head, hesitating to tell them what he wasn't sure he'd translated correctly—"near a branch of the lake of fire that burns at the center of earth." He gazed at them, assessing their belief but found only stunned confusion. He sighed. "Although I don't think the temple was there at the time."

Groaning, Hayden swallowed hard, his face growing pale.

"What is it?" James asked.

He took up a pace, eyes darting over the hut, mumbling something they couldn't hear over the storm. Finally he halted and faced them. "There was a priest in Rio. He told me there was a fire lake beneath the temple."

"A priest?"

"Yes, some odd man I bumped into on the street. It was nothing, really. He was muttering crazy things. But I do remember him mentioning the fire lake. I thought him mad at the time, but now. . ." Shock leapt in Hayden's green eyes as he gaped at them.

"Did this priest say anything else?" James moved to the edge of his chair.

"Something about six. I don't remember." Hayden rubbed his eyes.

"Surely it's a coincidence." Eliza hugged herself. "If all this is true, why would God allow these angels to be so easily released?"

"Not easily," James said. "If the cannibals hadn't built their temple in that exact location and then dug tunnels beneath it, these beings would still be locked below and we'd be knee-deep in sugarcane, coffee, and the utopia we sought."

Eliza frowned. "Then it would seem Satan told the cannibals exactly where to build their temple."

James nodded. "A reasonable assumption." Though he could tell from her clipped tone that she was being facetious.

Blake snorted. "But why didn't God bury them so deep they'd never be found?"

Tossing down his pen, James leaned back in his chair. "I don't know. Something to do with man's free will, I'd wager."

"I'm starting to hate this free will thing." Blake huffed.

"It does have its downfalls."

Hayden shifted his stance. "Do you know how crazy this sounds? Invisible evil angels buried beneath the earth?"

"You saw their prisons yourself. How else do you explain your visions? And what this priest said?"

"I don't know." Hayden scrubbed his face. "Perhaps something in the food?" Though his tone bore humor, his expression was one of desperation—desperation for the normal life they all longed for. "The mandioca root we've been eating can be poisonous if not cooked right. And Thiago has been instructing the women to grind it into flour since we got here."

Eliza smiled. "Your skepticism is good, Hayden. We should all question things. But ultimately, we must put the matter to God and see what He says."

Blake lifted the flap and glanced out onto the street. "Perhaps we ought to pray for the rain to stop before we all drown. Wha—?" He disappeared outside. Hayden ran after him. Rain pelted James's face as he followed and peered down the street—more like a brook for all the water streaming down it. A muffled shout came from the darkness. Blake charged ahead, his figure dissolving in the downpour. A man emerged from the shadows, another man hanging limp in his arms.

Eliza appeared beside James, lantern held high.

"It's Mr. Lewis. Help! He's hurt."

Hayden grabbed Mr. Lewis from the man's tired arms. Blood expanded on his saturated shirt and stormed down his trousers, coming so fast the rain couldn't wash it away.

James's throat closed. He stepped back.

"What happened?" Blake asked over the roar of the storm.

"Wolf! He was attacked by a wolf!"

James was a fish. A fish swimming through a lake plump with swaying ferns and dancing vines. He breathed in water. He coughed up spray. His boots sank in puddles up to his ankles. He yanked one from the clawing mud. If only he *were* a fish. It would be much easier to swim through this sodden jungle with fins and gills than plod through it with feet and lungs.

Dawn had crested the horizon over an hour ago, but you wouldn't know it for the cloak that settled over the thick brush. If only that cloak would protect them from the rain that continued to spew from angry black clouds broiling across the sky. Rain that speared the leaves overhead like a thousand arrows before pummeling the group of five men below in a hail of violent grapeshot—saturating, stinging, biting.

The musket slipped in James's hand. Readjusting his grip, he wondered if it would even fire if they found the wolf. Blake moved ahead of him, his soaked shirt plastered to his skin, water dripping from his black hair. To James's left, Hayden slogged through puddles, looking more like a sea otter than a man. Another colonist angled away on James's right while Thiago led the way up front.

James ground his teeth. He should be back at the clinic helping Eliza and Magnolia tend to Lewis's wound, but instead he was traipsing through the jungle, soaked to the bone, looking for a wolf that was no doubt long gone.

If only there hadn't been so much blood...

At least he had caught a glimpse of Angeline when she'd stormed from her hut, hooded cloak askew, at the sound of Lewis's shrill screams. Their eyes reached for each other through the gloom of night, and he thought he saw sorrow in hers before she snapped them away.

Thiago halted, knelt, and examined the muddy ground, water trickling from strands of dark hair hanging at his jaw. Blake and James caught up to him as the Brazilian stood and shook his head. "We lost him. He not come this way. The rain hide tracks."

As James had tried to tell the man before they left town. But Thiago had insisted they must hunt and kill this *Lobisón*, the man-wolf he claimed had attacked Mr. Lewis. If they did not, Lewis would become a wolf himself. Or so the legend said.

Rubbish. Just a ludicrous Brazilian superstition. One James supposed he should be thankful for since it had allowed him to escape a situation where his ineptitude would be on full display. He had a feeling Blake would rather be in the jungle than witnessing the bloody mess as well.

A guttural howl pierced the rain—distant and hollow. Thiago's dark eyes narrowed as he scanned the maze of dripping green. "He watches us." Rain beaded on his long lashes and slid down his jaw.

"What happens to Lewis now?" Hayden shouted over the din of the storm, the tremor in his normally staunch voice more than evident.

"We wait. If his blood is poisoned, he become wolf in three days."

Above them, a colorful bird squawked at the ridiculous statement. James couldn't agree more.

Hayden's brow darkened as he absently rubbed his arm where Magnolia had stitched up a wolf bite two months ago.

Blake leaned toward him. "What's that?" He pointed beneath his chin. "Is that fur growing on your neck?"

Hayden flung a hand to his throat, eyes flashing. Frantic, he brushed fingers over his neck, chin, and jaw before he released a long sigh. Blake, James, and even Thiago chuckled as Hayden gave them a look of annoyance. "Amusing. Very amusing."

On the way back to town, James caught up with Thiago. "You

realize that this myth of Lobisón is just that, a myth. Surely you don't believe that men become wolves."

The Brazilian interpreter shrugged. "Many of my people see Lobisón." Shoving aside a large fern, he gave James a curious look. "You are man of God. There is much we not know about world and spirits. Like evil angels you speak of."

James flattened his lips. The man did have a point, but his answer made James wonder at his spiritual condition. "Do you believe in God, Thiago?"

"Sim, Mr. James." He nodded.

"And His Son, Jesus?" A frog croaked, and James barely missed stepping on it as it splashed across the path.

"Jesus opened way to heaven." Thiago shook water from his hair. "We pay money to priests for family to go. That's why we must make many friends in life, so many will pay our way."

Shocked at the man's words, James felt an urgency stir his spirit. He was the town's spiritual guide, and he couldn't very well let this kind man continue in darkness. But how to reach him? "That isn't really how it works. There is no price to pay. Jesus paid it on the cross. Then He gives us power to live good lives. He delivers, heals, and protects us."

Thunder rumbled in the distance. One glance over his shoulder told James the other men followed close behind, heads bent against the rain.

"There are women in Rio who heal people too." Thiago sloshed through a rather large puddle. "Wise women use herbs and oils and many other things. One time they crush roasted worms and sing a chant to cure my toothache. They also make love potions. All you need is lock of hair from your beloved." He frowned. "Wish I had some of Miss Sarah's hair."

James grew sad at the man's beliefs that seemed to be a strange mixture of Catholicism and sorcery. "You don't need a potion to make a woman love you. Nor do you need incantations for healing. And you especially don't need anyone to buy your way into heaven." He longed to set the young Brazilian free from beliefs that entrapped him in fear. Worse than that, beliefs that would eventually send him to hell.

Lightning flashed, and James kept pace with Thiago as they shoved through a wall of slippery vines. "In fact, you can't buy your way into heaven at all," James shouted above the storm. "God grants everyone entrance as a free gift to those who receive His Son. There is nothing else you need to do except get to know Him and follow Him."

Another growl of thunder shook the sky, and for a minute, James thought he'd overstepped the Brazilian's bounds. But finally Thiago said, "I will think on this, Mr. James."

James smiled.

They stopped at the river before heading back into town. What once had been a smooth-flowing finger of blue and green gently caressing the land, now had transformed into the bulging muscle of a raging bully shoving his way through the jungle. The sandy beach that had once spanned several yards up to an embankment had disappeared beneath a torrent of rushing gray water. At its edge, foam clawed the sheer rock where they stood, licking and groping like a hungry child bent on having his way.

Spears of rain stabbed the water, bouncing and skipping over the surface, sounding like the clash of a thousand swords. James swallowed.

"You don't think it will overflow its banks, do you?" He glanced at Blake, whose stern expression formed his usual unreadable mask. Hayden stood frozen at the sight. "We *are* in the middle of a valley."

"True, but the river flows to the sea," Blake answered, yet James didn't miss the slight hesitation in his voice.

Hayden released a sigh of relief and kicked a stone into the frothing mass. "Right. There's always an outlet for the water, then."

Then why did James suddenly feel like he was sinking into the mud? And fast.

CHAPTER 13

Angeline sank into the murky water, deeper and deeper. Shapes of life beyond the surface above grew blurry and hypnotic. Dark and cold, silence invaded her soul. Her lungs screamed for air—clawed her throat for life's last breath. In a moment, death would grant her the peace that had eluded her in life. But the water continued to slosh and gurgle, refusing to be silenced.

Drip. Drip. Water splattered on her eyes. She popped them open. Darkness slithered over a thatched roof where the *rat-tat-tat* of rain had drummed a steady cadence for five days. *Drip.* Another drop struck her neck. Light burst. A baby cried. *Lydia?* Water splashed.

"Angeline!" Sarah screamed.

Lantern light blinded Angeline before Sarah's anxious face filled her vision. "Angeline! The river, it's rising! We must get up!" Holding a lantern in one hand, she gripped Angeline's arm in a pinch with the other, the pain finally forcing her to surface from her morbid dream.

"Get dressed!" Sarah shouted as she sloshed toward the other side of the hut. "I need to get Lydia."

Knot in her throat, Angeline swung her legs over the cot. They landed in a foot of water—cold water that smothered her skin and sent a shiver up her back. Water that was rising. Fast!

"What's happening?" She stood, grabbed a petticoat, skirt, and blouse off a hook and began putting them on as best she could. No time for a proper corset. Thunder boomed. Thatches quivered, sprinkling drops onto their liquid floor.

"It's the river!" Sarah shouted over the roar of water as she bundled

Lydia in a blanket and headed for the door. "Hurry!"

Before she could open the flap, Blake stuck his head in. "To higher ground! We haven't much time!"

Tying her skirts on, Angeline grabbed Stowy and followed Sarah out the door. Darkness haunted a scene ravenous with the gush of water. In the distance, she made out Blake ushering the townspeople toward a hill that rose to the north. Madness, chaos all around! Shouts and screams zipped past her ears. People sloshed in all directions through the surging torrent. Lanterns speared light onto angry water. Rain pelted the surface like rabid pebbles.

She felt her neck. Her father's ring! Swerving, she dove back into the hut, the river at her thighs now. Groping in the dark, she waded through water that felt as thick as molasses and found the table by her bed. She searched the chipped wood. There. The chain. The ring. She grabbed it and flung it over her head. Lifting her hair, she tucked it safely within her bodice. Stowy clawed her shoulder and meowed in protest.

The river reached her waist.

Stomach twisting, she plunged out of the hut, trying to settle the cat. Dark water swirled around her, tangling her skirts and shoving her legs backward. She lost her footing. Throwing out an arm for balance, she forced her shoes back into the mud. In the distance, dots of light ascended into darkness like angels flying back to heaven. The colonists had left her behind.

Her friends had left her behind!

She headed toward the lights, fighting both the rising current and her rising terror. The water surged, spinning its greedy claws round about her. Pulling, tugging, twisting. Ravaging her like an unwelcome lover. Rain lashed her head and arms. Her hair hung in ropes of lead. Lightning etched across the sky—a gray flash of death that left a vision imprinted on her mind: a liquid grave rising to swallow her alive, trees bowing in defeat, huts collapsing. Then all went dark again.

Nothing but the roar of the river and growl of thunder remained to keep her company. And Stowy's fearful whines. The water reached her chest. Terror sucked the breath from her lungs. Her skirts felt like chain mail. Her legs tangled in the heavy fabric. Clenching her jaw, she thrust through the river, trying to shove the raging water aside with her arm. Her muscles ached. Her head grew light. The lights in the distance faded. She wasn't going to make it. She was going to drown in the middle of the Brazilian jungle, her body swept away to be devoured by some beast when the waters receded.

A fitting punishment for her crimes.

Her eyes burned, but no tears came. Wasn't it enough she'd been forced to give up James? Give up any chance at true happiness? What else did God want from her? Would He never be satisfied until she had paid for her sins with her life? *God, if You're listening, I won't pray for myself, but please save the rest of the colonists. My friends. James. And please give him the happiness he deserves.*

Her breath rasped over a dry throat. Her chest hurt. Water gripped her shoulders. Stowy's nails clawed her skin as he clung to her neck. *God, please save Stowy!* The current grew swift. A shadow moved toward her. A thicket of branches and twigs. Sharp wood jabbed her. Knocked her over. Her feet swept out from under her. Water absorbed her face. Thrashing, she fought to keep her mouth and Stowy above the surface, gulping and choking as the river spilled into her lungs.

❧

Handing Mrs. Matthews—who'd been separated during the confusion—back to her worried husband, James raised his lantern and turned, scanning the remaining colonists hiking up the hill. Sporadic lanterns dotted the jungle, spiraling and bobbing haphazard trails through leaves and vines. He squinted to make out faces in the brief glimpse afforded him. Anxious, pale faces, some casting fearful looks over their shoulders at the liquid death rising behind them. A fountain of bubbling pitch that snapped twigs and broke branches, devouring all in its path.

Thunder blasted, accompanied by the screech of birds and howl of creatures abandoning the forest floor for the canopy. James's blood mimicked the mad rush of the river—hot and violent. And mind-numbing. Shock buzzed across his skin. Everything was ruined. Everything they'd worked so hard to build, destroyed. But he couldn't think of that now. The river had breached its banks so quickly, they all would have surely drowned if he hadn't been up translating more of the

102

book—the book he'd handed Thiago for safekeeping only moments ago, along with his father's Bible. Perhaps James should thank God for his obsession with the ancient manuscript.

After alerting Blake and making sure the eldest colonists were up and moving, James had gone in search of Angeline and Sarah, the only two single women in the colony, but poor Mrs. Matthews had latched onto him in hysterics, refusing to release him until he found her husband. Now, as James searched the colonists bringing up the rear, he thought he saw Sarah in the distance. Surely Angeline was with her.

Making his way down the slippery hill, he wiped rain from his eyes and batted aside sopping leaves, all the while encouraging colonists he passed—their arms full of clothing, tools, and weapons—to keep moving.

Thunder bellowed, shaking the ground. Shoving aside a cascade of vines, James nearly ran over Blake. Two muskets were strung over his left shoulder beneath which he hefted a sack of rice. Eliza, arms loaded with blankets and a satchel—no doubt full of medicines—clung to her husband's other side, her expression stiff with alarm.

"Keep moving, my friend. We don't know how far the river will rise." Blake's normally controlled tone was laced with fear.

Sarah stopped beside them, nestling Lydia to her chest against the rain.

"Where's Angeline?" James scanned the three of them. Their eyes grew wide. Dread swept over him as they all glanced at the rising river. Lightning scored the sky, flickering a deathly pallor over the scene and a shroud of terror over his heart.

"She was right behind me!" Sarah shouted over the roar of water and rain.

Blake's jaw bunched. He turned to Eliza. "Go ahead. I'll catch up."

James clutched his friend's arm. "No, I'll go back for her. You get your wife and Sarah to safety." Turning, he marched down the hill, not waiting for an answer. Below him, the jungle floor sped past in a mad dash, snapping branches from trees as if they were matchsticks. Somewhere out there, Angeline was fighting for her life. He would find her. He must. He could not fail. *God, please, not this time. I cannot fail at this.*

✎✟✎

Helpless to move, helpless to fight, Angeline allowed the swift current to carry her away. Terror had long since abandoned her, leaving a numb submission behind. Her only fear now was for Stowy. Somehow he had managed to hang on to her neck, his sharp claws digging into her skin. *Hang on, precious one. Hang on.* Maybe he could find a tree to leap onto and save himself.

Tumbling, twisting, turning, the angry river flung her onto rocks, bashed her against tree trunks, scraped her against branches until every inch of her screamed in pain. She prayed for mercy. She prayed she would drown. But every time her head went under the water and she almost lost consciousness, the river shoved her back into the air, forcing her to gasp for a breath. And Stowy to screech in terror. How long could this go on? If each bruise and cut were punishment for her sins, it was going to be a long night. Rain lashed the top of her head. Shadows rushed toward her like ghouls. She closed her eyes.

And heard her name. "Angeline!"

God? No, probably the other guy. She wouldn't answer him. She'd meet him soon enough.

"Angeline!"

She opened her eyes. The dark outline of a patch of trees rushed toward her like soldiers in a demonic army. A branch swung low from one in the middle. A man's arm extended. Water filled her mouth. Gasping, she choked it out and tried to focus. She struck the first tree. Pain seared across her side. Dipping beneath the surface, she bobbed up again and shook water from her eyes. The hand was definitely there. Unless she was dreaming. If not, she'd have one chance to grab it.

And once chance only.

"Angeline! Grab ahold!" Desperation screeched in the voice—a voice she knew.

Oh, God. Please help. I really don't want to die. I am not ready to be judged.

Lightning flashed, flickering over the lowered hand. Large and strong. She slammed into the tree's buttress. Water gushed over the top, shoving her over with it, legs and arms flailing. The hand flashed in her vision. She reached for it. The current pushed her under again.

No! Gathering what little strength remained, she shoved her feet against the buttress and lunged back up. She hacked up water. Stowy uttered a deathly wail. Angeline reached once more.

Fingers met fingers. Palms met palms. And a grip tighter than a corset fastened around her hand.

Water sped past her, bubbling in defiance of losing its prey. She glanced up. James looked down upon her. "Hang on! I've got you!"

CHAPTER 14

It was a miracle. That was the only explanation for Angeline's appearance beneath the very tree James had climbed in the hope of spotting her in the frothing waters. Now that he had a grip on her, he would never let go. Ever. He growled as he gathered every ounce of strength to pull her up toward him. Desperately, she clutched his arm. He reached down with his other hand, grabbed the belt around her waist, and hoisted her the rest of the way onto the wide branch where he sat. She fell against his chest, their heavy breaths mingling in the misty air as the river raged beneath them. A shiver wracked her body, and he thought he heard her whimper. Wrapping his arms around her, he leaned back against the trunk, encasing her in what little warmth he had left through his soaked garments.

A sandpaper tongue licked his cheek. Jerking back, he squinted in the darkness, smiling when he realized it was Stowy. How the cat had survived, James had no idea, but he was sure Angeline would have sacrificed her own life for her feline companion.

Lightning flashed, giving him a brief glimpse of the tree. A kapok tree, if he remembered Thiago's lessons on Brazilian flora. Thick branches reached up toward the angry sky like hairy dragon claws, their tips swaying in the wind. A sturdy tree, James hoped. The tree God had led James to after he'd done the only thing he knew in order to find Angeline—plunge into the mad, chaotic water, grab onto a piece of wood, and pray with everything in him.

Angeline shivered again and he gripped her tighter, squeezing her between his thighs to let her know he wasn't letting go. Wind fluted

106

an eerie tune through branches, stirring leaves into applause. Rain squeezed through the canopy above and drip-dropped on their heads.

Another blast of thunder shook the sky—farther away this time. Good. Perhaps the storm was passing. Perhaps the rain would finally stop and the river would recede. But what would be left of their homes? Their town? Their crops? He couldn't think of that now. Couldn't think of the watery beast just yards beneath their dangling feet, gobbling everything in its path. For now, he and Angeline were safe. And Stowy too. Whispering a prayer for the rest of the colonists, he leaned his head back on the rough bark and closed his eyes. A few minutes later, Angeline relaxed in his arms and snuggled against his chest. Stowy began purring.

James fell into a semiconscious slumber and dreamed he was on a ship full of cats pouncing over a sunny deck in pursuit of mice. Above him, bloated white sails sped them to some unknown destination. The gurgle and rush of the sea against the hull tickled his ears while voices clambered up hatches from passengers below. Yet no one but James was on deck. No captain, no first mate, no helmsman. Wind whipped his hair. The ship bucked over a swell, and he steadied his feet on the deck when he caught a glimpse of darkness in the distance. Not the type of darkness when a huge cloud covered the sun or when night approached, but a vast wall of black spanning the horizon. Flames burst through the ebony slate in a savage, frightening pattern. Like lightning. . .yet more ominous, more threatening. . .as if the jagged flares had a mind of their own.

James froze. A thousand needles punctured his heart. He leapt up the ladder onto the foredeck for a better look. The ship sped on a course straight for the dark menace. And somehow he knew that if he didn't stop it, everyone on board would die. His glance took in the sails, the wheel spinning out of control. He had no idea what to do! Even if he did, how could he lower sails and turn the ship all by himself?

The smell of coconut tickled his nose. The sweet scent filled his lungs and tantalized his memories. A bird squawked.

James snapped his eyes open with a start.

Angeline was staring at him. Sitting as far away from him as possible on the branch, she petted Stowy in her lap. Morning sun cut through branches and leaves and set her damp hair aglitter like liquid fire. A drop from above splattered on her shoulder, soaking into the fabric of her blouse. For a moment they simply stared into each other's eyes as if they were both lost in dreams they didn't want to end.

Finally she lowered her gaze. "You saved my life. Again."

A bird chirped above them and Stowy leapt from Angeline's arms in hot pursuit. She reached after the cat and lost her balance. James lunged to grab her waist and settle her. Their gazes met again, just inches apart this time. An emotion he couldn't name brewed within her violet eyes, but whatever it was, it made him never want to look away. His heart ached all over again from the loss of her.

She shoved his hands away as if he had leprosy.

"If you want me to apologize for coming to your rescue, I fear I cannot." James glanced down to see what his ears already told him. The waters had receded. Well, most of them. A shallow stream trickled over the land, shoving tangled nests of branches, twigs, and leaves through the mud, some bunching in knots to form beaver dams. The *tap, tap* of water from the canopy provided a cheerful accompaniment to the warble of birds. A pleasant tune so different from the mighty roar of the storm the night before.

But how could James possibly keep his focus on muddy water, birds, or storms when Angeline's lips were so close to his face he could feel her breath on his cheek?

"No, I. . ." she began and James leaned back against the trunk, lest he do what every impulse within him drove him to do—kiss her.

"I. . ." She lowered her chin. "How did you know where I would be?"

James shrugged, trying not to notice the way her damp blouse clung to her curves. "I didn't. When I saw you weren't with the others, I jumped in the river and prayed I would find you."

"You did?" Tiny brows collided above her freckled nose as her eyes searched his.

"Of course. I knew you must be out there somewhere. Either in the water or clinging to a tree."

"But the chances. . ." Moisture covered her eyes and she looked away.

"Are good with God." He smiled. When she didn't respond, he swung his leg over the branch and gripped the bark on either side.

Angeline sat inches from him, one hand pressed on the branch beneath her, one nervously fiddling with her tangled hair. Yet she seemed so distant and cold she might as well have been miles away.

A flock of orioles, plumed in brilliant yellow and black, landed in branches above them and began their morning serenade as if all was right with the world. Totally oblivious, it would seem, to Stowy who flattened himself, his ears back, his tail jerking as he slunk toward them. Yet were they oblivious? Were they too busy praising God to notice the danger lurking all around? Or did they simply trust Him to care for them? As God had cared for James and Angeline through the storm.

"You shouldn't have come after me, James. You could have died." Angeline's tone turned petulant as if he had dipped her hair in ink or put a frog in her stew.

Which completely baffled him. He knew he should be angry at her for her ungrateful attitude, but he couldn't find it within him. "I'm sorry for saving your life, your dragonship."

A smile peeked from her lips. "You said you weren't going to apologize."

"Force of habit, I suppose." His chuckle fell limp when he noticed her torn sleeves and the cuts and bruises marring her arms. "You're hurt." He reached for her, but she grabbed her arm and drew it close, wincing.

"I guess I hit a few trees."

James studied her, not able to imagine the horror she must have endured being helplessly carried away by the current. For him, he'd been more concerned about finding her. But she must have believed she would die. His gaze landed on the scar on her arm.

"But this"—he gestured toward it—"is old. What is it from?"

Her body stiffened. She attempted to cover it with shreds of her sleeve.

"Forgive me. I shouldn't have asked."

She raised a brow. "Another apology, Doctor? It does, indeed, appear to be a habit with you."

"Only when I'm with you, for I seem to constantly cross some invisible boundary that awakes the sleeping dragon."

She looked away but not before he saw her smile.

"Nevertheless, when we get back, have Eliza look at your wounds." Since it was obvious she wouldn't allow James to touch her.

She nodded, and James stretched the aches from his back and ran hands down his still-damp trousers, longing for her to understand the depth of his feelings, but she wouldn't look at him. Instead she peered through the lattice of shifting leaves and drew in a deep breath of air scented with sodden earth and salt.

"We are near the sea," she finally said before looking down and wobbling slightly, her face blanching.

"The river pushed us toward it. Here, grab this branch and don't look down." James guided her hand to a bough angling beside her shoulder then reached over to pull a scrap from her hair.

She snapped her eyes to his.

"Just a twig." He held it up before her horrified gaze. "I assure you, I wasn't taking liberties." Though he wouldn't mind coiling his finger around the lustrous curl he'd just briefly grazed.

Moments passed in silence. Surely she wasn't angry at him for saving her life! He'd never met such a puzzling woman. He longed for the camaraderie, the friendship they had formed the last time they'd been in a tree together, but that had drifted out to sea with the raging river.

"I cannot believe what happened," she finally said. "The river came up so quickly."

A breeze gusted through the leaves and chilled his wet shirt. He adjusted his position on the branch. "Too quickly. It doesn't make sense. It was as if someone broke a dam upstream." Yet he had his suspicions—suspicions that had nothing to do with natural causes.

"You don't suppose there's anything left of our town?" She bit her lip, her voice vacant of hope. "And the others. They are safe?"

"Yes. They all made it up the hill in time." He wanted to tell her all would be well. He wanted to kiss the worry from the freckles tightening on her pert nose, but he truly wasn't sure anymore. Not after all the disasters they'd suffered. "I don't know about our huts. Or our crops."

She faced him again, staring at him with sad eyes. Wind eased a curl across her cheek, and reaching up, he brushed it behind her ear. She took in a quick breath.

So he *did* have some effect on her.

Fear sped across her eyes before she attempted to scoot farther away from him. "We should go find out."

"We should wait until the water is gone. If the town is destroyed, there's nothing we can do about it now."

When another branch blocked her progress, she let out a huff of displeasure. What in the surefire blazes had James done to deserve such aversion? Whatever the reason, it wouldn't dull the pain lancing through his heart at the moment. She'd made it plain she didn't want a courtship. What he hadn't realized was that she also found him repulsive.

Moments passed in silence. Stowy sent another flock of birds scattering before he began pouncing on leaves instead. Finally Angeline attempted a smile. "How odd that we are stuck in a tree again. I wonder if this will become a regular occurrence?"

"I hope so. Apparently it's the only time you'll talk to me."

"I *talk* to you."

"Not since you told me our relationship was over."

"Not over. Just different." She stared down at the muddy ground. "I've been busy. And it's been raining."

He wished those were the only reasons. But he knew better. Regardless, he would cherish the time they had now. Even if she wished she were anywhere else but with him.

Gathering her mass of damp curls, she tugged them over her other shoulder. They tumbled to her lap where she attempted to untangle them with her fingers.

Red streaks drew his gaze to blood on her neck. "What are these?" He brushed more of her hair aside and examined what looked like scratches. Deep ones.

She fingered them absently. "Yes, I'd forgotten. Stowy. He hates the water."

As if on cue, the cat swatted at her from the branch above causing Angeline to giggle. A wonderful, delightful sound that helped loosen the tightness in James's gut at both her cold demeanor and the sight of fresh blood.

He swallowed, plucked a nearby leaf and pressed it on the wounds. "You may need stitches."

⟨⟨◈⟩⟩

James's voice sounded hollow and trembling, as though it came from within a cave—a very cold cave. Though she'd been trying not to look at him, she swerved her gaze to his, noting that his eyes were on anything but her neck and his face bore resemblance to white parchment.

Moving his fingers aside, she held the leaf in place, remembering all the times he had been paralyzed in the presence of blood. At first she'd thought it ludicrous and weak. Especially for a doctor, but now that she knew him—had witnessed his strength and bravery—she knew this was no simple phobia. "It must have been horrible for you on the battlefield," she mumbled the thoughts filling her mind.

"You would never know it now, but I used to be quite a good surgeon," James said with a sordid chuckle, still not looking at her neck. "They would send the worst cases my way. . .the ones with limbs blown off and entrails bubbling from bellies."

The visual sent a sour taste into her mouth.

"Forgive me, Angeline." He laid a hand on her arm, but she moved aside. The man had no idea how his every touch played havoc with her insides. And her emotions. When she awoke, cocooned in his arms, she'd felt safe and warm and loved. And she found herself wishing time would stand still and she'd never have to leave his embrace. But that could never be. So, she'd moved as far away from him as she could and watched him sleep—a restless, fitful slumber that tore at her heart to discover what caused him such angst and to put an end to it with her love.

"You were quite accustomed to seeing blood, I imagine," she said.

A drop of rainwater landed on his forehead from above and he shoved it into his hair—damp, chaotic hair threaded in strings of gold and tawny brown that curled when they reached his collar.

"Is it possible for one person to see too much blood in a lifetime?" His jaw flexed as he gazed into the jungle. "Perhaps there is some limit set by God that man cannot go beyond. Similar to the threshold of pain that thrusts men into the bliss of unconsciousness. I reached my limit is all." His bronze eyes searched hers, brimming with sorrow and shame, yet sturdy as the metal whose color they favored.

"I cannot imagine what you went through."

"I wouldn't want you to. I wouldn't want anyone to. Yet, it was nothing compared to what our soldiers saw on the battlefield."

"Yet you saved many lives."

"A few."

"How could there be shame in that? Or what happened to you afterward? In fact, you should be proud of your service." Unlike her. While he was saving lives, Angeline was ruining them. Her own included.

Stowy leapt onto James's leg, pouncing on a shifting spot of sunlight. They both chuckled, lightening the dour mood. Perhaps lightening it a little too much, for when the laughter died, their eyes met again, and his hand swallowed hers. This time, she allowed it. The rough feel of his skin, the warmth, the way his fingers folded over hers, protecting, caressing. Eternity was made of moments like these, moments when time halted, dangling on the line strung between their gazes. Moments when there were only two and the strength of their love seemed to power the universe. She soaked it in, storing the memory deep in her heart.

For it could never happen again.

She couldn't have this man. Or Dodd would ruin his chance at happiness, his chance at marriage and children with a true lady. Angeline must be strong. Breaking the trance, she turned and gazed below. "The waters are low enough now. Perhaps we should go. It isn't proper for us to be here alone."

"People will understand. Besides, you're safe with me." With a touch to her chin, he brought her to face him again. "You know my feelings for you."

She did. And it threatened to undo her carefully erected shield. But Dodd's ultimatum rose like a sword beside that shield—one she must use to keep James at bay. For his sake.

Sunlight angled over his jaw, over his dark stubble so at odds with his light hair.

She tugged her hand from his. "You must accept the way things are, James. I'm sorry."

"And how exactly *are* things?"

That I'd give anything to be loved by you. "We can be no more than friends." Moisture blurred her vision.

"I don't understand. You feel something for me. I see it in your eyes."

"You are mistaken." She waved a hand through the air. "I have a terrible fault, you see, of making everyone feel cared for. I've been that way since I was a little girl." She laughed to cover up the sob caught in her throat and turned from him.

"Does this character flaw include crying when rejecting someone you have no feelings for?" Again he moved her chin to face him. She lowered her lashes as two traitorous tears sped down her cheeks. He thumbed one away.

Oh, God if You're there. Please give me strength. She closed her eyes beneath his touch. His kissed the other tear away. Before she could jerk back, his lips descended onto hers. His breath filled her mouth.

And she lost herself in his taste, his male scent, the tender touch of his lips, so unlike other men who'd kissed her.

Her skin tingled. Her body grew weightless and drifted toward the sky. If only she could fly away with James, away from everyone, away from her past, away from Dodd.

What am I doing?

Shoving him back, she punched his chest, grabbed Stowy, and inched away with one thought in mind. Get as far from James as she could. The branch bounced, she shrieked, lost her grip, and toppled to the bough beneath her. Landing hard. Squashed between her chest and the bark, Stowy let out a painful howl.

"Don't move, Angeline. Stay there." She could hear the creak of wood as James made his way down to her.

No! He would touch her, hold her, rescue her again. She couldn't allow it. Her heart couldn't take it. "Stay away!" She struggled to rise. Cradling Stowy, she slid to the branch below. It was too thin, too slick from rain. She slipped. Her feet met air. One arm flailing, she reached for another bough, but her hand scraped over bark. Her leg caught on something. The rip of fabric filled her ears. Along with Stowy's mournful screech.

Splat! Angeline landed on her derrière in the mud. Stowy flew from her arms and alighted on a pile of broken branches beside her.

"Angeline! Are you hurt?" James shouted.

Water soaked through her skirts into her petticoat and nightdress. A croak brought her gaze to a toad sitting atop a rock to her left. A giggle burst into her throat, but she forced it back. "You! You made me fall!" She lifted her hands and shook off the mud as James skillfully navigated the tree, swung down on the final branch, and landed on the ground with a splash.

He started toward her. "If you hadn't been in such a hurry to get away from me—"

"Because you made improper advances!"

Stopping, James cocked a brow. "If I had made improper advances, you would not have fallen, I assure you."

"What is that supposed to mean?" She reached for the gun at her waist, but her hand met the empty belt around her skirt. "Are you saying you would restrain a woman against her will?"

"Missing your pistols, your dragonship?" He quirked a grin that made her want to giggle, to toss mud at him, to drag him down with her until they both burst forth with laughter. But instead she forced anger into her tone. "If you wish me to be a dragon, I shall oblige you!" She had no idea what that meant, but it was the only retort she found on her lips.

He chuckled. "Dragon or not, I would never restrain a woman."

"Why? Because you are so captivating, so virile, so exciting that women swoon in your arms?" Though honestly she couldn't blame them.

This, however, seemed to hit the mark as the grin faded from his lips and he lowered his chin with a sigh.

Angeline felt like sinking into the mud.

Instead, James extended a hand to assist her up. Refusing it, she struggled to rise, got caught on her skirt, fell down again, growled, then shoved herself up to stand. She wanted to thank him for saving her life, for risking his own for the likes of her, for being so wonderful and charming and honorable...

Reaching up, he wiped mud from her cheek. She stepped back. "We should get going. Come Stowy." She turned to gather the cat in her arms, but he leapt into James's instead.

Clutching her skirts, she started sloshing back toward town. *Traitor.*

CHAPTER 15

The crash and fizzle of ocean waves—normally soothing to Angeline—grated over her like a washboard on skin. Still, she was thankful to see the storm's retreat on the horizon, waving farewell in robes resplendent in amber, coral, and ruby—a promise for a sunny day on the morrow. Yet no amount of sun could brighten the colonists' dour mood. Especially after a day of scouring the jungle for castoffs left by the river, hidden booty shoved behind bushes and stuffed up trees in some kind of demonic treasure hunt. And always the trinket disappointed. A shirt here, a hat there, an iron pot over there, but not enough left of the things they really needed.

"Thank God we found some of our clothes scattered about." Ever the optimist, Eliza plucked a sopping pair of trousers from a bucket and flung them over the line the men had strung between palms.

Angeline finished hanging a petticoat and stretched the aches from her back. She'd given up on the ones in her legs long ago.

"Mercy me, Eliza." Magnolia stuffed a wayward hair into her bun. "Our entire town is destroyed. We have no homes, no food, no cots, and now we are forced to sleep on the sand like burrowing crabs. I hardly think a few clothes will aid our situation."

Angeline quite agreed, but she wouldn't say so. There was already far too much complaining firing about the camp.

"Without proper attire we'd be *naked* crabs burrowing in the sand." Eliza smiled, an infectious smile that caused all of them to grin, Sarah included, who assisted with the laundry on Angeline's left.

However, Magnolia's smile soon faded. "Honestly, what is to

become of us? The entire town is washed away. Not a single hut remains."

Angeline stooped to retrieve a dripping coverlet, her gaze drawn to James chopping wood down the beach. After the colonists had hauled everything they could find of use down to the shore, Blake had organized the men for different tasks. Some chopping wood, others building shelters, a few fishing. He'd asked some of the women to search for fruit, though most of it had been stripped from the trees by the mighty claws of the river. The rest of the colonists scoured the jungle for scattered goods. All except Dodd and Patrick, who insisted their time would be better spent looking for the gold that would—how had Patrick put it?—*rebuild the town into a thriving metropolis.* Angeline had met too many men like Patrick Gale in her life to give credence to a single word he spoke.

As if in defiance of her thoughts, Sarah added, "Towns can be rebuilt, Magnolia."

"And they can be destroyed again, as well," came the lady's retort.

Destroyed was a fitting description of New Hope. Demolished might be better. Every hut, bamboo pole, palm frond, and even the fire pit had been washed away. All that remained as evidence that civilized people had lived there was the stone oven beneath where the meeting shelter had once stood. In fact the ground was still so soggy and littered, there was no place to sleep. And it would take weeks to pick up all the debris in order to build again. Which is why they decided to settle on the beach for now. Though much of the sand near the mouth of the river had been washed away, this northern section of coast remained unscathed, save for mounds of wet sand and downed palm fronds.

So much loss. So much sorrow. As Angeline glanced at the colonists scattered across the beach set to various tasks, she wondered what would become of their attempt at a Southern utopia. Already she'd heard rumblings from some who wanted to quit and go home.

Two of those mumblers headed toward them now. Magnolia's parents. Mr. Scott, gray hair askew, face red, arms stiff by his sides, marched in front of his wife who scurried along behind him, wringing her hands while the torn fringe of her hem dragged over the sand. Mable, their slave, followed on her heels.

Magnolia released a heavy sigh as they halted before the clothesline.

"Magnolia," Mr. Scott began, lifting his chin as if addressing an assembly. "We have decided to return to Georgia on the next ship. Brazil is obviously no place for civilized people."

"And dearest"—Mrs. Scott placed a hand on her daughter's arm, her tone desperate—"we want you to accompany us."

"In fact, we insist," Mr. Scott added.

Magnolia released an annoyed sigh. "In case you have forgotten, I am married now, Father."

"Do you think I could forget such a travesty?" Glancing around, he restrained his rising voice, or rather attempted to. "Since you ran off with that ruffian, I haven't had a full night's sleep!"

His belligerent tone drew a few gazes from others down the beach, including Moses, who halted from chopping wood to wipe sweat from his face. His eyes latched upon Mable.

"I didn't run—" Magnolia began then gave a tight smile and faced her friends. "Why, excuse me, ladies." Her Southern drawl reappeared as she lifted her skirts, looped an arm through her father's, then escorted him and her mother out of earshot.

Angeline's pity rose for the lady. Though Angeline had lost her father at a young age, he'd been nothing like Mr. Scott. Perhaps Magnolia would be better off without him. Perhaps the entire town would. All except Moses, whose longing gaze toward Mable spoke of a growing affection that would be severed should the Scotts leave and take their slave with them.

While Magnolia argued with her parents, Eliza eased beside Angeline, flung an arm around her shoulder, and squeezed her close, causing her bruises to throb. But the affection of such a good friend was well worth the pain. "You are very quiet, Angeline. Such an ordeal you endured being swept off by the river. We were so worried for you."

Angeline smiled. "I thought for sure I would drown."

"It's amazing James found you at all."

"A miracle," Sarah said as a breeze nearly tore the garment from her grasp. "And you and James spending the night in a tree?" The mischievous twinkle seemed so out of place in the pious woman's eyes. Under normal circumstances, Angeline would have feigned a giggle or a blush or something else appropriate for maidens. Instead she only felt shame and sorrow.

Her traitorous eyes swept to the man in question, standing over a log, ax hefted above his head, muscles strained. And she remembered the feel of those muscles encasing her in a fortress of protection. Not since she'd been a little girl snuggled in her father's lap had she felt so safe. And loved. The loss of him joined the ache in her heart for her father. "He's a good man."

"And quite fond of *you*." Eliza shook water from a man's torn vest and held it up to the fading light.

A child's belly laugh drew Angeline's gaze to Thiago playing with Lydia in the sand. Anxious to change the topic, she gestured toward the Brazilian. "He's so good with her, Sarah. You must be pleased."

"Yes." Seemingly lost in her thoughts, Sarah smiled as she glanced at the handsome Brazilian swinging six-month-old Lydia around in a circle. Perhaps a woman like Angeline would never marry and have children, but a saint like Sarah certainly deserved happiness.

Leaves parted, and Dodd emerged from the jungle just feet from where they hung clothes. His wink sent a chill scraping down Angeline before another chill followed when Patrick Gale sauntered onto the beach after him. Had they found their gold? No. Not from the scowl on Patrick's face. Another man, one of the farmers, burst from the trees, his chest heaving, his eyes searching the beach and then dashing toward Blake, shouting, "Mr. Lewis is missing. We can't find him anywhere!"

⚜

James tried to keep his focus on the flames instead of on Angeline, who sat on a stump across from the huge fire. But his gaze kept wandering her way. Her hair, tied in a braid, tumbled over the front of one shoulder down to her waist, where Stowy batted the curled tips. Firelight reflected such sorrow in her violet eyes, it made him long to sit beside her and make her smile again as he had in the tree. Before she'd become a dragon and spurned his kindness. Ah, the woman's fickle moods! He would never understand her. Perhaps that was part of her allure. Yet, despite that allure and her insistence otherwise, he *knew* she felt something for him.

Resisting the urge to approach her, he lowered to sit upon one of the logs framing the massive fire, where colonists assembled for a town meeting. Or a beach meeting, since there was no longer a town. A salty breeze whipped the flames into a frenzy before blasting over James, filling his lungs with the smell of fish and brine and wood smoke. Crashing waves serenaded them, drowning out the drone of the jungle just yards away. One by one, the colonists took positions around the fire, some sitting, some standing, all looking hopeless and worn. It had been a long day of hard work—a long day of disappointment.

Stretching the aches from his back, James glanced toward the row of shelters he and some of the other men had managed to erect. Not nearly enough for everyone, but at least the ladies would have some protection from the elements.

"What are we gonna do, Colonel?" one of the ex-soldiers finally said when all were assembled. "What's the plan?"

"Plan? How can there be a plan?" Mr. Scott bellowed, thumbs stuck in his torn lapels. "The only reasonable course is to count our losses and head home."

Grumbles of assent followed.

Blake rubbed the back of his neck and stared into the flames. Was it James's imagination or did the colonel's shoulders sit much lower after this last disaster?

"That is one possible course, Mr. Scott," Blake said, glancing at his wife, Eliza, who stood by his side. "We could give up and leave, go back home like the failures the North claims we are."

"Better failures than dead," one man spat.

"But *have* we done our best?" Hayden spoke up, gazing over the group. "At what point do we give up on our dream?"

"When your dream is out to kill you, that's when," the blacksmith's wife muttered, followed by bitter chuckles.

"What do you make of all these disasters, Colonel?" another man asked.

Blake exchanged a glance with James, an approving glance followed by a nod James took as permission to share what he knew. He rose to his feet, shrugging off his hesitation. They were all in this together; they might as well know everything. Even if it sounded completely and utterly mad. "We think this may be the work of a supernatural force."

"Poppycock," Dodd scoffed, fingering his gold watch.

Ignoring him, James continued. "There's a book I've been translating written in ancient Hebrew. We found it at the temple."

"You talking about a curse, Doc?"

"Yes and no." James assessed the group, knowing full well most would think him unhinged. "We believe Mr. Graves released a supernatural being called *Destruction* and it is he, or *it*, who is wreaking havoc on our colony."

"Balderdash!" the baker shouted then scanned the group with a chortle. "I do believe the preacher's still got water on the brain from the flood."

Chuckles joined the crackle of the fire. Yet some of the colonists remained somber, staring intently at James, waiting for him to continue.

"Released from what?" one asked.

"A prison of some sort. . .where Graves was digging." James fisted hands at his waist while a gust of wind sent hair into his face. He snapped it away.

One of the women hugged herself. "What sort of being are you talking about, Doctor?"

Halfway above the dark horizon, the moon peeked from behind a heavy cloud, casting them in murky light. "An evil one, Mrs. Wilson. An invisible one."

More chuckles erupted.

"He speaks the truth." Blake's commanding tone silenced them. "I've seen this temple myself. It's a strange, evil place with broken chains that once imprisoned something, or someone."

"I have seen it as well," Hayden offered, much to James's surprise since the confidence man had been nothing but skeptical.

"And me." Angeline added, her gaze brushing over him—too quick for him to thank her.

Wind sprayed them with sand and Magnolia stood, brushing off her skirts. "Haven't we all had frightening visions? People long since dead appearing out of nowhere and talking to us?"

Nods bobbed around the group.

"Then why is it so hard to believe that some supernatural being is causing them?" She gave James a satisfied smile and sat back down beside Angeline.

"You mean there's more than one of them?" One of the farmers scratched his head.

As if she could stand no more talk of evil beings, Mrs. Scott released a blubbering whimper and leaned on her husband's arm. For once the man responded with kindness, drawing her close.

"Yes, we believe so," James said.

"All the more reason to leave." Mrs. Jenkins stood, drawing her young daughter into her skirts. "I don't want Henrietta exposed to some unearthly evil."

Though she said nothing, Delia, Moses's sister, nodded her agreement while gathering both her children close as well.

"Let's say this thing exists." Mr. Jenkins swung an arm around his wife. "How can we fight it?"

A crab skittered over James's boot. He flipped it aside. "I don't know yet. I need to translate more of the book."

"What if we can't fight it? What if it keeps trying to destroy us?"

Patrick, who'd been standing to the side keeping unusually quiet, now cleared his throat and pushed through the throng, fingering his graying goatee. "Come now, you can't seriously be swallowing this gibberish? Invisible creatures? Bah! There are no such things. We are intelligent, civilized people, not unschooled savages." He scanned the crowd with imperious green eyes. "I have not had a vision."

"Nor have I," Dodd added.

A cotton farmer from Louisiana stood. "Begging your pardon, Mr. Gale, madness or not, if this is something evil, all the more reason to leave. At least back home, I didn't have the devil to contend with."

"Indeed," one man yelled.

"I couldn't agree more," another added.

"Ah, I didn't say that you shouldn't leave. In fact, I think you should," Patrick added. "There is nothing for genteel people here."

James's anger boiled. "Have you considered that perhaps God brought us here to defeat this evil?" Shame burned in his gut that he hadn't thought of that until now. If that was true, God would make a way, wouldn't He?

Moses stepped out of the shadows from beside his sister. "I say we's got to try. God will be wid us."

"I ain't listening to no Negro," the cooper hissed, causing James to cringe and the crowd to start muttering.

"Sorry, Colonel, Mr. Gale," one of the ex-soldiers said, crossing his arms over his chest, "but I've made up my mind to leave. The next time Captain Barclay sails to our shores, me and my family will be on his ship headed home."

"Us too," a farmer said.

"And us."

While others stood and announced their intentions to do the same, James swept his gaze to Angeline, still staring at the fire. He wouldn't blame her if she wanted to return as well, yet she said nothing.

Mr. Scott moved to stand behind Magnolia. "You will return with us, Magnolia." His normally strict tone held a hint of pleading that drew his daughter's gaze and caused her to rise.

Hayden took her hand in his. "Perhaps you should go, Princess. There's nothing but hardship for you here right now. We will rebuild the colony, create better homes, bring a crop to harvest. And then I'll send for you when it's safe."

"Finally some sense from the man," Mr. Scott announced.

Ignoring her father, Magnolia gave her husband a look of reprimand. "Are you daft, Hayden Gale? I have no intention of ever leaving you. Not now. Not ever. We will get through this together."

Considering the way the woman had complained all day, James was taken aback. Yet even from where he stood, he felt the love stretching between husband and wife.

Blake turned to Eliza, glanced over her swollen belly, and started to say something, but she silenced him with a lift of her finger. "Don't you dare even say it. I'm staying with you."

"But the baby—"

"Will be perfectly all right. I will have this baby here in Brazil. And he or she will be the firstfruits of this new land. Proof that we can survive anything." Eliza glanced over the crowd. "And we *can* survive if we stay together."

James swallowed and lowered his gaze. Would a woman ever love him, be as devoted to him as Magnolia and Eliza were to their husbands? He glanced at Angeline. Her expression had changed from one of exhausted sorrow to tangible fear. James followed her gaze to find Dodd looking at her. . .no, more like leering at her. If he continued,

James's fist would pummel those eyes until they were too swollen to look at anyone for a very long time.

But that wasn't a very nice thing for a preacher to think.

"Sorry," one of the ex-soldiers announced, "but I still intend to leave."

"Us too."

"And us."

"Very well." Blake released a heavy sigh and circled an arm around his wife, ushering her close. "I understand. I won't try to stop you."

"We've lost everything, Colonel. Not only our homes and our meager belongings, but now our crops. Twice. And worst of all, our hope."

"We still have our lives." Hayden raked a hand through his hair. "And each other."

"What of Graves? What of Lewis?"

"Graves died from his own foolishness," Blake said. "And we will search for Mr. Lewis tomorrow."

The fire sputtered and snapped as a wave thundered ashore.

"He probably drowned when the river rose," one woman offered.

Thiago tossed a log into the fire, shooting sparks into the black sky. "Or he become Lobisón —Wolfman."

Groans and wide eyes filtered over the group. A woman gasped.

James chuckled. "Hogwash. Come now, everyone. Let's keep our wits about us."

"Wits? You go on about curses and temples and supernatural beings, and you're telling *us* to keep our wits about us?"

James rubbed his chin. The man did have a point. Yet he didn't have time to respond before a distant sound echoing through the trees made the hair on his arms prick to attention.

The eerie howl of a lone wolf.

CHAPTER 16

Angeline hefted the basket of fruit in her arms. With only one orange and a half-spoiled mango, it wasn't terribly heavy, but she had an ache in her shoulder that wouldn't go away. Perhaps it was sleeping on the sand these past two weeks. Or perhaps it was an ache to match the one in her heart every time she saw James and had to force herself to avoid him. Avoid talking to him, seeing him, being anywhere near him. Which was difficult to do when they lived on the same beach. On the occasions when their eyes met, she saw the hurt in his, the yearning. And she wanted to scream, to cry. . .to run into his arms. But that was not possible. Not with Dodd watching her every move, slinking around the beach and jungle, eyeing her like the wolf that serenaded them each night with its baleful howl.

Was it possible that Mr. Lewis had, indeed, transformed into the beast? For they had not been able to find hide nor hair of him since the flood.

She glanced into the canopy, searching for fruit, but instead saw dozens of colorful birds hopping from branch to branch, trilling their happy tunes. Always happy. Always carefree. Oh, how she envied them. They had naught to fear from flood or ants or invisible beasts. A verse from scripture rose in her mind. . .something about how birds neither sow nor reap, but God cares for them. She pushed it aside. Comforting words meant for others. Not her.

Lowering her gaze, she scanned the delicate green lace of life that surrounded her. Where had the other ladies gone? Magnolia, Sarah, and the two other women who'd been sent in search of fruit. Nothing

125

but ferns and vines and leaves large enough to be gowns met her gaze. Not to mention the occasional spider or lizard or frog. But they didn't bother her. She had bigger reptiles to deal with. Still, Blake had instructed the women to stay together.

In truth, she relished the time alone. Sharing a shelter with four other women had not allowed her any time to think, to decide what to do about Dodd. Even though, deep down, she already knew her answer. And that answer saddened her more than anything.

Batting aside a leaf, she moved forward, her boots sinking into the still-sodden ground. Perspiration dampened her neck and brow and made her long for the ocean breezes she left behind only moments before. Prying her shoe from the mud, a memory forced its way into her thoughts. Of a dark night and another muddy puddle. Of another pair of shabby boots—with holes in the toes—stepping into the muck as she made her way down the streets of Richmond. The icy mire had seeped into her stockings and crept up her ankles until her legs shivered. Not wanting to risk being recognized, she'd hid her face in the folds of her cloak as she kept to the shadows—hungry, cold, wet, and wishing for death. Angeline tried to shake away the memories. The depths to which she'd been reduced—begging on the streets like an urchin.

Little did she know, she would sink lower still.

She drew in a deep breath of the humid air so full of life, hoping some of that life would infiltrate her soul. But instead she heard crackling rising from all around. Fearing what it foretold, she stopped and squeezed her eyes shut. But the voice slithered over her ears nonetheless. It was the same voice of kindness, of charity, she'd heard that night over two years ago. The voice that had saved her.

And brought her to her doom.

She opened her eyes.

"Oh, you poor dear," Miss Lucia said, clipping Angeline's chin and turning her face side to side, just as she had done that dark night. "Such a fright. And so thin. Why, I declare, you are in dire need of a hot meal and an even hotter bath. I have just the thing for you, darling. Now, don't you worry."

Angeline could do nothing but stand and stare at the woman with her ample bosom and rounded hips, bedecked in glitter and feathers just as she had been that night. She'd been stunned by the woman's interest in her. Wary, of course, but too hungry and tired to care. Now, with Miss Lucia standing before Angeline looking as real as any of the trees that circled them, all the emotions of that night returned—raw and festering like open sores. She had allowed Miss Lucia to take her to an upstairs room at the Night Owl. She'd eaten her food, taken a bath, and slept in one of her feather beds. The woman had been so kind, Angeline wondered if this was what it felt like to have a mother, an older woman to care for her and love her and teach her the things women must know. On Angeline's fourth day at the Night Owl, she discovered Miss Lucia would skip over the first two and only provide the third.

Now, placing a jeweled hand on her rounded hip and tapping her fan to her chin, Miss Lucia sashayed around Angeline. "Yes. . .yes. . . you will do nicely." She had dressed her up in a lovely gown of creamy taffeta with a red silk ruche. And a bodice far too low for Angeline's tastes. "Now, you go out there, honey, and be friendly. That's all I ask in return for my hospitality." And then she'd smiled, that pearly smile of hers, made all the whiter by her brightly painted red lips.

The trees shrunk into tables, branches into men with tankards. The leaf-strewn ground into a floor strewn with other far nastier things: spit and ale and tobacco. And Miss Lucia nudged her into the crowd. All eyes shot to her like darts to a bull's-eye, leering, salivating. Hands reaching, swatting her behind, pulling her onto laps.

"Leave me alone!" She shoved them away. "Don't touch me."

A meaty hand gripped her arm. She struggled to free herself. "Let me go!"

"Angeline!"

She looked up and saw Dodd smiling at her with a grin of merciless victory. The tables and men faded. One glance over her shoulder told Angeline Miss Lucia was gone as well. Yet Dodd remained. She tore from his grasp and backed away, rubbing her arm. "You're real."

"In the flesh, my dear. But I believe you were having a dream. Or perhaps a vision?"

"A nightmare since you were in it." She reached for her pistol but remembered she'd lost it in the flood. Then, stooping, she picked up her basket and fruit. At least she'd have something to swat him with should he come nearer. "What do you want?"

"It's been two weeks, my dear. I must hear your answer."

"Surely you've seen that I'm no longer associating with James. In fact, I've told him to leave me alone."

A breeze lifted strands of his blond hair as his narrowed eyes assessed her. "What does that matter to me?"

"Your threat was due to our courtship, was it not?"

"*Threat* is such a nasty word. I prefer to call it an arrangement." He fingered a leaf by his side. "And yes, your pending affair with the good doctor prodded me to action, though I had hoped you would come to me on your own."

"And why would I do that?"

"Because of *what* you are." Incredulous, he looked at her as if the fact were inescapable.

Shame and fear burned in her throat. "I am not that woman anymore."

"Ah ah ah." He wagged a finger. "You can never erase such a blemish from your soul. What does the scripture say about fallen women. . . something about pigs with rings in their snouts?"

Perspiration slid down her back. "What would you know of the Bible?" What would *she*, in fact? Just snippets from her childhood when her father would read to her. Thankfully, she remembered no such reference to jeweled pigs.

"Regardless. The *arrangement* stands. You come to me twice a week and I keep your shameful little secret." Blue eyes scanned her from head to toe. He licked his lips.

She had no doubt the carnal letch would keep to his word if she complied. Even if he also knew the other truth about her, she doubted he'd give up her services to tell anyone. Nevertheless, she had but two cards to play with this huckster. She forced a complacent expression. "And why should I care if you tell everyone?"

He smiled. "Because I've been watching you, my dear, and I see how much you value your newfound friends. All that would disappear if they knew who you really were. In fact, the pious doctor may even ostracize you from the colony. He does seem to have an aversion toward trollops."

The word burned her ears and sped to the canopy, where birds gobbled it up and spit it back down. *Trollop, trollop, trollop.*

Dropping the basket, she covered her ears.

"Come now, it's not so bad. Why, you could even start up your own business in New Hope. Lord knows the town needs a little entertainment."

"Never! I came here to get away from that."

He cocked his head. "Yet we can't change who we really are, can we?"

Tears burned behind her eyes, but she forced them back. She had thought she could change. She had thought she could become a real lady.

"Perhaps you are right." She glared at him. "You are still the vulgar swine you always were."

He flinched as if wounded. But that couldn't be. The man had no heart to wound. "My point is proven, then."

Angeline stared at the ground, expecting to see her heart, her very soul bleed from her boots into the mud. She had but one card left, but it broke her heart to play it.

"I will leave."

Finally she got a reaction out of him. "What?"

"I'm going back to the States." She lifted her chin, enjoying her moment of power. "Thiago is taking a group to Rio tomorrow. I intend to accompany them." Back to a land where her past was known and she was wanted by the law. Back to horrid memories and a hopeless future.

But what choice did she have?

A slice of sunlight angled over his crooked nose as his eyes filled with malice. "I will still tell them."

"I'm sure you will." She knelt to pick up her basket and fruit and then pivoted on her heels. "Good day, Mr. Dodd."

Fingers as tight as bands clenched her arm and yanked her back. "No wench walks away from Dodd!"

Pain burned into her shoulders. She struggled against his grip and was about to kick him in the shin when James, hair askew, face red, stormed into the clearing. "What did you call her?"

James couldn't believe his ears. Or his eyes. He knew Dodd had a fetish for Miss Angeline. He'd seen the way he gaped at her, licking his lips as if she were his next meal. Which was why he'd followed the man when he plunged into the jungle. But this! Grabbing her. Calling her foul names! Charging forward, he shoved Dodd, sending him toppling backward. Eyes firing like cannons, Dodd righted himself and brushed his vest where James had touched.

Despite the heat, Angeline's face was white as frost. Her moist eyes, filled with terror, shifted between him and Dodd.

He'd kill the man for frightening her. "How dare you touch her!" He barreled toward him. Dodd's eyes widened, but he had no time to react before James clutched his collar and thrashed him against a tree trunk. "What kind of lawman are you?" He ground Dodd's back into the rough bark, but fear had fled the man's face, replaced by superior smugness that ignited James's rage.

"I did the woman no harm. Ask her yourself."

James glanced over his shoulder, expecting to find Angeline relieved, perhaps even grateful to have been rescued from such a monster. Instead she trembled like the leaves all around them. "Let him alone, James," she said almost sullenly.

"He should be taught how to treat a lady," James growled.

Dodd snickered, and James tightened his grip on his throat.

"I said leave him be." Angeline's voice turned commanding. "He did me no harm."

Something was wrong. Why would such a strong, independent woman like Angeline—one who became a dragon at the slightest provocation—allow a worm like Dodd to defame her good character? James released the fiend.

Stretching his shoulders, Dodd circled him with a wary eye.

"Nevertheless, you will apologize for insulting her character," James said.

Dodd and Angeline glanced at each other as if they shared a secret. "There is no need," she said. Pleading filled her misty eyes.

"There is *every* need." He grabbed Dodd's arm and squeezed until the man winced. "Apologize to the lady."

For some reason, Dodd found this amusing. "My apologies, *milady*." The title rode like a taunt from a jester's lips.

Releasing him yet again, James stepped back, resisting the urge to punch the smirk from his lips. Dodd winked at Angeline, cast a scathing look at James, then turned and sauntered away, whistling a happy tune.

Shoving a hand through his hair, James faced Angeline. "Why grant mercy to such a beast?"

She wouldn't look at him. "Everyone deserves mercy, James. Being a preacher, surely you know that."

"Mercy is one thing. Justice another. And if Dodd isn't taught a lesson, he'll try to harm you again."

Her gaze skittered across the jungle. "If you don't mind, I should be getting back." And without another word, another explanation, or even a thank you, she turned and headed down the trail.

James caught up to her. "I know I've gone and done the unthinkable and rescued you again. How will you ever forgive me?" He intended to bring some levity to the confusing situation, but her scowl only deepened.

"You didn't, and I do." Her tone was placid, her eyes straight ahead.

James forced down a groan of frustration. "What is it between you and Dodd?"

"I don't know what you mean. I hardly know the man." She brushed aside a patch of ferns, her shoes making *splat*, *splat* sounds in the mud.

"He's dangerous. I see the way he looks at you."

"As he does all the women. He's harmless, I assure you."

But the quaver in her tone spoke otherwise. They proceeded in silence for several minutes, James leading the way so he could move the thick foliage aside for her.

"Please do not wander off alone again." He held back the final leaves before they emerged onto the beach. "Will you promise me that?"

"There is no need. For I won't be here to wander." She stepped onto the sand and hurried forward, no doubt desperate to relieve herself of his company.

Stunned as much by her words as by the slap of bright sunlight, James followed and touched her shoulder, halting her.

"What are you saying?" He didn't want to believe her words—prayed he'd heard her wrong.

She glanced toward the waves washing ashore, a forlorn look on her face. "I'm leaving for Rio tomorrow with the others."

Her words scattered into nonsensical phrases in his mind. He'd accepted that she didn't want a courtship. That she found him repugnant. But he could not accept never seeing her again.

"If it's because of me, I have received your message loud and clear. I understand your sentiments, and I won't be pursuing you."

Wind tussled her fiery hair. "It's not you." A glint of affection sped across her eyes. . .ever so slight. Then it was gone. She started walking. "I'm tired of sleeping on the sand and eating fruit and fish. It was a mistake coming here. Our utopia has failed. I have the good sense to know when to accept that." She didn't sound convincing.

"But you have no one back home."

"That's none of your concern, Doctor." Shielding her eyes from the sun, she gave him one final glance before she swirled about and walked away.

Leaving James feeling like one of the empty seashells lying at his feet.

⚜

Angeline couldn't take another minute of this agony. It was bad enough she hadn't slept all night. Bad enough she had to witness the torment carved on James's face yesterday. Now she must endure the tears of her closest friends as they stood around her bidding her farewell. Magnolia, Sarah, and Eliza embraced her over and over, wiping tears from their eyes, begging her to stay. Another moment of such genuine affection and she might give in. Throw her past to the wind and remain with the only friends she'd ever had.

Yet how long would they be her friends once the truth was known?

The sun finally burst above the horizon, spreading its honeyed feathers over sea and land, and causing Angeline to blink. Good thing, for she didn't know how much longer she could hold her tears at bay. Releasing Eliza's hand, she hefted her satchel over her shoulder and glanced at Thiago, who was preparing his own sack for the journey. Only seven of the colonists dared to make the five-day trek to Rio, preferring to take their chances in the jungle rather than remain in the ill-fated colony waiting for a ship to arrive. She shouldn't be one of them. She didn't believe the colony was doomed. She believed they all had a chance at life and hope and new beginnings.

Her gaze landed on James in the distance. With trousers hiked to his knees, he stared at the sunrise, arms folded over his chest, waves swirling about his legs. Even now, she felt drawn to him like a plant to the sunlight. He glanced over his shoulder and their eyes met, though she couldn't make out his expression. Had he sensed her looking at him? No matter. Turning, he hung his head and started walking in the opposite direction.

She would never see him again. Now the tears finally came.

"See, you're crying." Magnolia looped her arm through Angeline's and handed her a handkerchief. "You don't wish to leave us after all."

"Of course I don't wish to leave such good friends." Angeline dabbed her cheeks and glanced over the three ladies. "But I *must* go."

"I still don't understand." Eliza tossed hair over her shoulder. "After all we've been through, surely it can't get any worse." She gave a sad smile.

"And you have been so strong." Sarah positioned Lydia higher on her hip. "Why leave now?"

"I wish I could explain, but I can't."

Lydia reached chubby fingers toward Angeline, gurgling happy sounds upon a stream of drool. Despite her tears, Angeline giggled and took the baby's hand in hers, planting a kiss upon it. "I will miss you, little one. Be good for your mother." Turning toward her friends, she opened her arms. "I will miss you *all* terribly." The women fell into her embrace. Over their shoulders, she spotted Blake, Hayden, and some of the colonists making their way toward them, no doubt to say good-bye. All except Dodd, who leaned against a rock cliff by the water's edge, scowling at her, and Patrick, who was engaged in a heated discussion with Magnolia's parents. What they argued about, Angeline could only surmise. Though the couple was anxious to leave the colony, they had opted to wait for the comfort of a ship rather than traipse through "the primordial sludge of Brazil," as Mr. Scott had put it.

Boom! Thunder split the sky. Releasing her friends, Angeline glanced upward. Nothing but white clouds against a cerulean background. Sarah scanned the horizon and shrieked. Eliza's wide eyes met Angeline's. Swinging her arms around her friends, she shoved them to the side and forced them to the ground. An eerie whine scraped Angeline's ears. The beach erupted in a fiery volcano. The dirt beneath them trembled. Sand showered over them like hail, pelting their backs as they huddled together. No one dared speak. In the distance, a woman screamed. Men shouted. Baby Lydia sobbed. The rain of sand ceased. Angeline glanced up to see a smoking crater just a few feet from where they'd been standing.

Struggling to her feet, she helped her friends rise, her mind numb with confusion and fear. Gunpowder and smoke bit her nose. Dazed, the women stood staring at the crater. A shout sounded. All eyes fixed on the sea where the outline of a tall ship drifted like a giant sea serpent before the rising sun. Smoke curled from her charred hull.

A man on the deck held something to his mouth.

"This is pirate ship *Espoliar*. Surrender or die!"

CHAPTER 17

Sweat streamed down James's back that no amount of sea breeze could cool. Not even the continual gust swirling about the colonists as they were forced to line up at sword point before the pirate crew and their captain. Some of the men, James included, had made a valiant dash to retrieve pistols and what few supplies they had left amid a spray of grapeshot. They'd succeeded too—had even managed to gather the hysterical colonists and dive into the jungle. What they hadn't counted on was the preplanning of the pirate captain in the form of a dozen muskets that greeted them through the leaves. Now, back on the beach, those same muskets, along with a mishmash of swords and pistols, in the hands of over thirty pirates dressed like colorful parrots, tore any remaining hope of escape to shreds.

The sun, high in the sky, set the sand aflame and sea aglitter as waves crashed on the beach with an ominous thunder that matched the pounding of James's heart. Several yards offshore, the *Espoliar*, complete with a dozen bronze lantaka rail guns and a jolly roger sporting an hourglass and cutlass, bobbed and dipped with each incoming wave.

Captain Armando Manuel Ricu brazenly strolled before them, pantaloons and loose shirt flapping in the wind. A mane of curly black hair framed a long face with a tuft of dark whiskers crowning the chin. Every time he moved, sunlight glinted off dozens of jeweled pins scattered across his embroidered waistcoat like stars across the night sky, blinding James.

The twisted scene could match any of those pulled from a storybook espousing an age of piracy long since dead. Yet it was a scene James had witnessed not three months before in similar grueling detail when this same Captain Ricu had stolen Magnolia and brought her aboard his ship. If not for Hayden's ingenuity and courage, they would not have rescued her in time. Even now, after nudging Magnolia behind him, Hayden stood, arms crossed, face like flint, an impenetrable fortress protecting his wife.

James hoped it would be enough to deter the flamboyant captain. Though Eliza eased beside Blake and met the pirate's gaze with valor, the remaining women stood behind the line of men, hugging the children close. Mr. Keen, the poor farmer on James's right, couldn't stop his hands from shaking. Down the line, another man kept muttering to himself. Dodd stared straight ahead as if he'd gone numb. Yet, Patrick Gale fingered his goatee and kept glancing toward the jungle as if devising a plan of escape. Only for him, no doubt.

Mrs. Scott's whimper brought James's gaze around to see the lady swooning in her husband's arms. Moses stood beside Mable, while his sister and her children cowered behind his massive frame. James's eyes met Angeline's. He'd assumed she was with the other women, but instead she'd moved behind him. Though the corners of her mouth tightened and her chest rose and fell like a billowing sea, she gave no other indication of fear. He smiled and nodded, hoping to offer her a reassurance he didn't feel before he faced forward again.

Captain Ricu stopped before Hayden, studied him intently, then drew a knife longer than his arm and pointed it at his chest. Hayden didn't blink.

"I remember you. You striked me in my cabin. And you. . ." He dipped his head, first to one side of Hayden—and when Hayden moved to block his view—to the other side, before he reached to pull Magnolia forward. "You be the pretty thing I took to bed."

One of the women gasped.

Despite the terror screaming from her blue eyes, Magnolia lifted her chin. "*I* was the one who struck you, not this man." In a valiant effort to protect Hayden, she placed a finger on the pirate's blade and moved it aside.

But Hayden was having none of it. Eyes like slits and jaw bunching, he shoved between them, tugging Magnolia from the pirate's grip.

"Almost," he ground out. "You *almost* took her to bed. But she's my wife now, and you'll not be taking her anywhere."

Captain Ricu chuckled, turned, and said something in Portuguese to his men, which caused an outburst of laughter among the slovenly band. He faced Hayden again. "One thing to learn"—raising his voice, he shifted his gaze over all the colonists—"all must learn. I am Captain Ricu and I take what I want when I want."

Hayden clenched fists at his sides. Not a good sign. James must do something before he slugged the pirate captain and mayhem ensued, no doubt ending in an early death for them all. Stepping forward, James opened his mouth to speak when Blake beat him to it.

"What is it you want, Captain?" The colonel's annoyance rang louder than his fear. "As you can see, we have lost everything in a recent flood. We have nothing of value. So, take what you want and be gone with you."

Captain Ricu sauntered toward him. "You are leader, yes?" He sized Blake up with eyes as dark as coal, waiting for Blake's nod of affirmation. "You remember me?"

"Of course." Blake frowned.

"Then you know why I come." He flung hair over his shoulder in a feminine gesture that defied his fearsome appearance.

Dodd, standing on James's left, took a step back, trying to hide himself in James's shadow.

"We have no gold," Hayden shouted over the wind. "We didn't have any the last time you came and we don't have any now."

The captain's eyes snapped his way but halted upon Eliza. He curled a finger around a loose strand of her hair. "What say you, *bela*?"

Stiffening, Blake flung an arm in front of her. She pushed it down. "I know of no gold, Captain."

"Search our things and see for yourself," James said.

"I no need your permit, *idiota*!" Captain Ricu barked at James then suddenly swung around and snapped his jeweled fingers. One of his men came running with a surprisingly white handkerchief, which the pirate took and swiped over his face and neck before he flung it back at the man. With a sigh, he faced the colonists again and took up a pace before them, eyeing them up and down as if they were slices of meat hung to cure. In defiance of his ominous presence, the jeweled pins

137

on his waistcoat made a delicate jingling sound. Or was it the bells he wore on his boots? He halted before Mr. Keen who stood beside James. "What be this?" His lip curled as he raised his knife toward the poor man.

Drops of sweat quivered on Mr. Keen's trembling jaw. James reached toward the farmer to tug him away, but sunlight blinked off the gold earring in Ricu's ear, temporarily blinding him. Mr. Keen's legs gave out, and he fell to his knees. The pirate leveled his blade beneath the man's chin and raised him to his feet, sniffing the air as if he smelled something foul. A drop of blood trickled down the farmer's neck.

Another string of Portuguese spilled from the captain's lips, ending with the emphasized word *covarde*, which brought the expected chuckles from his men.

"Leave him alone." Taking Mr. Keen's arm, James shoved him out of the pirate's reach. "Can't you see he's scared out of his wits?"

Captain Ricu turned to James with a chuckle. "And *você*? Are you scared out of these wits?"

"No."

Ricu swerved the knife toward James's chest. He felt the prick through his shirt but didn't flinch. Instead, he returned Ricu's staunch gaze with one of his own and was surprised by the intelligence he saw in the pirate's dark eyes. He also saw bloodlust. And something else that made him squirm—a crazed gleam. Uttering a silent prayer, James braced himself to be run through, to feel his lifeblood poured out upon the sand and end his days on this Brazilian shore. But the pirate suddenly whirled on his shiny heels and pranced down the line of colonists. Yes, pranced. Like a giddy schoolboy. " 'Tis a map I seek. Three maps in truth." He waved his hand through the air, the lace at his cuff fluttering in the breeze.

Patrick slid his boot across the sand and exchanged a frightful glance with Dodd. Captain Ricu, who seemed to miss nothing, headed toward them.

"What maps are these, Captain?" Blake asked. "I know of no maps."

Ricu spun about. "Three old maps. Three maps that need a fourth. Fourth one I have." He patted his pocket, dark brows flashing. "Maps that lead to vast gold to make a man rich for many lives."

James glared at Dodd. This blasted gold would be the ruin of them all!

A cloud gobbled up the sun, giving them a moment's reprieve from the heat. James rubbed the sweat from the back of his neck and scanned the pirates again. If only they could catch them off guard, storm them, and grab their weapons before they knew what was happening. But not these men. Though filthy and bearded and wearing clothes in every color imaginable, they stood soberly, some leaning on the tips of weapons thrust in the sand, others holding them at the ready, awaiting their captain's command—alert and loaded like a line of cannons on a warship.

Ricu snapped his fingers again, bringing another man with a handkerchief to his side.

A stream of angry Portuguese shot from his mouth as he flung the cloth back at the pirate, who plucked it from the sand and scurried away while another man approached with yet another cloth. This one seemed acceptable as Ricu again wiped his face and neck and tossed the cloth to the ground.

James's stomach knotted. Bad enough they'd been captured by a pirate, but a mad one?

A seagull squawked overhead as if laughing at the scene. One of the women behind James began to sob.

"They have the maps, Captain. I'm sure of it," one of the pirates spoke in perfect English before he spat a black glob onto the sand.

"I know, you *imbecil*." Ricu snarled at him then faced the colonists with a grin. A silver tooth winked at them in the sun.

A tic twitched in Blake's jaw.

James fisted his hands at his waist. He'd about reached his limit of this lunacy. "Map or no map, no one here has found any gold. Feel free, Captain, to search our things." Join Dodd and Patrick in their treasure hunt for all James cared. It would serve the two greedy curs right.

Charging toward James, Ricu pricked James's throat with his knife. Angeline gasped.

"I am free with or without your permit, *senhor*! You keep that in head, eh?"

James eyed the man. Yes, he would keep that in his head. Along with how the pirate's own head was a bit unhinged.

Blake stepped forward. "He meant no insult, Captain, merely that we will make no trouble for you."

A moan sounded from Dodd's direction.

Ricu snorted, withdrew his blade, and ran his disinterested gaze over the colonists. "No trouble! Ha!" He tossed his knife in the air. It flipped several times, sun glinting off the metal, before he caught the handle with expert precision. "Search them and their things." At this, half his crew scattered like cockroaches in sunlight. He stopped before Blake. "You have till sunrise tomorrow, senhor, to give maps to me."

Blake swallowed as Ricu paced once more before the colonists. His eyes locked on something behind James. Shoving James aside, he grabbed Angeline by the wrist. She squirmed as he dragged her across the sand. James charged him.

A dozen pirates leapt in his path. The smell of sweat and alcohol stung his nose.

Ricu wheeled about and glanced from James to Angeline. "Ah. . . she be your *amante*, eh?" He grinned, his gaze landing on Hayden. "Take him." He snapped his fingers, and two of his men hauled Hayden at sword point from his spot. "I hang him in morning."

"No!" Magnolia shrieked, reaching for her husband.

"For what?" Blake demanded, his face a knot of fury and fear.

"He stole woman from me, cut my anchor chain. For this he die."

Tears spilled down Magnolia's cheeks as she started for Hayden, but Eliza and Blake held her back.

"Can we have the other women?" one of his men asked.

"No!" Ricu snapped, glaring their way, before turning and fingering a strand of Angeline's hair. She turned away in disgust. "Not before I try all first. Captain's. . .how do you say. . .privilege." His gaze took in Magnolia then skittered to Eliza, Sarah, and some of the other women as if he were deciding in what order to ravish them.

Every nerve in James's body ignited. "If you hurt her. . ." he seethed, nodding toward Angeline. "And if you kill this man, you will never get your precious maps."

"So, you have maps?" One dark sinister brow rose. "Good. Bring them to me when sun rises and I may not hang this one."

"And the lady?" Blake said. "You will not touch her."

Instead of answering, Ricu grinned, a wide grin that reached his eyes in a salacious twinkle before he dragged Angeline away.

CHAPTER 18

G ive us the maps!" James gripped Patrick by the throat. The posh man stumbled backward, clawing at James's fingers, terror bloating his face.

Strong hands tore James from the villain and pushed him back. "This isn't the way." Blake's look was stern, but his eyes held understanding.

"What *is* the way with the likes of him?" James caught his breath. Fury pounded blood through his veins as Patrick coughed and gasped and finally rose to his full height, the fear on his face replaced by indignation that only further infuriated James.

"Give them the maps, Martin. . .Patrick. . .whoever you are!" Magnolia spat out through sobs. "If there is any decency in you, give them the maps. Hayden is your son!" She hung her head as more tears streamed down her cheeks. Eliza wrapped an arm around her and drew her close, trying to offer comfort that James knew was pointless.

Blake stood his ground between James and the two men who possessed the only things that might save Angeline and Hayden. Running a hand through his hair, James took a step back, uttering a silent prayer for strength not to kill both of them on the spot.

Night had flung a dark curtain over the beach, a heavy curtain that suffocated any remaining hope from the colonists. Hope that had leeched out during a day of watching the pirates scatter their few remaining belongings across the beach and then storm away, angry and spewing threats when they didn't find anything of value. A palpable terror buzzed through the camp. No one could eat. Few even spoke. And most had retired early for the evening. All except those who, unable to sleep, now sat around a fire.

His gaze sped down the beach where the pirates assembled around another fire, chortling and singing as they passed a bottle of some vile liquor. Two bobbing lanterns marked the location of the ship offshore where all was silent. No drunken ballads, no shouts, no woman's scream pierced the crash of waves on the sand. He prayed that was a good sign. He prayed the mad pirate was leaving Angeline alone. Perhaps he'd gotten drunk and passed out before he could touch her. The alternative was too horrible to consider. And he'd had nothing but time to consider it during the long afternoon. Only Blake's level head had kept James from plunging into the waves and swimming to the ship, where he would no doubt be hung alongside Hayden or shot dead as soon as his feet landed on deck. That would do Angeline no good. Though sitting here doing nothing at all was doing her no good either.

"Don't worry." Eliza followed his gaze. "We'll get her back." She hugged Magnolia. "We'll get them both back."

"You don't know that." James's hope, dare he say even his faith, had abandoned him the minute Ricu had dragged Angeline away. The look of terror in her eyes nearly did him in—would have caused his demise if several pirates hadn't blocked his path. Even then, he'd attempted to storm through them. If Blake hadn't restrained him, he'd probably be six feet under at the moment.

He could not lose her. Not like this.

"We *do* know that," Blake said. "Because we are going to give them what they want." Turning, he faced Patrick and Dodd with that commanding look of his that must have sent soldiers scrambling to do his bidding. "Even if I have to tear off every inch of your clothing, piece by piece, I will find those maps."

"Please!" Magnolia's misty eyes raised to both men. "How can you be so cruel?" She ran fingers down Stowy's fur, trying to calm the jittery cat in her lap. "Mercy me, what is a map compared to a human life? Compared to any of our lives?"

Patrick fingered his goatee. "Fools! Do you think if we give them our maps, they will be satisfied? Why, they'll probably kill us all anyway."

A gust of wind sent flames leaping into the sky as if in agreement.

James snapped hair from his face and glanced at the armed pirates commanded to patrol the beach lest the colonists try to slip away in the night. "I can't believe even *you* would allow your own son to die."

Patrick stared at the fire. "He was as good as dead the second they dragged him away."

"Don't you need their map to find this gold?" Eliza grabbed Stowy from Magnolia, trying to calm the agitated cat. "Ricu seems to believe you need all four."

Patrick eyed Dodd, and a look of understanding passed between them. "Indeed, it could be the reason for our lack of success."

A howl sounded from the jungle—a wolf's howl. An icy chill skittered across James's neck, joining the one in his heart.

"Then you have nothing to lose by giving them your maps," Blake said. "For all we know there might be no gold at all."

"There *is* gold, I assure you." Dodd nodded with a grin.

James clenched his jaw, trying to restrain his fury. "Have you any idea what Angeline might be suffering right now? Because of your greed!"

Dodd's expression was oddly remorseful. "The pirate would have taken her anyway. Just as he'll take the other women eventually."

A shudder passed over Eliza as she shared a glance with Blake. He slipped his hand in hers.

Patrick clipped thumbs in the lapels of his coat. "We could still plan an escape. Why not wait until they are well into their cups and the guards asleep and then slip into the jungle?"

"And leave your son to die, you gruesome beast!" Magnolia started to rise, but Eliza forced her down.

"There is nothing I can do about that, map or no." Patrick brushed sand from his shoulder. "In battle there are sacrifices to be made."

Shoving past Blake, James slugged the man across the jaw.

Patrick's head swerved, blood squirting from his nose. Firelight reflected flames of hell in his eyes as he righted himself and charged James. But it was Dodd, this time, who blocked the assault. "We will give you the maps. I could not bear it should the lady die." Thrusting his hand down one leg of his trousers, he plucked a wrinkled but carefully folded paper from inside what must be a secret pocket, and handed it to James. He jerked his head toward Patrick. "His are sewn into the back of his waistcoat."

Blake and James tore off the man's embroidered vest before he could protest.

"Of all the—! You have no right!" Patrick wailed. "This is thievery!"

Ripping the silk fabric, Blake pulled out two pieces of paper. Patrick, face erupting in rage, started for the colonel. James shoved him aside. He caught his balance and yanked his ruined vest from Blake's hands. "Thieves! The lot of you!"

Ignoring him, Blake nodded at James. "Let's go rescue Hayden and Angeline."

◦◦◦✟◦◦◦

Captain Ricu shoved Angeline onto the bed and then plopped in a chair to remove his boots. It was the fourth time he'd entered the cabin since he'd locked her inside. His cabin, the captain's cabin, she deduced from the size and lavish furnishings. Each time he'd returned, the stink of alcohol was stronger, his eyes more glazed, his threats more insidious. Yet each time she thought he would ravish her, each time he pinned her to the bed and started to rip her bodice, he'd shoved away and stormed out in a groan of frustration.

She didn't know how much more terror she could stand. Hours of pacing, fearing the worst, followed by minutes of horror when it seemed he would attack her, only to have the cycle start all over again. He was either completely mad, incapable of performing, or perhaps he actually had a heart beneath all that glittery bravado. She opted for the first one. Part of her wished he'd get it over with and then toss her to the sharks. What was one whore worth, after all?

Not much, according to Miss Lucia, who, when Angeline had begged for a few nights off a week, had responded with, "Honey, you're comely of face and figure to be sure, but I can find a dozen girls just as pretty to replace you if you'd rather go back on the street again and starve."

The woman's voice had been so casual and amiable as she sauntered about the upstairs parlor, long cheroot in hand, that Angeline hadn't felt the true impact of her words for several seconds. When she did, her heart crumbled in her chest. The woman Angeline had come to

144

care for as a mother had just told her she was replaceable.

Replaceable and expendable.

Ricu tugged off one boot and tossed it aside. Darkness coated the stern windows and squeezed the last of Angeline's hope from her heart. This time, the pirate would follow through with his threats. He removed his other boot and stood. Chest heaving, she braced herself against the ratty mattress. Lantern light oscillated over the fiend and shimmered off the jeweled pins scattered across the vest he now removed and pitched onto his desk.

She swallowed and wondered how Hayden fared. Once they had stepped on board, he'd been quickly dragged below. He'd cast one last glance at her over his shoulder, an attempt, no doubt, to reassure her, but all she saw was fear in his eyes. Though the thought of hanging terrified her, she envied Hayden his quick release from this earth. Her fate at the hands of this lecherous swine would be far worse.

That swine now wobbled before her, a lustful gleam in his eyes. Hair as black as night curled around his face and hung past his shoulders. Mighty shoulders. Thick shoulders that could subdue her without effort—that had no doubt subdued many women before her.

"Ah, you and me, we have good time, eh?" he muttered.

The ship rolled over a wave. He stumbled to the left. Took his eyes off her for a moment. Angeline flew from the bed to the other side of the cabin, avoiding the urge to open the door and run. Better to deal with one pirate than dozens. *Dear God, if You're there. . .* she began but then realized God would not be concerned with a prostitute getting ravished.

Ricu whirled about and grinned. "You wish to play chase?" He rubbed his hands together and took a step toward her.

"I wish for you to leave me alone."

"But I am Captain Ricu!" he bellowed, brows dipped as if he could not fathom such a thing. "I take what I want when I want." He staggered toward her.

Angeline darted behind the oak desk. Her eyes grazed over the silk handkerchief she'd seen there earlier, so delicate and out of place among the stained maps and rusty nautical instruments, and so different from the stack of common white handkerchiefs sitting beside it. An idea formed. Picking up the cloth, she waved it in the air.

Ricu halted and stared at it as if an angel appeared before him. Sorrow melted the glee from his features.

Angeline forced calm into her voice. "Who gave this to you, Captain? A lady friend, perhaps?" She drew it to her nose, inhaling the sweet fragrance of gardenias and lilac, then ran her fingers over the silk embroidered initials, AMV. There could be only two reasons a pirate would have such a thing. One, he'd stolen it from a woman he'd assaulted, or two, a woman he loved gave it to him as a remembrance. Angeline prayed it was the latter. And from the look on his face, she was right.

He snagged it from her grip, his angry scowl softening with its touch.

"Who is she?" Angeline dared to ask.

He ran his thick jeweled thumb over the initials. "Abelena Martinez y Vicario," he replied, still staring at the cloth as if he could materialize the woman from its fabric. "From Santo Domingo."

Angeline allowed a tiny smile. Inconceivable as it was, this beast, this pirate *was in love*! Completely mad but definitely in love. She thought of James. Perhaps insanity and love went hand in hand.

"She must love you very much to have given you such a personal gift."

Growling, Ricu marched to shelves built into the bulkhead. He grabbed a bottle, uncorked it, and tipped it to his lips. Angeline inched to the other side of the desk, as far away from this volatile man as she could get.

"Where is she now?" she asked, trying to settle her thrashing heart, desperate to say the right words to keep this man at bay.

He took another swig. "Home. Her father say I not have enough wealth to marry her."

"So that is why you need the gold?"

Without warning, he tossed the bottle across the room. It struck the door and shattered on the deck in a dozen glassy shards. Brandy dripped down the wood as the pungent smell filled the room. Angeline's heart crashed into her ribs. She swallowed and dared to glance his way, fearing he intended to toss her next. But his face had softened again.

"I get gold. Be very rich." He flung hair over his shoulder and swaggered toward her, his glazed eyes scanning her like a lion would its prey.

Angeline must think fast. "Would she want you to ravish women?" she blurted out.

He halted. "She will not know."

"She *will* know—deep down." Angeline placed a hand on her heart. "If she's a proper lady, she'll perceive the goodness of your heart. You cannot hide that from her. If she's a good, decent lady, the gold won't matter. It's your character, your heart that will please her most."

He cocked his head and gave her a quizzical look as if the thought had never occurred to him.

"She won't want to marry a murderer. She won't want to marry a man who hurts women."

He let out a loud belch and fisted his hands at his waist, studying her as if she were some freakish animal he'd never seen before.

Angeline lifted her chin, trying her best not to behave as frightened as she felt. "That is why you couldn't touch me all night. You love her, and you know she would be displeased."

"You not know her."

"But *you* do. Would she want your gold if she knew how you came by it?"

He fingered the dark whiskers crowning his chin. "But I am a pirate. It is what I do."

"Perhaps it's time to find another profession."

Turning, he gripped the edges of his desk and stared out the stern windows. Water purled against the hull. The deck tilted. Wood creaked and the lantern squeaked on its hinge as seconds counted down to her fate.

"Then I let my men have you." He pushed from his desk and started for the door.

Angeline's breath fled her lungs. "That would be the same thing as ravishing me yourself!"

He spun around, his brow wrinkled. "Not same. I get no pleasure from it!"

"But you would be allowing it, don't you see?" She took a step toward him. "It's the heart that must change first, proven by your actions."

He shook his head and kicked a broken piece of glass aside. "My crew will not understand."

"But you are their captain. They listen to you. They obey you. Unless of course"—she shrugged—"they do not respect your authority."

"Of course they respect!" He stretched his neck as if trying to make himself larger. Angeline allowed herself a tiny smile. This man may be a murderous, raping, deranged pirate, but he had an Achilles' heel. A woman named Abelena Martinez y Vicario. A woman who, even from a distance, could quite possibly save them all.

"And the man you have on board. You can't hang him either," Angeline said pointedly.

He suddenly looked like a young lad who'd just been told he wouldn't be receiving gifts at Christmas.

"Hayden was only protecting his lady when he came on your ship and fought you. Wouldn't you do the same for your Senorita Vicario?"

His gaze lowered to the handkerchief still clenched in his hand.

"If I not kill him, I look weak."

"If you *do* kill him, you will look weak to your lady. If you really want to change, Captain Ricu, you must start now." *Please start now!* her thoughts screamed above the blood pounding in her head. "Find your gold. Keep your men focused on that, and leave us be. That will show your lady your true heart."

"Humph." He fingered the handkerchief for several seconds, his thoughts taking him elsewhere. No doubt to his memories of this Spanish lady who dared to love a pirate.

A knock on the door startled him from his daze. He approached her and before she could stop him, clutched the fringe of her neckline and ripped her bodice down the front. Buttons shot to the ground like scattered seeds. Angeline leapt back, heart in her throat, wondering how she could have misread the man.

He shoved her onto the bed. She closed her eyes. Boot steps thumped. The door squeaked open. And a blast of salty air swept over her.

A man addressed the captain and said something in Portuguese. Angeline opened her eyes to see a sailor leering at her from the entrance. The captain replied then slammed the door in his face.

He turned and grinned. "Your people give me maps."

CHAPTER 19

J ames's worst fears became reality when, escorted by two rather rank-smelling pirates, he, Blake, Patrick, and Dodd stepped into Captain Ricu's cabin. Angeline sat trembling on the man's bed, gripping pieces of her shredded bodice to her throat. Her violet eyes lifted to his, and a hint of a smile graced her lips—which didn't make any sense at all. He dashed her way and pulled her into his arms. She fell against him with a ragged sigh as unavoidable visions of what the pirate had done to her screamed through his thoughts. Nudging her back, he marched toward Captain Ricu who stood behind his desk, arms crossed over his bejeweled vest and a smirk of satisfaction on his lips. James could get one punch in, maybe two, before the pirates could stop him. After that, he didn't care.

"You will pay for—"

Angeline pulled him back and shook her head, her eyes filled with warning, her expression telling him all was well. But how could that be?

"Pay for what, little puppy?" Ricu chuckled.

Blake stepped between James and the pirate. "The woman returns with us."

Ricu snorted and waved his hand at her in dismissal. "Take her. I am done."

Growling, James tried to shove Blake aside, but once again Angeline's gentle touch drew him back.

Still clutching torn fabric to her throat, she leaned toward him and whispered, "He did not touch me, James."

He scanned her once more for any cuts or bruises. What remained of her pins could not contain the tumble of russet hair falling past her shoulders. Her skin was flushed, shadows clung to her eyes, but otherwise she appeared unscathed. He removed his shirt and flung it around her shoulders. She thanked him and buttoned it up then sat back down on the bed, refusing to look at him.

Was she lying? Trying to keep him from getting killed in an altercation with Ricu? He wouldn't put it past the sweet lady. But at least she was alive. That's what mattered now. And getting her back to camp.

Taking a protective stance beside her, James turned his attention to Captain Ricu, who was demanding to see the maps and eyeing Blake, Dodd, and Patrick as if they were cockroaches who dared to crawl into his cabin. At his nod, the chime of metal on metal echoed off the bulkheads as three crusty pirates drew swords and aimed them at the intruders. Ricu opened his palm and gave a grin of victory.

Withdrawing the papers from his vest pocket, Blake tossed them on the desk. "No need for that, Captain. We will comply." Minutes passed as Captain Ricu carefully unfolded each map and laid them side by side on the desk. Out the stern windows, a murky ribbon of gray burst on the horizon as the sun attempted to rise on the macabre scene. Shadows of light and dark from the lantern above swayed over the four aged maps as everyone—even the pirates—inched closer for a better look.

Finally Ricu pointed a long black fingernail at the maps and declared, "These maps are forestries! They make no sense." He spat something in Portuguese, which was no doubt a curse.

"Forgeries," Dodd corrected.

Slapping both palms on his desk, the pirate leaned toward Dodd, his black hair dangling in twisted curls over the maps. "You try trick Captain Ricu!" One of his crew pressed the tip of his sword in Dodd's back.

Dodd's face blanched. "No, I was just correcting. . .repeating—"

"Captain, if I may," Patrick intervened. "These maps are genuine, I assure you. In fact"—he straightened his string tie and put on a superior look—"I know the secret to translating them, and if you are willing to bargain—"

The captain laughed, a disbelieving laugh that ricocheted off the deckhead. "Who are you to know such secrets?"

Patrick lifted his chin. "Why I—"

"Our deal was only the maps," Blake interrupted. "We have delivered them. And now we demand you leave us and our colony be."

"Demand!" Ricu gave a hearty chuckle, his pirates joining in. But then with a snap of his finger, his men silenced, and fury overtook his features. "No one demand Captain Ricu."

"But there's gold. I know there's gold," Dodd began to whine. "I got my map from a very reliable source. Paid good money for it. And he"—he thumbed toward Patrick—"has figured out how to read them." He picked up one map and placed it atop the other. "You see, you have to bend—*ouch*!" Dodd glared at Patrick who settled his foot back onto the rolling deck.

Ricu slapped Dodd's hand away. "No touch maps." Then, opening a drawer, he pulled out a bottle of amber-colored liquid, took a long draught, capped it, and slammed it on the desk before he glared at Patrick. "You tell me secret now."

Patrick fingered his goatee, his lips slabs of stone.

At the snap of Ricu's jeweled fingers, one of his men leveled a blade at Patrick's back. The normally composed man's eyes began to twitch.

The ship teetered over an incoming wave, creaking and groaning. While the rest of them stumbled to keep their balance, the captain stood, arms crossed over the trinkets shining on his waistcoat, like a statue of some Greek god demanding worship.

"I am Captain Ricu, and I take what I want when I want." Eyes as dark and hot as coals measured each one of them like a judge deciding a prisoner's fate. He rubbed the handle of a pistol stuffed in his belt, and James wondered if the captain was trying to decide who to shoot first. He knew they had nothing to bargain with. Pirates were notorious torturers, and James was sure Patrick or Dodd would sing like birds at the mere threat of such measures. He was also sure the captain knew that as well.

"Captain, we will gladly share our knowledge of these maps as long as you promise not to harm any of us and release Angeline and Hayden," James put forth.

For once Patrick didn't protest. Though it may have had something to do with the blade jabbing his back.

The creak and moan of timbers marked the unbearable passage of time as the mad pirate considered James's proposal. Or perhaps he was merely deciding the most painful way to kill them all. Golden sunlight cast an amber halo around Ricu's dark curls. Plucking a handkerchief from his desk, he wiped his face and neck, his gaze assessing each one of them in turn. Finally, he grinned and waved the cloth through the air. "I agree. You"—he pointed toward Patrick—"tell us how to read maps." He gestured for his man to lower his blade.

Patrick released a breath. "And what do I get in return?"

Ricu gave an incredulous huff. "Your lives."

"We accept," Blake and James said in unison.

Standing knee deep in water, James extended both arms toward Angeline. "May I?"

She knew he intended to carry her from the small boat, but just the thought of being held in those powerful arms, nestled beside that powerful chest, sent warning bells off in her heart. It was bad enough James had rescued her once again—along with the others—but then the man had gone and stripped to his bare chest in an effort to preserve her modesty. No man had ever wanted to preserve her modesty. Quite the opposite, in fact.

She nodded her assent. But as she feared, the way he lifted her as if she weighed no more than a cat, the feel of his muscles encasing her in steel, his masculine scent, and the look of protection and care in his bronze eyes threatened to break down all the barriers she'd so carefully erected between them. Thankfully, once he put her down on the sand, Eliza and Magnolia dashed toward her, flinging their arms around her and asking how she fared. After ensuring them she was well, both ladies flew into their husbands' arms. As the pirates rowed back out to the ship, Dodd and Patrick slogged off, grumbling under their breath.

"I'm all right, Princess." Hayden pushed his overzealous wife back. "Not a mark on me, see?"

"We are all safe, for now." Blake smiled at his wife, who quickly slipped from his arms and eased beside Angeline. "Are you sure you aren't hurt?" Eliza brushed hair from Angeline's face, her gaze suddenly dropping to James's shirt. Fear laced her eyes. "Oh, you poor dear. Come with me." She swung an arm around her and started off when Angeline stopped her.

"He never touched me." She faced her friends.

"But your. . .your bodice. . ." James said.

"He ripped it, yes, but only to make his men believe he had ravished me."

"I don't understand." Blake's dark brows bent.

"I can't say that I completely do either." Angeline leaned onto Eliza, suddenly feeling weak. "He fully intended. . ."—her voice muddled as if the fear of her predicament suddenly struck her—"intended to. . ."

Eliza squeezed her close.

Angeline drew a breath. "But the man has a weakness."

"Aye, he has barnacles for brains." Hayden snorted.

"Better than that. A lady." Angeline smiled. "Crazy as it sounds, Captain Ricu loves a real lady. And he wants to change his ways so she'll love him back."

Looks of shock assailed her, followed by declarations of disbelief.

"It's true. It's why he didn't touch me. It's why I believe he won't allow his men to harm the rest of the women either. They fear him. With good reason." She trembled as memories of his many attempts to ravish her saturated her thoughts. "I convinced him his lady would be abhorred at such a thing."

"You placated him for one night," Hayden said. "I don't trust him. Men like him rarely change."

"You changed." Magnolia smiled at her husband.

Without warning, Stowy leapt into Angeline's arms and began burrowing beneath her chin, bringing levity to the somber topic and a speck of joy to Angeline's heart. She kissed the cat on the forehead and stroked his fur as purring filled the air.

"Seems you were missed," Eliza said.

"By more than the cat." The tone of James's voice chipped away at her heart. But she couldn't allow it.

"I agree with Hayden," she said. "I was spared, we were all spared this time. But I have no faith this man's love or desire or whatever it is he harbors toward this woman will placate his passions forever."

"Indeed. He's as volatile as a rusty cannon." Blake shifted weight off his bad leg. "We must find a way to escape, to sneak back to Rio. Perhaps the emperor would allow us to move to another location."

"But we haven't paid a single *réis* for this one." James shook his head and squinted toward the rising sun.

Blake flattened his lips. "I'm not admitting defeat. Not yet. We can still start a colony elsewhere." Nods of affirmation spread among Angeline's friends. But she didn't join them. How could she? Though her heart seemed ready to crack in a million pieces, she still intended to part ways with these beloved people. She had no choice. Extricating herself from Eliza's calming embrace, she gave an excuse of exhaustion and walked away, ignoring their offers of help, ignoring the look of love in James's eyes, and ignoring the tears that now spilled down her cheeks.

CHAPTER 20

Angeline finished the final chorus of "Hark the Herald Angels Sing" and sat down in between Eliza and Blake on one side and Sarah and Lydia on the other. She could hardly believe it was Christmas Day. Dates seemed of little consequence here in Brazil, especially with all the tragedies of late. And with the sun blaring overhead, it certainly didn't feel like Christmas, neither in temperature nor in temperament, for no one was very cheerful. Yet when James insisted they hold a service, they'd all banded together to haul logs and stumps and a few chairs salvaged from the flood to form pews in their thatched-roof church.

With the crash of waves thundering behind him, James rose to stand before the crowd, open Bible in hand. His gaze landed on something behind Angeline, and his slight flinch caused her to glance over her shoulder at the two pirates sitting in the back. She'd seen them come up during the singing but assumed they'd leave when the sermon began. Yet, there they sat, arms crossed over their colorful waistcoats, scarves blowing in the wind, pistols and blades sticking out everywhere like bloodthirsty porcupines, and looking like attending church was a normal occurrence. In fact, the past two weeks of living among pirates had proven much easier than everyone had anticipated. Though they drank too much and their leering gazes caused some of the ladies to squirm, they kept mostly to themselves. Angeline was sure it was because the fear of their captain was stronger than their passing passions.

James's voice brought her gaze around as he began to recite a passage from scripture. Wind tossed strands of his wheat-colored hair in a chaotic dance that made him look like a little boy at play. No, not a boy at all. He was all man. Every six-foot brawny inch of him. Not to mention all the manly qualities stuffed within that handsome frame: courage, selflessness, determination, honesty, integrity. . .and the way he looked at her like she was worthy. Just like he was doing now.

She loved him.

If a woman like her could love a man. If the burning in her belly whenever he was near was love. If her desire for his happiness above all else was love.

James glanced over the assembly as he began his sermon. Something about Jesus and a woman at a well. An odd take on the Christmas story, but regardless, Angeline found herself mesmerized by the deep tenor of his voice, the way the sun angled over his shoulder and kissed the tips of his hair blowing in the breeze, how his bronze eyes flamed with passion while he spoke. Why hadn't she attended church more often? If only for the opportunity to gaze at him without anyone thinking her forward. Even Thiago had made an appearance today and seemed enthralled with the message as he sat on the other side of Sarah.

Angeline smiled at little Lydia asleep in her mother's arms then glanced at Eliza's rounded belly on her other side. What would it be like to carry the child of the man she loved? The thought shamelessly brought her gaze back to James. Despair threatened to send her running from the crowd, but instead she lowered her eyes to her hands clasped in her lap. She could entertain no hope of such joy as long as Dodd threatened her. Thankfully, the annoying rodent had been too busy searching for gold with the pirates to bother with her. It had been a nice reprieve, but she knew it wouldn't last. Whether they found gold or not. Whether the pirates stayed or left, Dodd was not the type of man to give up what he considered a worthy prize.

Which is why she must leave as soon as possible. Before her feelings for James grew to the point of shattering her heart. Before Dodd blurted out the truth and exposed her shame to everyone. She couldn't bear the rejection, the shock, the looks of disdain from people she'd grown to love. As if sensing Angeline's angst, Eliza gave her a tender smile and placed a hand over hers, bringing tears to Angeline's eyes. She gazed out to sea.

"She was a prostitute, a woman who'd had five husbands and was living with a man out of wedlock." James's voice sharpened in her ears. "Yet Jesus traveled a day's journey out of His way just to speak to her, just to tell her God loved her." He took up a pace before them, eyeing them each in turn. "To tell her to stop drawing from a broken well that did not satisfy, but to receive the living water He offered. " His eyes latched upon Angeline's. "Then she would never thirst again."

The light in those eyes seemed different somehow. Brighter, dazzling even. And they seemed to pierce her very soul. Forcing back the mist in her own eyes, she lowered her gaze to the sand by her shoes. Yet, his words kept repeating in her mind. Jesus traveled a day's journey out of His way for a prostitute. To tell her God loved her. Could the same be true for Angeline? She began to tremble. But if God loved her, why had He allowed so much heartache? Why had He allowed her to become what she'd become?

A fire crackled. A voice, distant and sounding much like the thunder of the waves called her name. Her eyes flew up and scanned the shore. A man stood with his back to her, staring at the sea. He turned around, his braided frock coat flapping in the wind and a suggestive grin on his rounded face. "Come here, Angeline. The water's warm."

Her heart dropped like a stone.

"Angeline," another man called, drawing her gaze to the other side of James, where the old trapper, Swain, stood beckoning her toward him with a curled finger. "Come for a swim, my precious peach." Perspiration dampened her skin. Her breath clogged in her throat. No. Not two of them here at the same time! And why now?

To remind her she wasn't worthy enough to sit in a church service. That she had no right to be here among proper folk. She glanced around the crowd to see if anyone saw the men when a third one appeared just feet away. Charlie Wilkins, one of her regulars. Smoke curled from the cigar hanging from his lips while he counted out dollars in his hands, just as he used to do when he paid for her services. He glanced down at her, eyes cold and void. "Go in the water, Angeline. You aren't clean. You must be clean to sit there."

Angeline couldn't breathe. She couldn't live with the memories anymore. She wanted to shut her eyes and never open them again. She *did* shut her eyes, but the voices continued. She covered her ears, but they rang in her head. "Whore. Hussy. You'll never change. The water, the water, it's the only way," all three men brayed in unison. Eliza squeezed her hand. James's voice grew distant. Sweat slid down her back. Every breath became a struggle. "Filthy whore. The water will cleanse you. The water, the water, the water—" Punching to her feet, she barreled straight through ole Charlie and dashed toward the sea with one thought in mind. To silence the memories. To end the pain.

James plowed into the sea. Waves assaulted him, stinging his eyes and shoving him back. In the distance, green fabric floated atop water where Angeline's russet hair had disappeared. He fought off the next wave and dove into the foaming churn. Memories of another rescue at sea flooded his mind. Of another attempt by Angeline to end her life. God be praised, this time they weren't in the middle of the ocean, this time he'd had enough warning. He'd seen her fidgeting in her seat, watched her frightened gaze skitter back and forth across the beach, saw her chest bellow like the wind, her lips tremble, her hands cover her ears. He had some idea as to the cause and intended to conclude his sermon posthaste in order to come to her aid. But no sooner had he glanced down at his Bible than she had already reached the water's edge.

No vision, no matter how terrifying, was worth her life. Something else affected this poor lady, and James had allowed his affection for her to get in the way of being her spiritual advisor. Curse him for being a selfish fool! He thrust upward for air, gulped it down, then dove again. His hand touched her gown. Grabbing the fabric, he pulled her toward him and circled an arm about her waist. He kicked and they sped upward, breaking through the surface with a mighty splash. She spit and coughed until air took the place of water in her lungs. A wave thundered over them. James fought to stay afloat. She slumped against his chest, weighing them down. Breath heaving, he swam to shore, inhaling more water than air. Strength slipped from him with each thrust of his arm through the water. They went under. They weren't going to make it. His feet struck sand. Gathering his remaining strength, he shoved against the seabed, burst through the surface, and hoisted her in his arms. Bracing against the crashing surf, he carried her to the women's shelter and laid her on a bamboo pallet. Eliza ushered him out, promising to care for her as the other women gathered around.

Lungs still wheezing for air, James took up a spot beside Blake just outside the hut. He wasn't going anywhere until he heard how Angeline was doing. He knew she was alive. He'd heard her breathing. But he was more worried about her emotional state. An hour later, Eliza and Magnolia emerged from the ladies' hut, concern darkening their faces. A crowd formed to hear the news.

"She's well, James," Eliza started. "No harm done. At least not physical." She frowned. "She spoke of seeing visions. More than one. And voices that told her to throw herself in the sea."

Blake's jaw tightened as he stared out over the waves. Magnolia brushed the back of her hand against a wayward tear. Hayden drew her close, and she gazed up at her husband then over the crowd that seemed equally stunned by the event. "Whatever she saw, it terrified her to the point of not wanting to live."

"I can't imagine." Sarah hugged Lydia to her chest. "The poor dear."

"I say the lady has gone quite mad," Mr. Scott's bellow fell limp in the wind.

"How can you say that?" Though her voice quavered, Mrs. Scott's unusual defiance of her husband had all eyes shifting her way. "We have all seen these visions. Why, you told me just this morning that—"

"Enough, Mrs. Scott!" He moved to stand behind his wife, his shout dwindling into nervous laughter as he pressed a hand on her shoulder.

"Indeed, Mother." Magnolia snapped angry eyes toward her father. "There isn't a one of us who hasn't seen something."

"I swear there's spirits haunting this place!" one of the famers said. "If it weren't for these blasted pirates, we could all leave, go home, and be done with these visions."

Thiago crossed himself and eased beside Sarah. Lydia lifted her chubby hands toward him, and Sarah gave him a coy smile as she handed him the child. "Even I see dead grandmother yesterday," he said. "Last week, I see brother who died of sickness."

Most of the colonists nodded, understanding glances exchanged between them. A few groaned and stared at the sand. Others gaped vacantly at the sea as if unwilling to even think about what they'd seen.

Confirming James's fears.

"The visions are getting worse." He ran a hand through his damp hair and released a sigh, heavy with dread. "I need to get back to the book. Interpret more." He lifted his gaze to the storm brewing behind Blake's gray eyes. The same one that brewed in James's stomach. "This has got to stop before we *all* drown ourselves in the sea."

CHAPTER 21

Magnolia eased her face over the surface of the water, searching past the ripples for any sign of youth in her reflection. Was it her imagination or was there a clarity to her eyes that hadn't been there before? A plumper look to her skin? A few blond hairs among the gray. She sat back with a sigh. Mercy me, becoming beautiful on the inside was sure taking a long time! *Lord, can You work a little faster?* She bit her tongue, wondering if she was wise to ask for such a thing. Didn't that mean more struggles and trials? *Oh, bother, Lord. You will be gentle, won't You?* Of course He would. He was her Father, and He had proven Himself loving and trustworthy. She smiled and ran fingers through the cool water as a flock of thrushes warbled a happy tune above her. Eliza had sent her to find some fresh water for Angeline, and along the way, she'd happened upon this lovely creek surrounded by clusters of multicolored ferns. Which made for a bit of privacy off the beaten track. Privacy that had become a rare commodity since they'd moved to the beach, and Magnolia couldn't help but stay just a moment and breathe in the peace.

If only peace would settle on the entire colony, but with everything that had happened and with pirates guarding their every move, how could it? Her thoughts sped to Angeline, and she lifted up a prayer for her friend. What could she have possibly seen that had stolen her hope and driven her into the sea? Perhaps it was a combination of the disasters that had struck the colony, the uncertainty of their future, the threat of pirates, and these hellish visions. If Magnolia hadn't found her strength in God, her peace in His watchful eye, she'd most likely go mad as well.

"Thank You for that, Father," she whispered. In fact, she had much to be thankful for. Her husband, for one. "And thank You, Father, for Hayden—"

"Someone call me?" The leaves rustled, parted, and her husband strolled into the clearing with the fluid assurance of a panther stalking its prey.

What a luscious sight he was. But she wouldn't let him know her delight, lest it go to his head. She feigned a frown. "You shouldn't sneak up on people. How did you find me?"

"You are not supposed to venture out alone, remember?"

"I know." She pouted. "But I wasn't going far. And Eliza needed water."

He knelt beside her, grinned, and ran a gentle thumb over her cheek. Their eyes met, and she saw a familiar gleam within his that sent an eddy of warmth down to her toes. Suddenly conscious of her appearance, she patted her windblown bun and stuffed wayward strands behind her ear.

"Where is your brush and mirror?" Hayden twirled one of her curls around his finger. "The ones your father gave you. I haven't seen them since the flood."

"Because I lost them in the flood." She stilled his finger and brought it to her lips for a kiss.

He gazed at her curiously, moving his hand to caress her jaw. "But during the mayhem, you insisted on going back into our hut for something. I thought it was to gather them. They were so important to you."

She reached inside the pocket of her skirt and withdrew the wooden toad.

Hayden's look of shock brought a smile to her lips. "You went back for that silly thing?" He chuckled.

"How could I not? You made it for me." She ran fingers over the smooth wood. "It reminds me of our time in the jungle. When we first fell in love."

Hayden swallowed up her hand with both of his and gazed at her with such adoration, she nearly melted into the sand. "I still cannot believe you are my wife." He sat beside her and kissed her cheek then leaned his forehead against hers.

Magnolia drew in a deep breath of him as her body itched for his touch. "It hardly seems like we are wed anymore." Not since all the colonists had moved onto the beach and she'd been forced into the ladies' shelter. Oh, how she ached for her husband each long night. But she wouldn't dare say such a thing. Women weren't supposed to have such longings, were they? She pressed a hand over her flat belly. "How am I to give you sons and daughters when we are never alone?"

He cocked a brow, a twinkle in his jungle green eyes. "We are alone now, Princess."

She gave him an inviting smile that lured him to trail kisses up her neck, across her chin, until finally his mouth claimed hers. Every cell within her tingled as he laid her back on a bed of soft leaves and consumed her with his love.

Dodd didn't like this one bit. Not one bit. Though he'd told the pirates there was nothing but evil and death here, warned them that a man had been decapitated by some unearthly being, still they insisted on descending into the tunnels beneath the temple. Now, as Dodd felt his way along the stone walls and attempted to find footing on the uneven ground with only a single torch to light their way, a heaviness settled on him like none he'd ever felt. It squeezed the breath from his lungs and made his soul feel clogged with soot. Patrick stumbled before him with pirates fore and aft, while Moses and a few other colonists brought up the rear. All excitement faded into silence as they descended into the oppressive heat.

These tunnels were their last hope. For two weeks, they'd folded the maps together in every possible combination. Four combinations, in fact, all leading to different locations. Three of which they'd dug up until they struck water or rock. Well, in truth, it was Dodd, three colonists, and Moses who'd done the digging, while Patrick and Captain Ricu attempted to best each other with exaggerated tales of conquest and valor. Patrick Gale could charm a snake into giving up its nest of eggs. Dodd only hoped his charm continued to work on the wily pirate.

As if in defiance of the thought, Dodd tripped and nearly barreled into the pompous shyster. A sharp crag on the wall sliced his hand. He cursed as they rounded a corner and began traipsing down a set of stairs hewn from the hard dirt. Why, oh why, did the final location for the gold have to be at this gruesome temple? Once Dodd had spotted the crumbling walls surrounding the shrine, his blood had turned to needles. He'd only been here twice before, but it had been enough to convince him he never wanted to return. At least not below ground. Something evil lurked down there. If there was such a thing. Good and evil. He'd never considered himself a religious man, but the sense of depravity that permeated these ancient walls was enough to make him reconsider his standing with God.

Perhaps Moses was doing enough praying for them both. Dodd could still hear the man mumbling petition after petition to the Almighty as he hobbled behind him. Forced below at sword point, the poor freedman's face had nearly turned white—if that were even possible for a Negro.

Sweat pasted Dodd's shirt to his skin. Colorful curses spewed from the pirates' lips, most in Portuguese. The ones in English made even ole tavern-inhabiting Dodd's ears curl. At least he wasn't the only one suffering.

Up ahead, Ricu's torch sputtered and grew dim. A darkness as thick as tar seeped into Dodd's lungs. He wheezed in air. Something skittered over his hand. Stifling a scream, he drew his arm close. A stench that seemed to emanate from an open grave rose with the heat and stung his eyes.

They trekked down another flight of stairs and in through a hole that led to the first chamber. Ricu snapped his fingers, sending men to light torches and search behind every rock, every stalactite and stalagmite of the cave. While the pirates examined the alcoves and chains and weird writing on the wall, Dodd, Moses, and the other colonists hovered near the opening, saying nothing. Patrick, however, strolled through the cavern seemingly oblivious to the fiery heat, putrid odor, and the foreboding heaviness in the air. Odd. Everyone who had ever gone this deep beneath the temple had complained of all those discomforts and more. Everyone except Graves, and look where he was now. Six feet under.

The eerie *tap*, *tap*, *tap* of dripping water grated over Dodd's nerves as Patrick returned to stand beside him.

"There's another chamber below," Dodd whispered as he gestured to a barely discernible cleft in the shadows of the rock wall. "If they don't find the gold here, it could be there."

Grinning, Patrick fingered his goatee. "Then we can come back later ourselves."

Precisely what Dodd was thinking. Though the idea of returning to this horrid place sent a hornet's nest buzzing in his chest. Yet, what was a little fear and heat when it came to finding enough treasure to make him a king? He was almost ready to believe that the torture of this place might be worth it after all when one of the pirates shouted something in Portuguese and pointed toward the other opening.

Confound it all! Dodd ground his teeth together as they descended into the lower chamber. Though similar in shape and size to the one above, it seemed smaller. But perhaps that was due to the wall of rocks—some small, others as large as a man—stretching nearly to the ceiling and cutting the room in half. Instead of two alcoves, only one was hewn from the cavern wall. The same broken chains lay at the bottom of a tall metal pole that poked through the top of the circular recess. James claimed invisible beasts had once been chained in these alcoves—the same beasts that now taunted the colonists with visions. Dodd thought the idea as ludicrous as the preacher himself. A preacher who hardly preached and a doctor afraid of blood. And they were supposed to listen to him?

Shoving the torch into one of the pirate's hands, Captain Ricu spread the maps atop a flat rock and beckoned to Patrick. After folding the scraps of parchment into place, he pointed at them, his long black fingernail forming a divot on the paper. "This is right place." His voice, normally commanding and belittling, held a hint of vulnerable excitement. "It must be!" He swirled around, studying the cave as a child would a toy store before he gestured back toward the maps. "Here, see drawing of—how do you say—*sepulture, caixão.*" His sweaty forehead wrinkled as he flung a clump of long curls over his shoulder and snapped his fingers.

A pirate appeared with a white handkerchief in hand. Without looking up, the captain took it, wiped his face and neck, and tossed it back to the man.

"Coffin," Patrick offered, eyeing the strange empty alcove. "I believe you mean coffin, Captain. Yes, it does appear to be a coffin of some sort, or perhaps a prison."

Curious, Dodd inched forward to peek at the map and saw a drawing of what definitely looked like a coffin standing on its edge. Why had he not seen that before?

Ricu folded up the maps, stuffed them in his pocket, then grabbed the torch from his crewman. "The gold be here! The gold be here!" he announced, the bells on his boots and trinkets on his vest jingling with excitement. Shouts and cheers rang from his men while a sharp snap of his jeweled fingers sent them searching every inch of the cave. Dodd made a pretense of joining them, trying to hide his own excitement at being so close to his dream. Indeed the gold must be here. But now to get rid of these pesky pirates! That's when he saw the blood—a large rust-colored circle staining the dirt. Graves's blood. Where Dodd had heard the man's head had been sliced clean off.

Phantom pain seared across his throat. Clutching it, he backed away and bumped straight into Moses. The Negro's eyes were as white and wide as eggs as he continued to mutter prayers.

"Frightened by mark in dirt?" Captain Ricu kicked the stained sand in some sacrilegious tribute to poor Graves before leveling a scowl at Dodd that would make a general whimper. "Get to work!"

Dodd darted away, nearly tripping over Patrick, who knelt to examine the chains at the bottom of the alcove. An hour passed—the longest hour of Dodd's life. His lungs were scorched, and his back had nearly split in two from hauling large stones back and forth across the chamber. But not one sparkle, not one glimmer, not one speck of gold was found. One of the pirates climbed the wall of rocks and shouted something in Portuguese to his captain. A conversation ensued, and finally Captain Ricu spewed a string of curses. "We come back tomorrow," he growled. "Bring tools to dig through rocks. Bring more men. It take many weeks to break wall down, but I know gold is here!"

And from the look of zeal in Patrick's green eyes, Dodd knew he agreed. That zeal was still evident as Dodd marched through the jungle beside Patrick on their way back to the beach. Thankful to be out of the hellish tunnels, Dodd drew in a deep breath of air saturated with life and earth and moss, so opposite the stagnant smell of sulfur and rot beneath the temple. The sun withdrew her light from the trees as she dipped behind the mountains, turning the pirates stomping before Dodd into shifting ghouls.

Ghouls or not, pirates or not, Dodd longed to find hope in the situation. Still both glee and gloom battled for dominance within him. Glee at finally finding the location of the gold. Gloom at knowing he'd probably never possess any of it. But why, then, did Patrick now whistle a happy tune beside him?

"If you're withholding some liquor from me," Dodd chortled, "I'll ask you to kindly share. I could use a drink about now."

"No drink, my friend, could produce such joy as fills my heart at the moment. Liven up, there, lad. We have found the gold and it is ours for the taking." A band of squirrel monkeys cackled overhead, mimicking Dodd's sentiments at Patrick's silly declaration.

"And how do you figure that, when you know as well as I these pirates will take it all for themselves."

"Because we shall steal it from them, of course."

Ducking beneath a spiderweb, Dodd shook his head, frustration bubbling in his gut. "For the genius you claim to be, you sure aren't so smart. How are—"

"Shhhh, keep your voice down, man."

Dodd drew closer and whispered, "How do you propose to steal gold from over forty well-armed pirates when we have less than thirty men and no weapons?"

"Simple. We swindle them." Patrick flashed his brows up and down in that sinister yet charming way of his. Then at Dodd's obvious look of confusion, he continued in a whisper, "We cause a mutiny, my friend. We offer some of the crew a higher share than their captain and then take over the ship."

Dodd restrained a laugh. "That's your brilliant plan? Become a pirate." He batted aside a rather large beetle. "But we know nothing about sailing, and we still have to share."

"Only with a few. The fewer the better, to my way of thinking. Besides, we have something else they want."

"And what is that?"

"Women. Their captain forbids his men to touch them, but we will offer them freely. Why, they'll be so immersed in their carnal pleasures, they won't even notice when we run off with the gold."

Women like Angeline. Dodd smiled. No, he hadn't forgotten about their little arrangement. He'd simply been too busy and too tired to take what was his. Now that the pirates were keeping the colonists hostage, she couldn't leave and therefore had no choice but to comply with his demands. Surely his request was not a terrible inconvenience for a woman of her immoral standing. Dodd would honor his bargain. He wouldn't tell anyone about her past as long as she complied. After all, he was not without compassion. Yet, just the mere thought of getting his hands on her luscious body made him giddy all over—almost as giddy as the thought of getting his hands on all that gold.

Patrick's elbow to Dodd's ribs brought him out of his musings. "What do you say, friend? Are you with me?"

Though he detested the man and hated being called his friend, Dodd had to admit, if anyone could pull off a mutiny, it would be Patrick. With the perfect timing, a lot of charm, and the right incentives, they just might convince enough pirates to side with them. And some of the gold was certainly better than the no gold they'd get from the pirates.

As if sensing his thoughts, Captain Ricu flung his ebony locks over his shoulder and glanced at Dodd, a menacing grin on his lips. Blood churning, Dodd tripped on a root, caught his balance, and looked away. Ricu laughed and faced forward again, slashing leaves aside with his blade as if he'd been born in a jungle.

A wolf howled in the distance. Dodd shivered and peered into the shadows. They'd never found Mr. Lewis. But the idea he had turned into a man-wolf, this Lobisón, was beyond absurd! Nearly as absurd as the belief that invisible beings caused army ants and floods and visions. Visions Dodd had yet to experience. No, he would not fall prey to such lunacy. He must keep his wits about him. Especially if they were going to swindle these pirates. For Dodd knew that if Captain Ricu even suspected their duplicity, he'd slit both their throats and hang them from a tree to rot.

CHAPTER 22

I'm sorry, James." Angeline stared at the sand. Embarrassment had kept her in the tent all day, along with a desire to avoid the man standing before her. But desperate for some fresh air, she'd finally emerged onto the beach after everyone had dispersed from supper.

And ran straight into the handsome doctor.

"No need to apologize." He shoved hands in his pockets, reminding her of an awkward schoolboy. Which only endeared him to her even more. "You are definitely keeping my swimming skills honed."

Though a slight upturn of his lips indicated he toyed with her, she couldn't help but feel ashamed. "You mock me."

"No." He withdrew his hands and touched her arms. "Forgive me. I shouldn't have made light of it. I'm just happy you're safe."

"Thanks to you." She moved from his touch. A gust of wind struck and she hugged herself. A few colonists wandered by, staring at her as if she were possessed with an evil spirit.

James took her elbow and led her aside. "What did you see, Angeline? Or perhaps I should ask who? Whoever it was and whatever they said, nothing could be so hopeless. Not when you have friends who care deeply about you."

Like you? Are you one of those friends? She searched his eyes. Flecks of gold sparkled against deep bronze in the setting sun. But she knew he was. And that made everything so much worse. She glanced at the jungle—a seemingly impenetrable fortress of green that moved and swayed and squawked and howled like a living, breathing entity. Perhaps if she dove into it, it would swallow her whole. Save her from

Dodd and her past and from making more of a fool of herself than she already had.

James reached out for her but then pulled back. "I fear I'm not very good at comforting people."

Angeline looked at him again, at the way the wind tossed his hair in every direction, at the dark stubble on his jaw. She smiled. "Yes, you are."

He shrugged. "What I meant to say before was, I'm a good listener if you'd like to tell me what's bothering you."

What was bothering her? Men from her past kept appearing out of nowhere, taunting her with words and crude gestures. Dodd was blackmailing her into sharing his bed. And she loved this man who stood before her with all her heart but could never tell him. She could never be his. "Nothing is bothering me. I thought I saw something in the water. I was tired, delirious... I wasn't thinking."

He blew out a sigh that spoke of disbelief.

She must lighten the mood before he delved deeper into her secrets, before that look of affection and love in his eyes made her want to tell him everything. She gave him a scolding look. "Now, what did I tell you about rescuing me, Doctor?"

He smiled, studying her. "Guilty, as charged. Do say you'll forgive me once again."

She would forgive him. She *did* forgive him. And though she was happy to be alive, she wanted no more rescues—from him or anyone else. Rescues meant trust and dependence on others. And she wasn't ready to allow herself those luxuries, to become vulnerable, open to betrayal.

Blake started a fire and the colonists began to congregate. Though the night was warm, Angeline continued to shiver.

"You're trembling," James said.

"I can't seem to stop."

"Come by the fire. We can talk later." He led her to sit on a log beside Eliza then sped off as if he couldn't get away fast enough. She didn't blame him. She not only spurned his every advance, but now she'd gone and proven herself completely deranged. A person could dismiss one leap into the sea. But two?

Stowy jumped into her lap and nudged her with his head. At least the cat didn't mind if she'd gone mad. She petted him as Eliza smiled and asked how she was feeling. Magnolia and Sarah did the same as they joined the group. Though some of the colonists stared at her as if she had a disease, Angeline found no hint of wariness or judgment on any of her three friends' expressions. Or even on Blake's or Hayden's. These people truly were her friends. She would miss them terribly. She'd heard the pirates return just after supper more excited than usual, declaring they'd finally found the location of the gold. Of course, they'd announced similar success on many an occasion, so Angeline wasn't allowing her hope to rise that they'd soon gather the treasure and leave. But if they did, that meant she could finally get away as well. Away from the voices and visions, away from the threats, and away from the torture of seeing the man she loved day in and day out, longing to be with him but knowing he would always be out of her reach.

Grabbing a blanket from among his things, James sped back to the fire and flung it around Angeline's shoulders. She looked up at him with the strangest mix of shock and sorrow. He wanted to tell her that he longed to hold her until she felt safe again. He wanted to tell her that if she'd allow him, he could love all her problems away, but Captain Ricu joined them at the fire, drawing all eyes and a few whimpers from the ladies. He'd not addressed them as a group since the first day he and his pirates had landed, and his presence now sent a tangible fear through the colonists.

"So you think you've found your gold, I hear." Blake kept his tone nonchalant.

"Aye, we have. We be sure of it." The twinkle in Ricu's dark eyes confirmed his statement as he planted hands at his waist and surveyed the crowd.

"Where?" Hayden asked as he took a spot in front of Magnolia.

"In the temple." Dodd clipped thumbs in his belt. "Can you believe it? Under our noses the whole time."

Silence, save for the crackle of the fire and sizzle of waves, permeated the group as nervous eyes skittered about. James shared a worried glance with Blake and Hayden.

"You mean the moon and stars above the altar?" Eliza asked, voicing the hope they all felt.

Pressing hair back at his temples, Patrick pushed his way through the crowd. "No. You may have those if you wish." He flicked his hand through the air. "It is the gold *beneath* the temple that is the fortune we've been searching for."

James couldn't believe his ears. Of all the places for this infernal gold to be located, why that heinous place?

"Did you actually see this gold?" Blake crossed his arms over his chest.

"Nay." Captain Ricu stepped over a log and stood before the fire. "But maps led us straight to it." He patted his colorful vest—where said maps were, no doubt, safely tucked—sending his pins sparkling in the firelight. "I should realize it before. The cannibals, the temple. It makes sense."

"I don't understand." James took a spot standing behind Angeline.

"I ne'er told you tale of how I came by map?" A blast of wind tossed Ricu's black curls behind him. "Aye, quite a tale it be." His eyes, the color of the hot coals in the fire, sped to Hayden. "Thanks be to this *estúpido* who cut my anchor chain."

Ricu, now having gained an audience, lowered himself onto a stump, leaned forward on his knees, and swept his gaze over the assembled colonists. "We drift for week, hoist and lower sails, try stay close to shore so we fix anchor and not run into ground. We find berth in inlet near the port of Itaqui. And while we fix anchor chain, we go to town's tavern.

"There we met Bartolomeu Henrigues or Blastin' Bart as he call himself, a Portuguese pirate, at least hundred years old. We had merry time drinking and playing cards into long night. But when I told him of gold I sought, he pull map from waistcoat. And this be the tale he told." The captain's eyes were alight with adventure while everyone leaned toward him to hear over the pounding waves.

"His grandfather be a fierce pirate who sail under Portugal flag and raid along coast of Brazil and Caribbean. Legends of vast amount of gold—enough to buy entire world—lure him to land on Brazil shores. A search of jungle brought he and crew to strange temple with stone obelisks and steaming water pool."

"Just like the one we found." Magnolia's voice came out numb with shock.

"Aye." Ricu nodded, fingering the tuft of dark hair on his chin. "Only few cannibals remain and pirates torture them to find where gold be, but they ne'er say a word, kept make gestures about fierce beast who come up from ground and made tribe go *louco* and kill each other."

A few of the ladies gasped, including Mrs. Scott, who leaned against her husband.

James swallowed a lump of dread.

"Then pirates see things. Dead people talk to them. Terrible nightmares. Yet they keep search for gold, dig where cannibals say it buried. But *visão* get worse and worse, and nightmares grow until pirates get crazy and shoot and stab each other." Red and gold flames danced over Ricu's face as he stared at the fire, mesmerized by his own tale. Or perhaps as frightened by it as most of the colonists seemed to be.

James gazed at Angeline, longing to see her expression, but her back was to him. Would that be their fate if they remained? If they allowed the visions and nightmares to continue? Would they all go mad and either kill each other or themselves?

"What happened to them?" Dodd asked, the joy of only moments ago slipping from his expression.

Ricu grunted. "Only four remained and fear to kill the others. They not care about gold, but they not want such fortune lost, so they draw four maps that when put together lead to gold. Then they each take map and leave Brazil. Go in different directions, get far from each other and temple. They say if God want, others bring maps together and get gold." Ricu patted his vest yet again and proclaimed, "Blastin' Bart gave me one map. These men"—he pointed at Dodd and Patrick—"had others. That is story."

Moonlight dripped pearly wax on Captain Ricu's ebony locks as the fire snapped and spit sparks into the night sky. Some of the colonists continued to gape at him as if they thought him as crazy as the pirates he spoke of. Blake gazed numbly into the fire. Eliza looped an arm through Angeline's, while Hayden drew Magnolia close, a fear rolling across his features that James felt in his gut.

"You can't dig there, beneath the temple," James spoke up, forcing authority into his voice. "You'll release the fourth beast."

Captain Ricu stared at him as if he were a two-headed fish that had just emerged from the sea. A similar expression twisted Patrick's features. Dodd, however, dropped his gaze to the sand.

Patrick released a long sigh. "Of course we can. And we will."

"Dodd, you know this to be true." James turned to the ex-lawman. "You've seen what we've seen. You know what happened to Graves when he released the third beast."

Though hesitation sparked in his gaze, Dodd shrugged. "I'm not sure what I've seen."

"Beasts! *Ridiculo!*" Ricu spit onto the sand, his outburst causing a few colonists to flinch.

James shook his head. "But, you just told us there *were* beasts, Captain, the ones who drove the cannibals and pirates mad."

A rumbling broke forth from the captain's throat. "You believe?" He tried to contain his amusement. "This be louco pirates' tale."

"But you believe the part about the gold." Eliza raised a brow.

Snorting, Ricu rose. "We dig up gold. You see. I am Captain Ricu, and I take what I want when I want."

And with that, he marched away.

Later that night, after everyone had retired, James sat alone by the fire with the ancient book in hand and his father's Bible lying on a log beside him. He alternated between praying, reading the Bible, and interpreting more of the Hebrew script. But his eyelids kept sinking, and he wasn't sure he was learning anything useful. He chastised himself for not studying Hebrew with more diligence when he'd been a young man learning to be a preacher like his father. But back then, he hadn't taken life very seriously, except the feel of a beautiful woman in his arms. What a wastrel he'd been and a disappointment to his parents. Especially when he'd run off to become a doctor and joined the war.

The wind had lessened, the waves now stroked instead of pounded the shore, their caress so soft, he could hear the pirates snoring down the beach. Sand crunching brought his gaze up to see Blake and Eliza heading his way, their drooping eyes telling him they'd lost their battle with sleep as well.

Blake acknowledged him with a nod before tossing a log into

the fire and taking a seat beside his wife. Moments later Hayden and Magnolia joined them.

"I *thought* you were still awake when I left the tent." Eliza patted the spot beside her for Magnolia, who sat, adjusted her skirts, and drew her long braid of flaxen hair over her shoulder. "I heard you leave and decided it was better to have company than lie in the dark alone with my thoughts." She gazed up at her husband standing by her side. "No sooner did I step outside than Hayden dashed up to me."

He winked at her. "At your service, Princess." He turned to James. "So, Doc, can the pirates release this fourth monster?"

"You finally believe?" James gave a grin of victory he didn't truly feel before he closed the book and set it down. "Only a man with pure darkness in his heart who speaks the phrase above the alcove can release the beast."

"Whose heart is darker than a pirate's?" Magnolia dug her toes into the sand.

"But what pirate knows Latin?" Eliza added with a hint of hope.

"What cannibals do?" James shrugged. "They don't have to know the language. They only need to speak the words out loud. We can't risk it. We must stop them from digging for that gold. If the fourth beast exists, we cannot allow him to be set free. From what I'm reading, his release would affect the entire world."

"The entire world? How can that be?" Hayden asked.

"Oh my." Eliza shook her head.

Magnolia grabbed her husband's hand and gazed at the jungle. "Look what *Destruction* has done to us already."

"Nearly destroyed us," Blake said.

Wind blasted over them, whirling sand through the air. Hayden coughed. "And I don't think he's finished."

"Then even if the pirates get their gold and let us go, leaving Brazil wouldn't help." Blake's forehead wrinkled.

"No." James glanced up to see Angeline emerge from the shadows, the same blanket he'd given her wrapped around her shoulders.

"I heard voices."

"We didn't mean to wake you." Eliza stood and gestured for her to sit beside her.

"I wasn't sleeping." She lowered to the log. "What are we discussing?"

When no one answered, she lifted her violet eyes to James, moist and glimmering in the firelight. Moonlight circled her head like a halo. James swallowed. Was there ever a more beautiful woman? "Pirates and beasts," he said. "Not exactly topics to aid restful sleep."

"But important ones we need to discuss," Blake added.

Stowy peeked out from Angeline's blanket and began pouncing on the firelight flickering over the cloth. "What I don't understand is how a fortune in gold came to be hidden beneath the temple," she said. "Whose gold is it?"

"I don't know," James said. "Perhaps it was put there as bait to lure men to dig up the beasts."

Blake nodded. "Good thinking, Doc. That makes sense. Why else would it be placed in the tomb of the last beast?"

"Mercy me, who would do such a thing?" Magnolia asked.

James rubbed the back of his neck. "It's almost like God Himself planted a test for mankind. Much like the tree of the knowledge of good and evil. Will man choose evil for riches? Or will he deny himself and choose good?"

"But the pirates drew the maps that led to the gold, not God," Eliza shot back.

James smiled at her defense of the Almighty. "No, but God knew they would. He also knew what the first two beasts would lead man to do. Beasts whom I believe the cannibals released accidentally."

"Is that to be our fate?" Angeline's voice caught. "Are we to end up killing each other?" She lowered her chin, and James knew she thought of her plunge into the sea.

"We won't allow it to get that far," Blake stated with authority.

An ominous growl sounded from the jungle, drawing all their gazes. Several minutes passed as the crackling of the fire joined the sound of waves lapping ashore.

"Wait, I just remembered something." Hayden rubbed the stubble on his jaw, his eyes wide. "Remember that priest I told you about? The one I met in Rio?"

James nodded. "You said he mentioned a fire lake."

"Yes, and something about a temple and pure evil. A force that could not be defeated." Hayden stared at the fire. "He also said something really odd. At the time I thought he was crazy. He told me I was one of the six. That I had to go back. That only the six could defeat the evil."

"Six." James thumbed the scar on his cheek. "Didn't Graves say something about six?"

"That's right," Eliza said. "I remember him saying that there weren't six yet. That there can never be six."

"Six what? People? Us?" Angeline asked.

"I don't know, but I'm hoping this book holds the answer." James gripped the large leather tome and drew it back into his lap.

"The answer to stopping pirates?" Hayden snorted. "I doubt it. We have no weapons and they outnumber us."

"No. Not pirates." James swallowed. "The beasts."

Hayden chuckled and ran a hand through his hair. "Yes, that's so much easier than defeating pirates!"

"Not by might, nor by power, but by my spirit, saith the Lord," James said, wondering where the phrase came from. Had he read it in scripture? Either way it poured from his mouth before he gave it a thought. The effect was astounding. Instead of snorting in disbelief or taunting him for uttering a religious platitude, his friends nodded and stared at the sudden explosion of sparks from the fire ascending into heaven.

James had no idea how they would get out of this mess. But he knew one thing: This was not just a battle against pirates. This was a battle against pure evil.

Chapter 23

Angeline's face hit the sand. Hard. Grains imbedded in her cheek. They filled her nose and mouth. Wind howled in her ear, holding her down. Muffled screams surrounded her. What was happening? She'd been dreaming of trains—large trains with their *chug-a-chug* clank of wheels turning on iron tracks, their huge snorts of steam filling the air, and their mighty roar when they reached full speed. It was that roar that woke her, sent her barreling from the women's shelter with Stowy in her arms.

Straight into a wall of wind that knocked her to the ground on her stomach, shoved the air from her lungs, and sent pain across her shoulders.

Through the blur of sand, she saw the pink hue of dawn lining the horizon, lifting the shroud of night. She tried to move, but it felt like a hundred bricks lined her back. Sarah dropped to her knees beside her, Lydia bundled in her arms. She tugged on Angeline's arm. Her mouth moved but the wind stole her words. Hayden clutched Angeline's other arm, and they hefted her to stand, only to be shoved backward. All three of them rammed into the women's shelter. The wood snapped with a loud crack, and the palm fronds that made up the roof flapped and flailed until the wind broke them free and they billowed toward the sky like wings of a giant bird. The other shelter beside it suffered the same fate, disappearing into the clouds as the tempest scooped up clothing and supplies and tossed them like an angry, spoiled child.

Thiago darted toward them gesturing toward a cliff down shore. Shielding her eyes from the wind and sand, Angeline scanned the beach. Blurs that must be people darted back and forth, falling to the ground and then struggling to rise again. Beyond them, the sea was calm, clear, and smooth. . .

Like glass. *What?*

The sting of sand and salt in her eyes was, no doubt, making her see things. She rubbed them, but it only made them hurt more. Still, the placid sea remained. Thiago wrapped an arm around Sarah and started toward the massive rocks at the north end of their beach where several people took shelter. James came alongside Angeline, while a call for help sent Hayden down shore. Protecting her with his body, James drew her close, shoving his back to the wind. But it kept changing direction. Stowy let out a chilling howl, and Angeline hunched to shield him between her and James as they turned and twisted their way over the sand. Or, more like, *through* the sand as there seemed to be more of it in the air than on the ground. Grains pricked her skin and clothes like a thousand needles.

Pieces of wood, clothing, even small tools flew through the air. A chunk of firewood struck James. He moaned and forged ahead. His scent of sweat, smoke, and James filled Angeline's nose, bringing her a modicum of comfort.

Once at the cliffs, he pressed her against the rock wall, kissed her cheek, and sped away to help others. The wind's violence reduced to but a slap as the cliff absorbed the force of its punch. Angeline hunkered down, along with other colonists, and shielded her face as best she could. Something struck her head. Loosening her grip on Stowy, she reached up to rub the wound. The frightened cat leapt from her arms and sprinted away. Within seconds, his black fur was swallowed up in a cloud of sand.

"Stowy!" Shoving from the cliff, Angeline dashed after him, fear cinching her throat shut. Someone called her name, but it didn't matter. This wind would toss Stowy around like a rag doll, and she couldn't stand to lose him. Dodging flying branches and half blinded by sand, she plunged into the jungle. "Stowy!" A flash of black fur up ahead kept her stumbling forward.

Leaves slapped her. Branches stabbed her. Dirt and sand assailed her. Her skirts billowed, then slammed against her legs, then flapped right, then left. Her hair flailed about her head as if someone tugged on it from all directions. She struggled for each breath, barely able to hear her own thoughts—even the ones that shouted the invisible beast's name, *Destruction*. Was he the cause of this mayhem?

"Stowy!"

The cat crouched near a boulder, his fur standing on end, his eyes skittery with fright.

Someone darted past her, dove onto Stowy, rolled onto his side, and came up with the cat in his arms. Wind tossed light hair in a frantic dance above sky-blue eyes.

Dodd.

He smiled, rose to his feet, and fought his way through flying debris toward her. Dodging a large frond, she reached for Stowy, but he held the cat back. Instead he leaned toward her ear and shouted, "I know a cave nearby. It'll be safe. I'll take you there." His spit splattered on her neck.

"I'm not going anywhere with you!" She tugged on Stowy until finally Dodd released him. He took a step back, disappointment burning in his eyes. Then grabbing her hand, he tugged her forward. "I'll keep you safe," he shouted, ducking a flying branch.

Jerking from his grip, she hugged Stowy and backed away. The wind drove her against a tree trunk, whipped hair in her face. Squinting against a blast of dirt, Dodd went for her again, but she turned and sped away. A crack as loud as thunder pummeled her ears. She spun around. Something above Dodd moved. A massive branch loosened from the canopy and came crashing down. Dodd's eyes met hers. She started toward him, gesturing for him to move. He looked up. Terror rang in his eyes just as the branch struck him.

⌁

James closed his eyes and drew a breath, hoping to steady the thrashing of his heart. But when he opened them again, the wooden spike still protruded from Thiago's chest. Blood gurgled from the wound around the chipped wood. James's stomach cycloned, feeling much like the windstorm that had obliterated their camp earlier that day. Sarah knelt beside the unconscious Brazilian, her eyes red rimmed. She grabbed his hand while Magnolia and Eliza stared at James expectantly. Rising to his feet, he glanced over the wounded—at least a dozen. All lying on the sand beneath a slapdash bamboo roof some of the men had hastily erected. All attended to by Magnolia, Eliza, Angeline, and a few other colonists, who now stared at him as if he held the patients' survival in his hands. But they were wrong. Avoiding Angeline's gaze, he ducked beneath the bamboo and darted down the beach.

She followed him. He knew, because her coconut scent drifted on the ocean breeze and swirled beneath his nose. He continued walking, lengthening his stride, too embarrassed to face her. She caught his arm and turned him around. But there was no pity in her violet eyes. Concern, determination perhaps, but no pity.

"Eliza and Magnolia need you, James. You can't just walk away."

He glanced across the beach where colonists scavenged for anything left by the wind. "I'm not a doctor anymore."

"They don't know whether to pull out the wood or not. They need you to tell them what to do." She squeezed his arm. "Dodd needs you too. And the others. You don't have to look at the blood."

In the distance, Blake marched across the sand, stopping to speak to one man, then slapping another on the back, before shouting orders to a group who combed the beach for goods. His commanding voice was an encouragement to a colony that no doubt wondered if maybe next the ground would open up and swallow them whole.

Sobbing drew his gaze to Mrs. Scott, sitting on a stump, her slave, Mable, trying to comfort her. The windstorm had stripped the colony of what little the flood had left them. James felt like crying himself, except that would make him appear even weaker than he already was. Useless as a preacher—evidenced by the woman standing before him who had tried to kill herself two days ago—and useless as a doctor.

"Will you at least try?" Angeline's windswept hair fell in tangled waves over her shoulders. A curl blew across her face and tickled the freckles on her nose. She slid it behind her ear and stared at him, her pleading eyes shifting between his. And he knew he'd do anything to please her. Even if it meant his own death.

Which is exactly what it felt like he faced as he headed back to the makeshift clinic. Rolling up his sleeves, he approached Thiago, saw the relief on Eliza's face, then shifted his gaze to the blood bubbling from his friend's chest. And froze. His own blood turned to ice. He glanced away, his gaze landing on Dodd, lying in the corner, a lump on his head the size of a lemon. Angeline said a branch had fallen on him. The man hadn't woken up or even stirred in the two hours since they'd carried him from the jungle. Beside him lay Mr. Jenkins, a gash on his arm. Mrs. Swanson had a broken leg. Next to her, two farmers suffered mild abrasions, and the rest had minor aches and scrapes.

But it was Thiago who caused James the most concern. And the most terror.

"Please, James." Eliza pressed a cloth on the blood and looked up at him. "Tell us what to do."

"We have to pull it out," he said without looking at the wound. Angeline knelt beside Thiago to help. Sarah dipped a cloth in a bucket and dabbed the Brazilian's head, her hand trembling.

"But what if it struck an organ?" Eliza asked.

James risked a glance. Blood pooled around the wooden spike. His breath beat against his chest. His head grew light. Cursing himself, he looked away. At least the location of the wood indicated no organs or major arteries had been punctured. "If it pierced his heart, he'd be dead. If his lungs, he wouldn't be breathing like he is." If it was another organ. . .well, James doubted he could operate. "Have lots of rags available, some alcohol if we have it."

"We don't," Eliza said.

"I have some." The shame in Magnolia's voice drew James's gaze as she pulled a flask from a pocket of her gown. "I don't drink it anymore," she offered as an excuse when all the ladies gaped at her.

James drew a deep breath. The coppery smell of blood sent his heart hammering. Sweat beaded on his neck and arms. "Get a needle and suture ready. Pull the wood out, dab the blood, pour the alcohol on the wound, and sew him up as best you can."

Silence answered his instructions, prompting him to glance their way. All four ladies stared at him in horror.

Sarah grabbed Thiago's hand, tears streaming down her cheeks.

Eliza tossed her hair over her shoulder, her expression tightening. "You make it sound so easy."

James stared at the palm trees blowing in the wind just outside the clinic, at the gauzy foam bubbling on shore, anywhere but at the blood. "It *is* easy." For anyone but him. "You can do this, Eliza. I know you can. I promise I won't leave."

Abandoned Memories

Angeline lifted Lydia to sit on her lap, caressing the soft skin of her cheek. So soft, so innocent. Had Angeline ever been this innocent? She couldn't remember. The baby uttered sweet gurgling sounds and grabbed Angeline's chin, staring up at her with a drooling smile and eyes as green as moss filled with trust and wonder. *Trust*. How trusting Lydia had to be. She was completely dependent on others for everything: food, water, protection, even for moving from place to place since she couldn't yet walk. Yet she had complete trust with no fear of harm or betrayal. How wonderful. How different from the way Angeline felt—from the way most people felt. What happened to people to make them so jaded and skeptical when they reached adulthood? Betrayal, rejection by someone they trusted. What a shame. Angeline hoped Lydia would not suffer such a fate. She hoped—dare she even pray?—that this little angel would never suffer abuse or a broken promise or heartache.

Or become what Angeline had become.

"You're good with children." James's voice jarred her from her musings and made her blood warm at the same time. Plopping to the sand beside her, he drew up his knees and laid his arms atop them. "Want some of your own someday?" His lips curved in a half smile that sent her mind reeling with possibility.

Angeline kissed Lydia's head and stared out to sea, where morning sunlight cast golden jewels atop waves. Of course she did. But she never would. The thought burned her throat with emotion, keeping her silent. It was just as well. Lydia pointed to Stowy perched on a rock beside them and said, "Day da."

"That's Stowy. He's a cat," Angeline said. "C. . .a. . .t."

James laughed. "I fear she's a bit too young to understand you."

"It's never too soon to start learning." Angeline smiled. She'd been taking turns with Eliza and Magnolia looking after Lydia for Sarah, who insisted on keeping vigil beside Thiago ever since they'd removed the spike two days ago. Angeline didn't mind. She cherished her time with the child. It gave her a chance to pretend, just for a moment, that she was a decent lady with a family of her own.

"How is Thiago?" she asked.

James tried to hide his concern, but she knew him too well. "He's over the worst of it. We shall see."

"And Dodd?" Dodd had not woken up in two days and she hated herself for being overjoyed.

James plucked a large shell from the sand and handed it to Lydia, who promptly stuck the edge into her mouth and began sucking on it. He released a heavy breath and squinted at the sun traversing across a cerulean sky. "I fear it's a coma. If he hasn't woken up by tomorrow, there's no guarantee he ever will."

"Poor man," she said, though her heart leapt at the prospect. Dodd's eternal sleep would solve all her problems. Well, the biggest one, anyway. She could stay with the colony—what was left of it. More importantly, she could stay with James. Start a new life like she always wanted. Abandon her memories to the past where they belonged.

"In the meantime, we must keep water and soft foods down him as much we can," James said.

James and Dodd had never been friends. In fact, quite the opposite. Yet the concern in his voice for the man put Angeline to shame. Because of his fear of blood, James thought himself weak. But he was the strongest, most courageous man she knew. Though sweat had beaded his brow, though his hands had trembled and his chest heaved, he had stood by Eliza and Magnolia, instructing them minute by minute while they tended to Thiago. He hadn't even left his post when his legs had begun to tremble. He'd just sat down and continued.

His eyes met hers. And in their depths she saw a life played out with the two of them—a life of love and passion and children and joy. A mist covered her own eyes, but she couldn't turn them away.

"What are you thinking?" He cocked his head as a breeze stirred the tips of his hair.

"I'm thinking about you."

Hope shone in his smile. Confusion formed a line on his brow. He brushed a curl from her face. "I thought you said. . ."

That she didn't want his courtship? "I can think, can't I?"

"As often as you want." He chuckled. "As much as you want."

Lydia pulled the tip of the shell from her mouth and tossed it at him.

He caught it, drool splattering on his hand. Laughing, he lifted his gaze to Angeline's. "As long as they are good thoughts."

"Always." She knew she shouldn't have said that. She knew she should keep her feelings to herself. But something broke free within her. Maybe it was all the near-death disasters the colony had suffered, maybe it was Dodd's coma, maybe it was the hope she saw in James's eyes. A hope she felt mirrored in her own.

Lydia grabbed Angeline's hair and tugged. She winced as James peeled back the chubby fingers to free the strands. Then relieving her of the child, he hoisted the baby in his arms and stood, twirling her around and around until she giggled so hard it made them both laugh. Angeline stared, mesmerized, at the child cradled in James's arms, her tiny hand splayed over his rounded biceps. He tickled her gently, and she laughed and drooled on his shirt.

He glanced at Angeline and smiled, and she wondered what it would be like to have children with such a man.

Oh God, if You're up there and You listen to women like me, please, please, don't let Dodd wake up.

CHAPTER 24

I t's the beast, *Destruction*." James glanced over the colonists and the few pirates who had assembled the following evening around the fire. "He caused the windstorm. I'm sure of it."

Snorts and chuckles ensued.

"Pshaw!" one colonist said.

Ricu planted his hands on his waist. "Ridículo! I should not told you my tale."

James had not expected—nor wanted—Ricu to join their meeting, but he was not in a position to stop the man from doing much of anything. Still, his presence would only make what James had to say more difficult.

Hayden looked up from whittling a piece of wood. "We knew about the beasts before you got here, Captain."

From Magnolia's lap beside him, Lydia flailed her chubby hands in the air and yelped in agreement.

"Humph!" Ricu uttered a curse, lifted his hand, and snapped his fingers. One of the pirates placed a white handkerchief in his grip. The captain studied it intently before dabbing it over his neck and forehead. Firelight glinted off his jewel-pinned waistcoat.

James gestured toward the pirate's ship anchored several yards offshore. "How do you explain your ship? Not a sail torn, not a timber rent. No damage at all from the wind."

"And the water was as smooth as glass during the storm," Angeline said, petting Stowy. "I saw it."

Ricu scratched his whiskers and studied his ship, fading with the

186

setting sun, before offering only a grunt in response.

"*Destruction* or not, we lost what little we had left," one of the ex-soldiers said.

"All that remains are some clothes, a couple of pails and baskets, a wagon and some tools," the blacksmith grumbled.

"And our lives," Eliza offered.

Moses added his "Amen," drawing the scowls of some. He stood beside Mable and slipped his hand in hers, making sure the Scotts couldn't see them from where they stood at the edge of the crowd, arm in arm, looking much older than their fifty-some years.

James smiled at the freedman. In fact he was smiling a lot these past few days. And all because of the alluring russet-haired beauty sitting on a stump beside him. Since the windstorm, something had changed for the better between them. He had no idea why, but he wasn't complaining. She gazed at him now, her eyes sparkling in the firelight and a smile curving her lips. And he found he didn't care whether they had no shelter or food or whether invisible beasts attacked them or pirates kept them prisoner. If Angeline continued to look at him like that, he could survive whatever came his way.

"Indeed." A cool breeze struck them as Blake stepped before the group. "We are all alive and have plenty of food. We should thank God for that."

"Some Southern utopia," a lady muttered under her breath.

Mr. Jenkins, a bandage wrapped around his arm, stood and cast a wary glance toward Ricu before turning to Blake. "There ain't nothing for us here, and you said the emperor might be obliged to relocate us."

"I don't want to start over on another plot of land in this dreadful jungle," another man said. "I just want to go home. Back to the States."

"Here, here," two people shouted at the same time.

"Ah, and with a quick stop at Rio de Janeiro," one woman added with a dreamy sigh. "What I wouldn't give to sleep on a bed again."

"And have a new gown made," Magnolia agreed but was instantly silenced by a look from Hayden.

James exchanged a glance with Blake. That was their plan. If the pirates ever released them, they would travel to Rio, take out a loan from the emperor, and purchase new supplies and a new plot of land. But that couldn't happen until the pirates left. And the pirates wouldn't leave without their gold. And James couldn't allow them to find it and release the final beast. If that fourth monster were freed—from what James had interpreted in the Hebrew book—it wouldn't matter where they went. Life would never be the same anywhere on the planet. But how to explain that to people who, though they'd witnessed the same things James and his friends had, thought the notion of invisible beasts utterly ridiculous?

Captain Ricu emitted a growl that would stir the hairs on a bear. "I say who leaves and who not leaves! If you go Rio, you will tell about gold."

"Ah, let them go, Captain," Patrick pushed his way through the crowd and gave Ricu a smile as if they were the best of friends. "They won't tell anyone. Who would believe them anyway? Look at them." He waved a hand over the group, his nose wrinkling. "They look like beggars and wastrels. And if they do say anything, by the time anyone gets here, you'll have dug up your treasure and been long gone."

Hayden shook his head at his father's performance and continued his whittling. What did Patrick hope to accomplish by siding with pirates? Did he actually believe they would hand over any of their gold to him? No, Patrick was many things, but he was not stupid. The charlatan was up to something. But what?

"I need men to help dig," Ricu returned, fingering the butt of a pistol stuffed in his belt as he scanned the colonists, no doubt seeking strong men he hadn't yet worn to a frazzle. For the past four days, he'd selected five of their men and dragged them to the tunnels. And each day they'd returned hungry and parched and covered in cuts and bruises. James wondered why he hadn't yet been chosen. Perhaps because Ricu knew he was a doctor and thought it best to keep him uninjured. Hayden had already gone twice, poor man.

The pirate captain drew his blade. "Tomorrow I take you, you, you, you"—he pointed the tip toward each man in turn, the baker, two ex-soldiers, Blake—"and you." Jenkins the farmer.

The chosen men's expressions dropped.

"*Capitão*, why not bring all the men?" One of the pirates rubbed his shoulder and winced.

"No room in tunnels. Too many to guard." Sheathing his sword, Ricu gazed out at his ship, the silhouette barely discernible in the shadows. "We will get gold soon." He sneered at the colonists. "Then I think about if I let you go." He waved his hand in the air, the lace at his cuffs fluttering in the breeze. And without another word, he turned and marched away, joining his fellow marauders already well into their cups down shore.

An eerie howl, more heartrending than frightening emanated from the jungle, drawing all eyes to the green fortress just yards away.

Hayden tossed another log on the fire. Sparks shot into the darkening skies.

"Wish they'd at least share their spirits," one man grumbled.

A cry for help, followed by "Doctor, Doctor!" shrieked from down the beach as Sarah flew at the group in a flurry of fear and hysteria.

She yanked on James's arm. "Thiago is much worse!"

And worse he was. His skin flamed. His breathing was ragged, and the wound in his chest had turned green and smelled putrid. Infection had set in. And James had no medicine. Nothing to give him at all.

The man fluttered his eyes open as he drifted in and out of consciousness. Sweat glued his black hair to his head and neck. His chest rose and fell like erratic waves at sea as he tossed over the sand in discomfort. Finally, he settled and his hazy gaze landed on James.

"Am I to die, Doc?" Thiago's voice came out weak and raspy.

James swallowed. One thing he swore he'd never do was lie to his patients. He had never done so in the war, and he wasn't about to now. "Unless a miracle happens. . .I'm sorry."

Sarah broke into sobs, and Thiago turned his head toward her. "No tears for me, sweet Sarah." She took his hand and raised it to her lips. James knew the couple had grown close. He just hadn't realized *how* close. His heart hung like a huge boulder in his chest as Eliza continued to dab a cool cloth on Thiago's forehead while Magnolia sat nearby, looking stunned. James rose just as Blake and Hayden arrived. He shook his head at their questioning looks. Then ignoring their anguished expressions, he stormed out of the clinic and kicked sand with his boot. "Truss it!"

"Don't blame yourself." Blake followed him. "It's not your fault."

James held up his hands and looked at his friends with disgust. "Maybe if I had been the one to operate on him, he'd have a chance."

A night breeze tossed Hayden's hair in his face and he jerked it aside. "And maybe not." He gripped James's arm. "Magnolia tells me you instructed them as well as if it were your hands doing the fixing."

Jerking from him, James took up a pace, rubbing the back of his neck. "If only I had some vinegar or mercury. Anything to treat him."

"Have you tried praying?" Blake asked as James passed him.

"Did you *see* him?" James halted. "He's beyond prayer."

"No one is beyond prayer," Hayden said.

James shook his head. He had never considered praying. Not once. And he was the colony's preacher! Shame doused him as he charged back into the clinic, Hayden and Blake on his heels. He gave a cursory glance at poor Dodd lying alone on the other side of the bamboo structure before dropping beside the Brazilian once again. He would pray for Dodd later. Right now, he laid a hand on Thiago's shoulder. "God, please heal this man. Like You did in the days of old. I command this infection to depart from him so he will live and know You. In Christ Jesus' name, we ask. Amen."

The others mumbled, "Amen."

Though she offered him a smile, even pious Sarah seemed skeptical. Minutes later, instead of a miraculous recovery, Thiago began to cough up blood.

CHAPTER 25

Thiago didn't die that night. Nor the next. In fact, after three days, he still barely hung to life with the thinnest of threads. Angry at God, angry at himself, James did the only thing he knew to do. He grabbed the Hebrew book and his father's Bible and headed into the jungle away from the incriminating glances that labeled him a failure at both doctoring and pastoring. Lowering himself to sit on a boulder by his favorite creek, he gazed up at the canopy where colorful birds engaged in a dance equal in style and grace to any waltz back home. A blue lizard skittered up a tree while a frog croaked from somewhere near the water. The gentle ripple of the creek soothed his ears, a welcome change from the boom and sizzle of waves. A glint caught his gaze, and he looked up to see a spiderweb that spanned between two trees, its silky threads sparkling in a ray of sunshine. A tiny black spider sat in the corner awaiting his prey. No doubt it had taken him days, even weeks, to spin such a magnificent web. Such patience, such ingenuity. All to trap some unsuspecting victim.

Is that what the fallen angelic beasts were doing to the colonists? Luring them into their web with the glint of gold? James released a heavy sigh, set his father's Bible aside, and opened the Hebrew book to the place he'd marked. Why, oh why, had God entrusted the fate of the colony, maybe even the world—if he were reading things correctly—to a failure like James? He had to do better. He had to work faster. The answer to stopping the beasts was in this book, and he had to find it.

After two hours of interpreting, James had achieved little more than an achy back, tired eyes, and sweaty skin. He slapped a mosquito that landed on his arm, wondering if he was wasting his time. But he *had* learned one thing: the name of the fourth beast—*Depravity*. He'd also learned that once *Depravity* was released, all four beasts would not be restricted to this small section of Brazil. Instead, they'd be free to travel the world, wreaking havoc and destroying lives wherever they went. He'd suspected as much from prior hints in the text, but now he knew for sure.

He knew another thing for sure. They had to stop *Depravity* from being freed.

Pondering why God would allow such awful beasts—or fallen angels or whatever they were—to be free in the first place, James set the book aside and knelt by the creek, splashing water on his face and neck. Sitting back, he opened his father's Bible and ran fingers over the pages. Oh, how his father had loved this Book. Not a day had passed when James had not seen him sitting by the hearth absorbing its words as if his very breath depended on them. James had read the Bible too. When he'd had time. And of course his father had forced him to study it, training his son to become a preacher. But James had never been quite in awe of the Holy Scripture as his father had been. Perhaps that had been his problem all along. Yet now, could the answer to his current dilemma with the beasts be found within?

Flipping to the Gospel of Matthew, he started reading when crackling sounds tightened his nerves. A woman's voice, cooing his name, made his blood run cold. He brought his gaze up to see Abigail Miller, standing in the middle of the creek, water up to her neck, golden locks floating like silk atop the liquid. She smiled, that sultry smile that used to melt his insides but now made them turn into slime.

"You're not here." Setting the Bible down, he stood and rubbed his eyes.

"Of course I am." She started for him, water slipping off her like the layers of clothing she had shed for him on many a night. When she reached the shore, her wet chemise molded every curve of her glistening skin. He turned away, cursing his body for reacting even as disgust soured his mouth.

"Reading your Bible, I see. Like a good little preacher's son." Her tone was teasing, playful, like she'd always been with him. "But it never really did you any good, did it? You're too passionate a man to be restrained by some distant God."

"What do you want?"

She sidled up to him. "I want you. I've always wanted you."

Pulse racing, he stepped back. "You only wanted to ruin me."

"Of course not, James." She pouted, water sliding down her face like glistening diamonds. "I only wanted to make you happy. Weren't you happy with me?"

He had been. At least he thought he'd been. But what he'd mistaken for love had been only lust. And what he'd mistaken for a lady had been nothing but a trollop. A devouring trollop. Much like the spider he'd seen earlier, Abigail had cast her web for the young preacher and snared him without resistance. Widowed and older than James, she had opened up a new world to him—a world that was exciting and passionate, filled with carnal pleasures he'd never imagined. But it was all an illusion. A deadly one, for when his father, along with their parishioners, discovered his immorality, he'd been removed from the pulpit. "*For a time of correction*," his brokenhearted father had said. But shame drove James away. To become a doctor and join the war.

He stared at the leaves, the vines, the rays of sun spearing the canopy, desperate not to glance her way, desperate to give her no opportunity to entice him again. Women like her had ruined him. Twice. Abigail, who had driven him to war, and Tabitha who had ruined his life afterward.

"Thinking of me?" The new voice startled James into daring a peek. He wished he hadn't, for now both of them stood staring at him with innocent eyes that belied their scantily clad bodies.

Growling, he covered his own eyes, pleading with God to get rid of them, when a new voice, a male voice, added to his misery. He should just turn and leave, run as fast as he could back to the beach, but this particular voice owned a piece of his heart. And that piece forbade him.

"Father." He opened his eyes to see the man who had sired him, the man he had respected most in the world, standing by the creek, face pale, agony burning in his eyes and blood oozing from a pistol shot to his heart.

"Why did you let this happen?" Blood dribbled from his father's lips. "Where were you?"

James's chest caved in. The scar on his cheek began to throb. He rubbed it and fell to his knees, drowning in his agony and shame. He could not bear the sight, the memory of what he'd done. Would it never escape him?

It had been the most horrible night of his life.

And the most incredible. He'd faced a crossroads that fateful evening. One path led to death. The other to life. An angel had come alongside him—a woman who had ministered to him during the night, who had sang hymns and quoted scripture and helped him choose the right way.

"James, are you all right? James." Someone touched his arm. Small hands, gentle fingers. Abigail, Tabitha? Could visions touch? He jerked away and scrambled backward only to see Angeline staring at him, her face creased with worry.

He blinked the moisture from his eyes and looked away. "Yes. Forgive me."

"You saw a vision."

He nodded and slid a thumb over the scar on his cheek. The one he well deserved for what he'd done.

"Who was it?" Her eyes flitted between his, searching, caring. . .as her hand reached up to caress his jaw.

He took her in his arms. He couldn't help himself, and for once she allowed his embrace. She felt so small, so fragile. Here was a real lady. Pure and honorable and innocent. Not the kind of woman who lured men into traps and destroyed their lives. This was exactly the kind of woman who could redeem him.

⚜

The fear Angeline expected to feel locked in a man's embrace never came. Even though James was much bigger than she was, much stronger, able to do whatever he wanted with her, she felt no apprehension. Instead, she felt cherished, protected. And loved. This preacher-doctor stirred her heart and soul like no man ever had. And now, dare she hope for a chance to stay in these arms forever? She drew in a deep breath of him and gazed into his bronze eyes still filled with angst from whatever horrifying vision he'd seen. If only she could erase the memory and bring him the comfort he always brought her.

But then he smiled and the agony left his eyes, replaced by such affection, it brought moisture to her own. He slid a strand of her hair behind her ear, and even that slight gesture sent her senses whirling. She'd never known a man's touch could evoke such feelings. She'd always thought women merely endured lovemaking, that it was nothing but an unpleasant burden for the sake of bearing children. Or in her case, surviving.

But James had woken things within her that bordered on a bliss not of this world. It was *that* bliss that forced her to step back from him now. It would be too easy to give in to his charms, but she was not that woman anymore. She was the lady she saw reflected in his eyes, the proper lady, the virtuous lady. She wanted *so badly* to be that lady.

Approval beamed in his expression as he took her hand in his. "Forgive me for being forward." He gazed down uncomfortably. "You have captivated me, Angeline. I know I shouldn't ask again, but I can't help it. These past few days, you've given me reason to hope that perhaps you've changed your mind about our courtship?"

He looked so hopeful, so vulnerable, as if his heart teetered on the cliff of her answer. And, oh, how she wanted to say yes to keep it from falling. And hers from falling with it. If only. . . She hated herself for even thinking it, but if only Dodd would never wake. . . How cruel of God to dangle the gift of happiness before her on the thread of another's death.

Her breath came rapid as he lifted her hand to his lips for a kiss. Hadn't James said that the longer Dodd remained asleep, the less the chance he would ever wake? Maybe God wasn't cruel at all. Maybe He was giving her a chance at love. But what of Dodd's chance? He was a vile man who deserved what he got, wasn't he? If that were the case, then she deserved an equal fate. A person could go crazy with such thoughts!

James smiled and lowered her hand. "It wasn't that difficult a question to answer."

"My answer is. . .yes." She breathed the word before her good senses smothered it.

James shook his head as if he hadn't heard her correctly. "What did you say?"

She raised a sly brow. "I said yes, I accept your courtship."

His smile was blinding. His eyes alight with glee. Taking her other hand, he brought them both to his lips and kissed them over and over.

Warmth sped down to her toes as a giggle rose in her throat.

"I don't know what changed your mind, and I don't want to know as long as you don't change it again," he said, lowering her hands but not releasing them. "I do not have a perfect past, but I will make every attempt to make myself worthy of you."

She already knew a part of that imperfect past and wondered at the rest. Yet all of it would seem like a monastic interlude compared to her former life. She was the one who must prove herself worthy of him. Or at least forever hide from what she had once been.

"May I kiss you?" he asked.

No one had ever asked her that before. They'd simply taken what they wanted. She could feel his pulse throb in his hand, could hear his deep breathing, could smell his scent of wood smoke and salt and James. And she could stand it no longer. She pressed her lips against his. Unlike the few stolen kisses they'd shared before, this one had meaning. It carried a devotion and a passion free to express itself within commitment. Each stroke, each caress of his lips on hers held the promise of unending love. Her toes wiggled. Her head spun. She pressed against him. Those beefy arms of his she loved so much surrounded her, hands running down her back, fingering her errant curls. All the while his mouth drank her in with such affection, she thought she would explode in pleasure. Was this what real love was like?

Then suddenly he was gone. He backed away and turned to the side, gathering his breath. "Forgive me. I lost myself."

Forgive him? For what? Angeline blinked to clear her head, waiting for her body to settle.

He looked at her. "I should not have taken such liberties with so fine a lady as you." Shame haunted his eyes as he took her hands once again in his. "It won't happen again. You deserve more respect than that. You deserve my utmost respect."

Respect? Her?

He ran a thumb down her jaw, and she leaned into his hand. He trusted her. He believed her to be pure and innocent. And, oh, how she loved pretending that she was. Even for a moment. But how could she base their courtship on such a horrific lie?

Yet there would be no courtship without the lie.

Her brain hurt from the conundrum. Besides, how was she to think clearly with him so close, with the taste of him on her lips?

Footsteps and the swish of leaves broke into her dream as Hayden crashed into the clearing. His glance took in their locked hands before he turned to James.

"It's Thiago. Come quickly!"

Grabbing the ancient book and his Bible, James darted after Hayden, pulling Angeline behind him, but after a few minutes of her skirts getting stuck on every passing branch, she insisted he go ahead without her. They were almost at the beach anyway, and she needed time to think. But no sooner had James and Hayden disappeared into the greenery than the crackling sound of a fire burned her ears. She shut her eyes, knowing what was coming, but then decided it would be best to hurry along and join the others rather than face whatever heinous vision was about to appear. Unfortunately, it wasn't just one vision, but a half dozen of her former clients who took up a stroll on either side of her. Clutching her skirts, she tried to ignore them.

"Your beau there thinks you're a lady," the oldest one remarked, whose name she couldn't recall. Though she did recall his stench.

"You sure got him fooled!" Mr. Keiter slapped his hat on his knee.

One of her more refined clients brushed dust from his suit of fine broadcloth. "If I were him, I'd want to know what sort of woman I was marrying. It's only right, you know."

Grief and fear stole her newfound joy. She covered her ears.

Milton Daniels, one of her regulars, leapt in front of her, halting her in her tracks. He swept strands of greasy hair to the side and frowned. "You never kissed me like you kissed him. You was holding out on me!"

You're not here! You're not here! She screamed inside her head. But his words stung, nonetheless. All of their words pierced a place in her soul where light had risen, where hope had begun to shove the darkness aside. It crowded back. Closing her eyes, she barged right through old Milton, feeling not a whisper of his body on her skin. They weren't real. But what did it matter? They had done their damage.

Tears spilling down her cheeks, she shoved through leaves and burst onto the beach, hoping they wouldn't follow her.

"Ah, why don't you try and drown yourself again? That's the only way out." A shout and morbid laughter trailed her onto the sand, but when she spun around, no one was there.

CHAPTER 26

"Healed?" James blinked at the sight of Thiago leaning on Sarah's arm as they strolled down the beach. He would shrug it off as yet another vision if not for the fact that everyone saw the same thing. Blake and Eliza stood arm in arm, beaming smiles on their faces. Hayden, Magnolia, the Scotts, and Moses also stared at the wondrous sight.

"Is it so surprising?" Blake slapped James on the back.

Magnolia cocked a brow. "You *did* pray for God to heal him, did you not?"

James swept his gaze to Thiago. The Brazilian glanced up, and upon seeing James, a huge smile broke his tight expression as he and Sarah started back toward the group.

Waves crashed onshore, tumbling and foaming, much like the thoughts in James's head.

"You heal me, Doc!" Thiago exclaimed on heavy breath as he and Sarah stopped before him.

Shaking his head, James scanned him from head to toe. Though his face was pale, he'd lost weight, and he seemed weaker than an overcooked noodle, he was indeed very much alive. "May I?" James gestured toward the bandage on his chest, and at Thiago's nod, he peered behind it and sniffed. No bad smell, no discoloration. He stepped back, his mind trying to make sense of what his eyes told him.

"You heal me," Thiago repeated.

"God healed you," Sarah said with a smile.

"Yes." James shook his head to shake off the trance that had overcome him. "It was God who healed you, not me. I didn't do anything." Nothing at all, in fact, except direct Eliza and Magnolia to make a mess of his wound. And then say a simple prayer. "This is truly a miracle," he mumbled in disbelief. Slowly, the realization sank into his thick head and then trickled down to his heart, where a spark ignited. He glanced over the crowd. "This is a miracle! This man was dying." He gripped Thiago's shoulders and shook him. "You were dying!"

"I know." Glistening white teeth shone against his tawny complexion. "And now I am not. It is your God."

Moisture clouded Sarah's eyes as she clung to the Brazilian's arm.

From across the beach, Angeline approached and eased beside James. "What's happen—" Her eyes latched upon Thiago. "You're well again!"

"Sim, Miss. Mr. James pray and God heal me."

An adorable line formed between her eyebrows. "Indeed? Healed?" She blinked and exchanged a shocked look with James. A gust of wind blasted over them, cooling the sweat on his brow.

"God healed many people in the Bible." Hayden shrugged and snapped hair from his face. "Why can't He heal now?"

James stared at the sand by his feet. "I'm ashamed I didn't have faith that He would. I just prayed and went away without hope."

"None of us truly believed." Eliza gazed up at the sun, now high in the sky, as if she could spot the Almighty Himself, smiling down at them. Perhaps He was.

"God is bigger than our weaknesses." Magnolia's smile spoke of an intimate knowledge of that fact.

"Aaaa-men!" Moses proclaimed.

"There must be another explanation," Mr. Scott grumbled. "God no longer heals or does miracles. Those were only stories in the Bible."

"The evidence is to the contrary, sir." Blake jerked his head toward Thiago.

"Come along, Mrs. Scott." The elder man dragged his wife away, but her eyes were on Thiago, and her smile said she believed.

"This God," Thiago began, his voice weak but the light in his eyes strong, "He loves me. Just like you say, Doc. In your sermons. He loves everyone?"

"Yes, He does." James smiled.

"Indeed." Eliza gave Thiago a hug.

Magnolia wiped a tear from her eye.

"You need your rest." James placed a hand on the man's back. "Have Sarah take you to lie down, and Eliza and I will be there in a minute to examine your wound."

"And someone get the man something to eat!" Hayden shouted, causing them all to chuckle.

Angeline couldn't sleep. Whether it was the thrill of accepting James's courtship, the haunting visions of her clients, or the excitement of Thiago's healing that kept her awake, she couldn't say. But finally, growing bored listening to the blissful slumber of the other ladies, she crawled off the leaf-strewn bamboo that served as their bed and stepped out from under the palm frond roof. The shelter the men erected didn't afford much privacy, but at least it would keep them dry should it rain. Speaking of. . . She drew in a deep breath and was sure she smelled the sweet scent of rain on the wind. Her legs began to quake. She used to love the rain, but after the flood, even the slightest hint of it made her nervous. Yet there were no clouds on the horizon. Just a full moon that hovered like a pearl atop black glass, sending ribbons of milk onto water and sand. So peaceful. Peaceful except for the snoring from the men sleeping on the beach and one pirate belting out a ditty from the ship.

She wondered which of the shadowy mounds was James but thought it best not to seek him out. A flicker caught her eye from a lantern at the clinic and she headed that way, hoping for some company. Anything was better than being alone with her thoughts. Or worse, being alone should any of her former patrons return to haunt her.

Sarah smiled up at her as Angeline ducked beneath the roof.

"How is he?" She gestured toward Thiago, who lay fast asleep on one of the homemade pallets while Sarah kept vigil beside him.

"He finally fell asleep." She gazed at him adoringly before snapping her eyes back to Angeline. "Lydia is all right?"

"Yes, yes." Angeline cast a quick glance at Dodd's shadowy form at the other end of the clinic before she sat beside Sarah and adjusted her skirts. "She's sleeping peacefully beside Eliza. I think Eliza is practicing for when her own baby comes."

Sarah smiled and pressed a hand atop Angeline's. "And you? Why are you not able to sleep?"

"Too much on my mind, I suppose."

A breeze swept in and flickered the lantern sitting on a stump beside them.

"Like pirates and evil beasts?" Sarah raised one brow at Angeline. "Or is it the good doctor who invades your thoughts?"

Heat creeping onto her cheeks, Angeline lowered her chin. "Am I that obvious?"

"That you both care deeply for each other is quite obvious." Sarah squeezed her hand.

"He is such a wonderful man. I fear I don't deserve him."

"Don't be silly." Sarah's face scrunched. "Of course you do."

"No." Angeline pulled her hand from Sarah's and began toying with her hair. "You don't know me. Not really."

"I know you are kind and thoughtful and intelligent and strong. Any man would be fortunate to gain your affections."

Angeline gave a tiny smile. "Perhaps I am some of those things now. But. . ." How much should she disclose to her friend? Lantern light glimmered on the cross Sarah always wore around her neck, reminding Angeline that this pious woman had probably never done a single vile thing in all her life, nor even thought a single vile thought. "My past—"

"Oh, pish posh, who cares about your past?" Sarah dipped a rag in a bucket of water and rang it out.

"I've done terrible things, Sarah. Things that if James knew about them, he'd never speak to me again."

Sarah's gaze snapped to hers. "I doubt that very much. He's a man of God, and God is in the business of forgiveness."

Angeline couldn't help the snort that emerged from her lips. "There are some things I'm sure even God does not forgive."

Wind whipped through the makeshift clinic, sputtering the lantern and stirring the sand.

Setting the rag atop a pile, Sarah slipped a strand of hair behind her ear. "There is nothing God doesn't forgive except rejecting the sacrifice of His Son." Brown eyes as warm and soft as a doe's assessed her.

Angeline studied those eyes now, searching for some hint of doubt, some hint of insincerity, but all she found was concern. Swallowing a burst of emotion, she concentrated on the rhythmic lap of waves onshore.

Sarah leaned toward her. "Do you want to know a secret? A deep, dark secret that I've never told anyone?"

Angeline could not imagine this woman having any secrets, especially nefarious ones.

"Lydia is not my husband's child," Sarah said.

Angeline lifted her gaze to Sarah's, sure she hadn't heard the woman correctly. "What do you mean?"

Frowning, Sarah glanced down at Thiago. "You see, I didn't love my husband. Not the way a wife should. I know that now." She fingered the ripped fringe at the edge of her sleeve. "After he went off to war, I got terribly lonely. There was a man who helped out on our farm. He was strong and protective and kind. I don't know how it happened, but. . ."

Angeline squeezed her hand. "No need to go on. I understand." And she truly did understand. She understood too well how one moment—one weak moment—and one foolish decision could have dire consequences for the rest of your life.

Distant thunder rumbled as the *tap, tap* of raindrops danced over the roof.

Sarah folded her hands in her lap, refusing to meet Angeline's gaze. "Do you think differently of me now?"

"No." Angeline touched her arm. "I think of you as human." Her eyes moistened. "I always thought you were so perfect, Sarah."

Sarah chuckled and wiped a tear from her cheek. "Oh my, how we do make assumptions of others." She smiled. "Thank you, Angeline. You are a true friend." She squeezed Angeline's hand. "Now, I've told you my secret. Yours cannot be half as bad."

Withdrawing her hand, Angeline grew somber. "Far worse, I'm afraid." Minutes passed. Lantern light flashed over Thiago's sleeping form as the pattering of rain tapped all around. "I don't think I can speak it out loud."

"Then you don't have to," Sarah said. "But you must know that God forgave me, Angeline. I knew what I'd done was wrong. I dismissed the man and repented. Truly repented. And I've never felt such love and peace." She touched Angeline's chin, bringing her gaze up to meet her own. "Whatever you've done, it doesn't matter. If you repent and change your ways, God promises to forgive and remember your sins no more."

If only that were true. Angeline desperately wanted it to be true. She glanced at the man sleeping so peacefully beside them. "If you marry Thiago, will you tell him about Lydia?"

"Marry?" Sarah's brows lifted, but a sparkle took residence in her eyes. "Where did you get that fool idea?"

Angeline squared her shoulders and raised her chin. "That you both care deeply for each other is quite obvious," she repeated in a voice much like Sarah's, which caused them both to laugh.

When they ceased, Sarah took Thiago's hand in hers. "I do care for him. And now that he's truly following God. . .well, who knows what will happen? But to answer your question, yes, I must tell him. You cannot base a marriage on a lie."

CHAPTER 27

The smell of fire-roasted fish made James's mouth water as he led Blake toward the edge of the jungle to speak to him in private. But no sooner had they stopped when just a few feet away, leaves parted and Patrick made an entrance onto the beach with his usual aplomb, feigning an exhaustion James was sure was not caused by hard work. Separating from Patrick, Captain Ricu and his band of pirates sped toward their end of the beach, no doubt anxious to drown themselves in rum, while five colonists glared at Patrick as they passed and nodded toward Blake and James. Patrick waved at two single women from his original colony who'd been awaiting his arrival like giggling toadies. They came running with a bucket of fresh water and towels in hand.

"Why, of course the excavation is going well!" Patrick answered Blake's question as he drew cupped hands of water to his face and neck. "It's this fiendish dust that disturbs me. Not to mention being forced to live in such squalor like an ignorant native, sleeping in the sand and eating food only fit for a monkey." He took the towel a young lady handed him and dried his face. "The things I do for gold, Colonel."

Blake rubbed his sore leg, annoyance written on his features.

"How close did they get today to unearthing the fourth alcove?" James crossed his arms over his chest.

Patrick dried his face and handed the towel back to the woman, whose look of silly adoration threatened to ruin James's appetite. How the man managed to garner such devotion, he could not fathom.

"Thank you, my dear." Patrick's sickly sweet smile caused the lady's face to redden. "Now if you ladies wouldn't mind getting me a drink while I talk to these men, I'd be so appreciative."

After casting him flirtatious smiles, they both flounced away. His eyes followed them. "Such lovely creatures, don't you agree, gentlemen?"

"I have a wife, sir"—Blake gave a sigh of frustration—"and she is all the lovely I need."

"Oh, quite. I forgot how prudish you religious sorts could be." Patrick planted hands at his waist and stared over the sea that was transforming from turquoise to gray in the setting sun. "The alcove. Ah, yes. Surely you don't still believe it is the tomb of this fourth invisible beast? Come now, gentlemen. I'm surprised men of your intelligence have succumbed to such balderdash." Winking, he elbowed James. "I've got some prime farmland in the swamps of Louisiana for sale, if you're interested." He laughed at his own joke but then sobered when neither of them joined in.

How could this buffoon be Hayden's father? The physical resemblance was uncanny, but inside they were as different as the Rebs were from the Yanks.

In the distance, James spotted Hayden heading their way.

"All right. All right. Lost your sense of humor in the war, I see. Now, let me think." Patrick tapped his chin. "The alcove. Indeed, we are almost upon it. Another few yards of rock to be cleared. I'd say a week or two at the most and then"—he rubbed his hands together—"we'll find the gold. Enough gold to rule the world."

Hayden halted before his father, his jaw tight. "But you won't see any of it, Patrick. So why the excitement? Why do you volunteer to help every day?"

"To benefit us all, of course! Do you think I do this for myself?" Patrick placed a hand over his heart as if wounded. "The sooner these vile pirates find the gold, the sooner they are gone. And the sooner we are all free."

"Wonderful performance. Bravo, bravo." Hayden clapped. "But you forget who your audience is."

Patrick frowned and brushed sand from his shirt.

"You're up to something," Hayden added. "I just can't figure out what it is yet."

James agreed. He hadn't known the man very long, but he'd discovered two undeniable traits. One, Patrick only thought of himself, and two, he was only in Brazil for the gold.

Patrick gave a feigned look of guilt like a little boy caught with his finger in a pie. "I suppose I do have a plan to get some of the gold for myself." He shrugged. "But what does it matter whether I take it or the pirates take it, either way you and your pathetic little colony will be left alone." He grinned as one of the women returned with a mug of water. "Why you're sweeter than a peach pie, Miss Belinda."

James groaned inwardly. How could he get across to this greedy blaggard the danger he faced—the danger they all faced—should the fourth beast be freed? "All I'm asking, sir, is that you consider what you are doing. There are forces at work which we cannot see in the natural."

"Of all the lunacy!" Patrick laughed, Belinda joining him. "Invisible monsters and visions and the destruction of the world. Pshaw!" A devious look twisted his features as he leaned toward James. "I fear the sun has addled your brain, preacher or doctor—or whatever you are."

Belinda's giggles grew louder. James's heart turned to lead.

"Now, if you'll excuse me, gentlemen." And off he strolled, the young lady on his arm.

Hayden glared after his father. "Good thing I've forgiven him, or I'd probably kill him on the spot."

James flattened his lips. "It must be difficult to live so close to him after all the damage he caused you and Magnolia."

"He'll be gone soon enough. But I do wonder what he's about. He has a plan to get that gold, a good one. You can bet on that."

Blake shook his head. "He'll probably get himself killed."

A breeze spun around them, cooling the sweat on James's neck as crickets buzzed from the darkening jungle. In the distance, colonists began to gather around the fire for supper.

"I interpreted more of the book last night," James said. He'd wanted to discuss his findings with his friends all day, but they'd been busy building huts and foraging for food. Besides, he needed time to ponder the new revelation, to ensure he was right, to ask God what to do.

Wind stirred sand at their feet as Blake and Hayden stared at him in expectation.

"I've discovered who these four beasts are." James hesitated. He knew this would make him sound like the addlebrain Patrick had just called him, yet it was no crazier than the idea of invisible beings in the first place. "They are four of Satan's fallen angels. In fact, they were—or are—generals in Satan's army." He glanced at his friends, but their expressions were unreadable. "Apparently, I was correct in my assumption that they stepped outside the boundaries God had placed on them, did something they had no permission to do, so God sent Gabriel with a contingent of warring angels to battle and subdue them."

Only the crash of waves and snap of a distant fire responded. James tightened his jaw, bracing for the laughter he expected from Hayden.

Instead, Blake moaned and gave an agreeing nod. "Perhaps that charred area behind the temple was the battlefield."

"My thoughts exactly." James turned to Hayden. Skepticism screamed from his eyes, yet he remained, waiting to hear more.

"Like I told you before, the angels' punishment was to be imprisoned underground near a hot spot until the end of this age."

"The fire lake the priest I met spoke of," Hayden said.

"Yes." James rubbed the back of his neck. "The book speaks of a river of fire that runs through hell in the center of Earth then flows up to the Earth's crust in only three places."

"Then the cannibals came along," Blake said. "Erected their temple right on top of it, dug tunnels, and happened upon these beasts."

"As I said before, I don't think they understood what they'd found or what they'd released."

"Not until it was too late," Blake added, gazing at the surf.

Hayden cursed, his mood growing sullen. "You told us that the person who recites the Latin phrase must have a black heart, an evil heart." He glanced at his father sitting on a rock, entertaining a group of people with some embellished tale. "If anyone has an evil heart..."

Blake groaned. "Tell us again what happens if this fourth beast is released?"

"He is called *Depravity*. Need I say more?" James heard the fear in his own voice as darkness settled on the beach. "And from what I've read, his release multiplies the power of the others and enables all four of them to leave this place and wreak evil over the entire planet."

"There's no telling how much damage they will do. How many lives will be lost." Hayden's gaze remained on his father.

Blake's body stiffened. "We've got to stop the pirates. We've got to stop Patrick from releasing that fourth beast."

James glanced at Captain Ricu climbing the rope ladder to his ship. "Pirates have gunpowder. . .do they not?" He lifted his brows and scanned his friends.

A slow grin spread over Hayden's lips while Blake nodded his understanding.

"We blow up the tunnels," they all said in unison.

"It's the only way," James added. "God is on our side. I believe He sent us here to stop these beasts." He'd been sensing that for days. But now he hoped his friends would agree.

Blake squeezed the bridge of his nose. "Perhaps. But even if we can destroy the tunnels, the pirates won't give up on the gold. Not when they know it's still down there."

"But it will buy us time." James stared at the ship, a shadowy leviathan floating offshore. "But how do we get on board and steal enough gunpowder to blow up those tunnels?"

CHAPTER 28

James glanced over his shoulder at the pirates guarding the beach. Though a few of them had left at sunrise for the tunnels—along with several of the colony's men—the rest stayed behind in order to keep the remaining colonists from escaping. "They are sneaking aboard tonight," he answered Angeline, who had asked about their plans to steal the pirate's gunpowder.

"Who?"

"Hayden and Blake," James said as he slammed the ax through a thick piece of bamboo. He'd been attempting to reinforce the women's shelter when Angeline approached. Storm clouds on the horizon portended rain, and he wanted a dry place for the ladies to congregate.

"Why aren't you going?"

Wind tore a curl from her pins and sent it bouncing over her neck as her concerned gaze snapped to the pirate ship. James set down the ax and wiped sweat from his brow. Since she'd agreed to their courtship, she'd been seeking him out, starting conversations, sitting with him at meals, strolling with him on the beach, looking at him with those exquisite violet eyes so full of admiration. He felt like he was living in a dream, a dream ripe with hope and love and every possible joy. Yet at the same time he felt guilty for feeling such happiness in the midst of so much struggle and danger.

He took her hand in his and caressed her fingers, thrilled when she no longer pulled away. "They need me here to protect the colony should. . ." He stopped, not wanting to alarm her.

"They get caught." She finished, her lips tightening. "I'm thankful you aren't going. Is that selfish of me?"

"Is it selfish of me to wish I *was* going?" He chuckled. "To want to do something—anything to stop this madness."

Swaddling his hand in both of hers, she brought it to her chest. "I fear for them. I fear for us all."

He ran a thumb over her cheek. She was so small, but he knew inside her petite frame, a dragon lurked—a dragon filled with strength and determination. And he loved her all the more for it. "They will be all right. God will go with them."

She smiled. "I wish I had your faith."

James squinted toward the rising sun. A handbreadth above the horizon, it scattered droplets of gold onto the restless sea. *Did* he have faith? Though Thiago had been healed and had come to believe more firmly in God, James hadn't been sure either would happen. Did he truly believe that Hayden and Blake would be safe, or was he just reciting the expected platitude? Another trite proverb sat ready upon his lips—something about how Angeline could have faith too if she only believed—but it tumbled unspoken onto the sand. More proof that he wasn't a very good preacher at all.

"Thank you for working on our shelter." She peered behind him at the tilting stack of bamboo and fronds.

Running a hand through his hair, he gave a lopsided grin. "If that's what you call it. But yes, I'm trying. I may even erect a front wall today so you ladies can at least enjoy some privacy."

"Doctor, preacher, and home builder. Is there no end to your talents?"

He withheld a skeptical snort. He'd never had a woman look at him the way Angeline did. Other females had looked at him with interest, appreciation, fury, and even desire, but never with such admiration that his heart nearly burst. If he told her the truth—that he was good at none of those things—he feared the sparkle would fade from her eyes. And he didn't think he could bear to see it go. "At your lady's service." He gave a mock bow.

When he resumed his full height, her eyes were locked on his bare chest. She looked away and began fingering a wayward strand of hair. So accustomed to wearing minimal clothing in the sultry environment, he'd unwittingly forsook proper etiquette that morning. Still he found her innocence refreshing. And alluring.

"Sweet saints," she whispered then bit her lip.

"What did you say?"

"Nothing." Shielding her eyes from the sun, she returned her gaze to his. "I actually have a purpose for disturbing your work, James. To invite you to a picnic lunch." She gestured to her left. "Just beyond the cliffs. In an hour? Just the two of us?"

Heart leaping at her suggestion, he turned and grabbed his shirt from the sand and gave her a teasing smile. "Without a chaperone? I do hope you're not trying to seduce me?"

⁂

Chastising herself, Angeline begged James's forgiveness and turned to leave. She truly had no idea how real ladies behaved. Maybe it was his bare chest that prompted her to ask such an improper thing. What was she thinking? Inviting a man to lunch! And without a proper escort? He must think her wanton.

His hand on her arm stopped her. His look of remorse stilled the pounding of her heart.

"Forgive me. My poor attempt at humor was completely un-warranted." He searched her eyes. "I would love to join you."

"Very well." Her insides unwound at his loving look. "On one condition."

"Anything."

She wanted to tell him—to insist—that he put on the shirt he held in his hand. His bare chest was driving her to distraction. Not because it was thick and corded with muscle. Not because it was tanned and lined in strength. But because it was James's. And he was so close. A sturdy rock of manhood—a cave into which she longed to crawl and never come out. And she hated feeling that way. Needing him made her vulnerable. Did all women suffer such uncontrollable longings during courtship? As if they couldn't get enough of their beau? As if they'd shrivel up and die without him?

When she didn't answer, he placed a finger beneath her chin and raised her gaze to his, one brow lifting. "Your condition, Miss?"

"Oh, yes." She attempted a smile. "That we don't discuss any of our problems."

He nodded his agreement.

And like a gentleman, he kept his word. For two hours Angeline and James—and Stowy—escaped the world with all its problems and stresses: the temple, the beasts, the visions, the disasters, the pirates. And most of all, Dodd. For two hours she sat on an old quilt in the sand and memorized every curve of James's mouth; the scar that angled down the right side of his lips; the flex of his jaw; every sparkle in his eyes; the way the wind played havoc with his hair, making it poke out all over; the sound of his voice that reminded her of the thunder of waves. And his laughter, which brought a lightness to her spirit she'd never known. After sharing some of their meal, Stowy curled up in James's lap, something he rarely did with anyone but her. Sweet saints, if the cat trusted this man so much, what reason did she have not to do the same?

She discovered they both enjoyed the writings of Emerson and Thoreau, the artwork of Frederic Edwin Church, the sound of a violin, and fruitcake. They spoke little of their past and shared dreams for their future. A future that was beginning to form out of the haze of Angeline's memories. Like the bright sun, it shoved aside the bitter cloud of her past and shaped her dreams into sparkling possibilities.

She could spend a lifetime on this blanket with this man on this beach. And die happy.

Finally he leaned toward her and planted a kiss on her lips. A soft, chaste kiss, his breath feathering her cheek, as if he touched precious porcelain. She drew in a breath of him and felt her pulse race, imagining what it would feel like to be loved tenderly and gently, not harsh and rough like an animal satisfying an impulse. Memories invaded, sullying the moment. Voices shouted insults in her mind. James cupped the back of her neck and ran a thumb over her cheek, luring her out of the darkness.

"Angeline, sweet, sweet, Angeline," he breathed over her lips before tasting her again. Angeline's world spun. What she wouldn't give to be pure and innocent for this man. To be the lady he believed she was. Perhaps she could wish her former life away, abandon all her bad memories to the past where they belonged.

James tasted of mango and salt and she pressed against him, wanting more and more, trusting him like she'd trusted no other. It began to rain. Small drops at first but then larger and larger, until the two separated, gathered their things, along with Stowy, and ran back to camp laughing like children.

Hours later as the sun sank behind the tips of the trees, Angeline sat on the beach, Stowy in her lap, studying the webs of foam each wave created upon the shore. Each one was so delicate, so beautiful, so unique, it would put the finest Chantilly lace to shame. Yet how many exquisite designs bubbled over the sand one minute and then were gone the next? If she hadn't been sitting here to observe, no one would have seen their beauty. How true of their own lives. Tossed upon the sand by God, some forming gorgeous patterns, others fading away too soon. But did anyone notice? Was something beautiful if no one ever saw it to proclaim it so? If it was swept away before anyone realized its value?

"May I join you?"

Startled, Angeline glanced up to see Hayden standing beside her, a friendly yet concerned smile on his face. "Of course."

He plopped to the sand and stretched out his legs, planting his hands behind him. For several minutes he stared at the sea, his jaw bunching then relaxing, then bunching again. No doubt, he was anxious about sneaking aboard the pirate ship in a few hours. Yet, why would he come to her and not his wife?

"Is there something I can do for you, Hayden?" She caressed Stowy's fur.

He glanced over his shoulder at camp, where some of the colonists were starting the evening fire and several others were cutting fruit for supper. "You and James have an understanding?" He faced her.

The topic took her by surprise. "We are courting." Curiosity caused her to search his expression. Why would Hayden concern himself with her and James's relationship? Especially in light of the danger he faced that night.

He blew out a heavy sigh and gazed at the horizon. "I don't know how to say this, but I feel I should discuss it with you before. . ."

"Before you risk your life tonight?"

"Indeed." He rubbed the stubble on his jaw. "I don't know what will happen, but I care deeply for both you and James. And, well, I suppose there is no delicate way to say this. Back in the States, I saw your likeness on a poster at the Norfolk sheriff's station." He stared at her. "You were wanted for murder."

Angeline's heart collapsed. Her blood turned to ice. She gazed out to sea, trying to force breath into her lungs, trying to put on an expression of shock, of indignation. Anything but reveal the terror gripping her.

"The name wasn't yours," he continued. "Clarissa somebody, but I'd know your face anywhere."

She dug her toes in the sand, staring at the wavelets stroking the shore, not finding them as beautiful as she had only moments before. "My face is a common one."

"Hardly."

She looked at him, at the way his lips curved in that alluring smile, and she knew why Magnolia was smitten with him.

Angeline gave a huff of resignation. "What do you wish to know?"

"What do I wish to know?" He gave a cynical chuckle. "Well, if you're going to marry James, I suppose I'd like to know what your real name is and whether you are, indeed, a murderer."

A crab skittered across the sand. She followed it with her gaze.

"Just tell me it isn't true," he continued. "Tell me it was a mistake and I'll never mention it again."

A torrent of emotions clogged Angeline's throat: fear, sorrow, anger. She opened her mouth to answer him, but nothing but a squeak emerged.

"Angeline. I know you. You aren't capable of murder. Tell me they had the wrong woman."

The crackle of a fire sounded in the distance, and she fully expected to see her clients appear to taunt her. She wanted to lie to Hayden. Wanted to shout that she had no idea what he was talking about. But it seemed that no matter how hard she tried, no matter that Dodd remained in a coma, her past would find a way to ruin her future.

"Zooks, Angeline. What happened?"

She closed her eyes, wishing the crashing waves would sweep over her and carry her away. "It's a long story, Hayden." Tugging on the chain around her neck, she pulled out her father's ring and rubbed it gently with her thumb. The ruby and topazes barely shimmered in the fading light. "It started when my father was murdered. Thrown out the window of his shipyard by some madman claiming ownership."

She expected more questions. She expected the typical expression of sympathy. What she didn't expect was to see Hayden's face turn a shade of white to match the sand.

"What was your father's name?"

"Frederick Paine. Why?"

Hayden seemed to be having trouble breathing. "And the man who fought him?"

"A Mr. Carson, I think. He took off afterward. We never saw him again. Why? What do you know of this?" She laid a hand on his sleeve. His arm trembled. "If you know something about my father, please tell me."

"I never met your father." Hayden stared at the sand, his shoulders taut. "But I know about the deal that sent him to his death. The felonious accord which made Mr. Carson believe he owned your father's shipyard."

Angeline's thoughts spun in a whirlwind. "How could you possibly know that?"

"Because I was the man who struck that bargain."

CHAPTER 29

What are you saying?" Leaning forward, Angeline palmed the sand and shoved to her feet, still not believing her ears. Stowy circled the hem of her skirts, howling in annoyance.

Hayden rose and brushed sand from his trousers. Guilt dripped from his expression.

"You murdered my father?" Blood boiled through Angeline, muddling her thoughts and inflaming her anger. "You murdered my father!" Hot tears spilled down her cheeks.

"Not directly." Agony stretched across Hayden's eyes. "I had no way of knowing Mr. Carson would react the way he did."

Raising her hand, Angeline slapped him across the cheek. Her hand stung, but it felt good. Hayden rubbed his jaw. She backed away and broke into sobs.

"I'm so sorry, Angeline. I was a swindler, a confidence man back in the States. I hurt a lot of people, God forgive me." He took a step toward her, holding out his hand.

She shoved it away. Then batted tears from her face. She would not let this man see her cry. "You swindled this Mr. Carson?"

"Yes, I sold him your father's shipyard."

"But it wasn't yours to sell."

"No." He lowered his chin.

"What did you think would happen?" Leaning over, she grabbed a handful of sand and tossed it at him. The grains struck him and slid down the fabric of his shirt. He never flinched. "What did you think!?" she shouted.

"I didn't." His eyes misted. "I had no way of knowing Carson would shove your dad out that third-story window." Wind tossed hair into his face and he snapped it away. "I'm not that man anymore."

Angeline didn't care. All that mattered was that he was responsible for her father's death. He was responsible for what she'd been forced to do afterward in order to survive! "Do you know what happened to me after my father's death? Do you?" She thrust her face into his. "I was an orphan. Went to live with my uncle. A terrible man." She turned her back to him. She wouldn't tell him anymore. Wouldn't give him the satisfaction of knowing the pain he had caused her. Instead she stood seething, longing for the pistol that used to sit in her belt.

"I'm so sorry, Angeline."

Turning, she charged him and pounded both fists on his chest, her only thought to make him suffer as he had made her. But her thrusts merely bounced off thick muscle. He grabbed her hands and forced her to stop. Tearing from him, she dropped to her knees, gasping for air. Stowy hissed at Hayden.

"Angeline." He took a step toward her.

She snapped her fiery eyes his way, feeling as though they could shoot darts at him if she so willed. "Don't come any closer."

"I hope you can forgive me."

She scooped up Stowy. "If you're truly sorry, then do me one small favor."

"Anything."

"You must not tell James. Not about the poster. Not about our talk."

He hesitated, drew in a deep breath, and glanced out to sea. "I make no promises."

Angeline stood and stiffened her spine. "I hate you, Hayden Gale. I will never forgive you. Ever."

Hayden slid into the dark water and dove beneath an incoming swell. Thank God the waves came in strong tonight. The thunderous sound would hopefully mask any splashes he and Blake made as they swam toward the pirate ship. Well past midnight, clouds covered a waning moon and a smattering of stars, keeping light at bay and the night reigning in darkness—another sign God was on their side. Well, of course the Almighty was on their side. Surely He wasn't on the pirates'? Hadn't they prayed with James, Eliza, and Magnolia before they'd left? If God could heal Thiago, certainly He could make their mission to steal gunpowder successful.

Cool water gushed around Hayden, gurgling and slushing past his ears. Saltwater filled his mouth. He spit it out. The scent of brine stung his nose. Every muscle was tight. Every nerve coiled. Every sense heightened. *Oh, God, please just get me back to Magnolia in one piece.* Not hanging from a yardarm.

He broke the surface and spotted Blake just ahead of him. Getting to the pirate ship shouldn't be a problem. Getting past the few pirates on board was another story. Hopefully it wouldn't be as difficult as his encounter with Angeline had been earlier that day. An encounter he couldn't shove from his mind, no matter the present danger.

He'd swindled many people in his past, made a thousand spurious deals that had relieved people of their fortunes and lined his own pockets. But he'd never hurt anyone he cared about.

Until now.

Not only hurt, not only stolen money from, but apparently his actions had destroyed her life, had possibly led her to murder and God knew what else.

Drawing in a deep breath, he dove beneath a roller, wishing the waves would wash him clean of his past. But he supposed God didn't work that way. God forgives, God redeems, but He doesn't always sweep away the consequences of one's bad choices. Like everyone in the colony, Hayden had hoped to escape the horrors of war by coming to Brazil. He had also hoped to escape his equally horrifying past. But it had found him anyway. First in the form of his father, and now in the form of precious Angeline.

He plunged upward through the surface, his eyes stinging from salt, his lungs gulping air, his heart heavy with guilt. He could do nothing but apologize to both God and man. God had already forgiven him. Hayden prayed Angeline would do the same someday. Water slapped him in the face like she had done earlier. He deserved that and more for what he'd done. Even still, he could not abide by her wishes and keep silent. James deserved to know the truth—whatever that truth was.

Hayden could not allow one of his best friends to marry a murderer.

All such concerns fled him when he and Blake struck the side of the ship. He must focus on their mission or all would be lost. Waves lapped the wood and spread foamy claws upward toward a railing that disappeared into the thick black of night. The oaky smell of moist wood filled Hayden's lungs as Blake nodded and began climbing the rope ladder.

Captain Ricu was on board. At least they'd seen one of his men rowing him to the ship at nightfall. That was hours ago, and by now, the flamboyant captain was surely sound asleep in his cabin. The long days spent in the tunnels seemed to steal his ostentatious vitality. Most of the pirates ashore were asleep as well, save the few that guarded the camp. Since they were preventing the colonists from escaping by land, not by sea, it had been easy to slip into the water without drawing their attention.

Hayden gripped the thick line, propped his bare feet on the hull, and followed Blake. Coarse rope, which felt more like a dozen needles, burned his hands. The ship creaked and groaned beneath each incoming wave, mimicking the ache in his muscles. Above him, the night soon swallowed up Blake. Hayden continued until finally a hand gripped his arm and hauled him over the bulwarks. He landed like a wet fish on the foredeck. The *drip, drip* from his clothes and his heavy breath echoed like alarms over the ship.

Thankfully, the guttural snores of several men rose to drown out the sound—pirates, who with bottles clutched to their chests, lay in haphazard positions across the deck like marionettes whose strings had been severed. Even the watchmen, muskets strewn across their laps, slouched against masts and gun carriages as if God had poured a sleep potion on them from heaven.

Lifting a silent prayer of thanks, Hayden inched his way around prostrate forms, eyeing the pistols and swords strapped to their bodies. The colonists could sure use some weapons, but he dared not risk waking the sleeping miscreants. The gunpowder was far more important. Destroying the tunnels and—if what James said was true— keeping the final beast imprisoned was their top priority. Then perhaps Captain Ricu would give up his quest for gold and leave them alone. If not, they'd find another way to deal with him.

Hayden dropped down a hatch, ignoring the foul stench that bit his nose. He'd been on this ship twice before. Once to rescue Magnolia and the second time to deliver the treasure maps to the captain. Both times, he'd taken note of the layout—knew the ship's magazine must be located between the second deck and the hold. He only hoped it wasn't locked. Grabbing a lantern from a hook on the bulkhead, he led Blake into the bowels of the ship, past the wardroom and the pantry until they stood before a bolted door.

Apprehension stormed across Blake's gray eyes. He yanked a small ax from his belt and raised it above the iron lock. It would make noise. They both knew it would. What they didn't know was whether that noise would penetrate the pirates' blissful slumber. But they had no choice.

Blake slammed the ax down.

Clank!

The lock swung on its hinge but didn't break. Groaning inwardly, Hayden exchanged a look of frustration with his friend. They waited. The ship rolled over an incoming wave. Blake rubbed his sore leg. Wind whistled through the hallway, joining the creak and grate of aged wood. But no human sounds met their ears. The lantern sputtered, casting ghoulish shadows on the bulkhead. Blake raised the ax again.

Clank! Thud!

The lock snapped off and fell to the deck. Lifting the lantern, Hayden pushed the door open to reveal a dozen kegs of gunpowder, piles of muskets, pistols, grenades, cutlasses, and cannonballs. He exchanged a grin with Blake. Now the hard part began. Getting one of the heavy kegs up the ladder to the main deck, over the bulwarks, and into one of the cockboats tied to the ship without getting caught. Once in the boat, it would be a short trip down shore away from camp where they could hide the keg until they could formulate the best plan to put it to use.

Clipping the lantern on the deckhead, Hayden grabbed a pistol and shoved it in his belt then slid a handful of shot in his pocket. All these weapons. All this gunpowder. It seemed a shame to leave most of it behind.

"We could blow up the ship if we wanted," he said without thinking.

Loosening his tie, Blake ran the ends over the sweat on his neck.

"Everyone on board would die."

They stood staring at each other, the possibility of enacting such a heinous task weighing heavy in the air between them. The deck tilted. The lantern swayed. A chill bit through Hayden's wet clothes.

Blake shook his head. "You don't have it in you either, Hayden. Not anymore."

Hayden's tight chest unwound. Before he'd come to know God, he wouldn't have hesitated to kill men who were intent on killing him. But something *had* changed within him in the past few months. Well, a lot had changed, if he was honest. But one thing he'd come to know with certainty—human life was precious. Every human life. Each person a unique masterpiece of the divine Creator.

Even pirates.

He released a breath and nodded at his friend while Blake snatched a couple of pistols and a sword and shoved them into his belt. Then together, they carried a keg of powder down the hall and up the ladder onto the main deck where a blast of wind flapped Hayden's damp trousers against his leg and sent ice up his spine.

Something didn't feel right. Yet when Hayden glanced around, the pirates remained sprawled in the same positions as before. A lantern swinging from the mainmast cast ribbons of dark and light over the deck as it screeched in harmony with the creak of wood. They set the keg down and glanced over the port railing at the dark shape of a boat thumping against the hull. Blake grabbed the rope dangling over the side and began tying it around the keg while Hayden kept watch.

Just a few minutes. That's all the time they needed in order to lower the keg to the boat and be on their way. Just a few more minutes and their mission would be completed. Hayden shook his head at how easy it had been. Thank God the pirates had grown overconfident and become complacent in their vigilance.

Blake finished tying the rope and tugged on it to test the knot.

Squatting, Hayden helped him lift the keg, his muscles straining as they set it atop the bulwarks. They were about to lower it over the side when boot steps clapped over the deck and a shadow emerged from the darkness. Lantern light glimmered off a jeweled waistcoat and winked at them from a gold ring in one ear.

"And where you think to go with that?"

Hayden's body turned to mud. And like mud, he wanted to spill to the deck, squeeze between the planks, and disappear. Instead he set down the keg, wondering if the despair in his own eyes matched the despair he saw in Blake's.

Captain Ricu graced them with one of his annoying, insolent belly laughs. "What be this? You think to make idiota out of Captain Armando Manuel Ricu?" He stomped his boot on the deck, jingling the bells that adorned it.

Hayden cursed himself silently. Why hadn't he heard the man coming? Rum and sour fish wafted beneath Hayden's nose. Why hadn't he *smelled* him?

Four pirates swarmed them, relieving them of their weapons and leveling pistols at their chests. Ricu planted fists at his waist and stared at them, though his expression was lost in the shadows. Probably for the best as Hayden could feel his anger from where he stood.

"I treat you well and this be how you repel me?"

Blake shifted the weight off his bad leg and huffed. "Repay. And we could have blown up your ship, Captain. And you, along with it."

"Instead you steal to blow up later."

"No," Hayden began. "We—"

"Enough!" Ricu stormed, swung about and charged through his sleeping men, kicking them as he went and shouting words in Portuguese.

Groaning and grunting, the pirates scrambled to rise, rubbing their eyes and standing at attention once they saw their angry captain.

Further Portuguese words were brandished about before Hayden and Blake were escorted back to shore, along with the captain and a few of his men. At least he didn't hang them from the yardarm or enact any other vicious pirate torture Hayden had read about. Such as the rosary of pain that made a man's eyes pop out or flogging with the "cat," a whip made from knotted strips of rope that ripped open a man's flesh. He suddenly wished he hadn't read any of those fanciful pirate tales as a kid. Trying to evict them from his mind, he glanced at Blake who sat beside him in the jostling boat. Stiff and stone-faced like a warrior, a tic in Blake's jaw was the only indication of his angst.

Whatever Captain Ricu had planned for them, it couldn't be good. Pirates jerked them from the boat and hauled them through tumbling waves onto dry sand. With a snap of his fingers, Ricu sent several of them marching toward the colonists' camp.

Hayden's heart stopped. Beside him, Blake's breath came hard and rapid.

Captain Ricu took up a pompous pace. "Since you not know to behave. Since I cannot trust you, I take what is most precious to you."

Hayden's mouth dried. He had nothing precious but Magnolia.

Within moments, women's screams pierced the night. Both he and Blake started forward, but the tips of two swords held them back.

"Now you listen. Now you behave." Ricu grinned.

"Please, Captain," Blake's voice came out in a desperate growl. "They had nothing to do with this. Punish us. Not them."

Heart in his throat, Hayden squinted into the darkness where the pirates took form, dragging two women across the sand, one with brown hair, one with flaxen.

"Leave them be!" Batting aside the blade and ignoring the pain slicing his hand, Hayden charged forward with one thought in mind: kill the man who handled his wife so harshly. But he only made it a step when something hard struck his head. He toppled to the sand, barely conscious.

Conscious enough to hear Magnolia scream and the captain's glum pronouncement:

"I take your wives prisoner aboard the *Espoliar*."

CHAPTER 30

Y ou can't go." James clasped Angeline's hands. "The pirates may not allow you to return."

Violet eyes, moist with tears yet sparking with defiance, raised to his. "They are my friends. The only friends I've ever had." She swallowed as the rising sun highlighted the smattering of adorable freckles on her nose. "If Captain Ricu is allowing me to bring them food and see how they fare, how can I refuse?" She squeezed his hand then released it. "I *know* you understand."

Of course he understood. If Ricu would allow him to go, he'd row out to the *Espoliar* in a second. "I still can't believe you talked him into it." James had seen her speaking to the flamboyant pirate yesterday evening after supper. A brief conversation in which Angeline did most of the talking and Ricu did most of the staring, giving her a look as if he wished to swat her away like one of the sand fleas that inhabited the beach. By the time James was halfway there to rescue the foolish woman, Ricu had shrugged and walked away while Angeline turned to face James, a smug look on her face.

"I had merely to mention his lady's name and how he would wish someone to care for her should she find herself in such a predicament."

"You have that pirate wrapped around your finger." He eased a lock of her hair behind her ear, constantly amazed by this woman. "But what else would I expect?"

She smiled. "By a tenuous thread, I assure you."

"All the more reason not to deliver yourself into his hands," James growled. It had been two days since Eliza and Magnolia had been imprisoned aboard the ship, and everyone in camp was overwrought with worry. Each evening Blake and Hayden had returned bone-weary and bruised from the tunnels where Ricu had dragged them as part of their punishment. Unable to sleep or even to eat, both men spent the night pacing the beach in frustration while dipping their heads in secret plans to rescue their wives. Yet after contemplating a thousand scenarios, nothing seemed feasible. Nothing that wouldn't put their wives in more danger, and risk all the colonists' lives. The worst part—James knew from experience—was imagining what Captain Ricu and his men were doing to Magnolia and Eliza. Though Angeline tried to comfort them with hopeful words of Ricu's desire to change, Blake and Hayden suffered immensely, their haggard faces reflecting the torture they felt within. Captain Ricu was far smarter than James had given him credit for. Sure, he could have killed Hayden and Blake on the spot, but that might have caused the rest of the colonists to rise up in rebellion. This way, Ricu kept them all in check on the threat of hurting two of the colony's favored women.

A breeze tossed a curl across Angeline's shoulder as she squinted at the *Espoliar* rocking offshore, the golden sun rising behind its stark masts. "I will be all right, James. Don't worry."

Yet *she* was worried. He saw it in the tightness around her mouth, in the way she bit her bottom lip. "I can't lose you," he said.

"You won't." She tried to smile.

"You stand barely above five feet tall, and you forget you don't have your pistol anymore."

"I haven't forgotten." She frowned as if she truly did miss the weapon. "What good would it do against a dozen pirates, anyway?" She gave a little shrug.

"That is exactly what I am saying!" James said.

Which only made her smile all the more. She brushed sand from his shirt. "Is this our first squabble?"

"No."

She seemed to ponder that for a minute. "Indeed, I fear you are correct. We've had many before. Are we to spend our entire courtship quarreling?"

"Not if you stop being so stubborn."

"Hmm. I'm not sure that's possible."

"Something we agree on at last." He grinned.

She reached up to caress his jaw. "There are many others, I'm sure."

When she touched him like she was doing now, James believed he'd agree with anything she said. "We'll have a lifetime to discover our many areas of agreement." He placed his hand atop hers but suddenly frowned. "That is, if you don't go getting yourself killed by pirates."

She smiled. "I better go." Bending, she picked up the sack at her feet containing fruit, smoked fish, and a few of Eliza and Magnolia's personal items then headed toward the cockboat where Blake and Hayden waited to see her off.

James followed after her. *Mule-headed, reckless woman!* The frayed hem of her emerald skirt sashayed back and forth over the sand as she marched dauntless into unknown danger.

Courageous, beautiful woman.

Angling a wide circle around Hayden as if he had a disease, she stopped to speak to Blake before she allowed the pirates to assist her into the craft.

Captain Ricu appeared at the railing, doffing his red-feathered hat in his usual colorful greeting, but his eyes were on Angeline approaching in the boat.

"If he lays one finger on her!" James huffed and kicked the sand then glanced up at Hayden and Blake, their sullen gazes glued to the ship.

"Forgive me, I'm being thoughtless." When he should have been comforting his friends, he was the one demanding comfort. Once again, he'd failed as a preacher.

Blake slapped him on the back. "We will all feel better when Angeline returns with a good report."

If she returns. He watched as the pirates assisted her up the rope ladder and then over the railing, where she disappeared from sight. *Please, God, watch over her.*

⤙⟡⤚

Not since her father had been alive had anyone cared whether Angeline lived or died. James's raw emotion, so often worn on his sleeve—and one of the things she loved about him—had kept her warm all the way out to the ship. Kept her legs moving even now as Captain Ricu, after sifting through the contents of her bag, escorted her below. The massive man smelled of port, gunpowder, and tobacco. He repeatedly glanced over his shoulder at her, licking his lips as one would when selecting a choice cut of meat for supper.

Angeline had met men like him—men far more prolific in stature than brains. Men who, decked in garish pretention, swaggered their authority about in order to mask a wavering confidence within. To say she was not frightened would be a lie. Her jittery stomach was evidence of that. But to say she couldn't handle herself with such men would also be a lie. She had proven that already with this particular man. But would the allure of his lady-love's approval continue to restrain his nefarious passions? That was the question that had her heart in a knot.

"You no bigger than sprite." He guffawed. "A bela sprite, I say."

"But I should warn you, Captain, this sprite has a vicious bite."

At that, he swung around, his frame filling the narrow hallway. Two lanterns creaked as they swayed from hooks on the walls, their shifting light barely chasing away the gloom. The pirate behind her bumped into her, but Angeline steadied her thrashing heart and stood her ground. Instead of striking her as she expected, Ricu laughed, a deep husky laugh that bounced over the bulkheads like thunder. "I bet you have bite, little one." He turned and continued down a ladder. Hoisting the sack over her shoulder, she tried her best to navigate the rungs as carefully as possible while holding her breath against a stink that would send even the staunchest sailor reeling. The last thing she wanted was to slip and tumble down on top of the man.

"Perhaps we try your bite soon." Ricu stopped at the bottom and held up his lantern. Maniacal threads of light twisted across his face as eyes as dark as onyx assessed her.

The pirate behind her chuckled.

Angeline resisted the urge to kick him in the groin. "Where are my friends?" she demanded.

Grunting, he jerked the lantern to his right. "Faro will show." Then turning to the rotund pirate behind him, who had more hair on his chin than his head, Ricu spouted off a string of Portuguese before climbing up the ladder with a groan as if every step caused him pain.

Down the hall, the pirate unlocked a door, shoved Angeline inside, and slammed it shut. A squeal of delight etched across Angeline's ears before arms surrounded her in a strong embrace. *Eliza*. Or at least Angeline thought it was Eliza in the darkness, for the woman could embrace like no other. She could also grip quite hard as she shook Angeline's shoulders. "What are you doing here?" Her tone had turned from delight to anger.

Finally her face came into focus as Angeline's eyes grew accustomed to the shadows. Muted light drifted in through a tiny porthole near the deckhead, offering the only reprieve from the gloom. A pile of sailcloth was stacked against the bulkhead on the left. Beside it, a chamber pot fumed from the corner. Atop the rickety table hooked to the wall sat an empty pewter plate and an old book. Two chairs framed it, providing the only place to sit, aside from the narrow cot on her right—the cot from which Magnolia now rose. The Southern belle flung an arm around Angeline's waist and squeezed. "How fares Hayden, Blake, and everyone else?" The woman's attempt to keep her tone light failed as desperation rang in her voice.

"Everyone is well. Tormented with worry, but well. How are you both?" Angeline squinted to see her friends in the shadows and, thankfully, saw no cuts or bruises, nor additional tears to their already tattered gowns. "The pirates haven't. . .they haven't. . ."

"No," Eliza said. "Not yet, anyway."

Magnolia hugged herself. "That beastly captain drags both of us to his cabin each night and then just sits there staring at us while he drinks his brandy."

Relief settled over Angeline. "That's good news. He's keeping you from the other pirates as well."

Eliza drew a ragged breath. "I fear one of these nights he will drink too much and forget about this woman you say he loves."

Angeline feared the same. The ship teetered over a swell, creaking in complaint. Balancing her feet on the deck, she flung the sack on the table. "I brought gifts." Opening the pouch, she pulled out the fruit and fish and set them on the plate, then reaching back into the sack, she withdrew a small wooden object and handed it to Magnolia. "Hayden said this would bring you comfort." Though Angeline couldn't imagine why. What woman preferred a carving of a toad over fresh underthings or soap or a hairbrush? But as soon as Magnolia saw it, she clutched it to her chest, her blue eyes pooling.

"He also said he loves you very much and bids you be strong."

Brushing aside a tear, Magnolia nodded, her face beaming with such intense emotion, Angeline looked away. That same emotion, a desperate longing, now burned in Eliza's eyes—so unusual for the stalwart woman—as her gaze shifted to the sack.

"And Blake sent this." Angeline pulled out a Georgia Army belt plate, which Eliza gobbled up in her hands as if it were made of gold. "Strange gifts, if you ask me."

"Not strange at all." Eliza pressed the belt plate to her chest. "This is Blake's most prized possession. I'm surprised he risked it falling into the pirates' hands."

"He told me to tell you that he would have sent his heart, but you are already in possession." At the time, Angeline had thought the phrase too sentimental and trite for the staunch colonel to say, but now as she repeated the words and saw their reaction on Eliza's face, she knew it had been the perfect message.

Eliza laughed and cried at the same time, and Angeline wondered if she'd ever share such an incredible bond with James.

"I can't believe Captain Ricu allowed you to come." Eliza finally gathered her emotions, still staring at the belt plate, but then her gaze snapped to Angeline. "You aren't a prisoner too, are you?"

"Possibly."

"You risked too much." Magnolia sat in one of the chairs, the toad still cradled in her hands.

"Not too much for my friends," Angeline replied. "Besides, Hayden and Blake would go utterly mad if they didn't hear word of your well-being."

"I fear I will go mad if I do not see my husband soon." Magnolia sighed. "Please tell us you bring word the pirates will release us soon."

Captain Ricu's voice bellowed from above decks, followed by the stomping of feet. Angeline bit her lip. "I wish I could, but I have no idea."

"It doesn't matter." Golden light from the window oscillated over Eliza with the sway of the ship. "God told me we will soon be returned to the colony."

Magnolia lowered her chin. "I wish I could believe that."

"I have faith for us both, Magnolia." Eliza knelt before her friend and gazed up at her. "We *will* get out of here."

Angeline wasn't so sure. How could God speak to people? He was way up in heaven and, obviously, completely unaware of what was happening here on earth. But it would do no good to shatter her friends' hopeful illusions.

Rising, Eliza faced Angeline. "But you. You shouldn't have come."

Angeline shrugged. "Even if they keep me here, I deserve it more than either of you."

"Why would you say such a thing?"

Unaccustomed to the wobbling deck, Angeline lowered onto the other chair. She was so tired of keeping secrets, pretending to be someone she was not. "You think you know me, but you don't. I've done terrible things."

"I doubt that," Eliza said.

"It's true."

"Whether it is or not, the past no longer matters." Magnolia reached for her across the table. "God has forgiven you."

Had He? Angeline hadn't asked Him for forgiveness. Mainly because she wasn't sure He would give it, but also because if she was honest, she was angry at God for what had happened to her. "Perhaps I haven't forgiven *Him*," she said. "He hasn't been very kind to me. Why did He allow my father to die? Allow me to become—" She stopped. "Allow all the horrid things that happened afterward."

"Did you ever ask Him?" Eliza said. "Did you ever seek His will during those difficult times?"

Angeline shook her head.

Eliza sank to the cot and stared at the belt plate. "I fear we are very much alike, Angeline. I spent most of my life making my own decisions, going my own way, thinking I didn't need God. I wanted to live my life without anyone telling me what to do. And I made such a mess of things. I caused myself and a lot of people tremendous pain."

Angeline studied her friend. Eliza caused people pain? Unlikely. At least not the enormous amount of pain Angeline had caused. Tugging her father's ring from beneath her bodice, she fingered the beautiful jewels. "I assumed God didn't care what happened to me. He wasn't there when I became an orphan, when my uncle tried to. . ."—she gazed at her friends, who both stared back with such loving eyes, she couldn't help but continue—"ravish me."

Magnolia raised a hand to her mouth. Eliza remained silent, listening.

Waves rustled against the hull.

"What happened?" Magnolia asked.

"I ended up begging on the street." Angeline hugged herself and stared at the stained deck. "I became a trollop." There, she'd finally said it. The words floated through air thick with stink and steam before the weight of their shame plunged them to the deck. Wind whistled against the window. The ship canted to the left. Angeline cursed herself for a fool. Why, oh why had she said anything? She could feel Magnolia and Eliza's eyes piercing her—eyes, no doubt, filled with disdain and disgust. She couldn't bear it another minute. Rising, she clutched her skirts and started for the door, intending to bang upon it until the pirates released her.

Magnolia grabbed her hand before she took a step. "God was there with you."

Eliza blocked Angeline's path. "There and loving you as He is now."

Overcome by the concern on their faces, tears filled Angeline's eyes. "With me? God was with me? Then why did He allow me to become. . .what I became?"

"You never asked Him for help," Eliza said. "God hated what your uncle did to you, but afterward, I know He was there waiting to love and help you. But it sounds like you ran away from Him instead. You wouldn't allow Him in your life. How can you blame Him now for the choices you made?"

Tugging from Magnolia's grip, Angeline swept past her friends.

"I don't mean to be cruel, Angeline," Eliza continued, spinning to face her. "Just honest. It will do no good for me to placate you with comforts or flatter you with kind words that don't get to the root of the problem. Life is cruel. Terrible things happen, but it's how we react that matters. It's who we run to for help that makes all the difference."

Like a sharp knife, the words sliced through Angeline's heart, leaving a winding trail of pain and shame. She backed away from her friends until she struck the hard bulkhead. Could her life have been different if she'd turned to God, begged for His help? Would He have answered her? Taken care of her?

The ship creaked and groaned, mimicking her tormented conscience. Eliza and Magnolia gazed at her with nothing but love and concern. Not disgust. Not repulsion. Not condemnation. Her throat burned. Her vision blurred. Shock sent her thoughts whirling. Shame for her own stupidity gutted her. She wobbled, and instantly her friends led her back to the chair.

Magnolia sat beside her. "Ask His forgiveness and start anew. I did. And it has changed everything."

Angeline couldn't argue with that. Just months ago, Magnolia had been nothing but a spoiled, vain, selfish lady. Yet, here she sat, imprisoned on a pirate ship, concerning herself with Angeline. Giving hardly a thought to her own predicament.

Maybe God could do that for Angeline. Change her. Make her new. Maybe He *had* been with her the whole time. A tiny spark of hope pushed away the blackness in her soul. . .like a match struck in a dark room. "You aren't shocked, appalled, disgusted?"

"Hardly," Eliza said. "We've all done horrible things."

"But this. . ."

"Is no worse than my selfishness." Magnolia rose. "Or my vanity, pride, or boorishness."

"Or my rebellion, stubbornness, and independence," Eliza added.

Angeline smiled and sobbed at the same time. "I'm so sorry." She wiped moisture from her face. "I came to comfort you, and here I speak only of my own problems."

"It's quite all right." Magnolia shrugged and shared a smile with Eliza. "What else have we to do?"

"Perhaps this is why God allowed us to be brought here," Eliza said. "Just to have this talk with you. In that case, it is worth it."

Angeline's throat clogged with emotion even as her heart seemed to swell. This was certainly not the reaction she'd expected from her friends—not the reaction she usually received from proper women. Would God equally surprise her with His response? Warm arms enveloped her as both Eliza and Magnolia pulled her into an embrace. All three ladies stood teetering with the rolling deck, crying and laughing and encouraging one another until the clank of lock and key jarred them from their camaraderie and the entrance of Captain Ricu separated them. With narrowed eyes and a grunt, he dragged Angeline from the cabin.

"Thank you for allowing me to visit my friends, Captain," Angeline remarked as he led her through the narrow hallway.

His only reply was another grunt.

"And I also thank you for not harming them. Your lady—*Senhorita* Abelena was it?—would be pleased."

He wheeled around, his coiled black mane swinging about him, his eyes darts in the dim lantern light. The hall closed in on Angeline, and for a moment she'd thought she'd lured the mad pirate out from hiding. But then his shoulders lowered and he breathed out a sigh.

"I run out of rum to keep men happy. Soon they will want their turn."

"Then release the women, Captain. Their husbands have suffered enough for their crimes."

"Humph." Turning, he continued up a ladder to the main deck where a blast of wind flapped Angeline's skirts and swept away the foul smell from below.

His gaze took in the open sea as if he longed to be as free from Brazil as some of the colonists were.

"You can't fool me, Captain," she said, risking his anger but sensing something in his eyes.

He snorted and faced her.

She pointed toward his chest. "There's a heart growing in there. You *are* changing." She leaned toward him and whispered, "But your secret is safe with me."

"Beware your words to me, bela sprite. I am still Captain Ricu, and I take what I want when I want!" He spat the words with venom, but there was no sting in his eyes as he shoved her toward his waiting men who assisted her into the boat below.

Somewhere between ship and sand, as the waves struck the small craft, showering her in mist, as the rising sun sprinkled her in gold dust, Angeline whispered her first prayer to God in years. Just a quick "hello" to see if He was listening. A tingling began deep within her. A burst of light. A flood of love raced through her veins, pumping them full of life. By the time she met Blake, Hayden, and James ashore, she could hardly think, could hardly form a coherent thought.

No sooner had she reassured them of their wives' safety than Ricu and his men hauled them off to dig in the tunnels. The rest of the day went by in a blur as Angeline's mind and heart whirled with thoughts of God, of being loved by her Creator. Excusing herself from supper, she retired early. But she couldn't find sleep. How could anyone sleep with such a glorious feeling bubbling up inside? All warmth and love and peace and protection. Angels' songs called to her in the night, celebrating, rejoicing, inviting her to a feast.

It was the voice of her heavenly Father welcoming her home.

Tears dampening her cheeks like the water dampened her bare toes, she strolled among the waves till well past midnight, one minute begging for forgiveness, the next laughing and singing, and the next dancing through the lacy foam, until, exhausted, she finally dropped to the sand and fell deep asleep.

She dreamed she was a princess captured by an evil magician who had imprisoned her in a dark dungeon for years and years. But one day a prince came. White-robed, with gleaming sword in hand, He stormed the fortress, fought for her, and loosed the shackles that bound her hands and feet, drawing her from the dungeon into the light. She shrank back, ashamed of the filth that covered her. The prince drew her close. She resisted. How could she allow someone so clean and beautiful to touch her grime and muck? He persisted, and finally she fell into His embrace. Instantly, the dirt cracked as if made of dried clay and fell off her, piece by piece, until she stood wearing the white robe of a princess.

A light pierced her eyelids, flooding them with gold.

She slowly opened her eyes to see the edge of the sun arc above the sea. She was clean. Clean at last! She chuckled. All these years, she'd never wanted to trust anyone, never wanted anyone to rescue her. But as it turned out, she needed God to sweep in and save her most of all. And He *had* rescued her. In every possible way.

Rising to sit, she drew a deep breath of the salty air and allowed the gentle breeze to finger through her hair. She'd never felt so free, so light, so loved. *Thank You, Father. Thank You!*

No more bad memories, no more guilt. No more lies. She must tell James. Regardless of the consequences, she could not continue their courtship without telling him the truth. He was a man of God, after all. Surely he would understand.

CHAPTER 31

James lifted the basket toward Angeline. She dropped an orange inside. He'd been thrilled when he'd spotted her climbing over the railing of the ship yesterday. He'd been more thrilled to find her unharmed when she returned to shore, bearing a good report from Eliza and Magnolia. And he'd been equally thrilled when she'd invited him to accompany her this morning to scavenge for fruit. She rarely enlisted his help for much of anything, especially something as easy as picking fruit. Which could only mean that she enjoyed his company and she was serious about their courtship. Maybe this time she wouldn't change her mind and push him away. The thought put a smile on his face as he watched her scour the low-hanging branches. Rays of morning sun cut through the canopy and formed ribbons of shimmering ruby in her hair as her graceful arms reached to pick a mango. Standing on tiptoe like a ballerina, she cast an alluring smile at him over her shoulder.

Yet there was something even more alluring about her today. A lightness to her step, an unusual joy on her face. Was there ever a more innocent and chaste lady? She was the perfect woman for him. And he thanked God every day for allowing him to court her, to hopefully marry her one day. Soon, if he had his way of things.

"When you were on the ship, did Captain Ricu say anything about Eliza and Magnolia's release?" He raised his voice above a particularly loud burst of squawking coming from the canopy.

"No, but I do have a feeling it will be soon." She glanced up at a pair of blue and green macaws who seemed to be scolding them for trespassing. Stowy leapt on the tree trunk beside her and started toward them.

"I hope you're right." James pointed at a papaya hanging from a high branch to their right. "I'll get this one." He plucked the fruit, dropping it in the basket, then met her gaze. A shadow crossed her violet eyes, a momentary hesitation before she smiled and continued onward.

Perhaps she thought about the pirate gold and the fourth beast and what would happen to them should it be released. Something James never ceased to fret over. Though he'd recently tried interpreting more of the Hebrew book, his progress was slow. Ever since Ricu had taken Eliza and Magnolia aboard his ship, James had trouble keeping focused. And Blake and Hayden had been so consumed with getting their wives back unscathed, they'd all but forgotten why they'd gone after the gunpowder in the first place.

Or perhaps the beasts, the angelic battle, the prison alcoves, and fire lake were all just silly myths from an ancient book and none of it was real. He ran his hand through his hair and sighed. On days like today, when he hadn't seen a vision in a week, when the sun was shining and the birds were singing and his heart burst with love for Angeline, it was easy to entertain a smidgeon of doubt about the supernatural war they found themselves entangled in. Perhaps the disasters were just that, disasters. Perhaps Graves had been murdered by a *bandido*. Perhaps the visions were caused by bad water, as Hayden had inferred.

But James knew that wasn't true.

Still, he didn't want to think about it now. For the moment, he was strolling through a lush jungle with the woman he loved, serenaded by an orchestra of birds and breathing air fragranced with sweet orchids. He would allow himself this bit of pleasure.

The gurgle of water drew them to a brook tumbling playfully over rocks. Setting the basket down, he squatted and cupped water to his mouth. Fresh and cool, it soothed his throat as he splashed some on the back of his neck. Angeline knelt beside him and did the same then flicked droplets at his shirt, giggling.

He cocked a brow and shook his wet hand in her direction. Drops sparkled like diamonds in her hair and on her skin, making her look even more angelic—if possible. She feigned indignation and sprayed him again. They continued for several minutes, laughing and showering each other until water dribbled from their chins and hair. An odd, wonderful feeling bloomed within James and began to swell through every inch of him. Something he had never felt before—happiness. Not only happiness at the moment but hope for many more happy moments with this precious woman.

Stowy jumped onto the pebbly bank and began batting at tiny bugs floating in the stream.

"I'm glad you invited me to come along. I was so worried about you yesterday." James kissed the water from her lips, drawing in a deep breath of her coconut scent. Circling a hand around her back, he pressed in for more when she nudged him away. Her sad smile dissipated the gaiety of the moment like the water drying on her skin. "I need to speak to you about something, James."

"Sounds serious."

"It is." She flattened her lips, those luscious lips he'd just kissed and longed to do so again.

He sat back on a rock, leveling his elbows atop his knees. "Very well." The look on her face caused his gut to clench as she picked up Stowy and stroked the cat's fur.

"It's something about my past that you should know before. . ." —she glanced at the stream—"before we continue courting."

Relief washed over him. Whatever sin she'd committed, it couldn't be worse than what he'd done. Perhaps she had lied, cheated, even stole something. Though he doubted such an angel could even do that. "Whatever it is—"

"Let me tell you, please." She drew a deep breath and bit her lip. "There's no polite way to say this, James." Her eyes misted, and she glanced down.

James reached for her hand, hating to see her so distraught. "There's no need to tell me."

"Yes, there is." She met his gaze, wiped a tear from her cheek, and swallowed hard. "I was a prostitute."

The word spun gibberish in James's ear before the breeze carried it away. "If that was meant as a joke, I don't find it amusing in the least."

Yet he found no teasing, no humor, in her eyes—eyes that had dried to a hard sheen.

He stared at her, unable to process what she'd just said. It bounced around in his head like some intoxicated balloon.

"It was only for a short while, a little over a year," she continued, looking away. "I was cast out on the street. I had no food, no home, no means of support. I would have died, James." She searched his eyes, pain and hope screaming from her own.

But he had gone numb. Finally the balloon struck the tip of his reason and popped. Jerking away from her, he punched to his feet, his heart imploding. Shock became anger. Anger became disgust. All three stormed through him like the horsemen of the apocalypse, trampling everything in their path. His reason, his sympathy. . .

His love.

Releasing Stowy, Angeline slowly stood, fear appearing on her face for the first time.

James wiped the back of his hand over his lips and spit. He'd kissed her! A tramp! "I thought you were a lady." His voice came out strangled. "I thought you were pure and innocent."

Pain scoured her eyes. "Are any of us really innocent, James? Are you?"

"I never sold my virtue to strangers for money. I never sold my soul to the devil!"

Feminine laughter drew his gaze over Angeline's shoulder to Tabitha, sashaying about the clearing, her lips upturned in a coy smile. *Of all the times for a vision!* Ignoring her, he glanced back at Angeline, whose expression had sunk into that look that had become so familiar to James during the war. The same look that had appeared on many a soldier's face when James had told them they wouldn't make it through the night.

"Is that what you think of me?" Angeline asked, her voice barely a whisper. "That I am allied with Satan?"

"What am I to think? You led me to believe. . .you accepted my courtship, knowing what you were. . ."

"What I *was*, yes. And what I am no longer." Strength permeated her trembling voice, and James looked away, unable to bear the sight of her—the thought of her with another man.

Many men.

"I'm sorry to have bothered you, Mr. Callaway." Her voice came

239

out wooden. Turning, she started to leave. He gripped her wrist. She winced and tugged from him, tearing her sleeve, exposing the scar on her arm.

"This scar. It's a knife wound." He grabbed her again. "Who did this to you?"

"A man."

"What man?"

She met his gaze. "One of my clients, if you must know. Turns out he preferred to slice women rather than enjoy them." Her breath came heavy. Her lip trembled, but she stood her ground.

He wanted to feel sorry for her, wanted to consider how horrible her life had been, but he was too angry. Everything was starting to make sense. Her aversion to being touched, the pistol she used to carry around, the distance she kept. It wasn't because she was chaste and timid around men. It was quite the opposite. He felt sick to his stomach.

And to make matters worse, she merely stood there with shoulders drawn back and chin stiff. Not dissolving in shame, not begging his forgiveness, and not even lashing at him in anger. Which only increased his fury.

How could she have deceived him? How could she have allowed their courtship? Heat raged through him, tightening his jaw and forming sweat on his neck. He'd come to Brazil to escape women like her, to start a new society without the immorality and decay they caused. And then he fell in love with the only prostitute on the journey! What was wrong with him? "Do you know what women like you have done to me?" He tightened his grip. "Ruined me! Tore my life from me. Made me a failure." And caused his father's death. But he wouldn't tell her that.

She raised her chin. "It seems to me, Doctor, that you give a great deal of power to women who, in your assessment, possess none at all."

Tabitha giggled. "Oh, touché, my dear. She's good, James. I must say, I'm growing quite fond of her."

"Shut up!" James shouted at the insidious vision.

"I'd be happy to if you'd kindly release me." Angeline yanked from his grasp. Stowy circled her skirts, looking as if he would pounce on James.

"I wasn't talking to you." James let go of her wrist, his frustration at the boiling point. He waved a hand at her. "Go."

Angeline glanced around the clearing, wondering who else was present, then took a step back from James, rubbing her wrist. Inside, a storm of agony raged. Outside, she maintained control. She'd learned that useful skill during her time working in a brothel. She'd also learned how to deal with enraged men. She should leave as he'd ordered. Yet he looked so distraught, so lost. And all because of her lies.

James took up a pace. "I trusted you. You knew how I felt about immoral women."

"Which is why I didn't tell you until now." She drew a breath for strength. "And I am no longer immoral. I am forgiven. As a man of God you should know that and forgive me too."

"Don't you dare"—he pointed a finger at her—"Don't you speak of God to me." His bronze eyes hardened. "Women like you know nothing of God. Women like you lure men to their deaths."

Angeline's heart crumbled to dust. She had expected shock, perhaps a bit of disgust, but she hadn't expected hatred. *Oh, Father, help me. Please help me cope with this pain*, she breathed a silent prayer as all her dreams of happiness shriveled beneath the rage spewing from James's lips. . .from his eyes.

"I will lure you no further, sir." She took another step back, intending to leave, when he grabbed her shoulders and shoved his mouth onto hers. Forcing her body against his, he clutched bunches of her hair and kissed her rough and angry, not loving and gentle as before. Agony screamed within his groans. She shoved her hands against his chest, trying to free herself, but he was too strong.

He withdrew, his breath stinging her face. "Is that the way you like it, Angeline? Is this what your clients did to you?" His voice bit like a viper.

He released her and stepped back, shame flooding his eyes before he turned and wiped his lips as if her taste was poison.

Angeline couldn't breathe. Couldn't feel her legs, her arms. Darting to the water, she scooped up Stowy and stumbled from the clearing, tears finally pouring down her cheeks.

James stayed in the clearing until the sun set. Ignoring the taunts flung his way from Tabitha and Abigail, he dropped to the sandy dirt and stared at the water flowing past, dashing over rocks and plummeting into troughs, sparkling when the sun alighted on it and turning ashen when clouds hovered overhead. On and on it flowed, no matter the obstacle, no matter whether the sun shone or gloom set in. Much like life. Or was it? For he felt as if the obstacle before him was much too large for him to ever get past.

He stayed in the clearing because he couldn't move. Whether it was rage or fear or despair that kept his legs locked, he didn't know. Perhaps it was shame. Shame for the way he'd treated Angeline. Shame for the things he'd said. For the way he'd forced his kiss on her. The thought of her allowing men to grope her, touch her—bed her—had ignited a rage in him he could not control. Something dark and evil had come over him, shoving aside all decency. But he wouldn't blame some unseen force. He wouldn't blame anyone but himself.

Once again he'd been played a fool by a beautiful woman. Once again, he'd given his heart only to have the vixen tear it to shreds and destroy his life in the process.

A chill came over him as the sun sank behind the trees and shadows crept through the jungle, stealing the light. Finally he rose and trudged back to the beach. But instead of joining the others, he borrowed some rum from one of the colonists and made his way beyond the cliffs to a private section of beach. Hours later when the night was spent and the sky spun around him, he toppled backward in the sand. The last thing he heard before he drifted into a welcome oblivion was the eerie howl of a wolf.

He was on a ship. The smell of salt and fish swirled about him as he balanced on the swaying deck. There was peace out at sea. In the purl of the waves, the creak of the ship, the endless horizon, the snap of sails that sped the ship on its course far away—far away from all life's problems. James allowed that peace to roll over him as sunlight stroked his eyelids with warmth.

But then it was gone. The light, the warmth. Even the scent of the sea had turned putrid, metallic. He opened his eyes, gripped the railing, and glanced over endless swells of dark red—*blood* red. Panic sent his thoughts spinning. He barreled down the foredeck ladder. "Is anyone here? Hello!" But the ship was empty. Only a single rat scampered across the deck and disappeared below. A grating sound drew his gaze to the ship's wheel spinning in its casing as if directed by some maniacal sailor.

James sped to the railing again. Blood clawed the hull, maroon fingers reaching for him. His stomach convulsed and he wretched its contents into the sea. Hanging over the bulwarks, he gasped for air, his heart thumping in his chest. Lightning arched a white blade across the sky. In the distance, a gaping darkness loomed on the horizon. No, it wasn't darkness at all, but rather a complete absence of light. Like a hole in the universe that sucked everything, including the earth and sea, into its black void.

And the ship was heading straight for it.

Dashing onto the quarterdeck, James grabbed the gyrating wheel and struggled to keep it steady, but it leapt from his hands and spun wildly, first to the right and then to the left. A *meow* shot his gaze up to see Stowy perched atop the binnacle, wind tossing his black fur while his amber eyes stared off the bow.

A scream penetrated the rush of wind. James leaned over the starboard railing to see a small boat just ahead of the ship filled with people. Grabbing a telescope, he leveled it upon the craft. His heart sank. His friends. Blake, Eliza, Magnolia, Hayden, and Angeline sat in the dinghy, gripping the thwarts, fear blaring from their eyes. Blake and Hayden rowed and rowed, their faces sweaty and red, but the boat continued to drift toward the darkness. Angeline stared at James. Struggling to stand, Magnolia waved her arms. "Help us! Save us, James. Save us!"

Panic sent him racing across the deck, seeking another boat he could lower. There were none. He tried to stop the wheel again but to no avail. A rope. There must be a rope. He found one coiled by the foremast. But what could he do with a rope?

One thing he knew. If he didn't get to his friends in time, they'd fall off the edge of the earth and be swallowed up in darkness. And in that tiny boat, they would never survive.

"James!" Someone gripped his shoulder. "James, wake up!"

But he didn't want to wake up. He had to save his friends. He swatted away the offending hands and moaned, "Leave me alone."

"It's Blake. Get up." But it wasn't Blake's voice. It was Hayden's. James pried his eyes open, immediately sorry he did. Sunlight pierced straight through them and stabbed his brain with a dozen hot pokers. Pain radiated down his back into every limb. He blinked, and Hayden's face came into view.

"Get it together, man. We need you." Urgency branded Hayden's tone.

"Bother someone else. I was having a perfectly good nightmare."

Clutching his arm, Hayden pulled James to sit. His stomach did a flip, and something foul-tasting flooded his throat. "What on earth is the matter?"

"It's Blake. He's been attacked by a wolf."

CHAPTER 32

Blood bubbled from Blake's side where fangs had torn flesh and muscle from bone. Despite Angeline and Sarah's furious efforts to restrain the life-giving fluid, it dripped onto the pallet, sliding over bamboo and soaking into the sand beneath. James sped from the shelter and heaved into the bushes—only the third time since Hayden had woken him twenty minutes ago. Of all the nights to drink to excess. . .something he hadn't done since he'd recommitted his life to God.

Hayden slapped him on the back, not a friendly smack, but one that harbored a threat in its sting. "Get in there and do something. Now."

James glanced over his shoulder at the women hovering over Blake then at the crowd of worried colonists swarming the front of the makeshift clinic. Thiago, Delia and her children, even the Scotts and their slave, Mable. Others too, nearly the entire colony, save those men Ricu had dragged to the tunnels.

James faced the bushes again, air vacating his lungs until he could barely breathe. "We must get Eliza and Magnolia from the ship."

Clutching his shoulders, Hayden jerked him around. Dark strands of hair wavered over fierce green eyes that pierced James's very soul. "We can't. You have to do this. *You* have to save him."

Sarah approached and touched his arm. "You are the only one who can, James."

Angeline glanced up from where she pressed a bundle of rags to Blake's wound, her eyes hollow and distant. He stared at her, wondering how she could even look at him after the way he'd treated

245

her—wondering how he could even look at her. Yet, he couldn't seem to pull his gaze away. A spark of pleading penetrated the distance between them and went straight for his heart.

James rubbed the scar on his cheek and cursed under his breath. *NO! I can't do this, God. Why have You put me in this situation—again?* Visions of his father lying in a puddle of blood burst into James's mind, reminding him that no matter how much he'd wanted to save him, he'd been unable to move. Or even breathe. And his father had died in his arms. What would make this time any different? Lowering his chin, he squeezed his eyes shut, searching for another solution, someone who could perform the surgery, anyone with enough skills to follow his command. But there was no one. No one but him.

And he could not let his best friend die.

God, please don't let me fail. He drew a deep breath, opened his eyes, and lifted his hands before him. They trembled like leaves in a storm. His eyes met Hayden's.

"God can calm the storm," was all the man said before dragging James back to Blake's side.

James pressed a hand on his roiling stomach and stiffened his jaw. "I need boiling water, needle and sutures, clamps, a strong lantern, plenty of clean rags, and any alcohol you can find." He snapped stern eyes to Hayden. "Steal it from the pirates if you have to."

Hayden gave an approving nod and sped off.

From the outskirts of the shelter, Thiago crossed himself. "I hope Lobisón not bite him."

"Surely you don't believe that nonsense anymore," Sarah chastised him as she gathered a pile of clean rags. Without looking at James, Angeline found scissors, clamps, needles, and sutures and laid them all neatly on a tray.

Thiago lifted one shoulder. "I believe there is still evil in world, yes?"

"Indeed." James swallowed, trying to settle his nerves, still not looking at Blake's wound. Evil he could deal with. But blood?

"What can we do to help?" Mrs. Jenkins shouted.

Sarah exchanged a glance with James before turning to answer. "Pray."

"Now, if you please, I need room to operate without a dozen eyes upon me." Though the colonists were at least four yards away, James felt as though he stood in the center of a courtroom, surrounded by accusers. And he, on trial for his life. His pulse throbbed. Sweat slid down his chest.

The crowd retreated, but only inches, as Angeline placed the last instrument on the tray. Her hand quivered.

"Can you handle this?" James asked her.

Violet eyes assessed him. "Can *you*?"

He flattened his lips as Hayden returned with a bottle of rum. "The pirates left it on the beach."

Blake coughed. Blood trickled from his lips. At least he had lost consciousness. James couldn't be sure he wouldn't do the same. He released a ragged sigh, concentrating on the crash of waves, the soothing chorus of myriad birds, not on the hammer of his heart and the tremble in his hands.

"James." Angeline gazed up at him, her hands pressed on blood-drenched cloths. "I can't stop the bleeding. He's growing pale."

"Do something!" Hayden's shout stiffened every nerve. Bracing himself, James nodded for Angeline to remove the rags then lowered his gaze to the gaping wound. A mass of mangled flesh stared back at him. Broken ribs floated atop a pool of blood, where it appeared a pulmonary vein had been nicked. Blake didn't have much time before he bled out. *God in heaven, help me. I can't do this without You.*

Can a lady admire a man who broke her heart into a million pieces? A man who had insulted her in every way possible, who had *assaulted* her in body and soul? The answer, Angeline discovered, was yes. For she could not help but respect the man who, with erratic breathing, sweat streaming down his face, and quaking hands, had diligently worked for hours, sewing up the insides of a man he loved more than a brother—a man whom they all loved more than a brother.

While doing her best to quell the agony of her heart, she obeyed his every command, stood by his side, ignored her own queasiness, and watched him as he grimaced, winced, huffed, and concentrated harder than she'd seen anyone do. Sarah also assisted, while Hayden stood to the side, his face mottled in agony and fear one minute, while in the next, he bowed and whispered prayers to the Almighty.

They could not lose Blake. The colonel had been their leader since they'd begun this journey. The only man who could guide such a mishmash of grumbling, erratic, fanciful personalities. He was the strong warrior who had led armies on the battlefield to victory and who now refused to accept defeat for their decimated colony. They would fall apart without him. Eliza would fall apart. The poor woman— Angeline bit her lip—she had no idea that at this very moment her husband's life teetered on the cliff of eternity. Would their child be born without a father? *Oh, God, no. Please, no.*

James blinked back sweat from his eyes, and Angeline dabbed his brow. He didn't glance at her. Hadn't glanced at anyone for hours. He'd just kept his eyes locked on Blake's mauled flesh as if looking away for one second would break the trance that had come over him as soon as he picked up the first instrument. After that, he'd worked methodically and precisely, each movement the practiced step of an elegant dance. Every slice, every squeeze, every suture skilled and beautiful in its simplicity and grace, even amid the horror of nicked veins and a punctured liver. Tirelessly, Sarah held the lantern above Blake, keeping it steady against the occasional wind gusting through the shelter, ignoring the sweat dotting her neck and soaking the fringe of her collar.

Rays of sun reflected off crystals of sand and dappled the bamboo roof with light, hypnotizing Angeline as she tried to keep her focus should James need something. The metallic smell of blood mixed with sweat and alcohol threatened to turn her stomach inside out, but her silent vigilance of prayer kept her strong. Kept her hopeful.

Finally, James closed Blake's loosened skin, ordered her to pour alcohol over the needle and sutures, and then began sewing up his friend's side. His bronze eyes remained as hard as metal as he completed the work. Then grabbing the rum, he doused the wound, wrapped it tightly in clean rags, and stepped back. Finally his gaze lifted off Blake and scanned the three of them. Worry formed creases at the edges of his eyes.

Hayden stepped forward. Sarah set down the lantern and rubbed her arm. Angeline drew a stool over for James to sit, all of them breathless for a word of encouragement.

Whatever had held James's spine in place during the long

procedure suddenly liquefied and he dropped to the chair. He released a breath so deep, it seemed he'd been holding it the entire time. His shoulders slumped and what looked like tears glazed his eyes before he lowered his chin. Sniffing, he rubbed those eyes before glancing up again. "We wait now. If he doesn't get an infection, he will live."

Hayden gripped James's arm and shook him. "You did good, Doc. Real good."

"Wonderful," Sarah added. "God be praised."

"Thank you for all your help." James gave a sad smile. "All of you." His eyes landed on Angeline, but as if it the sight of her repulsed him, he lowered them to the dirt by his boots. Which was, no doubt, what he still thought of her.

Finally he struggled to stand. "Keep an eye on him. I'll return later." Then stretching his shoulders, he turned and walked away. Sarah began cleaning up bloody rags, but Angeline couldn't pull her gaze from James as he headed down the beach—the way the last vestiges of sunlight cut across the sharp angles of his back, his confident gait, the wind whipping his tawny hair into a frenzy, the way he dipped his head as if deep in thought. She should be angry at him. She *was* angry at him. But it didn't matter—he still held her shattered heart in his hands.

"What happened between you two?" Sarah dropped the scissors into a bucket of bloody water.

"Nothing. It doesn't matter." But it did matter, more than anything. She just couldn't talk about it or she feared she'd collapse into a puddle and melt into the sand to be lost forever. She busied herself helping Sarah while Hayden covered Blake with a tattered quilt and said a prayer over his friend.

When the mess had been cleaned and Sarah had taken the dirty instruments to the creek to clean, Angeline turned to go, but her gaze landed on Dodd, still unconscious in the corner. Oddly, she found no anger rising at the sight of him. No hatred, or fear. Only pity. Since Eliza and Magnolia had been taken aboard the pirate ship, Sarah and Mrs. Jenkins had been looking after him, trying to force broth down his throat as much as possible. Yet after eight days, the poor man grew thin and gaunt.

Kneeling by his side, Angeline dabbed a moist cloth over his face.

Once, she had been happy about his condition, had wished him dead. Now, she repented of that horrid desire and said a silent prayer for him. Besides, he could no longer cause her harm.

Dipping his hands in an incoming wave, James grabbed a fistful of sand and started to scrub blood off his skin. Astonishing. The sight of it no longer sent icicles up his spine. He shielded his eyes against the sun now dipping low over the mountains. He'd been operating on Blake nearly all day. *Operating.* Like he used to do on the battlefield. When he had saved lives. Some lives, at least. Hopefully, the one he'd sutured up today.

If not, he would never forgive himself.

He sat back and allowed the waves to wash over him, soaking through his trousers and rippling up his sides. Cupping a handful of the foamy saltwater, he splashed it over his face and neck. The cool liquid leeched the tension from his body and seemed to carry it out to sea with each receding swell. He drew a deep breath and bowed his head. *Thank You, Father. I know it was You who helped me today. No one else could have calmed me down like that.*

As soon as he'd picked up the scalpel, a cloud of peace had enveloped him. Like a warm cloak on a winter's day that shielded one from icy shards and brisk wind, it had permeated his skin, settled his nerves—and his soul—and suddenly he knew what he must do. And he had the confidence to do it, and do it well.

Why hadn't he ever thought of praying before? Back when the blood had overwhelmed him and the terrors had begun, back when his hands—and his body—had quivered at the mere mention of blood? Why had he not turned to God for strength then? All these wasted years he could have been saving lives. *Forgive me.*

He'd been too proud and too angry to ask for anyone's help. Especially God's. How foolish was that for a preacher? Snorting, he rubbed the back of his neck. Foamy waves lobbed a shell against his foot. He picked it up and flicked it between his fingers. For years he blamed his fear of blood on the war, on the horrors he'd witnessed.

A thought seared a trail through his conscience.

For years, he blamed his nefarious liaisons on the loose morals of the women he'd consorted with, never taking responsibility for his own actions, never asking God for the strength to resist them. Never leaning on the only One who could help him with his weaknesses. All his weaknesses.

Was he any better than the women he'd taken to bed? Hadn't he committed the same immoral act? Yet all this time he'd blamed them while holding himself innocent, believing his only sin was falling for their beguiling traps. Blaming them for destroying his life when it was his own weakness and lack of trust in God that had caused his undoing.

James tossed the shell into the sea and hung his head.

"He doesn't appear to be getting better." Hayden's voice startled Angeline as she sat tending Dodd. She glanced up, saw the hesitation in his eyes, and offered him a welcoming smile. Hayden had caused her father's death, sent her life spinning like a cyclone into the darkness. She should be furious with him—*had* been furious. But all that had changed when her Father in heaven forgave her and washed her clean.

"Poor fellow." He knelt beside her. "I wonder if he'll ever recover his senses."

She returned her gaze to Dodd. "He better do so soon. I doubt we can keep him fed enough much longer."

"I can't say I miss him very much," Hayden said. "Though I suppose that's not very kind."

"He was"—she bit her lip—"or rather *is* a hard man to like."

Silence, save for Dodd's shallow breathing and the wind whipping through the frond roof, settled on them both. Shifting across the sand, Angeline dampened her rag in a nearby bowl of water.

"No doubt, after our last discussion, you feel the same way about me." His voice lowered in shame.

She searched his green eyes, seeing only sorrow and remorse.

"What I did was reprehensible," he said. "Unforgiveable."

Angeline swallowed, allowing herself a moment to consider how different her life would have been had her father not been murdered. She would not have gone to live with her aunt and uncle. She would not have been forced onto the street, constantly on the run. She would not have become what she had become. And then James and she would still be together. Or would they? She wouldn't have come to Brazil at all. In truth, she would never have known him. And that thought hurt most of all. "I have discovered recently that nothing is unforgiveable." She smiled, dousing her few remaining coals of anger with undeserved grace—the undeserved grace God gave to her and that she must give to others.

"I don't know what to say." Hayden's brow wrinkled. "But—"

She placed a finger on his lips, praying he didn't misinterpret the intimate gesture. "Then say nothing more. What's done is done. You didn't murder my father directly. I don't think you would have done it if you had known." She drew a deep breath of the new life within her. "I forgive you."

A mixture of surprise and admiration rolled over his face. "You've changed, Angeline."

"Let's just say God and I had a long talk."

Hayden chuckled. "Indeed. He's been chatting with me lately, as well."

She wiped Dodd's face and neck as minutes passed by in silence. She felt Hayden tense beside her, knew he had more to say, but she didn't want to talk about her past anymore. Wasn't it enough that it had already ruined her future?

"That *was* you on the wanted poster then, wasn't it?" Hayden asked.

Releasing a sigh, she faced him. What difference did it make if she told him the truth now? She was done with lying. "Yes."

His lips grew tight, and he stared at Dodd. "Wanted for murder. Did you do it?"

"Yes." She gauged his reaction but he didn't flinch, hardly breathed. If only she could go back and change things, choose another action, lean on God for help instead of trying to do things herself.

Wind gusted through the shelter, stirring sand and flapping the coverlet on top of Dodd. "It was self-defense. My uncle attacked me. I grabbed a bookend from the table and struck his head." Memories flashed. The lust in the man's eyes, his rough hands grabbing her and forcing her against the wall. "I was just trying to get him off me."

Hayden was silent. Would he tell everyone? James? Her friends? She dreaded the looks they would give her. She dreaded the loathing that would follow. She had so wanted to remember the sweetness of their friendship when she was back in the States, not be haunted by their hatred. Waves sizzled ashore. A gull squawked overhead.

"No one need know," Hayden finally said, drawing her gaze. "I believe you, Angeline. I've come to know you. You aren't a murderer."

She laid a hand on his arm, hardly daring to believe. "Thank you, Hayden."

Placing a hand atop hers, he helped her to her feet. "We all came here for a new start. You deserve one like the rest of us. Now, go rest." He jerked his head toward the women's shelter down the beach. "It's been a long day. I'll take first watch over Blake."

Dodd listened to the sound of their footsteps shuffling away before he opened his eyes. He'd woken up several hours ago but had found himself too weak to move or even speak. Soon, he'd realized something must have happened to the colonel because he could hear James stitching him up. It must have been a serious wound from the sounds of things. Probably an injury from the windstorm, which was the last thing Dodd remembered. Regardless, Dodd had kept his peace. Then afterward, when Angeline had sat beside him and dabbed a cool cloth on his head, he'd thought to enjoy her sweet ministrations for a while before making himself known. But, oh, what a heavenly miracle had then occurred! The words he'd overheard passed through his mind, awakening memories that the woman's beauty must have forced him to forget. Angeline Moore was Clarissa Paine! The infamous woman who'd murdered her own uncle—bludgeoned him in his own house. Every law officer in Virginia had been put on alert, wanted posters had been handed out. Dodd couldn't imagine how he had missed it. Ah, sweet justice would finally be served. At least the kind of justice Dodd would choose to enact. Despite his weak condition, he lifted his lips in a devious grin.

CHAPTER 33

A burst of wind caught the crinkled pages of the Hebrew text and shuffled them across James's vision. With a huff, he shifted back to the end of the book and flattened the papers with his palm. An ache etched across his shoulders from leaning over the manuscript all day, and he sat up straight and attempted to stretch the kinks from his neck. Foam-capped rollers curled toward shore and spread creamy gauze over the sand, sending crabs skittering into their holes and the colony's children running in laughter. Ah, to be young and carefree again without a worry in the world. Without concern for food or shelter or pirates or invisible beasts who could plague the world with terror.

Which was why James had spent the past week studying the ancient Hebrew book, desperate to find a way to stop the pirates from releasing hell on earth. Yet he'd found nothing useful. Or perhaps he was missing something, some crucial piece of information that would make sense of it all.

Down shore, two men chopped wood while the women prepared supper around a blazing fire. The Scotts sat beneath a palm, looking quite peaked as Mable fanned them with a frond. Laughter drew James's gaze to Delia chasing her children through the tumbling waves. Beyond them, Thiago and Sarah held Lydia's hands as the child teetered along in her first attempts to walk. Children grew up fast. Too fast. Too soon they would have to face the hardships of life. The heartbreak.

Heartbreak. His eyes latched upon Angeline, hanging wet clothes with some of the other women, her hair ribbons of sparkling ruby in the waning sun. A viable pain seared his heart at the loss of her. He no longer blamed her for what she'd done—what she'd become. He understood. He forgave her. But he still couldn't bring himself to receive her back into his life. Or his heart. Though, in truth, he doubted he could ever banish her from that tender spot. Still, he had vowed to start over in Brazil, become a great preacher and spiritual guide to the colony.

And how could he do that married to a prostitute? Wouldn't that make him just as much of a failure as he'd always been?

He couldn't shake the images bombarding him day and night of her in other men's arms. Many other men. Of them groping her, fondling her, kissing her. . .and God knew what else. He'd wanted a pure woman, an innocent woman to make a fresh start with. A godly start.

Blake broke from the group of colonists and headed toward him. Holding his side, he moved slow and hesitant, pain lining his features. James shook his head. He'd commanded him to stay in bed and rest for at least another week, but the colonel wasn't accustomed to taking orders. Still, not a minute passed in which James didn't thank God for helping him save Blake's life. It was truly a miracle.

A miracle like Dodd waking up from a coma after eight days. The man's recovery was astounding. After eating every piece of fruit and fish in sight, he was back to his impertinent, greedy self. In fact, he'd even been strong enough to join the pirates at the temple today.

Thoughts of the ex-lawman vanished when the colonel stopped beside James, shifting weight off his bad leg and staring out to sea.

"Sit." Closing the book, James slid off the boulder and gestured for Blake to take his spot.

"Don't coddle me, Doctor." He grinned.

"That's an order, Colonel," James returned. "From someone who has had his hands inside your gut, I believe I have the right."

Blake pressed his side and eased himself to the rock. "If you'd stop reminding me, it might stop hurting."

"It will stop hurting when it heals, and it will heal when you rest."

"You sound as bad as Eli—" His gaze jerked to the pirate ship, anchored offshore, its stark masts golden columns in the setting sun.

"Blast it, I miss her."

James should say something here, quote some comforting scripture about how God would rescue her and all would be well. But James had learned two things in the past months: One, God's ways were often not what anyone would expect, and two, God needed no defending.

Blake stomped his boot in the sand, the leather soles sinking into the grains. "Would that those pirates would find their infernal gold and release Eliza and Magnolia. Yet if they *do* find the gold, they are likely to free the final beast." Blake squeezed the bridge of his nose and grimaced. He nodded toward the book in James's hands. "Have you discovered anything of value?"

James sighed and shook his head. "The beginning told how the beasts came to be imprisoned and how they can be freed. The middle consisted of nothing but poetry, songs of praise, and a tale of a mighty prince coming to rescue his people. I can't make sense of how it connects to the rest."

"And the end?"

"Talks about 'the six,' whoever or whatever that is," James said. "Something about the *six* being the only ones able to put the fallen angels back in chains."

"But who are these six? How are we to find them and what exactly can they do?"

"The book doesn't say. At least not yet, but I do have a few more pages to interpret."

Blake nodded. "Best get to it. I fear we don't have much time. I want my wife back. And I want this madness to end. I'm tired, Doc." His normally stormy gray eyes had turned dull as fog. "So tired."

"We all are. But we can't give up now."

Wincing, Blake rose to his feet and gripped James's shoulder in a brotherly squeeze just as shouts of glee and raucous laughter down shore caught their attention. The pirates, Captain Ricu in the lead, his red feather aflutter atop his hat, burst from the jungle, jugs of liquor in their hands. Songs in Portuguese filled the air as the band stomped across the sand to their side of the beach where the captain and three of his men began rowing one of their cockboats out to the *Espoliar*.

Dodd, Patrick, Moses, and three more colonists brought up the rear and headed toward them.

Acid welled in James's belly. Nothing good could come from the pirates' joyful mood.

Nothing good but gold. And lots of it, according to Dodd and Patrick—gold that filled the fourth alcove from floor to ceiling.

"Filled? The entire alcove?" James asked as the other colonists assembled around the two treasure hunters.

Dodd smiled and rubbed his hands together then winced at the cuts covering them. Shaking dirt from his hair and shirt, he glanced at Patrick, who remained as unsoiled and modish as one could in the middle of a jungle. He fingered his goatee. "Stuffed full. A veritable fortune! Just like the old pirate who gave me the map said."

"What of the chains?" Blake eyed the man with suspicion. "The shackles?"

"Don't worry about them." Dodd took a sip from a canteen one of the colonists handed him. "If they are there, they're buried. And probably lying in the dirt like the others. Nothing's there but gold, I assure you. No imaginary beasts that will destroy mankind." His chortle filled the air, drawing a few chuckles from the crowd, before he slid to sit on a stump, his breath coming hard and his face paling. Even in his weakened condition, his vulgar gaze searched the mob and latched upon Angeline, where it remained for far too long.

James's insides bunched in a knot. Hugging herself, Angeline turned and walked to the other side of the group where Dodd couldn't see her, causing James to wonder once again whether they had met in the States. The thought of the circumstances of that meeting made bile rise in his throat. He squelched the vision and focused on Patrick, who was continuing to prattle on about how rich they were all going to be.

Hayden crossed arms over his chest and snorted. "You are bigger fools than I thought if you think you'll see any of that gold."

Dodd and Patrick exchanged a knowing glance. "We shall see," Patrick said. His grin sent ice down James's spine. It seemed to have the same effect on Hayden as he studied his father with suspicion. Regardless, James had bigger problems than Patrick and Dodd's greed.

And from the look on Blake's face, he agreed.

Though James had entertained doubts—many doubts—along the way, and though everything within him wanted it to be false, he knew the fourth beast was still chained in that alcove. He wasn't sure how he knew, but he did. He also knew that the removal of the gold would no doubt aid in the monster's release. Especially if someone read the inscription above the tomb. In fact, now that James thought of it, the gold had probably been hidden there as bait for greedy men—just the type of men whose hearts were dark enough to free the fallen angel.

Everything he'd read in the Hebrew book, everything that had happened, finally started to make sense.

Dodd slowly stood, color returning to his face. "We start pulling out the gold first thing in the morning." He peered through the crowd looking for someone. James didn't need to turn around to know Angeline had slipped behind him. He could smell her coconut scent, feel her presence in the way his heart leapt, his throat burned, and every sense came alive.

"I don't care about the wretched gold!" Mr. Scott shouted. "My daughter is held captive by pirates! I want her back and I want to leave this loathsome jungle." Mrs. Scott clung to her husband, looking as though she'd aged a decade in the past few weeks. Poor woman. Mr. Scott was looking none too well himself, his lack of interest in gold speaking volumes as to his present discomfort.

Mumbles of assent bounced through the mob.

"The pirates won't keep us here any longer will they?" Mrs. Jenkins drew her daughter into her skirts.

Blake scanned the crowd. Though most wouldn't spot it, James knew his friend, could see the angst roll over his face. "I have no idea. But I urge you not to give up on our colony just yet."

"What colony?" Mr. Scott's ensuing chuckle was contagious.

"Oh, I almost forgot," Patrick's assured voice, along with his eyes, flew over the group—both finding a perch on his son, Hayden. "The pirates said they'd release your *wife*." He hissed the last word before turning to Blake. "And yours, Colonel. Right now, in fact." He flicked fingers in the direction of the ship. "Ricu feels you have learned your lesson and won't attempt any more tomfoolery."

Hayden needed no further impetus to take off in a spray of sand, parting the crowd with his exuberance. Blake, though equally exuberant, followed at a much slower pace. Within minutes the two ladies were rowed to shore and deposited in their husbands' arms. James turned away from their tender reunions, feeling his own eyes mist at the intensity of affection between husbands and wives. Unfortunately, those eyes landed on Angeline standing in the distance, staring at him. She tore her gaze away then strolled down the beach, her green skirts swaying in the breeze. At the very least, he owed her an apology for his cruel words and abominable behavior. But he couldn't face her. Not yet. And definitely not alone. Not until he had a better grip on his emotions and wouldn't fall prey to those pleading violet eyes of hers.

Besides, he had a far more pressing matter at hand. Somehow they had to stop the pirates from removing the gold and releasing the fourth beast. If they didn't, James feared all would be lost.

The moon floated atop the horizon, draping glittering silver over the sea. Her stomach a torrent of angst, Angeline had skipped supper and gone for a walk, in desperate need of some time alone—to think, to mourn, to pray. She'd hugged Eliza and Magnolia, laughing and crying for what seemed like hours before Blake and Hayden demanded their wives back. At least some good fortune had finally shone upon the colonists. Some sign that God had not forgotten them—that perhaps this whole nightmare would come to an end. Another sign was that the pirates had lessened their sentries around camp. No doubt they no longer cared if the colonists escaped to Rio, for by the time any of them made it, the pirates would have gathered their gold and sailed away. Which also meant that perhaps they didn't intend to murder them before they left.

Stowy nestled deeper against her chest. Running fingers through his soft fur, she thanked God for the stray cat who'd wandered into her life aboard the *New Hope*. Even back then, God had known she would need a comforting companion. Lifting her skirts, she dipped her toe in the bubbling foam of a wave, smiling when it tickled her skin. Wind pulled hair from her pins and tossed it behind her, and she drew a deep breath, filling her lungs with the salty, fresh smell. She'd grown to love Brazil, its creamy-sanded shores, emerald waters, verdant, steamy jungles, and high, lofty mountains. There was a wildness, a purity, that lured her heart away from the pretension and conventions of society. She could be happy here.

If only James would love her.

And if they could conquer these beasts.

But neither of those things was likely. Hence the reason for her walk. If they didn't find a way to restrain the fallen angelic monsters, things would get worse—far worse, according to James. If they *did* defeat them by the grace and wisdom of God, James would still not love her. And she couldn't live with that. At least not side by side with him in the same town, eating meals together, seeing him every day.

Either way, she would have to leave this beautiful place. Go back to a land where she was wanted for murder and had no way to support herself. But this time, God would be with her, though she supposed He'd always been. But this time, she would call upon Him, rely on Him, trust Him.

A shadow emerged from the sea like a mermaid coming ashore. Water dripped off his hat and coat as he headed toward her. The visions no longer startled her. In fact, whirling around, she hurried in the opposite direction, ignoring the man she recognized from her past, ignoring the lurid suggestions bubbling from his lips like the foam atop the waves. Laughter bellowed from down shore where a flickering fire and a bawdy ruckus told her the pirates were already deep in their cups celebrating their impending wealth.

The colonists still circled their own fire, partaking of their meager meal of roasted fish, coconuts, and mango mandioca pudding. Off to the side, James sat on a rock. Hayden held a lantern while he finished interpreting the book. As if that would do any good. Angeline quickly chastised herself for her lack of faith. She'd felt the love and power of God the past few days, she truly had. But she couldn't imagine what He expected any of them to do against such evil.

Oh, Lord, protect us all. Protect James.

"Come now, Angel, make ole Neal happy like you used to." Still dripping from the sea, the heinous man leapt in front of her.

Ignoring him, Angeline walked the other way. She wasn't ready to join the others. In fact, she must—no, she desperately *needed to*—put as much distance between her and James for the remainder of her time in Brazil.

Another shadow leapt out at her.

Not bothering to lift her gaze, she brushed past it. Sweet saints, was she to have no peace at all tonight?

"Now, that ain't very friendly." The voice halted her.

Dodd. She slowly turned to see his predatory smile gleaming in the moonlight. "I thought you were a vision." She lowered her shoulders. "But now I see you are only a nightmare."

"Ah. . ." He laid his hat over his chest. "The lady pains me greatly."

Stowy perked and stared at the man. "What is it you want?" She continued walking.

"Did you miss me while I was unconscious?" He slid beside her.

"No."

"Yet, I distinctly remember you caring for me, sitting by my side and washing my face." He caressed his own cheek and moaned in delight. "I can still feel your loving touch."

Angeline longed to slap the moan from his lips. "I suppose I might have." In fact, she could only remember one time she'd done so, and that was when she and Hayden had spoken about. . . she snapped her gaze back to Dodd's.

He grinned. "I see you remember." Jumping in front of her, he faced her and walked backward as she proceeded, skimming her with lurid eyes.

Swinging hair over her shoulder, Angeline stiffened her jaw. "What do you want?"

"It's simple, really. You see, I'm about to be a very wealthy man. Much wealthier than the good doctor."

"I care not for your financial standing." Stopping before she bumped into him, she stared out to sea, wishing more than anything for the kraken to emerge from the foamy waters and drag her down to the depths.

He grabbed her arm. "Hmm. I don't think you do. In fact, you're becoming quite the bore, Angeline. Playing the righteous prude does not become you." He released her and slid fingers up to her neck. "I much preferred the harlot."

Stowy hissed at him.

Frowning, he backed away.

Angeline lifted her chin. "The harlot is gone, sir. I am a new creature. I have been cleansed and forgiven by God."

His shoulders shook as laughter barreled from his mouth. "Well,

I'll tell you what, then, *Clarissa*. Just for old times' sake and since I like you, I really do, I'll not tell a soul that you are a murderer as well as a prostitute if you give me just one night. Just one night with dear old Dodd. Is that too much to ask for?"

She felt Stowy tense in her arms, nails springing from his paws. Perhaps she should release him and allow him to gouge Dodd's eyes out. But that wouldn't be pleasing to God. "Are you so desperate and so pathetic a man that you have to threaten to ruin a woman's life for one night's pleasure?"

"Desperate, aye," he said. "Pathetic. . .well, why don't you let me show you just how pathetic I am?"

Angeline was suddenly glad she had skipped supper. "I wouldn't spend the night with you if you could make me queen of England."

Dodd's face fell. His eyes narrowed and the lines at the corners of his mouth became spears.

"You are too late, Dodd. James already knows." She wouldn't tell him just what he knew. "So you have no power over me."

"Whether that is true or not, you forget one thing, my dear." He slid fingers down his thick sideburns. "I am a lawman, bound by duty to bring murderers to justice. And if you don't give me what I want, that's just what I intend to do, bring you home and make you stand trial for murder."

CHAPTER 34

Thank you all for meeting this late." James circled the fire and tossed another log into the flames. Sparks leapt into the air, disappearing into the darkness where the moon seemed to absorb them in its advance across the sky. Snores rumbled over the thunder of waves from both pirate and colonist alike, ensuring James all but the six of them were asleep. For what he had to say was not for prying ears. Nor for the faint of heart.

"We have no choice." Blake's tone grew solemn. "We must do something."

Hayden led Magnolia to sit on a log. "Are you sure about this fourth beast?" He scratched the stubble on his chin. "I haven't seen many visions lately. None, in fact, last week."

"*I* have." Holding his side, Blake eased to sit beside his wife. "And my nightmares have increased."

Eliza glanced at Magnolia. "We saw many visions while on board the *Espoliar*. Aside from the rats, they were our constant companions."

Magnolia squeezed her husband's hand. "If Eliza hadn't been there, I would have gone mad."

"If we hadn't been together, we both would have," Eliza said.

"And you, James?" Blake asked. "Have you been spared these torturous apparitions now that your fear of blood is gone?"

James stared into the fire, wishing to God that were true, but lately he'd been seeing his father everywhere. . .chopping wood in the distance, walking down shore, dashing through the jungle. But every time James rushed to confront him, he disappeared. If only he could speak to him, tell him how sorry he was. Just once. "It was God who took my fear from me, and no, I have not been spared."

All eyes turned to Angeline as she lowered to a stump and adjusted her skirts around her feet. "I've seen many," she finally said. "Too many."

James scrubbed his face, battling the irresistible pull to look at her, not wanting to see the pain on her face that he heard in her voice, not wanting to see the sorrow and anger in her eyes every time she looked his way.

Wind sent the flames sputtering and brought a welcome chill to the sweat on the back of his neck.

Hayden snapped hair from his face. "So, what are we to do about this beast, Doc? I assume that's why you asked us to forego our sleep."

"Yes. I finished interpreting the book." Drawing a deep breath, James sat and leaned forward on his knees. "From what I have learned, I believe it is possible to send the freed beasts back to their chains and keep the fourth one from being released. The Hebrew text speaks over and over of the six." God help him. He had studied and prayed and studied and prayed, asking for wisdom to interpret the words correctly. If he was wrong—even in a verb tense or the meaning of a single word—it could mean their doom.

"The six?" Eliza fingered a locket around her neck, her voice tainted with the skepticism she so often tried to hide.

James stared at the sand by his boot and wondered how to continue, how to share what sounded like complete lunacy, but what he knew in his gut was the truth. Picking up the book, he opened it to where he'd placed a leaf as marker and began to read from his translation. " 'The six are known to the six, yet not known. Called from afar. A destiny from above. And only through them can evil be chained.' "

He glanced at his friends. All eyes were upon him, sparkling in the firelight. Some were narrowed in confusion, others wide beneath arched brows, while others shifted to stare at the dance of flames.

Magnolia scrunched her nose. "What does it mean, 'known. . .yet not known'? And who are these six?"

James drew a deep breath, hesitated, then decided he might as well just say it. "I believe *we* are the six."

Hayden chuckled. Eliza slipped her locket within her bodice and folded her hands together. James didn't look at Angeline, but he could feel her eyes on him.

"What makes you say that?" Blake asked, lines forming on his forehead.

A howl echoed from the jungle, deep and malevolent, setting James's nerves on end. As if they weren't already tight enough. "I've prayed and prayed about this. I know this sounds absurd, preposterous even. But hear me out. When we all came aboard the *New Hope* eight months ago, we were complete strangers to one another, correct?"

Blake nodded. Eliza shared a glance with Magnolia while Angeline lifted her gaze to Hayden, who was oddly staring at James. James shifted uncomfortably on his seat, hoping that the reason for Hayden's interest was not that he had known James from before. Closing the book, he set it down on the sand and continued. "Yet, somehow our lives are connected." He faced Eliza. "I saw your husband commit a horrible act on the battlefield." She swallowed and gave a slight nod. "An act that affected Blake greatly and changed his life." Releasing a sigh, the colonel swung an arm around his wife and drew her near.

"That's three of us who affected each other's lives before we even knew one another." James turned to Magnolia. "You told me that you knew Eliza before you boarded the *New Hope*."

"Yes"—she smiled at her friend—"we met at a party at Eliza's aunt and uncle's hotel."

"You introduced me to Stanton..." Eliza's voice trailed off, her eyes growing wide. "I would have never married him..."

Magnolia winced.

"I would never have run away from home, been disowned by my family." Eliza lowered her chin, and Blake brought her hand to his lips. She looked at him in horror. "Who knows, maybe Stanton would never have murdered your brother."

Blake eased a curl from her face. "What's done is done, love. It doesn't matter now."

Hayden's gaze shot to his wife. "And you were engaged to my father."

"I need no reminder of that huge mistake." Magnolia stuffed hair into her bun.

"But don't you see?" James stood, his blood pumping fast. "That links Hayden to Magnolia and Magnolia to Eliza and Blake to Eliza and me to Blake and Eliza." He dared a glance at Angeline. "But what I cannot determine is how you are connected in all this."

"I'm not." Angeline swept pointed eyes his way. "You of all people should know that a woman like me could never be used to defeat evil." Her sharp tone sliced through James's heart. Yet even as she said the words, her gaze brushed over Hayden before returning to the fire.

Withdrawing his arm from Magnolia, Hayden picked up a chip of wood and began fingering it. Seconds passed as another gust of wind kicked sparks from the fire into the night. "Angeline and I have only recently discovered a prior connection," Hayden finally said. "I swindled the man who murdered her father. Inadvertently causing her father's death, in fact." He tossed the wood in the fire as everyone stared at him in disbelief, eyes shifting from him to Angeline.

But she refused to look at any of them, her eyes downcast, her arms looped around her waist, her hair sparkling in red and gold like the fire itself.

"I didn't know what had transpired after I tricked the man." Hayden's tone weighed heavy with remorse. "I simply left town with my pockets full."

Angeline finally raised her gaze to Hayden's. The moisture covering her eyes threatened to undo James and send him dashing to her side. "You couldn't have known." She smiled and glanced over the group. "Hayden and I have made our peace."

Shoving down yet another burst of admiration for the lady, James tore his gaze away and instead focused on his growing excitement as the pieces of the puzzle were coming together. Yet at the same time, sorrow also consumed him at the horrible way each of his dear friends had affected the other ones. All except him. Aside from seeing Eliza's husband kill Blake's brother, James had no direct connection with any of them. Perhaps it was *he* who wasn't part of the six.

"Before you go thinking you are innocent, Doc..." Hayden shifted his boots in the sand. "You and I crossed paths once."

James studied his friend. He would have remembered a man like Hayden. "You must be mistaken."

"Nope. I snuck in the back of your church in Knoxville on a cold night in February. I didn't stay long. I needed to find some meaning to my life. I'd grown tired of swindling people, of searching for my father."

A burst of dread formed in James's gut, even as hope dared to spark. What had he preached that night? Had his words been a comfort to Hayden?

"You preached on how God was a father to the fatherless, a husband to widows. How He adopts us into His family so we are never alone. Your words really spoke to me that night, Doc. You have a gift. I left that church wanting to change my life and give God a chance."

James would have allowed his heart to lift at the great testimony except for the look of despair resident in Hayden's eyes. And the frown tugging at his lips.

"Until I saw you in a tavern later that night slobbering over some woman."

Night birds and insects buzzed from the jungle, making James hope that he'd heard the man wrong, but when all eyes snapped toward him, he knew he hadn't. A brick landed in his stomach. Closing his eyes, he prayed for the ground to open up and swallow him whole. Anything to avoid the looks of shock and disgust on the faces of those whom he'd come to love and admire. He shook his head and rubbed the back of his neck. He had so wanted to start anew, to be a good preacher and spiritual guide for the colony. But how could he do that when his friends knew the truth?

As if things weren't bad enough, Hayden continued. "I know you're not that man now, but when I saw your hypocrisy, I gave up on God, moved to Norfolk, and ended up achieving my greatest swindle...the one which caused the murder of Angeline's father."

Could things get any worse? Now James had indirectly caused Angeline's father's death! His heart became an anchor in his chest. He dared a glance her way, but she stared at the fire, a tear sliding down her cheek.

Behind him, angry waves tumbled ashore, thundering and frothing like his insides—like his mind. Here he'd thought he had no real connection with his friends, and it turned out he'd had the worst connection of all.

"I knew you, as well, before our trip." Angeline's honeyed voice brought James's gaze up to her. No, impossible. James couldn't take any more bad news. His body felt numb, his mind dazed. He merely stared at her, feeling as if it would be best if he just floated into the night sky alongside the sparks from the fire.

Her freckles tightened like they always did when she grew angry. "You were drunk, stumbling through the streets of Knoxville, blood splattered on your shirt, muttering something about your father."

The night his father had died. James lowered his chin, feeling the pain even now.

"I brought you to my room, cleaned you up, and took care of you."

James stared at her in shock. This woman—this trollop—had been the angel who had changed his life that horrid night over a year ago? The night he'd wanted to kill himself. If not for her, he might have succeeded. Vague memories like shadowy figures slipped in and out of his foggy mind. When he'd found his father shot in a tavern and James couldn't save him, his anger had gotten the best of him, and he'd drawn his sword on the man responsible—Tabitha's husband. They'd fought. James stared at the fire and rubbed the scar angling alongside his mouth where the man had sliced him, where the man had bested him and could have run him through, but he'd granted James mercy and ran off. Laden with guilt, and wishing the man had ended his life, James drank and drank and drank until he couldn't feel anything. But an angel had come to his rescue. Or at least he'd thought it was an angel. When he'd woken the next day, he was in a room above a tavern, the night's rent and a hot meal paid for. And his memories full of an auburn-haired woman ministering to him in the night, holding his head while he tossed his accounts, wiping his forehead, singing gently.

"You tended my wound. You knew all along where this scar came from."

"No. I only knew when it happened, not why or how."

And James wouldn't tell her now. Or any of them. He'd already brought more than enough shame on himself. Yet further memories of that night invaded as he stared at her in shock. "You spoke scripture to me."

She nodded. "I remembered a psalm from my childhood. My father's favorite, Psalm 23. It was the only thing I could think to do. You seemed so distraught. . .so. . ."—pain misted her eyes—"so hopeless."

"That scripture, your kindness that night, it changed my life." James fought back the burning behind his eyes. "I made a decision to be a better man. To leave my home and start anew."

She blinked, her eyes shifting between his.

The fire crackled and spit like his conscience was doing. Though he'd bedded women without benefit of marriage, he'd thought her profession made her a worse sinner than he. He'd looked down on her, thought of her as too stained to become his wife. Yet, all along, she possessed the heart of an angel, while his was as black as coal.

Blake struggled to rise. "This is incredible. Unbelievable! Before we ever met, each of us affected the others. Our paths crossed in ways we could never have imagined, and the encounters changed each of our lives dramatically."

"For the worse," Hayden spat.

"No, you're looking at it all wrong," Blake continued. "Yes, our associations caused bad things to happen. But, don't you see? None of us would be here in Brazil at this time and place if we hadn't met before." The colonel scanned them, determination firing from his eyes. "If my brother hadn't died, I wouldn't have started this expedition. I would be home with Jerry. Angeline, if your father hadn't been murdered, you would have never ended up an orphan on the streets. You would have never met James. You wouldn't have joined this venture."

Angeline nodded. "Indeed. I'd be with my father."

"Magnolia." Blake spun to face her. "If Hayden's father hadn't stolen your family's money, you and your parents would still be on your plantation in Georgia, or at the very least, still in Roswell, living a good life. If you hadn't introduced Eliza to Stanton, she would have never run off with him and been disowned by her parents. She would have never become a nurse. She would have never been ostracized by the South and in need of a new start." He shifted his gaze to Hayden. "If you hadn't been disillusioned by James's hypocrisy—sorry James"—he added over his shoulder—"you wouldn't have swindled the man who caused Angeline's father's death. Then not only would she have never come to Brazil, but she would have never saved James that night, changed his outlook, his purpose to want a moral society, which eventually brought him here as well. All these chance meetings and events have led us to this exact moment. To this exact place."

Thoughts and memories spun a web in James's mind of impossible encounters, of strings of time and place and plans and devices that when looped together formed a perfect lattice of will and purpose. "Not known but known," he repeated the words from the book, his heart hammering. "That's us! Called from afar. A destiny from above. Six is the number of man. It makes sense now. God gave dominion of earth to man. Man handed earth's keys to Satan when Adam rebelled against God. God chooses to work through man to defeat evil on earth."

"I don't understand," Magnolia said.

"Never mind." James shoved a hand through his hair and took up a pace. "God knew this would happen. He knew the beasts would one day be released. Before we were even born, He chose us for this task, adjusted the course of each of our lives to bring us here to this place at this time for this purpose. Don't you see?" He glanced at his friends, their expressions frozen in shock and amazement.

"We are the six. God brought us here to defeat the evil beasts."

CHAPTER 35

Trying to settle her restless thoughts, Angeline made her way to the shelter she shared with the colony's women. She must remember to thank Hayden for not mentioning their other connection. Though it would bolster James's theory of the *six*'s prior associations—or not so much a theory anymore as incredible fact—it would do more harm than good to disclose that she was a murderer. After all, how much of her sordid past could her friends tolerate? They might even lock her up if they thought her capable of killing someone. She wouldn't blame them in the least. Of course they'd find out soon enough if Dodd followed through with his threat. She had resigned herself to that. And then she would leave this beautiful land, along with her only friends in the world. No, not her only friends. God loved her. He would always be with her. Even if she had to stand trial for murder.

Skirting around sleeping colonists, she was nearly at the entrance to the hut when footsteps sounded and a touch on her arm wheeled her around. She raised her hand, ready to strike.

"Whoa, whoa, it's only me," James whispered as he grabbed her wrist and lowered it. "Why so skittish?"

"Force of habit, I suppose," she breathed out then tried to see his expression in the darkness. Could he fathom what her life had been like working for Miss Lucia? The disgust and shame she faced each day, the constant fear, the customers who'd enjoyed beating her as much as they had using her body? It was why she'd always carried a pistol, until she lost it in the flood.

A cloud shifted, and moonlight revealed a spark of understanding

271

in his eyes. Followed by sorrow—overwhelming sorrow. "Will you walk with me?" he asked.

A breeze showered her with his musky scent and tossed his hair in every direction, just like his touch and the kindness in his voice were doing to her thoughts. Jumbled and anxious, they churned with ideas of destiny, purpose, battles against evil, and now with her feelings for this man before her, who had the power to destroy her. Should she go with him? Allow him a doorway back into her heart?

Yet in the end, she knew she could not deny him. She nodded. They hadn't gone far before he spoke. "I am a buffoon." He stopped before the waves that spun arcs of silver filigree on the dark sand. Angeline's heart ceased beating.

"The hugest buffoon ever to live," he continued.

She shook her head, afraid to hear any more. Afraid her heart could not ride the wave of yet another crest of hope, only to be plunged to the depths of despair.

"I have misjudged you, Angeline."

Angeline's lungs beat against her chest. She sought his eyes in the darkness, but he lowered his gaze.

"I believed it was an angel who tended me that night." He took her hands in his, caressing her fingers. She withdrew, not ready to receive his touch, not ready to erase the hurt he'd caused her.

"I was right. It *was* an angel. It was you, Angeline, my angel." He released a heavy sigh. "I'm so sorry. Can you ever forgive me for the cruel things I said, for forcing my kiss on you? I behaved like a monster. A complete cad."

Yes, he had. And he had broken every piece of her heart. But at the moment, she found the memory fading beneath the soothing baritone of his voice, the brief look of love in his eyes afforded her by the shifting moonlight. Dare she hope?

"But I cannot erase my past," she said. "I was—"

"You *are* a proper lady." He leaned to gaze in her eyes. "With a good heart and a kind spirit and an honor and decency that I've come to realize far exceeds mine."

He shamed her with his praise, and she looked out to sea where the moon flung diamonds atop ebony waters. "You go too far."

"Not far enough. For years I've blamed my troubles, my sins on others, only to discover it was my own weakness, my own lack of faith, which caused my pain."

She smiled. "I have discovered the same."

He cupped her face and brushed fingers over her cheek. Warmth trickled in pleasurable eddies down to her toes.

He leaned to whisper in her ear. "Let us start fresh, you and I. Please, Angeline."

She closed her eyes, cherishing the feel of his breath on her neck. "Start afresh? We may not even survive tomorrow."

"Which is why I cannot wait another minute without begging your forgiveness." He raised her hands to his lips. "And without telling you that I'm absolutely mad about you. I love you, Angeline."

She tried to cling to the words spinning in her mind, but her anger kept them out of reach. "You hurt me, James." She tugged from his grip. "You hurt me badly."

"I know." His voice caught. "I'm so sorry. I never meant to."

"How can I trust you? How do I know my past won't cause you to hate me in the future?"

"Because God has shown me what a hypocrite I've been. My past is far worse than yours, my heart far darker." He took her hands again, holding on tight. "If there is to be any loathing of pasts, it will be me loathing mine."

Minutes passed in silence as his calloused fingers caressed hers. "I don't deserve your forgiveness or your love, Angeline. But I want you to know that you are the angel I've been seeking my entire life."

Could a heart leap beyond a body and soar into the skies? For that's what it felt her heart was doing at the moment. She was hardly an angel, but the way he was looking at her right then made her believe she *could* become one.

"I love you too, James. Perhaps from the very first time you pulled me from the sea."

He smiled. "May I erase my last foolish kiss with a new one?"

Tossing propriety to the salty breeze, Angeline flung her arms around his neck and drew him close. This time, his lips pressed tenderly on hers, caressing, exploring, delicate yet hungry. Waves crashed over their feet, soaking her hem and tickling her legs, but she didn't care. She felt like she was a thousand miles away, floating on a blissful cloud.

The bristle on his jaw scratched her cheek, delighting her even more. He ran fingers through her hair, gripping the strands hungrily as if he couldn't get enough of her.

"Ah, how touching." Dodd's voice etched an icy trail down Angeline. She shoved from James, her heart racing, her mind reeling.

His breath coming equally hard, James shielded her with his body and faced the intruder. "Have you no manners, Dodd?"

He snorted. "Why don't you ask the lady? She and I are *well* acquainted."

Not now, Dodd. For a few moments. . .a few brief, wonderful moments, Angeline had forgotten about Dodd and his threats. Passion bled from her body and dripped into the foam at her feet, replaced by a chill that threatened to bite her heart in two. It wouldn't take long for James to put the pieces together. Even now, as his gaze shifted between her and Dodd, she saw understanding tighten his features.

She might as well say the words that thundered silently between them. "Dodd was a client many years ago." Turning toward the ex-lawman, she stiffened her chin. "I told you James already knows." Yet, she was afraid to look at him now. Afraid to see his reaction to this new discovery. To her surprise, he took her hand in his. Tears flooded her eyes—tears of joy that quickly turned to pain when Dodd flung his next arrow.

"But does the preacher know that you're a murderer as well as a trollop?"

Her heart crumbled. Sweet saints, would the man never leave her be? James snapped his gaze to her, his eyebrows bent. She tried to tug her hand from his, but he wouldn't let go.

"It's true," she said, her voice trembling. "I'm sorry, but it's true."

James shook his head, still staring at her.

Dodd stuffed thumbs in his belt. "She killed her uncle, you know. Her own flesh and blood. What sort of woman does that?"

Confusion burned behind James's eyes. Should she try to explain what happened? Would it make a difference? "I went to live with my uncle and aunt after my father died. He abused me, beat me, barely gave me enough food or clothing. . .made me a slave in their home."

Dodd huffed, pulling out his pocket watch and snapping it open as if bored with the story.

"One night he forced himself on me." She swallowed down a burst of fear at the memory. "He shoved me against a wall in the library and told me if I didn't do what he said, he'd kill me. I couldn't let that happen. I was only eighteen. An innocent girl."

Dodd chuckled. Ignoring him, she continued. "I missed my father so much and hoped my uncle would love me as his own child." She wiped a wayward tear, hating her own weakness. "We struggled. I grabbed a bronze bookend and struck his head. I didn't mean to kill him." Her legs wobbled and James steadied her. "After that I ran away." She lowered her gaze, unable to bear his steely eyes anymore. "You know the rest."

"Lovely story, don't you think, Doc? I so adore the slight quaver in her voice, the tremble of her lips. It adds that extra tug on your heart. She's very good at what she does. Very good, indeed."

James released Angeline's hand. The loss of him, of his strength and warmth, crushed her to the bone. She gazed out to sea, feeling the lure of its peaceful depths.

Thunk! Snap!

She turned to find Dodd toppling backward, arms flailing and curses spewing from his mouth before he landed smack on his derrière in the sand. James shook his hand. Despite the circumstances, Angeline couldn't help the smile that curved her lips or the sense of satisfaction that welled in her belly. Or the thrill at seeing James defend her honor.

Dodd, however, was not of the same mind. Struggling to rise, he rubbed his jaw. "Fool! Before you make the wench any promises you can't keep, Doc, you should know that after I get my share of the gold, I'm taking her back to the States to stand trial for murder."

⊸⊷⊹⊶⊸

He'd left her. James had left her standing on the beach beneath an umbrella of moonlight, with but a kiss on her hand to seal his feelings. But at the moment, he had no idea just what those feelings were. Aside from his overwhelming love for her. *A murderer!* Despite the circumstances—horrific as they were—she still had taken a life. Self-defense, yes. But how could he come to terms with such a crime? Yet, indirectly, hadn't he done the same?

He needed to think. So after Dodd had scrambled back into the hole he'd crawled from, James had excused himself. He had too much to sort out. Too many fears and dreams and hopes and memories and shocking news cycloned in his head. Not to mention he must go over their plan to defeat the beasts tomorrow.

Defeat evil angelic generals. How ludicrous did that sound?

It was too much for one man to handle. Or at least for *him* to handle. So he'd left her there, hope lingering in her eyes and an unspoken plea upon her lips.

Now, hours later, after pacing and praying along the distant shore, peace still eluded him. Falling to the sand in a heap, he drifted into a fitful slumber. He was back on the ship, pitching and rising through a sea of blood. With each flap of white sail and each thrust of the bow, the mighty vessel advanced toward the black, broiling horizon. Shards of flames shot across the darkness, followed by deep growls, ominous and fierce. Stowy perched on the binnacle, his amber eyes latched on James. Ignoring the cat, he dashed to the starboard railing. Foamy blood thrashed the sides of the small dinghy where his friends sat, staring blankly at the gaping dark mouth just ahead. Somehow they kept pace with the ship, though they had no oars or sails.

James cupped his hands. "Ahoy there!" They turned as one and stared at him, fear sparking in their gazes. Fear that turned to pleading. Angeline waved. Hayden shook his head at James in disappointment. Magnolia cried out for help. Eliza clung to her husband who faced the darkness once again, his jaw a bone of defiance.

James spun around and searched the ship. He must help them! He needed rope. He needed to increase the ship's speed to draw closer. He gazed up at the sails, stark white against a blood moon. Making his way to the ratlines, he tripped on something. The cat sped by him, emitting an eerie meow.

"It wasn't your fault." The familiar voice came from behind.

James slowly turned. His legs turned to mush. He stumbled backward. The hard wood of the mainmast prevented his fall. "Father. What are you doing here?"

The man hadn't aged. No, of course he hadn't. He was dead. But he looked younger than he ever had. Gone were the lines of grief and tension from his face. Gone was the weariness in his eyes, the gray from his hair. He even seemed to stand a bit taller.

And he smiled now at James as he'd never done when he'd been alive—a smile of love and approval and forgiveness.

"Son, I've been sent to tell you something." He adjusted the white tie he always wore over his black frock. "Something important."

"But you can't be here. Not really." James swallowed. "This is nothing but a dream, a vision." He rubbed his eyes.

"Dreams have meanings, son."

The ship crested a scarlet wave, creaking and groaning on the ascent. James steadied his boots on the deck, drinking in the vision of a man he thought he'd never see again.

"My death was not your fault," his father repeated.

James looked away. "It *was* my fault, Father. I should have been the one at the tavern that night. I should have been the one to come to the aid of Mr. Reynolds. Not you. But I wasn't at the church when his message came." James swept guilty eyes toward his father. "Do you want to know where I was, while you were dying from a gunshot wound? While you were lying in a puddle of spit and ale and drowning in your own blood?"

The words bore no effect on his father's loving look.

Which only angered James. Anger at himself. "I was with a woman. Mrs. Tabitha Cullen, to be exact. The wife of the man who shot you."

"I know, son." His father smiled—not a smile of victory or sarcasm but one of forgiveness.

"How can you stand there and look at me like that? Don't you see? Tabitha's husband accused Mr. Reynolds of compromising his wife. But it was me who was with her. With her that very moment when you went to stop the brawl. It was me." James's insides twisted into a hopeless knot. He should toss himself overboard. A fitting punishment.

To drown in the blood that he had shed.

As soon as James had heard the news, he'd raced to the tavern, knelt before his father. There was already so much blood. James might have been able to save him, but the terrors had gripped him, and instead he'd sat frozen and watched his father die.

"I failed you, Father." Tears filled his eyes. "As I failed you my entire life."

"No, no, no." James's father laid a hand on his shoulder—a solid hand, a real hand—one that bore the gold ring with the cross in the center that he'd worn to his grave. "You were never a failure. 'Twas I who demanded too much. Expected more than any son could give. I am sorry, James. I finally know what grace is." He smiled, and there was such peace in his eyes, James longed to dive into them and be lost forever.

The sails thundered above. A roar brought both men's gazes to the blackness swallowing up the horizon. "Your friends need you, James," his father said. "Gather them aboard and fight the darkness. You have been chosen. You and you alone can lead them to victory."

Dread sent James's heart pounding. He rubbed the scar on his cheek. "Me? Why me?"

"Why not you?" His father stepped back and began to fade.

"Please don't go." James wiped a tear away.

"We will meet again." His father smiled. "You can do this, son. God is with you." He gave him one last approving nod before he turned, stepped off the railing of the ship, and disappeared into the mist.

Something bright appeared at the prow of the ship. A white figurehead in the shape of a lamb—a lamb with a lion's head and a sword in its grip. A glow beamed from within it, casting light upon the bloody sea. Why had James not seen it before?

A fiery arrow shot across the darkness as if the stars themselves were falling. Then another and another. Thunder roared as the ship sped toward the horizon, pitching and rolling and sending scarlet foam washing over the bow. Heart thrashing, James clutched a rope, tied it to the railing, and spied his friends now drifting just yards off the ship. He flung it toward them. Blake caught it, and within minutes his friends climbed over the bulwarks and joined him aboard. Their frightened gazes sped over one another and then to the black hole about to swallow them alive. With determined nods, they took one another's arms and formed a defiant line at the bow just as the ship broke into the darkness.

⸙

"Will you marry me?" It was James's voice. At least Angeline thought it was, though the words jumbled in the wind.

She turned to find him standing there looking like a schoolboy, his face hopeful, his eyes filled with love, his fingers twitching by his side.

By the looks of his wrinkled shirt and trousers, he had passed the night much like she had—restless and filled with nightmares.

"I beg your pardon?"

The rising sun sparkled off his wide grin as he took both her hands in his. "Will you marry me?"

She searched his eyes, firing with golden flecks of hope, and found no trace of betrayal, humor, or anger.

"You want to marry a murderess and a prostitute?" Squelching down the thrill blooming within, she had to be sure he knew what he was asking.

"No, I want to marry *you*, Angeline."

Emotion burned in her throat: hope and fear and excitement all jumbled together. "When you left last night. . ." She'd thought it was over between them. He'd accepted her past as a trollop, but a murderer? How could she expect a man of God to tolerate that?

"I'm sorry. I needed to think. Not about my love for you. About what Dodd said, yes, but also about my own life." He flattened his lips. "I had a dream about my father." His eyes grew glassy, and he gazed out to sea. "He always expected me to be perfect, and I always failed him."

"No—" she began, but he silenced her with a gentle finger to her lips.

"I've done bad things, Angeline. That night back in Knoxville, you saw me at my worst. Yet despite my own past, I still expected everyone around me to be perfect." He glanced at the jungle. "I wanted to create a moral utopia where nobody fell away from grace." He chuckled and shook his head. "But I have discovered recently that where imperfection lives, God's grace abounds."

A tear slipped down Angeline's face.

James continued to caress her fingers. "I have also discovered that none of us will ever be perfect. That's what grace is for. I will never create a perfect utopia here on earth. I will never be perfect, and you will never be perfect. But God covers all our imperfections if we merely turn to Him."

Angeline squeezed his hand as a laugh-cry emerged from her lips. She could hardly believe her ears. This was precisely what she had prayed for during the long night.

"So, will you marry this imperfect man who doesn't deserve you?"

He raised her hand and placed a gentle kiss on it.

She batted her tears away as reality set in. "You heard Dodd. He intends to take me back for trial."

"Then let him. I will go with you. As your husband."

She searched his eyes. "I can't ask you to do that."

"Then don't ask. Just answer me."

A giggle burst from her lips. "You're mad."

"Incredibly, wonderfully, and hopelessly."

"James, Angeline!" A call came from the camp.

James glanced over his shoulder to where Blake, Eliza, Magnolia, and Hayden prepared to head into the jungle. Eliza had woken Angeline before dawn to inform her of their plans. Though the scheme sounded crazy, Angeline agreed and had slipped down the beach to pray. Pray for James. Pray for protection. Pray for God to empower them. Yet she feared her faith was too small to be of any effect.

Down shore, a few colonists stirred from their sleep and began stoking the fire for breakfast. Though the pirates drank and sang well into the morning hours, their greed had woken them early to head to the temple. Along with Dodd and Patrick and a few other colonists they had dragged from their beds.

Blake gestured for Angeline and James to join them. He had thought it best not to tell the rest of the colonists their plans. No need to spread unnecessary alarm when there was nothing anyone else could do. But the six of them must leave soon before the others started to question.

James faced her, a questioning look on his face.

"I will give you my answer later." When her heart stopped flipping and bouncing through her chest like an acrobat and when her thoughts descended from the clouds onto reason. Then maybe she could think with her head and not her heart. And pray. Yes, she must find out what God wanted. A first for her. But a habit she intended to foster for the rest of her life.

"Very well." He extended his elbow as if they were going for a stroll in a garden. "Shall we go defeat some demonic beasts?"

CHAPTER 36

I feel so helpless," Blake muttered as he trudged beside James through the jungle. "Not bringing anything with us but the shirts on our backs. No weapons—not that we have many—no clubs or spears or even iron skillets to slam over the fallen angels' heads." He gave a nervous laugh.

"The battle is not yours, but God's." James quoted from Second Chronicles. "We need only Him." Which is why he'd left the Hebrew book back on the beach. They didn't need it anymore. He'd read it over and over but still found no particular instructions for defeating the beasts, save commanding them back to their chains. At first he'd found that rather alarming, but then God had led him to the story in Second Chronicles where the Israelites faced a massive army of Moabites and Ammonites. Outnumbered and overwhelmed, the people trembled in fear. But God was with them.

"Ye shall not need to fight in this battle: set yourselves, stand ye still, and see the salvation of the Lord."

That verse had flown off the page and embedded itself in James's heart. And he knew that they had only to show up in the tunnels beneath the temple and God would do the rest. Yet now as they made their way through steamy leaves and branches and vines laden with all manner of skittering, crawling things, a small part of James began to skitter as well. Had he really heard from God? Had his father been correct when he'd told James he'd been chosen for this task? Or had it just been a silly dream?

Doubts saturated him, like the sweat trickling down his back. Tabitha sauntered out of the leaves on his left, Abigail on his right.

She winked at him, her dark lashes fanning her cheeks. "You haven't changed, James. I see the desire in your eyes." Tabitha sidled up to him, pressing her curves against his arm. Both ladies giggled. James turned to see if Blake noticed, but the colonel kept walking, face forward. Ignoring the women, James pressed on.

And nearly bumped into his father.

The man blocked the way with a body that looked more real than the trees. Yet the colonel strode right through him as if he wasn't there.

"Who do you think you are, boy?" His father clicked his tongue in disgust. "You're leading these people to their death. Just like you led me."

Guilt gripped James's heart, threatening to squeeze his remaining courage. He brushed past him. He appeared in front of him again, looking more like James remembered—tired, aged, and worn. "That wasn't me last night," he snarled. "That was just a foolish dream. I don't forgive you at all. You're nothing but a failure."

James halted, gut clenching. Those words were more what he'd expected to hear from his father.

"*Believe the truth, reject the lie*," a voice within him whispered.

But what *was* the truth? The truth was God's Word: forgiveness, love, grace.

Clamping down his jaw, James charged forward. "I don't believe you. Leave me alone," he said as he passed right through his father.

That's when the wind picked up.

⋘⟡⟡⟡⟡⟡⟡⟡⟡⟡⟡⟡⟡⟡⋙

Blake glanced up to see patches of dark sky through the canopy. He'd grown accustomed to storms rising quickly in Brazil but not this quickly. Wind whipped leaves and dirt in his face. The wound in his side ached. Ignoring it, he shoved aside a swaying branch, drew Eliza close, and continued forward. They wouldn't allow a little storm to stop them.

But he would allow his brother.

The boy appeared ahead on the trail in his Confederate uniform, leaning against a giant fig tree, unaffected by the battering wind. A vision. Only a vision. Blake stiffened his jaw and proceeded, but the boy's call to him halted him in his tracks. How could he ignore his only brother? He missed him so.

Jerry lifted blue eyes—so like their mother's—to Blake. "Why did you marry the woman whose husband murdered me?" Those eyes, now burning with hate, shifted to Eliza. "Why?"

Blake's heart shriveled. Thunder shook the ground. Drawing a deep breath, he led Eliza forward.

"How could you?" His brother's voice haunted him. "Do I mean so little to you?"

Blake's breath clogged in his throat. Agony burned behind his eyes. But he kept going. *Father, help me. Please, help me.*

"I love you, Blake. Don't you love me?" Sobbing came from behind, and Blake turned and stared at the boy he would gladly have given his life to save. But it wasn't his brother. Jerry was dead and in heaven. This was a monster. No matter what form it took.

"Leave me alone!" He yelled above the rising tempest. Then drawing Eliza close, he lifted an arm to protect them from flying debris, and proceeded.

Lightning scored the sky.

⋘⊹⊱

"Did you see something?" Eliza shouted over the wind. She'd felt her husband stiffen beside her several steps back, had witnessed him stop and stare at a tree, then stop again and shout something. Now, he gripped his stomach as though someone had stabbed him.

Another flash of lightning lit the darkening skies. Thunder roared. Eliza jumped and dodged a flying branch as she huddled beneath her husband's arm.

"It's nothing." Blake gave her a reassuring smile and kissed the top of her head. "I wish you didn't have to come along. Especially being with child. It isn't safe."

"I would be in more danger if I didn't come." She hoped her words reached his ears in the torrent of wind. His nod confirmed they had.

She glanced up to see how the others fared and wished she hadn't. Her father crossed the clearing up ahead, one hand behind his back, the other rubbing his chin. Turning, he started back the other way, deep in his musings, pacing as she had so often seen him do in his study back home. The sight of him stole Eliza's breath. He was young once again, strong, determined, so handsome in his suit of gray broadcloth, his thin mustache and dark hair clipped to style, his regal stride. She knew he was a vision, she knew she should ignore him.

But she couldn't.

Finally his eyes met hers. "You left me. Disobedient girl! Left me all alone. Ran off with that Yankee! Broke my heart." Anger turned to despair.

Eliza reached out to him. He withdrew. Lines creased his skin as it folded and drooped. His dark hair shriveled and turned gray, falling out in clumps until all that remained were feeble wisps atop his head. His shoulders stooped, his eyes grew cloudy. And she turned away as she and Blake passed him by, unable to bear watching him age. Seeing the agony in his eyes. The loneliness she had caused. She tossed a hand to her mouth to subdue a sob.

"Resist it!" Blake shouted, squeezing her shoulder. "It isn't real."

Nodding, she drew a deep breath and faced her father, who now walked beside her. "Go away. I want nothing to do with you." It was the hardest thing she'd ever said, yet as soon as she spoke the words, hatred fired from her father's eyes before he became a dark mist and blew away in the wind.

The sky broke open, releasing an army of rain.

Droplets stung like pinpricks. Magnolia ducked beneath a banana tree. Stopping beside her, Hayden plucked a giant leaf and held it over her head. "We should keep going!" he yelled above the tapping of rain and roar of wind.

Oh, how she hated what the rain did to her hair! Matted it to her face like strands of oily rope, making her look like a wet cat. But why was she thinking of that now? She hadn't been overly concerned about her appearance in months. Still, she hated that Hayden saw her like this. Would he still love her looking so hideous? Taking the leaf from him, she shielded her face from his view and dashed onto the trail again. Up ahead she spotted the blurry shapes of Blake and Eliza.

And someone else.

Someone wearing a gray cloak and limping across the trail. Splashing through the growing puddles, Magnolia drew near, curious who the intruder was. Perhaps a colonist who had followed them? A gust of wind nearly knocked her down. Clutching her close, Hayden tried to use his body as a shield, but the tempest shoved them both to the side as if they weighed no more than a feather. Leaves and twigs struck them from all around. Batting them away Magnolia peered once more toward the strange person.

Gray, spindly hair flowed from beneath a hood covering the woman's head—a hood that stayed put, despite the tempest. A flash of white light blinded Magnolia. *Crack! Snap!* Magnolia followed Hayden's gaze above to see a wide branch cascading through the canopy, heading straight for Blake and Eliza.

Releasing Magnolia, Hayden charged forward and barreled into the couple. All three of them tumbled into the middle of a large fern as the branch struck the ground with a thunderous roar, flinging mud into the air.

The earth shook. The cloaked figure reappeared. With a long pointed fingernail, she slid the hood from her face. Rain pummeled skin, shriveled and blotched. Drooping, sunken eyes met Magnolia's. The skin beneath them hung in blue, veiny folds. Magnolia gasped. It was her! Her old self that appeared in her reflection.

She screamed. Wind whipped her skirts against her legs, stinging her skin. Rain slapped her face. And an overwhelming terror gripped her that she would never be beautiful again.

"The LORD seeth not as man seeth; for man looketh on the outward appearance, but the LORD looketh on the heart."

Yes. Yes. She closed her eyes and hunkered down against the wind. That was true. She knew that. And with God's help, her heart was getting better every day. Hadn't she noticed improvements in her reflection? It might take a lifetime, but she would end up looking like a princess in the end. Bracing against the buffeting wind, she drew a breath and stood. The old woman gave her a malicious grin. But Magnolia waved a hand at her. "Be gone. I'm beautiful in God's eyes."

The vision faded, but Magnolia couldn't help the tears flowing down her cheeks.

◦◦◦❦◦◦◦

Hayden darted to his wife and absorbed her in his arms. Sobbing, she buried her face in his shoulder. When he nudged her back to ensure she wasn't hurt, her sapphire eyes skittered over the jungle seeking something. Or someone. Wiping wet strands from her face, he kissed the droplets of rain from her eyes. "They aren't real!" he shouted. "I love you." Then dipping his head to brace against the wind, he led her forward. Water rose on the soggy ground, gripping their ankles and making it difficult to walk. A branch struck his shoulder. Pain throbbed across his back. Covering Magnolia with his arms, he continued.

A silver slipper appeared in his vision, enclosing a very delicate foot dangling from a tree limb. Hayden glanced up to see Miss Sybil Shilling, casually sitting atop a branch as if she were a little girl on a summer's day. Her satin gown with velvet trim fell in lavish folds over her legs, completely dry. Her hair, a bounty of chestnut curls, remained untouched by wind or rain. He remembered her well. He'd swindled her out of a dowry that would have provided the homely, bird-witted girl the only means of a good match.

Before she even opened his mouth, Hayden said, "I'm sorry, Sybil."

"You're sorry!" She leapt from the tree as if she were a monkey and landed before him. "I never married, you know. Old spinster Sybil, the joke of the town."

Magnolia stared at Hayden, but he knew she couldn't see the woman. All the more reason for him to ignore her as well, ignore the guilt that tore his gut, ignore the look of anguish on her face.

"You told me I was beautiful. You told me you loved me."

He had. He'd flattered her more than any of his other victims. Perhaps because he'd felt sorry for her. But in the end, he'd not only broken her heart, but her life as well. How could he have done such a thing? How could he have been such a monster?

"Forgive me." Halting, Hayden's legs gave out. He lowered his chin and fell to his knees in a puddle. A chill soaked into his trousers. And his heart.

Magnolia gripped his drenched shirt, forcing him up to face her. Water slid down her face, dripped from her lashes and chin, as her sodden curls lashed about her cheeks. "You aren't that man anymore!" She shouted, tugging on his shirt. "Do you hear me? You aren't him anymore!"

How did she know what he'd seen? But then again, she always knew when he was hurting. Drawing her close, he pressed her head against his chest and kissed her sopping hair. She was right. He *was* a new man in Christ. The old things had passed away. Strength returned to his legs. He stood. The vision of Sybil crumbled to dust and blew away in the wind.

Swoosh. Swoosh. Swoosh. The beat of many wings filled the air. Dark blotches covered the canopy, swooping, diving, screeching, and stealing what remained of the light.

⋯⟨❦⟩⋯

Angeline rarely screamed. She'd seen too much horror, suffered too much at the hands of unscrupulous men to shriek like a fribble-hearted female at every frightening thing. But when the bats started diving for her, she screamed louder than she ever had. The hideous creatures' shrieks pierced through the rumble of the storm, sounding like tortured mice—murderous mice.

James grabbed a fallen branch and began swatting them away. A few fell into the puddles at her feet, twitching from their wounds. Bile rose in her throat, and she covered her head with her hands.

"They are trying to stop us!" Spinning to face their friends behind them, James cupped his hands over his mouth and shouted, "It's the beasts! They don't want us going to the temple! Keep moving. They can't harm us!"

In defiance of his words, lightning flashed, thunder blasted, and the rain thrashed down harder than ever. Wind shot droplets through the air like pellets, stinging Angeline's skin through her gown. Water gushed over the ground, picking up the dead bats and carrying them away as if they were leaves.

James pulled Angeline to her feet. Shielding her with his arms, he sloshed forward down the trail.

Above them, the bats disappeared into puffs of black smoke.

Which only made her heart beat faster. She knew they faced an unearthly evil. She'd just never witnessed it firsthand. Not like this.

James squeezed her. "It will be all right. Stay close."

The confidence in his voice, in the way he held himself, emboldened Angeline to ignore the dozens of customers who now assailed her at every turn, their eyes hungrily licking her, their mouths voicing obscenities.

"Whore! Trollop!" one shouted.

"Filthy slut!" another spat.

Covering her ears, she slogged through the rising water. Above her ankles now. *Oh, God, not another flood.*

"You think you're cleansed, eh? You think God forgave you?" Her uncle's wicked chortle echoed through the storm, transforming into thunder.

Halting, Angeline closed her eyes. She couldn't face the man she'd killed. She couldn't face the man whose assault had led her down the path to darkness. Not now. Wind whipped her blouse, her hair, branding her skin. Rain hammered her like punishment from God.

Branches, twigs, and leaves flew at them from all directions.

James covered her with his arms and led her onward, ducking and diving beneath the onslaught. The din of the storm grew louder. The force of the wind and rain more violent. Doubts rose within Angeline that she knew if she entertained, would surely send her running back to the beach. Sweet saints, how could they ever fight such power?

Yet James believed they could. She could feel his faith in the steel of his arms, the rock-determination of his body next to hers, in every confident breath he expelled. And it gave her strength to go on. On and on, head lowered, ramming into the wind, dodging wooden missiles and slogging through a river of water, until finally the crumbling walls of the temple appeared.

And a darkness invaded Angeline's soul. No. More than darkness. A heaviness weighted with despair and hopelessness.

She hated this temple.

James stopped to wait for the others and pressed her against the wall, shielding her with his body. There, battered by the elements and about to do battle with unimaginable evil, terror squeezed all hope from Angeline. Were they all about to die? What if these were her last moments with James? She couldn't bear the thought. There, barricaded by his strength and warmth, she knew there could be only one answer to his question. The answer God had reassured her was the right one during their trek there.

She lifted her gaze to his, but inches apart. "Yes."

"Yes?" His breath wafted on her cheek. His hair whipped his forehead. He searched her eyes before understanding widened his own. "Are you agreeing to marry me?"

She nodded, smiling.

He drew her to his chest. A rumble of joy burst from inside him, caressing her ear. Thunder cracked the sky. The ground shook. Water tugged at her gown. But Angeline didn't care.

Nudging her back, James cupped her face in his hands. "You have made me so very happy." He kissed her forehead, her nose, and proceeded down to her lips—would have kissed her as she so desperately wanted if someone hadn't coughed.

Hayden's hair flailed in the wind like sodden pieces of rope, but his grin and subsequent wink sent heat flooding Angeline's cheeks. She stepped back from James as the others approached. No time to celebrate.

Covered in scratches, their clothes torn, and with water dripping from their hair, the six of them looked as if they'd fought the kraken and lost. James turned and barreled through the wind and rain, leading them around the wall. The water hugged their ankles as, one by one, they slipped inside the broken gate.

No sooner had they entered the courtyard than the wind stopped, the rain ceased, and the water receded. The sky, however, remained black and ominous, still emitting its menacing growl. Dripping and panting, they stared at each other in numbed shock.

Blake's features tightened as he donned his warrior's mask. "Let's do this."

Trying to settle her beating heart, Angeline slipped her hand in James's as he ushered her onward, slogging in the mud past the gruesome obelisks and into the temple. Steam rose from the stagnant pond, and a glimmer drew her gaze to the gold moon and stars hanging above the altar. James led her into the tunnels, followed by Blake and Eliza, and finally Hayden and Magnolia. Angeline lifted up a silent prayer for God's protection and help. She knew her faith was weak, and she suspected Hayden and Eliza also struggled. Would God still honor their mission? Could He use such weak people to accomplish His will? If not, at least she would die trying to do the right thing. For the first time in her life. For the first time she would battle evil and fight for good. For the first time she believed in something larger than herself, believed in destiny and purpose, and that life had meaning.

She only hoped that life would not end today.

A roar much like an approaching train blared through the narrow passageway. The ground shook. Torches fell from hooks on the walls and sputtered on the wet dirt. Darkness swamped them. Rocks pelted Angeline. Ducking, she covered her head with her hands. They were going to be buried alive.

Chapter 37

James covered Angeline with his body. The ground leapt like a wild pony. Sharp pebbles stabbed his back and arms. Pain lanced through him. Something large struck his head. Momentarily dazed, he shook it off and gathered his wits. *God, help us!*

"No weapon that is formed against thee shall prosper."

The silent words swept through him, sparking to life places shriveled in fear. God was with them, and He was more powerful than any beast. "Keep going!" James shouted over his shoulder. "They can't harm us."

Though the pain burning in his head spoke to the contrary. Though he couldn't see a thing but thick, inky blackness. Drawing Angeline close, he stumbled forward over the heaving ground, their bodies shoved into sharp stone on one side then slammed against barbed rock on the other. Bruises formed. Angeline moaned, and he wished more than anything he could shield her from all harm. Rocks tumbled over them. Sizzling heat belched up from below like dragon's breath. Gripping the wall for support, James shuffled forward on the pitching dirt. Knife-sharp rock sliced his hand with each jolt. If only he could see.

"My Word is a light."

Yes. James drew a deep breath. "Thy word is a lamp unto my feet," he repeated the scripture from Psalms. "And a light unto my path." Though the roar of the earthquake muffled his words, a glow appeared from above. A soft glow like the glimmer of predawn, dousing the tunnel in a golden hue just bright enough for him to make out their surroundings.

Thank You, Lord. Heart swelling with awe, James sped ahead. He'd been down these tunnels enough times to know his way, and the quicker he went, the sooner this mad quaking would stop. Or so he hoped. Still, no matter how tightly he held Angeline or how fast he went, their bodies flopped back and forth against razor walls like corn through a prickly sieve. The shaking forced them to their knees one minute then tossed them in the air the next. Dust filled James's lungs until he could barely breathe. Angeline moaned. Magnolia shrieked, only heightening James's fear for all the ladies, especially Eliza so far along with child. *Oh, God, are You sure we are the six?* It wasn't so much a prayer, but a doubt he realized he shouldn't have entertained. A doubt that whipped his fears as out of control as the ground was doing to his body.

Halfway down the second stairway, a dozen pirates appeared, torches in hand, the flames distorting the terror on their faces as they pushed past them, shouting, cursing, and scrambling on top of each other to get away from the mayhem. Four colonists—three farmers and the cooper—followed fast on their heels in much the same condition.

"Doc, Colonel!" Mr. Jenkins shouted as he passed. "The walls are caving in. Get out now!" The others nodded their agreement as they shoved by them.

Angeline trembled in James's arms. Dust filled the air. Bending over, she coughed. But they couldn't go back now. God had sent His light as confirmation they were doing the right thing. Hadn't He? Ah, why so many doubts? When James had been so full of faith just that morning. When all these troubles should prove they were in God's will. Why else would the enemy be coming so hard and fast against them?

James squeezed through the opening into the first chamber and turned to assist Angeline. A jolt caused him to lose his balance. They both went tumbling to the dirt, barely missing a row of sharp stalagmites. Flickering light from torches on the walls wove a kaleidoscope of devilish shapes over the craggy ceiling. Dizzy, James closed his eyes. The ground rattled beneath him. The foul stench of sulfur and death stole his breath. Coughing, he tried to rise, but nausea churned in his belly. He had to get up. He had to go on. His friends depended on him. God depended on him.

Yet fear kept him paralyzed. Fear of failure. Fear of dying. Of losing Angeline, losing his friends, people who counted on him. Heat enflamed him. Overwhelming heat, as if he'd been thrust into an oven. His skin prickled. Blood boiled through his veins. He looked at Angeline beside him. Like a wilted flower, she melted on the ground.

What was he doing? Who did he think he was? He'd failed at everything in his life, what made him think he could succeed in defeating such powerful beings?

Angeline's gaze locked upon his. She must have read his thoughts for she struggled to rise and tugged on his arm. "Get up, James! Get up. We need you!"

Her violet eyes sparked with life, determination, and something else. . .faith. In him?

Forcing himself up, he gathered her in his arms. "Thank you," he said as Blake and Eliza poked through the opening, followed by Hayden and Magnolia. Sweat matted hair to their heads and darkened their torn clothing. Scratches lined their arms and faces—faces stark with fear but also set with determination. All four of them swayed in his vision as if he'd had too much to drink. But it was the ground still moving beneath them, rising and falling like ocean swells. Blake gave him a nod of encouragement.

Rattling drew James's gaze to the broken irons at the bottom of the two empty alcoves. They leapt over the dirt with each thrust of the ground. But no. Not with each thrust. Their movements were driven and angry as if something. . .or someone. . .moved them. His throat closed.

A missile fired from above, spearing the dirt beside him. Then another and another. The stalactites loosened, one by one, and shot to the ground. Tucking Angeline beneath his arm, he ducked and dodged, making his way to the opening that led to the chamber below. Magnolia screamed.

"Run!" Blake yelled, shielding Eliza with his body as he stumbled forward. Spears rained down upon them like lightning rods.

A growl spun James around. A shard impaled Hayden's foot. He yanked it out. Blood squirted, which would normally have sent James cowering. He started for his friend, but Magnolia knelt and pressed her handkerchief over the wound.

The hail of spikes continued.

Eliza and Blake disappeared through the opening. James shoved Angeline through and then turned to help Magnolia and a limping Hayden before jumping in behind them. More darkness. The shaking increased. James felt as though he were trapped in the hold of a ship during a mighty squall. No, much worse than that, for at least the hull of the ship was made of wood not rock as sharp as spears. He groped to find Angeline but lost his footing and was thrown against his friends. They fell, tumbling downward, screaming, legs and arms reaching, bodies scraping against rock and one another until they barreled through a hole, like rag dolls, onto the dirt of the final chamber.

Torches danced on walls that were cracking and sliding as if made of dough. Their shifting flames flickered over a stack of gold coins and trinkets that filled the top of the fourth alcove and spread out to a circular wall of rock that kept the treasure at bay. If the treasure indeed filled the alcove all the way to the ground as Dodd had claimed, then it was enough gold to own the world—if one wanted such a thing. Which Captain Ricu apparently did as he clung to a boulder to keep his balance, while four pirates, along with Dodd, removed the final layer of rocks that kept the gold out of reach. Beside them lay a pile of empty burlap sacks. Shouts of glee drew James's gaze to Patrick, who, down on all fours, bracing against the quake, looked like a hunting dog about to be released from his leash. None of them noticed James and his friends.

Assisting Angeline to her feet, James started for Ricu. He had no idea what he would do, but he must stop him or anyone else from speaking the Latin phrase. Even though all of them seemed more interested in the gold at the moment. But he couldn't take that chance, not when the phrase was clearly seen etched in stone above the alcove. Etched in more than stone, from what James could tell. The phrase above this final tomb was ingrained with gold that now glittered in the torchlight, making it all the more visible. And desirable. Even if the pirates hauled off all the treasure, their greed would drive them to scrape every ounce from the wall as well.

The ground tilted, and James slipped. Captain Ricu turned. His eyes narrowed, and his shout brought the tips of several cutlasses oscillating before James and his friends. James retreated to stand beside Angeline.

Another jolt struck, and Ricu leaned against a boulder for support. Sweat and fright made the mighty pirate captain shrivel before their eyes. Still, his voice rang through the chamber like a gong. "Leave at once!"

The pirates advanced.

Sweat stung James's eyes. He wiped it with his sleeve as the shaking settled to a gentle sway. Surely the addle-brained pirate could see that the walls of the chamber were about to collapse. Did he put so little value on his own life and so much on the gold that he was willing to risk being buried alive just to possess it? Pain lowered James's gaze to a sword jabbing his chest. The tip sliced a trail over his skin with each roll of the ground. The rest of the pirates leveled their blades at his friends. Yet they all stood bravely. Even Magnolia, whose trembling lips were the only indication of her fear. Angeline slipped her hand in James's. They were all going to die. Either by the blade or by the quake. *God, why did You bring us here if we are to fail?*

But then he remembered. . .and he prayed. . .and he hoped. . .

"No weapon formed against us shall prosper." James spoke the words God had given him earlier.

The swords flew from the pirates' hands. They twirled through the air, round and round, glittering in the torchlight before landing in a heap of *clanks* and *clangs* in the far corner. The pirates stared at them, then back at James, then over to the blades again, fear screaming from their wide eyes.

"Well, I'll be. . ." Hayden exclaimed. Blake shouted an "Amen!" Eliza laughed with joy, and James squeezed Angeline's hand.

"How you do that?" Ricu's face grew pale beneath a sheen of sweat.

Clanking drew James's gaze to the broken irons in the empty third alcove. They rose and fell and leapt and plummeted as if they had a life of their own. The stink of rotted flesh and feces swept over him. It burned his throat and lungs and he doubled over, gasping for air. His friends did the same. Even the pirates and Dodd coughed and wheezed—all except Patrick who had risen to his feet and stared at them as if they were all mad.

Wave after wave of heat swamped them. Sweat streamed down James's back, gluing his shirt to his skin. Skin that felt as though it were being roasted alive. His friends withered beside him. A mighty roar echoed through the chamber. The room lurched as if a giant slammed against the walls. Stalactites fell from the sky, piercing one of the pirates through his chest. He dropped to the ground with a moan. Magnolia screamed. Eliza started toward him, but Blake held her back. It was too late anyway. The man's vacant eyes stared at the ceiling. The floor tilted left then right, tossing them back and forth like a seesaw. The boulder beside Ricu rolled on its side. He backed away, eyes bulging.

Dodd stumbled toward Blake. "Don't you see the gold?" he shouted, pointing toward the alcove. "I told you it was here!"

Ignoring the buffoon, James watched as Patrick and one of the pirates struggled to remove a loose rock in the middle of the wall surrounding the alcove. The ground jolted, aiding their efforts, and the stone slid to the side. Gold coins poured from the opening like water from a faucet. Laughing with glee, Patrick grabbed a sack and held it beneath the hole while another pirate scrambled to collect the coins on the ground—both seemingly oblivious to the fact that the cave was about to collapse. In fact, there wasn't a drop of sweat on Patrick, not on his skin nor dampening his clothes.

The ground stopped shaking. The rest of the pirates darted to the wall and yanked and pulled until another stone loosened, creating a bigger hole through which goblets and jewelry poured along with coins. Ricu smiled and ordered them to fill the sacks as fast as they could.

James started toward them, his plan to keep them focused on the gold and not the Latin phrase, but the earth jolted once more and sent him careening backward. Dirt began swirling in eddies across the ground. Whirling and spinning and rising until columns of dust cycloned all around them. The pirates ceased gathering gold. Everyone backed away as the shapes coiled in a mass of mud and rock, rising higher and higher until each one slowly coalesced into a human form. James's parents, the women who had caused his downfall, the soldiers he'd lost on the operating table. And many other people he'd never seen before, but from the looks on his friends' faces, they were people they each recognized. People who now began to berate them with insults and taunts and accusations. James ignored them, as did his friends. They knew how to deal with these lies. But Ricu, the pirates, and Dodd saw them as well, for they stared at them in horror, while Patrick continued gathering gold into sacks.

The broken irons in the third alcove clanked and rattled as if enraged. The swords in the corner leapt in the air. They turned and pointed at James and his friends, each tip aimed at their hearts. Blake leapt in front of Eliza, but she eased out to stand beside him and took his hand. Hayden and James exchanged a nervous glance. Magnolia's chest panted like a bellows.

Captain Ricu crossed himself. Dodd jumped behind a boulder, and the pirates crouched to the ground.

James swallowed. There was no place to hide. No place to run. His gaze locked on Angeline, who stood bravely by his side. She smiled. The blades shot through the air. Angeline closed her eyes. Magnolia shrieked. *Swoosh!* Air wafted against James's arm. A dozen clanks sounded behind him. No screams. No pain. He glanced at his friends. They examined themselves for wounds, but no blood appeared. Either the swords had missed or, miraculously, had gone through them without any damage. James couldn't help the chuckle that spilled from his lips. God was, indeed, with them. And by the looks of confidence on his friends' faces, they now believed the same.

The visions collapsed into piles of dirt on the ground.

"Meu Deus! Deus salve nos!" Ricu gazed up toward heaven in an appeal to a God James was sure he rarely addressed. "Hurry, take gold. We leave!" he ordered his men. Then withdrawing a handkerchief from his vest, he turned and watched the third alcove chains continue to dance, shaking his head in disbelief.

The poor man. If James didn't believe in the power of God, he'd assume he was fast becoming a madman at what he'd seen today.

The ground swayed. The heat and fetor rose. Halting his greedy harvest, Patrick grabbed one of the pirate's pistols, cocked it, and leveled it at Ricu's back.

"Captain Ricu, behind you!" Magnolia shouted. James shifted curious eyes her way. But, no doubt, she favored the flamboyant pirate over her ex-fiancé.

Ricu wheeled about, bells clanging and trinkets sparkling. "What be this?" He stared agape at the pistol then snapped his fingers toward his men. "Kill this man."

But the pirates only chortled and continued shoving gold into their sacks.

Patrick grinned. "I do apologize, Captain, but I'm afraid this *be* a mutiny."

Magnolia gasped. Angeline grew tense beside James.

"We not on ship, idiota. Cannot be mutiny."

"Well, perhaps a prelude to a mutiny, then." Patrick called one of the pirates to his side. "Relieve your captain of his weapons, and tie him up, if you please, Eduardo." He glanced around the chamber. "These crumbling walls give me an idea. We were simply going to kill you, dear Captain, but I believe I'll let the chamber do it for me."

James exchanged a glance with Blake that said he agreed they should stay out of it. They were here only to keep the fourth beast from being freed. Nothing more.

"What?" Captain Ricu's eyes sparked fire. "Branco, Faro!" he called to his men and spat a string of angry Portuguese.

"Sorry, Capitão." One of the men shrugged. "He offer larger cut of gold. How could we say no?"

Ricu growled, his eyes burning embers. "I am Captain Ricu, and I take what I—"

"Want when you want." Patrick waved the pistol in the air. "Yes, yes, we know, Captain, but I fear your reign of narcissism has come to an end."

"Traidor desleal, patife!!" Sweat streamed down Ricu's face. Plucking another handkerchief from his pocket, he wiped his forehead and neck as further Portuguese curses flew from his mouth. Finally he settled. His face grew tight. His hand inched toward the pistol stuffed in his belt.

"Ah, ah, ah, Captain." Patrick braced his feet on the rolling earth. "I *will* kill you. Don't think I won't. I'm giving you a choice here, Captain. I can shoot you dead on the spot, or I can tie you up and leave you here to take your chances with the"—he took in the walls where chips of dirt and rock started to break free—"crumbling earth."

Two pirates approached their captain and relieved him of his sword, knife, and two pistols before grabbing rope and turning him around to tie his hands. Ricu's face bloated as red as a beet. He cursed and spit and growled like an animal in a trap. A violent jolt struck the chamber, sending the men off balance. Ricu kicked behind him, striking one of the pirates' legs. He fell to the ground. Without glancing back, Ricu plowed toward the opening, stumbling over the teetering earth. Patrick fired. The shot cracked like a whip, echoing off walls. Ricu's terror-streaked eyes glanced over James before he disappeared through the opening.

Angeline's breath came hard beside James. Hair clung to her face and neck in sodden braids. Her skin was pink, her gown was damp with sweat, and she seemed to be fighting for every breath. He kissed her forehead. She wouldn't make it much longer. Neither would Eliza, who sat slumped across a boulder behind them, hand on her rounded belly. *God, please, help us.*

"I'll be all right, James," Angeline whispered with a nod. He smiled and wanted to tell her how proud he was of her, how much he loved her, but Patrick's sarcastic voice brought him around.

"Never fear." Patrick waved off Ricu with his smoking pistol. "We will kill him later. Now, get that gold! And you"—he leveled the weapon at James and his friends—"get out! Or I'll shoot all of you. I don't know what tricks you are playing. I don't know how you made those swords fly, but you won't make this pistol move before I shoot one of you through the heart." His hard gaze took them all in. "Why are you here, anyway? Want to steal the gold for yourselves?"

James braced himself on the quivering ground. Sulfur and gun smoke stung his nose. He wouldn't answer the man. Nor would he leave. Not when there was still a chance someone could read the Latin phrase. But his eyes betrayed him as they shifted above the alcove.

Patrick fingered his goatee and glanced up. Grabbing a torch, he leapt onto a boulder and held it toward the alcove. "Writing in Latin. How odd. What would Latin be doing beneath this old temple?"

Dodd finally emerged from behind a boulder, shook dust from his coat, and cast wary eyes over the scene.

The ground canted. The rock walls shook. But Patrick seemed unfazed. "My Latin is a little rusty, but I think I can manage it."

Chapter 38

Hold hands!" James shouted. With Patrick about to speak the Latin phrase, James had no other choice. He must do the only thing he knew to do. His heart seized in his throat as Blake helped Eliza rise and the six of them formed a line with linked arms. "We command you beasts to return to your chains!" James shouted.

The quaking increased, tossing them over the ground. Larger rocks broke from the walls and ceiling and thundered to the dirt. An eerie *thwack* that sounded like the snap of a thousand whips sent a rod of steal down James's spine. A crack etched through the rock wall on their left as if an invisible hand drew a chaotic design. Frozen in place, James watched as water trickled from the cleft, slow at first like a lazy stream, then faster and faster until it gushed from the ever-widening fissure. Chunks of rock broke from the wall in the torrent that now surged into the room, cascading onto the floor, splattering mud into the air.

"What's happening?" Magnolia yelled.

Dodd leapt onto the boulder beside Patrick, but the man shoved him down, the first hint of fear appearing on his face. The pirates stopped their work.

"Why isn't it working?" Blake shouted. Eliza stood firm beside him. Hayden, Magnolia trembling in his arms, inched back toward the entrance.

The ground canted. Balancing himself, James shook his head. "I don't know! This is all the book said to do. Besides something about a prince."

"A prince?" Angeline stared down at the water swarming around her shoes. "What prince?"

"There was a story in the book about a prince who came to rescue his people, but his name was never mentioned." James had gone over it several times, praying for help with the interpretation, praying he hadn't missed something.

The water soon flooded the chamber floor and began to rise. "Hurry!" Patrick shouted at the pirates. "Fill the sacks, take the gold above and come back for more!" Snatching a pack of gold from one of the pirates, he sloshed through the water and disappeared through the entrance, only to return within seconds for another. The pirates followed suit. Dodd knelt to fill his own sack, water gushing around his knees.

James squeezed his eyes shut. Perhaps in all the mayhem no one would say the Latin phrase now, but they still needed to imprison the other three beasts. Terror like he'd never known drained the blood from his heart. Not terror of drowning or being buried alive, but terror of failing. Failing God, failing his friends. Hot water, brown with dirt, licked his ankles, seeped into his boots.

The ground tilted. Water sloshed left, then right, shoving them into the filthy mire. Shaking sludge from his hands, James rose and helped Angeline. Mud splattered her arms and neck and slid down her gown. She lifted her eyes to his, and for the first time he saw her confidence waning. *God help me. What do I do?* James had no idea. Panic fired idea after idea into his mind. None of them sticking. None of them making sense.

Patrick, Dodd, and the pirates continued to fill their sacks and carry them above. Instead of pouring out in a stream, the gold now only trickled from the holes with each leap of the ground. One of the pirates tried to pry loose another rock lower in the wall.

That's when the snakes appeared, dozens of them slithering through the muck. Magnolia screamed and leapt into Hayden's arms. Eliza scrambled to stand atop a boulder. Angeline buried her head in James's shirt. Reaching through the water, Dodd grabbed one of Ricu's swords and began hacking the reptiles. But still the snakes slithered around their trousers, around the women's skirts, slinking between their legs. One of the pirates leapt atop a pile of rocks and shot his pistol into the water.

"Behold, I give unto you power to tread on serpents and scorpions, and over all the power of the enemy: and nothing shall by any means hurt you."

The scripture blared in James's mind. "They can't hurt us. They aren't real!" he yelled as a jolt sent both water and snakes to the left, splashing against the wall, only to return and flood them once again. One of the slithering beasts coiled around James's leg. *It sure feels real! God, please help!* Terror choked him. He kicked the snake off. And the next one. And the next. His friends did the same.

The snakes were harmless, just as God had said. Another tremor struck. James caught his balance and steadied Angeline. Hayden lowered Magnolia to the water as the reptiles disappeared.

Eliza grabbed her wet skirts and waded toward James. Stark golden eyes met his. "The prince who rescued his people!" she shouted, kicking one of the remaining snakes away. The ground tilted, sending her tumbling back. Blake caught her and held fast. "The prince who rescued his people!" she repeated with more exuberance, nodding at James as if he knew the answer.

The answer Magnolia must have also just realized as she lifted wide eyes to James. "Of course!"

Angeline gripped James's arm. "You know. The prince who rescued his people!"

James's thoughts were as muddied as the water now clawing his knees, splashing on boulders and up the sides of the chamber. His dream of the blood ship played in his mind. He and his friends had linked arm in arm as the ship approached the darkness. But it wasn't completely dark. There had been the figure of light at the bow. The lion-lamb. *The Lion-Lamb!* The name lit the shadows of his mind like a flame in a dark tunnel. With a nod, they all joined arms again. James cleared his throat and shouted at the top of his lungs: "We command you to return to your chains in the name of Jesus!"

"In the name of Jesus," Angeline repeated, and each of them followed, ending with Blake who shouted, "In Jesus' name!" with vehemence.

Patrick faced them, gold coins spilling from his arms while laughter spilled from his lips. But his chuckle was soon muffled by a thunderous growl that sounded like a mortally wounded animal. A very large animal. A very angry animal. The force of it shoved James and his friends backward into the hot muck.

Water ceased pouring from the wall. The roar silenced. The ground became still. Chains in the empty alcove lifted in the air around the pole that stretched from top to bottom. The sound of rattling metal echoed through the chamber as the irons shook and trembled with such violence, it seemed they would burst. Then as if by invisible hands, the lock looped around the thick clasp and clanked shut.

No one uttered a word. Only the sound of breathing and the *drip*, *drop* of water filled the cave. All gazes remained on the lock. The third beast was imprisoned again. And James had no doubt the first two had also returned to their chains in the room above.

They had defeated the four demonic generals!

With God's help. In the name of His Son.

James glanced at his friends, all bloody, bruised, muddy, and sweaty. And they all began to laugh, to cry, to praise God!

Patrick, Dodd, and the pirates stood, mud dripping from their shirts, disbelief dripping from their expressions.

A snapping sound drew James's gaze to the chasm where the water had poured forth. The crack widened and jetted upward then spiked across the ceiling like lightning, etching a rut that grew larger with each turn and twist. Rocks chipped off walls and stalactites fell into the receding water. The earth jolted and the crevice expanded, arching down the opposite wall and jutting across the muddy ground. The floor split open. The remaining water poured down. Steam shot into the air.

"The room is collapsing!" Hayden shouted.

"Get out! Get out!" Blake yelled, holding his side and grabbing his wife.

They hurried back through the hole. Dodd brought up the rear, carrying two sacks of gold. Once back in the first chamber, James glanced at the alcoves. Chains hung suspended in air, locked tight. He smiled, longing to shout at the beasts, to tell them they could no longer hurt the colonists—that they couldn't send visions and nightmares and floods and snakes. But there was no time for gloating. The earth still shook like a carriage on hilly terrain as the walls around them crumbled.

Drawing Angeline near, James scanned the group, bouncing and jostling in his vision. "Where's Patrick?" he yelled. The celling of the first chamber began to crack. Halting, Hayden glanced back toward the opening. "Go ahead! I'll get him!" He started limping toward the lower chamber. James handed Angeline to her friends and insisted—against their protests—that they keep moving. Then turning, he followed Hayden. He wouldn't let his friend deal with Patrick alone. Or risk getting killed by staying too long.

"Father, please! Come with us!" Hayden shouted as he ducked to avoid falling rocks. "You'll be buried alive."

"Go on without me!" The imperious man pulled another empty sack from the pile, knelt at the base of the rock wall, and scooped gold into it.

The water was gone, replaced by a sea of mud sliding across the chamber with each leap of the earth. Some fell into the steamy fissure that grew wider with each passing minute. Balancing on the trembling ground, Patrick wiped a sleeve over his forehead and yanked a rather large goblet from the pile.

Perhaps they could hit him over the head with one of them and drag him above. But James doubted they had time. He must ensure the others made it safely to the surface. Yet how could they leave Patrick here? Hayden started for his father when a jet of steam shot from the crevice, forcing him back.

"Go on, Hayden...I'll be along." Patrick grinned. "And richer than you ever imagined."

The room split. Pebbles showered them from above. The rock wall shielding the gold shifted. Some of the rocks tumbled from the top into the mud beside Patrick. Another tremor struck. The wall teetered like a heap of pudding. Patrick gazed up in fear, started to leave, but it was too late. Raising his arms to cover his head, he crouched as an avalanche of rocks struck his shoulders and back and piled around his feet. Momentarily stunned, Patrick shook his head and raised his gaze as gold—finally freed from its barricade—showered over him. Ignoring the gashes on his arms and shoulders, he grabbed handfuls of the treasure and flung it in the air, laughing.

The chasm widened. Steam spit in his face. He screamed and fell backward. The ground opened up. Rocks and gold slid into the opening. Terror pinching his face, Patrick tried to move away from the growing fissure, but the weight of the rocks and gold surrounding his feet and legs kept him in place. Coins slid into the crevice as the mouth opened wider and wider, gobbling up the chamber.

"Father!" Hayden shouted, agony spiking his voice.

In that split second between time and eternity when life hangs between the living and the dead. . .Patrick's gaze met Hayden's. And for the first time since James had known them, a thread of affection spilled from father to son.

Hayden saw it too. He dashed toward his father.

But the ground widened, and the man slid into the steaming fissure, along with all his gold. His scream silenced within seconds.

Heat seared them as Hayden stood staring at flames leaping from the opening. No. Not flames anymore, but molten lava bubbling over the edge.

Clutching Hayden's arm, James hauled him back into the chamber above, angry when he saw his friends had waited. "Go!" he shouted. Magnolia grabbed her husband, and the two darted forward.

Elation, terror, and heartache battled in James's chest as he clutched Angeline to his side and followed the others through the tunnels. Was it his imagination or was the passageway narrowing with each step? Heat pursued them—heat that could turn them to ash in seconds. Heat and the roar of a mighty fire. He didn't look back. Didn't want to see what he assumed was a sea of flames chasing them up the shaft.

Ahead, Blake assisted the others through the final hole back into the temple. Turning, he reached down for Angeline and James. The ground trembled. The entrance crumbled, filling with dirt and stones. Heat scorched James's back. Angeline struggled through the opening. The bottoms of her muddy, seared shoes were the last thing he saw as the hole narrowed even more. He thrust his arm through, and Blake hauled him up. Rocks scored his skin.

A tremor struck the temple. Debris rained down on them. Something sharp speared James's shoulder. Pain radiated across his neck. The temple columns began to quiver like noodles. Water sloshed out of the steamy pond. The moon and stars dislodged from the wall above the altar and clanged to the ground.

"The temple's collapsing!" Hayden yelled as they all darted for the front.

"Where's Dodd?" Angeline shouted.

James glanced back toward the tunnel entrance. The opening was barely wide enough for a person to squeeze through.

"Get out!" He nudged her forward, grabbed a shovel one of the pirates must have left and dug around the entry. Steam poured from the shrinking hole. A mighty roar sounded. Dust erupted from the opening. The tunnels must have collapsed. No one could survive that. Hand covering his mouth and nose, James turned to leave, but Angeline darted past him. "There he is!"

A flash of light hair appeared among the rubble. Dodd's face, barely recognizable beneath the mud and blood, gazed up at them. "Help me!"

"Give me your hand!"

A sack of gold appeared instead. Disgusted, James shoved it back. "Your hand, man. Your hand!"

"Take the gold first." He breathed out. "I can't lift it."

"Leave it! Leave it, or you'll die."

Dodd closed his eyes. The entrance toppled in on him. Dirt and rocks filled the space where he'd just been. Dust filled the air.

Angeline coughed and batted it aside. "No!"

A hand burst through the rubble.

James grabbed it. Angeline clawed away the dirt. Groaning, James tugged with all his might. Dodd's shoulder appeared.

The ground shook. Temple walls cracked. The dirt loosened, and Dodd's other hand punched through the debris. Bracing her shoes on the wall around the entrance, Angeline pulled, she on one side, James on the other. Dodd's chest popped through. Finally his legs appeared. But his feet remained. Fire leapt up from below. Dodd screamed. James yanked him the rest of the way. Looping Dodd's arm over his shoulder, James hoisted him up and dashed toward the portico, whispering a prayer. Angeline ran at his side as they both dodged slabs of stone and tumbled down the stairs and across the courtyard. Obelisks fell left and right. Weaving around them, they burst through the gate into the arms of their friends at the edge of the jungle. All seven of them fell in a heap on the ground, covered in mud, blood spilling over face and arms, chests heaving.

But clinging to one another in victory.

The roar of a thousand cannons pummeled the sky. A plume of

flaming rock fired into the air above the temple. James shot to his feet and hauled the others up, ready to run. The wall surrounding the temple collapsed with a thunderous crash. The temple shook as if some giant child thought it nothing but a toy. Then it flattened as if that child stepped on it. Stones larger than a house folded inward and sank into the ground. A wave of dust blasted over them. James squeezed his eyes shut. Coughing, he clung to Angeline as they both fell to the dirt, gasping for air.

The shaking stopped. All grew quiet. Not a breeze stirred, not a bird sang. Afraid to open his eyes and discover he was dead, James sat there holding Angeline, listening to her breathe. He felt her move and push from him. Finally he opened his eyes. Ash and soot showered over them like snowflakes.

The temple was gone.

CHAPTER 39

Wilt thou, Angeline Moore, have this man to be thy wedded husband, to live together after God's ordinance. . ." Angeline smiled at James as he continued, half reading from the *Book of Common Prayer*, half gazing at her with his bronze eyes so full of love they seemed ready to burst. Was it proper—or even legal—for him to perform his own marriage ceremony? Angeline supposed if they were breaking some cardinal rule, God would make an exception in their case. For she wouldn't be able to stand another day—another night—without this man. Especially not the time it would take to travel to Rio de Janeiro to see a priest.

James took her right hand in his. Strong, bruised fingers intertwined with hers, the sensual action sending her breath spinning. A salty breeze tossed his hair over the collar of his shirt. The shirt that was missing two buttons and was singed in one spot where the heat from the tunnels had burned him. A badge of honor for his godly mission to restrain evil. One that he had accomplished with great courage and God's power. They all had, in fact. But James had been their leader. The prophet, the forerunner.

And she couldn't be more proud.

Nor could she be more excited that today he would become her husband. This preacher-doctor who looked more like a sailor stranded on an island than a groom. A sailor who had picked a fight with otherworldly beasts from the looks of the cuts and bruises on his face, neck, and arms. But as he stood there on the sandy beach beneath a bamboo arbor laden with orchids and red ferns, his hair and shirt blowing in the wind, he was the most handsome man she'd ever seen. The thought that within minutes he would become her husband made a tingle spread clear down to her toes.

"I, James Callaway, take thee, Angeline Moore, to be my wedded wife, to have and to hold from this day forward, for better for worse, for richer for poorer, in sickness and in health, to love and to cherish, till death us do part, according to God's holy ordinance; and thereto I plight thee my troth."

Someone sniffed in the audience, and Angeline saw Magnolia lift a handkerchief to her eye. Beside the Southern belle stood all the people who mattered most in the world to Angeline: Hayden, Eliza, Blake, Sarah, and Thiago. Next to them, Moses shadowed Mable who perched beside the Scotts. In the distance, Captain Ricu watched along with a group of his pirates. Those who had sided with Patrick— apparently over half his crew—were conspicuously absent. They had been "reward their due" Ricu had explained when asked, and Angeline hadn't wanted to inquire what that meant.

Dodd, bandages on his feet and legs, sat on a boulder to the right. She smiled at Mr. Lewis, who sat beside him, having reappeared from the jungle yesterday, dazed and with no remembrance of the past two months. Had he turned into a man-wolf, this Lobisón, as Thiago still insisted, and then somehow changed back when the beasts were imprisoned? Angeline didn't know, nor did she want to think about it on such a glorious day.

The crash of waves and serenade of birds provided the music. An overskirt the ladies had woven from purple and pink flowers made up her wedding gown. Yet she might as well be wearing taffeta silk for the way James looked at her.

Shifting his stance he turned to Blake, who fumbled inside his waistcoat pocket for a ring. A band of gold? Yet what else could shimmer so beautifully in the afternoon sun?

"With this ring I thee wed, with my body I thee worship." James slid it on her finger and adored her with his eyes. "And with all my worldly goods I thee endow." His lips slanted. "As scant as they are."

Tears glazed her eyes. She smiled up at him. He brushed a thumb over her lips in such an intimate, caring gesture, her knees turned to mush.

"I now pronounce us man and wife, in the name of the Father, and of the Son, and of the Holy Ghost. Amen."

Cheers of joy filled the air. Yelps and whistles and a few Portuguese words emanated from the pirates as the colonists flooded the couple with congratulations.

But Angeline couldn't take her eyes off her husband.

Not during the excruciatingly long celebration that followed, not when they entered the private hut prepared for their honeymoon. And not even an hour later when, to the gentle lull of waves, James and she became one in flesh in the eyes of God.

Afterward, they held each other and talked and loved and prayed and spoke of their adventures, their God, their future, and their dreams. They were both still awake when the first blush of dawn creased the horizon. Pulling aside the canvas flap that faced their private beach, Angeline sat to watch the sun rise on a new day, happier than she'd ever been. James inched behind her, straddling her with his legs while encasing her with his arms. She leaned back on his chest and sighed, thanking God for cleansing her, for forgiving her, for loving her. And for making all her dreams come true. "I never want this night to end."

James nibbled on her ear. "We will have many more nights together. A lifetime."

She sighed as wind tossed her curls that smelled of coconut and orange blossoms over his face, tickling his skin. He twirled a finger around one of the delicate strands, longing to wrap his entire body in the silky web.

And remain there forever.

Last night, his eyes had been opened to what real love was. Not selfish pleasure, but giving everything of oneself. The melding of soul, spirit, and body in a love that was as close to perfection this side of heaven. No wonder God held marriage so sacred, so holy. It was a taste of paradise, of God's unconditional love, a bonding that was more spiritual than physical. And to dishonor it by using it only for one's pleasure, to fulfill a physical need, absent of real love, was to spit in the face of God Himself and His incredible gift to man. It was also to do great harm to one's own body and soul.

James hadn't understood that until now. But God had cleansed him. He had cleansed Angeline. And together throughout the night they had danced across the heavenly realms.

The golden arc of the sun peered over the horizon, curling ribbons of saffron and scarlet over sky and sea. Squeezing her against him, he trailed kisses up her neck, his body reacting in delight when she moaned.

"If you keep that up, Mr. Callaway, I fear we will never leave this hut."

"If that were to happen, Mrs. Callaway, I fear I will die a very happy man."

⤜⟡⤛

"Upon your honor, Captain Ricu, please assure me that you aren't kidnapping these people." Blake squinted into the sun and stared at the ostentatious pirate, his red plume fluttering in the wind, his Portuguese bark sending men to assist the colonists into two waiting boats. "I wouldn't want them pressed into piracy."

Ricu faced Blake. "Colonel, do I lie? I take them to Rio, of course! Though you give me good idea. I can always use more men." His eyes twinkled mischievously.

Angeline chuckled at the disconcerted look Blake exchanged with James.

"No fears," Ricu continued with a grin, sunlight winking off his silver tooth. "Your God has much power. More even than me." He chuckled as if that were beyond comprehension. "I no cross swords with Him. Deliver people safe."

"What of your gold, Captain?" Angeline asked. "And your lady?"

He waved a jeweled hand through the air. "Gold stay buried with monsters. I value life more than wealth. Wealth I find. Life, I have one." He shrugged. "Perhaps two. Besides"—he grew serious and leaned toward Blake and James, crossing himself—"I see much evil as I cross seas. And what I see in tunnels should not be free. Not for gold." He stood back and shouted an order to one of his crew. "And my lady? If she prefer gold over golden heart"—he laid his hand over his heart and winked at Angeline—"then she not the lady for me."

Angeline gave him a smile of approval as sobbing drew her gaze to Magnolia and her parents. Poor Mrs. Scott wilted like a sun-bleached

311

flower in her daughter's arms. Mr. Scott stood beside them, looking as if he attended a funeral. They had decided to leave with the rest of the colonists—first to Rio and then on a ship back to the States. Angeline couldn't blame them. The jungles of Brazil were no place for landed gentry so unaccustomed to discomfort.

An argument ensued that seemed to have something to do with Mable, but finally the slave slid behind Magnolia while Magnolia's father planted a kiss on his daughter's cheek and led his weeping wife to one of the boats.

Other tearful good-byes were performed in morbid playacts across the shore. Most of the colonists had opted to go home. Good food—anything but fish and fruit—a soft bed, new attire that wasn't stained and torn, a house that didn't blow away in the wind, libraries and plays and concerts, all the pleasures of society, lured them to abandon the fledgling colony for civilization. Even with James's assurance that there would be no more visions or disasters.

But Brazil had burrowed deep within Angeline's soul. It had changed her. Shown her that she was more than a comely face and figure to be used by men. It was here where she had met God and found her freedom. It was here where she had fallen in love. And it was here where her husband remained. She would stay with him, follow him wherever he went. Forever.

Her throat burned watching the mournful partings as the colonists settled, one by one, into the boats. She'd already hugged the ladies who had meant so much to her, who had treated her like one of them, and she'd bid farewell to all the men who were leaving. Except the one heading straight for her now.

James saw him too and slipped beside Angeline.

Dodd tugged off his hat and swept a hand through hair too long and unkempt for the civilization to which he headed. He wiggled his crooked nose and lowered his gaze. "I came to say good-bye."

Though his tone was penitent, the sound of his voice sent a spike of dread down Angeline's back. Surely he was up to something. Despite his recent promise that he wouldn't take her home to face charges. Perhaps he had changed his mind, saving the cruel announcement until the last minute when he would clap her in irons and haul her aboard the *Espoliar*. She could almost see his malicious grin of victory.

But when he raised his face, all she saw was remorse.

"Good-bye, Mr. Dodd." Angeline forced lightness into her tone, though her voice came out scratchy.

"I have no doubt you're not sorry to see me go," he said.

"I can't say that I am."

He smiled.

Hoping to discourage any last-minute change of heart, Angeline added, "I do thank you, however, for not turning me in."

Dodd's eyes shifted toward the sea, where incoming waves collapsed into bubbling foam. "You came back for me. Both of you." He glanced at James. "You saved me, after all I've done." He fumbled with his hat.

James held out his hand. "All is forgiven, Dodd."

Surprise creased Dodd's forehead as he gripped James's hand in a firm shake. "Doc, I saw some things back there in the tunnels...things I need to consider. Things that got me thinking there's more to life than gold."

James grinned. "Indeed, there is, Mr. Dodd."

Angeline spotted a light in Dodd's eyes she'd never seen before. Was it possible God could change even Dodd? Well, of course it was.

"I'm sorry you didn't get your gold," she said.

"Are you now?" He grinned. "Where do you think that wedding ring on your finger came from?" He winked, plopped his hat atop his head, then turned and leapt into one of the boats.

Fourteen. Fourteen colonists. That was all that was left of New Hope. Yet, as James led them through the jungle to the spot where he hoped to reveal his plan, he couldn't help but feel that these fourteen souls—together with God—could accomplish miracles.

Would accomplish miracles.

His father's Bible tucked beneath his arm, he entered the rubble-filled clearing and was relieved to not feel the usual heaviness. Turning, he faced his friends. Blake stood behind Eliza, his arms circling her and resting atop her rounded belly as both their confused gazes assessed James. Hayden, his foot bound from his wound, assisted Magnolia over a pile of rocks before they both stopped and scanned the clearing with alarm. Angeline sidled up to James with a look that said, *I don't know what you're doing, but I believe in you.* It warmed him even more than the heat of the day. Moses, hand entwined with Mable's, sweat marring his forehead, approached the desolation with caution. Delia and her two children followed behind. And lastly, Thiago stepped beside Sarah, Lydia hoisted in his arms. As James's gaze took in the way Thiago looked at Sarah and Moses looked at Mable, he wondered if he might be officiating more marriage ceremonies in the near future.

The thought brought another smile to his face, which quickly flattened when all their questioning eyes latched upon him. He cleared his throat and ran a sleeve over his forehead. Why did it always seem hotter here where the temple had once stood? Gazing up at the wispy clouds floating across the sky, he listened to the chatter of wildlife and chirp of birds filling the air—life's constant lullaby.

"This is where we must build New Hope," he finally said.

Blake's forehead crinkled. "Here? Where the cannibals used to sacrifice"—he swallowed—"you mean on top of the tunnels?"

"Yes." James said. "I believe we must. I believe we have to." He gestured to a heap of remains where the temple had once stood. "I'm going to build a church here. A grand church with a steeple that rises high into the heavens."

Silence, save for the buzz of insects, met his declaration, yet when he faced his friends again, the skepticism on their faces gave way to understanding. And finally to nods of affirmation.

"I says it a good idea," Moses said.

Hayden gave a slanted grin as he scanned the area. "There's plenty of good farming land. Much of it already cleared."

"And it's close enough to the river," Eliza added.

"We build road to river. Good road," Thiago said, tickling Lydia who responded with a giggle.

Sarah shrugged. "If we must start over, this place is as good as any."

Angeline gazed up at James. "We must build a fountain in the middle of town. A glorious, sparkling fountain."

For her, he would build a lake.

Magnolia twirled a lock of hair and frowned. "But why here? Why this morbid spot? It still makes me tremble."

Lengthening his stance, James glanced over the ruins. "We must protect it. No one must ever dig beneath this land again. No one must ever come near those beasts." He hesitated, not wanting to sound like a madman, but yet needing to share what he believed God had told him. "We are the guardians of these fallen angelic generals. That is why we were sent to Brazil. Not only to confine them. . .but to keep them confined."

He half expected laughter, perhaps snorts of disbelief, but instead his friends stared into the clearing as if remembering the battle they'd so recently fought, remembering the horror of seeing such evil on the cusp of being released. Slowly, one by one, each determined gaze locked upon his.

Eliza smiled. "And we will teach our children to protect it, and they will teach theirs after them."

Blake gave an approving nod and drew his wife close.

"Indeed," James said, joy swelling within him. He raised the Bible in the air—the one his father had given him all those years ago. He'd not appreciated it back then. He'd not realized the power that existed in the Word of God. But he wouldn't make that mistake again. "So what do you say? Shall we build New Hope on this place? Shall we make it the Southern utopia we always dreamed of? Shall we put a church atop the gates of hell? A symbol of good triumphing over evil?"

"All in favor, say aye," Blake shouted.

"Ayes" fired into the air.

James turned to Angeline and nearly melted at the look of admiration in her eyes. He was no longer a failure. Not in her eyes. Or in the eyes of God. He had found his God-given purpose. And what a purpose it was! To protect the world from an evil that, if unleashed, would kill thousands, maybe more.

And to cherish and love this woman beside him with all of his heart, forever.

EPILOGUE

Present day

There is a quaint little town in Brazil called New Hope. Located just south of Rio de Janeiro and a short distance from the coast, it boasts close to thirty thousand inhabitants. Some are farmers, some tradesmen, some workers, some teachers, doctors, priests. At first glance, there is nothing special about the town. Yet if you decide to stay awhile, you might hear pockets of English spoken here and there instead of Portuguese. You might notice that grits, fried chicken, vinegar pie, and cornbread are found on restaurant menus, that the city seal has distinct markings of the US Confederate flag, and that once a year on the fourth of July, the local women get dressed up in hoop skirts for square dancing and singing. If you lend an ear during the celebration, you may even hear the familiar tune of "Dixie" floating on the city streets.

In the center of town sits a church made of stone—a church more than one hundred and fifty years old. Though its stone walls are chipped, and one of its wooden doors is rotting, its white steeple thrusts toward the heavens, strong and bright. Stained glass decorates the windows, and some say in certain light you can see scenes form in the colored glass, depicting an ancient battle between humans and angels, complete with floods and fire and lightning bolts. If you are ever cold, just slip inside that church and I guarantee, you'll be warm before you know it. What causes the heat when there is no electricity in the building, no one can explain to this day.

In front of the church stands a fountain with an angel carved in stone standing in its center, sword in hand. Water pours from the tip of the sword back into the fountain, where steam rises to meet the day. They say the fountain has curative properties, and you'll often see locals and visitors alike dipping their hands in the unusually warm pool.

If you're lucky, you'll meet the old pastor of the church, a man by the name of Aleixo Callaway. A tall man in his eighties with a shock of gray hair and bronze eyes that can see right through a person. The kindest man you'll ever meet. Honorable and wise, he is highly revered among the locals. In fact, it's on account of him that the city council hasn't torn down that old church and put up a new one. If you see him, ask him why. But make sure you have an hour to spare, for he loves to tell the tale of how his great-grandfather, along with five others, defeated four of the fiercest evil angels ever created, and entombed them beneath the church. It's his job to keep them there, he'll tell you. A job he'll pass down to his son Cristovao when Aleixo passes on.

A bunch of malarkey if you ask me.

But it sure makes for a good story.

AUTHOR'S HISTORICAL NOTE

New Hope, of course, is a fictional town, but it may interest the reader to know there is a real city in Brazil called Americana, located in the Brazilian state of São Paulo, very near to where I positioned New Hope. The town was originally populated by American Confederates fleeing the South, desperate to preserve their Southern way of life. They came to be known as *Confederados*, and the town became thus popularly known as *Villa dos Americanos* (Town of the Americans).

Though the majority of the Confederates who sailed to Brazil eventually returned home to America, many thousands remained. Their unique influence and culture are still evident throughout the country today. These immigrants didn't just bring their Southern way of life, they brought new agricultural innovations and introduced the Georgia Rattlesnake watermelon, which flourished in Brazil. They also brought the buckboard wagon and Protestantism, as well as improvements in education and medicine.

If you happen to visit Americana, there is a small Confederate cemetery nearby in the city of Santa Bárbara named Campo. Take a stroll among the graves and view names such as Carlton, Cobb, Green, Moore, Smith, and tons more—all common names in Alabama, Georgia, and South Carolina in the nineteenth century. Inscribed on one of the headstones you'll see the words:

"Soldier rest! Thy warfare o'er. Sleep the sleep that knows no breaking. Days of toil or nights of waking."

Four times a year, a group of people gather at this cemetery and hold a service in a nearby chapel, where they sing Protestant revival hymns and gaze at an altar covered with three flags: Brazilian, Confederate, and American. Afterward they dress in costumes of nineteenth-century America and enjoy a huge meal of biscuits and gravy and Southern fried chicken. If you look real close, you'll see that some of the people have red hair, freckles, and blue eyes, and many of them speak in a quaint English dialect. An odd sight, indeed, in the middle of Brazil! Although these American descendants have been meeting for years, it wasn't until 1955 that this group of Confederados formally became the *Fraternidade Decendencia Americana* (American Descendants' Fraternity), dedicated to preserving both the history and the culture of their Southern descendants.

ABOUT THE AUTHOR

MaryLu Tyndall, a Christy Award Finalist and bestselling author of the Legacy of the King's Pirates series, is known for her adventurous historical romances filled with deep spiritual themes. She holds a degree in math and worked as a software engineer for fifteen years before testing the waters as a writer. MaryLu currently writes full-time and makes her home on the California coast with her husband, six kids, and four cats. Her passion is to write page-turning romantic adventures that not only entertain but open people's eyes to their God-given potential. MaryLu is a member of American Christian Fiction Writers and Romance Writers of America.